Praise for

The Scent of Distant Worlds

"County creates a masterful novel with plenty of inspired plot twists, for an elaborate and exhilarating space adventure." —Self-Publishing Review, ★★★★

"…innovative and wildly entertaining… an emotionally intense and page-turning read." —Blue Ink Review

"Delving into the potential biology of life on other planets with empathy, *The Scent of Distant Worlds* is a unique work of science fiction." —Clarion Review

"With a taut plot and unpredictable twists… Hard science is blended with vivid characters in circumstances that become more threat-filled by the hour." —Sue Burke, author of *Semiosis*

"As a private astronaut and creator of online virtual worlds, I can say that W. D. County weaves a tale that is more than possible as we expand into the vastness beyond the cradle of humanity." —Richard Garriott, first of the second-generation astronauts, veteran of the MIR and ISS

"Mr. County expands his range into the universe in this very readable novel." —James Gunn, science fiction writer, editor, scholar, Hugo award winner and member of the Science Fiction and Fantasy Hall of Fame

Also by W. D. County:

Sammi

Quest for the Blue Crystal

Oasis at the Bottom of the Sea

The Scent

of

Distant Worlds

Acknowledgments:

Special thanks to Olena Ilnytska for the cover art. Thanks and gratitude to the Profits & Scribes writing critique group for their insights and recommendations on this novel.

Published by Summit Scribes Press. Lee's Summit, Missouri.

Summit Scribes
Press

The Scent

of

Distant Worlds

by

W. D. County

Prologue

When the nurse entered his room in the middle of the night, the old man pulled the sheet up to hide the knife and half-carved totem. The action also hid the dusting of black powder released from the meticulous shaving and scraping of the ebony that would soon reveal the figure concealed within the wood. In the morning, after breakfast, he'd tell the dayshift he'd spilled pepper. It wouldn't fool them, but it allowed them to overlook the whims of a dying man.

The night nurse took his pulse, temperature, and blood pressure. She asked if he were comfortable, to which he answered yes. It wasn't a lie. Pain could be mastered and subdued by those who knew how, and the aged shaman of the Seminole tribe knew many *hows* and almost as many *whys*.

In truth he missed his own bed—the familiar lumps, sags, squeaks, and sage-scented pillow that made it a friend. The hospital bed felt and smelled sterile. In this house of healing, it sadly held no life of its own. A portent, perhaps, since there would be no healing for him. He had chosen to die here, rather than pass away at home, to humor his granddaughter. Cassie's hope for his recovery was endearing but foolish. He did not regret his decision, for it was altogether fitting.

The nurse left and he resumed carving the totem. He wielded the knife cautiously, as the obsidian blade was exceedingly sharp. He worked in darkness, caressing the wood, for the shape inside revealed itself more to touch than sight. As the totem gained form, he filled it with his spirit and memories. Cassie needed these to temper her headstrong belief in science as the sole path to truth.

Though science wasn't inherently evil, it was a jealous god and did not play well with other beliefs.

Cassie's voyage to the stars would be a vision quest far more challenging than the one she'd attempted in her youth. That failure had caused her to turn her back on tradition and leave the tribe. He hoped the memories infused within this talisman would remind her of lessons learned. An occasional look back gives insight when peering ahead.

The totem told him it was finished. He strung a rawhide cord through tiny holes he'd made earlier. In the morning when Cassie came to visit she would take it, not because she believed in it but because she believed in him. That was altogether fitting. Reasons were less important than actions.

He closed his eyes and let his spirit soar, following the faint trail of the Thunderbirds through the heavens. Neither space nor time constrained him. A footstep of the spirit spanned light years, especially when his body clung so loosely to his soul. The trail led to a black planet circling a blood-red star. The silent life of that dark place brooded over ancient memories, shunning all things new. The unwelcoming world offered danger, diamonds, and death. He returned to Earth to warn Cassie.

She was already in his room. The journey of a few minutes had taken hours. His breakfast tray sat untouched.

"Grandfather, I got the job!" Her enthusiasm bubbled like a fast-flowing stream. "Science Officer on the *Far Traveler*."

"Dark is my vision," he said, her future very much on his mind.

A look of concern clouded Cassie's face. "Shall I get the nurse?"

She worried about the wrong person. He forced a chuckle. "Not me. Outer space and the worlds that lie beyond. You don't fear the void between the stars; you sail eagerly upon it. But some planets have a dark side, granddaughter. You may find your quest begins after you reach your destination."

"A quest for what?" Suspicion tinged her voice.

"Your spirit guide."

Her frown vanished as quickly as it formed, but not so fast to escape his notice. "Hear me well, Cassiopeia. Trust your heart when your brain is confused. Unexpected guidance comes in many forms, as do allies."

"I outgrew superstitions a long time ago."

"Travelers to strange lands must keep an open mind. That's all I ask."

"I do. That's why I'm a scientist."

So proud. "This may help you find your way." He pressed the totem into her palm.

She gazed at the inch-long intricately carved head of a thunderbird and touched the leather thong that passed through the totem's eyes and ears. "Blind and deaf?"

"When darkness comes, we do not walk by sight. We walk by faith."

Her fingers traced the face of the totem. "You know I don't believe in this any more."

So stubborn. He sighed and told her the story of Great Spirit and how he hid the nature of reality, knowing humanity wasn't ready for such knowledge. She'd heard the tale many times before but listened respectfully as he told it again.

When he finished, she smiled and called it a lovely story. She lied terribly, but he'd done all that he could. Her fate now pivoted around a much younger, stronger man. This was altogether fitting. He closed his eyes, so very tired after his journey. He felt the kiss she placed on his forehead and the deep affection it carried.

He thanked Great Spirit for this loving endpoint. He waited until she left the room and then released his spirit with a long, gentle sigh. This time it would not return. And that, too, was altogether fitting.

Newton's Third Law:

For every action, there is an equal and opposite reaction.

Part One:

ACTION

Chapter 1

Ship Time: Day 13. 0900 hours.

Cassie Clearwater floated at the apex of the upper dome of the observation deck, so close that her breath fogged the glass, blurring the orange ball of Teegarden's Star. With the ship in ghost phase, outer walls stayed much colder than the rest of the *Far Traveler*. The chill rarely bothered her. Distant worlds called to her like the sirens of Greek myths, and she answered as often as her duties as science officer permitted.

She wedged a foot between the bulkhead and a grab bar to anchor herself and then wiped the window with her sleeve. Yesterday the dark of space gave the illusion of flying among the stars like the magic spirits of her grandfather's stories. But today she felt trapped, caught between the smoldering flames of an ageless sun and the cold embers of the ancient planet locked in orbital embrace.

The memory of her grandfather spoke. *You are Seminole. You are stronger than this.*

Five meters beneath Cassie's feet, a pneumatic door hissed open. She grabbed the bar and rotated to face the room, grimacing as her stomach threatened to turn inside-out. The anti-nausea pills didn't work. None of the damn pills worked.

Doc and Li entered the room and drifted to the lower dome where they gazed at the planet below. Black and featureless as charcoal, the planet seemed less welcoming than the pock-marked surface of Earth's moon or the frozen badlands of Pluto.

Cassie willed breakfast to stay put. The last thing she wanted was to unleash a cloud of half-digested food in zero-gravity. Cleanup was a bitch. Stuff went everywhere.

Neither crewmember noticed her hovering above their heads. Doc cleared his throat. "Hard to believe it's sunny side up."

His long fingers circled the handrail like a bird clutching a branch, and his nervous, neck-twisting reconnaissance of the room reinforced the avian impression. The anxiety puzzled her. Sure, they were twelve and a half light years from home, farther than anyone had ever traveled, but the doctor had spent a decade making house calls to asteroid mines and remote planetary outposts. Space travel shouldn't bother him in the least.

Li gestured upward. "Blackened by prolonged proximity to the sun as well as past eons of volcanic activity."

Cassie winced as they glanced up, certain they'd see her, but sunlight pouring through the dome hid her in its ruddy glare even as it highlighted the faces below. They turned back to the view of the planet.

As usual, Li eschewed customary crew dungarees in favor of flamboyant attire. An embroidered satin robe caressed her petite body, several silk scarves danced on swirls of air, and long, black hair beckoned with each movement. Cassie's mind filled in what she couldn't see—a perfect, wrinkle-free face (stem cell gene therapy), unnatural green eyes (intraocular tattoos), and exquisite knock-off jewelry (fresh from the 3D printer). Despite the artificial enhancements, the fifty-year-old Asian exuded genuine erotic allure.

"I suppose we'll find out soon enough," Doc said. His tone turned serious. "Why did you want to meet here?"

Li stared through the lower glass wall. "Daiyu would be a good name, yes? It means black jade. Do you know why the planet is so black?"

"Carbon. Coal, soot, whatever. Overcooked, I'd say."

"Yes. There is evidence of vast volcanic activity in the distant past."

Doc grunted. "You really think diamonds are down there?"

"Great stress can forge beauty and hardness from common material."

"Or make a rubble pile. Get to the point, Li."

"So blunt. No finesse, no charm." Disapproval soured her voice.

He turned toward the exit.

Li said, "I know you spoke to Tobias on the ansible."

Intrigued, Cassie moved a few centimeters closer. A marvel of technology, the ansible used quantum entangled particles to provide instantaneous communication with a twin device on Earth, at a cost upwards of a thousand dollars a second. The initiator paid the expense. No one here made outgoing calls.

Doc paused, still facing the door. "So?"

"You have no money, no real power. Yet the richest man in the universe calls you."

"He wanted a status check."

"He talks to Jonas daily," Li said. Half true—the time dilation effects of travelling near the speed of light meant that from Earth's perspective, the father-son chats were *annual* events. "Never before has Tobias called for you. Or am I mistaken?"

Doc whirled toward Li. "It doesn't concern you."

She laughed, the sound like bells tinkling. "Forgive my curiosity. It is in my nature."

"Didn't work out well for Pandora." Doc turned again to the door.

"Wait. Please." Li grasped his sleeve and gently spun him around. "I know you find me attractive."

Cassie suppressed a snort. Li believed *everyone* found her attractive.

"You have been so tense, so alone, and you need not be," Li said. Her fingers combed through the doctor's blond locks.

He pulled away. "I should get to sickbay. Get things ready for touchdown."

"You don't know what it is like," she said with a theatrical wringing of her hands. "Desire enflames me, but the captain is a charmless brute and Jonas is infatuated by Cassie."

Not infatuated. In love. Stop being a drama queen.

Doc said, "You have Lyra."

"Lyra. Yes. I have her, she has me. But it is not enough. I have certain... appetites... that can only be satisfied by a man."

Why was Li acting this way? She wasn't stupid. Her PhD in geology was merely the first of many vetting requirements to land a place on the crew. Did she really think she could learn Doc's secrets through seduction?

Doc placed a hand on Li's shoulder, smoothing down a cascade of her silken black hair. "I am not getting involved with you or anyone else on this ship."

"Why? Surely you have no woman waiting on Earth. She would be an old hag when you return. For what do you save yourself?"

"I'm being professional."

A toss of Li's head sent the silky strands fleeing from his fingertips. "You would have me suffer—have both of us suffer—for lack of a few moments of physical intimacy? I am not looking for more than that."

"I can give you something to suppress the libido." He floated toward the exit.

Li sprang upward in a half-summersault, stopping face-to-face—but upside down—in front of him. "No one will know. They are all on the bridge." Her arms circled his head, constricting like a python until their lips touched. Doc's arms flew up, fingers spread.

Seconds passed. Doc's hands rose to grip Li's head. Cassie expected him to push her away. He didn't. The kiss grew passionate.

It ended with Li cartwheeling to align herself with Doc's body. Her fingers traced a slow path from his chest to his waist. Using his belt as a handhold, she lowered her body while maintaining eye contact. "It has been at least two weeks with no one ministering to your needs. The pressure must be terrible. Or have you taken matters into your own hand?" She laughed at his discomfort as her right hand danced on the crotch of his pants. "Are you ready for the ecstasy I can bring?"

Doc said something too soft for Cassie to hear. He seemed to be paralyzed as Li's hands opened his fly. "What did Tobias say?" she said casually.

"Damn it, Li. Go back to your cabin."

Her hand slipped inside his pants, turning his protest into a gasp. A few seconds later Li withdrew her hand and slid the middle finger slowly across her pursed lips. She stared expectantly at Doc.

"I can't," he said, though the words carried a distinct whine. Microgravity inhibited erections, but the tent in Doc's pants argued that impotence wasn't the source of Doc's unease.

"Is one of us ill?" Li asked. "Why else would he call you?"

"Everyone's fine."

"Perhaps he is ill and wishes you to break the news to Jonas? Whatever it is, your secret will be safe with me." Li's hand disappeared again. She murmured musically as Doc squirmed.

Cassie felt like a voyeur, unable to turn away. She hoped they weren't going to fuck right in front of her. Doc's hands descended to Li's head, those same hands that so thoroughly examined Cassie's most intimate parts in the pre-flight medical checks. A fresh wave of nausea surged through her stomach. Could she escape unnoticed through the upper door? No, not without puking. She longed for a breath of fresh, sweet air, not the sterile recycled atmosphere of the ship.

Li pulled away. "Quid pro quo, doctor?"

"What?"

"Or shall I ask Jonas why his father would rather talk to you than his own son?"

He growled. "I don't like being threatened." He caught one of the scarves and pulled her against his body.

Li twirled away, leaving him with a limp scarf. "Merely teasing." She stretched a hand toward the door, which hissed open. "Delayed gratification yields more intense pleasure." She somersaulted, gracefully pushed off the wall, and floated from the room. Doc followed, cursing and careening off the bulkhead as he fumbled with his zipper. The door closed behind him.

Cassie found herself breathing hard with the memory of JJ's dark muscular arms, his gentle fingertips, and the spiral of kisses he had planted on her body as she spun slowly in the air. What could Li understand of ecstasy? Sex in zero-G could be great, but it took patience and effort. And ecstasy required more than sex. It took trust, empathy, and commitment. Jonas listened to her, cared about what she felt. He knew her favorite color was green and her cactus was named Burt.

We took precautions. How could this have happened? She sighed and pushed her thoughts in another direction. Why had Tobias called Doc?

They'd been in space for two weeks, ship time, while twelve years passed on Earth. A lot could have happened back there, but what news would Tobias entrust to Doc and not JJ? Nothing came to mind.

The nausea finally subsided. She pushed away from the window and descended to the walkway. She lingered there as the orbit of the ship moved past its alignment with the star, smothering the room with blackness. Her mood darkened as well.

The *Far Traveler* was Earth's first starship. No one knew for sure the effects of living for weeks at a time in ghost phase, but data from decades of shorter interplanetary hops proved space travel had cumulative harmful effects on the body. Especially developing bodies.

She hadn't decided what to do. Her options sucked. She hadn't told Jonas, hadn't told anyone, including Doc. In a few weeks they'd be back on Earth and she'd be forced to reach a decision and devise a plan. Until then, she would focus on immediate goals and adapt as conditions changed. The ship would land soon. Duties would replace flights of fear and fantasy as gravity reasserted its authority, drawing untethered objects and dreams to the ground.

Chapter 2

Ship Time: Day 13. 1000 hours.

Cassie moved weightlessly onto the bridge. Unlike the empty, blank-slate feel of the observation room, the bridge bristled with displays and control panels. A sense of expectancy charged the air as electronic hums harmonized with beeps and whines like an orchestra of equipment warming up prior to a performance.

Captain Maxwell Kazakov sat in the command chair, ready to conduct the next movement. The chair's position on a central, elevated dais gave an unobstructed view of the crew and instrumentation.

He glanced at her and then the wall clock. The fingers of his right hand drummed on the arm of his chair. *Tap, tap... tap. Tap, tap... tap.* The quickness almost masked the missing middle finger. Cassie took her seat at the science console and strapped herself in. Images and data from the sensors—visual and infrared telescopes, radar, gravitometer, external temperature, hull pressure, radiation level—filled her screens. The readings hadn't changed since entering orbit. The planet had no moons, no magnetic field, no current volcanic activity. The oxygen-nitrogen atmosphere and an orbit in the Goldilocks zone made it a near-perfect destination for exploration and potential colonization.

The stations for the five crewmembers formed a semicircle in front of the captain. JJ sat in the foremost seat, ahead and left of Cassie. His dark hands moved confidently over and through the mix of real and virtual consoles. The transparent bow of the ship showed a field of stars over a black disk. JJ twisted around and flashed a smile. "Hi, Cassie. Got Burt tied down?"

A tingle rippled along her arms and legs. She had secured the cactus with the two bungee cords they sometimes used in zero-G sex. Overcoming the tendency to drift apart required a form of mutual bondage. "He'll stay put."

Lyra Sullivan sat at the engineering station behind and to JJ's left, parallel with Cassie. The engineer's IQ soared somewhere in the stratosphere, and she was one of the very few people Tobias trusted with the knowledge of the inner workings of the Inertia Dampening Field generator. Neither that trust nor the knowledge of the IDF translated into popularity. Lyra's intellectual prowess tended to alienate people, as did her androgyny. Thin lips cut across a square, unadorned face dotted with freckles. Red hair, cut short, made no attempt to conceal a thick neck set atop broad shoulders. Denim coveralls hid curves that probably weren't there anyway. Lyra's quick temper did nothing to win friends, either. No wonder Li wanted to hook up with Doc. The wonder was why Li had bonded with Lyra at all.

The bridge doors gave a mechanical sigh and Cassie twisted in her seat to watch the remaining crewmembers, Doc and Li, drift into the room. Doc's disheveled hair and flushed face hinted of recent activity. He took his seat behind Cassie without saying a word or making eye contact.

Li floated past Doc in pristine elegance, smiling as she passed Cassie. She stopped at the pilot's console and touched JJ's shoulder. "Our fate is in your skilled hands, Jonas."

Cassie considered tossing a verbal barb, but Max spoke first. "Wu, you have ten seconds to strap in. This isn't a pleasure cruise." He barked at the engineer next. "Sullivan! Ship status?"

Cassie glimpsed a frown on Lyra's face. It vanished when Li kissed the engineer, whispered something in her ear, and moved on to her own seat. Lyra blushed and lowered her gaze to the instrument panel. "Reactor power in the green, Captain. IDF on max. Thrusters on auto. External sensors on-line. All systems go for landing." The slight Irish lilt carried a hint of pride.

Adam, the disembodied tenor voice of the ship's computer, said, "I am monitoring all systems as well, and ready to assume control as needed."

"I'm ready, Captain," Jonas said.

"Transfer IDF control to the pilot. Take us down, Mr. Jefferson."

Jonas nudged a lever on his panel. "Exiting ghost phase in five, four..."

Cassie suppressed a shiver. *Ghost phase*—a nearly perfect permeable state where meteors and cosmic rays could pass through the ship in silent, harmless, impotence. Objects in ghost phase stayed solid with respect to each other but lost inertia and gravitational attraction with respect to the rest of the universe. In theory, a spaceship in such a state could accelerate at thousands of Gs and quickly approach the speed of light. The *Far Traveler* turned theory into reality.

She clutched the totem dangling from her neck. The phase change took six seconds—six seconds of extreme vulnerability. Any outside object that entered the IDF and remained inside for six seconds also transformed into ghost phase. It would materialize inside the ship with catastrophic, often explosive results. Safety protocols required that ghost phase be entered and exited only in the vacuum of space and at speeds sufficient to ensure transient objects passed through the ship in less than six seconds. She held her breath as Jonas counted.

"...two, one." The ship lurched slightly as a maneuvering thruster fired, confirming they now had mass and inertia, albeit reduced, with respect to the rest of the universe. Cassie exhaled.

"IDF at ninety-nine point nine," JJ said. "Thrusters on manual."

Inertia pressed Cassie gently against the side of her seat. The onset of weight and motion felt comforting after nearly two weeks of weightlessness.

"Reducing forward speed," JJ said. "Starting vertical descent." Cassie felt the seatbelt restrain her levitation as the black curve of the planet expanded. A band of white flashed by on its surface, denoting the six-hundred-kilometer wide belt of ice and snow that vertically wrapped the planet from pole to pole. The nausea pills were doing a better job. She felt only the barest bit of queasiness.

"Entering the atmosphere. Elevation two hundred fifty kilometers, descending at five kilometers per second."

The glow of ionized particles filled the windows as they blazed like a meteor through the atmosphere. The titanium hull could handle the heat—for a while, at least. She kept tight hold of the totem.

"Cass, you holding up all right?" asked Doc.

"Fine." An invisible hand pressed Cassie to the opposite side of her chair. Jonas must be banking at five or six Gs. The traitorous pills threatened to concede defeat.

Lyra said, "Jonas, quit showing off."

"The ship needs a workout." His hands were a blur, adjusting thrust, pitch, yaw, speed, and a dozen other variables. "Reducing speed to twenty kilometers per hour."

The invisible hand let go of Cassie, but seemed to have left a finger stuck in her throat. She covered her mouth and swallowed a bit of reflux.

"A dry area at sector three appears suitable for landing," Adam said. "The geological features satisfy the criteria set by Dr. Wu. It also satisfies Dr. Clearwater's request for liquid water. The site is two hundred meters from a small lake."

A few breaths calmed her stomach. She focused on a HUD of green grid lines that appeared in the air over the pilot's station. The display tilted and shifted forward it perfectly overlaid the view of the planet in the window. One square of the grid blinked yellow.

"Got it," Jonas said. "Elevation fifty kilometers." His confidence and her own fear of embarrassment convinced her stomach not to heave.

"Forty," continued Jonas. "Thirty. Twenty. Ten. One. Point five. Point two. Hovering at fifty meters. Adam, give me a radar bounce. What kind of surface is under us?"

"Checking," said the ship. "Layer of dust or loose soil, depth varies from zero point two meters to four point one meters. Bedrock under the soil. The surface is essentially flat, with a zero point seven degree slope toward the lake."

"Good. Keep me away from the water and the deep soil." JJ's fingers pushed a translucent lever floating in the air. "Landing struts extended. Touchdown in three. Two. One."

A slight jolt shook the ship. Panel lights blinked and displays shifted rapidly as the propulsion drive shut down and the ship's attenuated weight settled onto the landing struts.

"We did it!" squealed Li.

"Pop the cork and call me happy," Doc said.

"That's my girl," Lyra said with evident pride.

"The first landing outside our solar system," said the captain. "We're the world's first interstellar veterans. Good job, everyone. Sullivan, shut down the IDF."

"Please remain in your seats," said the computer. "You will soon experience the planet's full gravity. Items may have shifted during flight."

Doc groaned in mock irritation. Cassie grunted as she sank into the flight seat.

Jonas looked over. "You okay?"

"Feels like someone's sitting on me."

He grinned. "Wait until you stand up. It'll feel like a gorilla sitting on your shoulders."

Cassie tried to smile back.

JJ's brow rose. "Sure you're okay? You look pale."

Captain Kazakov barked questions in his gruff voice. "Hull integrity? Environmental readouts, internal and external?"

"Integrity one hundred percent, Captain," Adam said. The ship moved slightly. "No leaks, no structural deformations. Landing struts are leveling the ship. Ground surface has compressed approximately fourteen centimeters under the weight of the ship. This is within design parameters."

Cassie studied her own console. "External environment is consistent with the readings from orbit. Twenty-three degrees Celsius. Atmospheric composition: nitrogen seventy-three percent, oxygen nineteen percent, water vapor five percent, argon one percent. Carbon dioxide is a bit high at zero point nine percent. Hundreds of trace compounds, mostly aromatics."

"Most excellent," Li said. "We will not need to wear those ugly plastic suits!"

"Yes, you will," Cassie said. "We don't know enough about those trace compounds. There could be unknown poisons or microscopic pathogens. Until I finish the analyses, we treat this world as a BioHazard Level IV."

"Which is?" Doc asked.

She locked eyes with him, irritated because he of all people knew the protocols. His knowing smile and a shifting of his eyes said, *the others need a reminder*. Cassie nodded. "No one goes out without a biosuit. Nothing from the outside comes aboard. The airlocks stay in decon mode until I say otherwise. Samples go straight to the hot side of the inflatable lab."

"We know the drill," Max said. "Adam, give us a video feed of the outside."

"Of course, Captain." A semi-transparent image formed in the air above JJ's work station. The initial view matched the scene outside the window—a twilight sky with a few stars pressed down on an expanse of black ground, like a field of crushed coal, empty and desolate for hundreds of meters. The image panned, showing more of the same until the sky lightened and Teegarden's Star appeared low in the sky. The terrain now looked like thousands of black bubbles of different sizes. Adam increased the resolution to reveal umbrella-like domes that sat atop thick stalks of various heights and diameters.

"That looks like... plant life?" Doc said in a questioning tone.

Cassie's heart skipped a beat. Planetary explorers had found single cell organisms before. She'd studied some of them on Europa during graduate school. She had expected similar life here, something akin to cyanobacteria or blue-green algae responsible for creating the oxygen in the atmosphere. She hadn't expected life forms the size of bushes and trees.

"Increase magnification," she said. The view zoomed again but didn't help. The black objects provided almost no contrast with the black soil. "I'll have to get out there, Captain."

"Do you think the Prime Directive applies?" Doc asked.

When life—albeit simple, one-celled organisms—had been found on Mars and then on Europa, the United Nations had passed the so-called "Prime Directive" resolution, which stated humanity would take a hands-off approach to any planet found to harbor intelligent life. No complex extra-terrestrial life had ever been found, much less any sign of intelligence.

Lyra said, "Don't mess with my commission."

"Protecting life is more important than one percent of the gross," Cassie said.

Lyra's gaze shifted between Cassie and Jonas. "Easy for you to say."

"They're just a bunch of weeds," Max said.

"Too soon to say." Cassie ignored the scowls from the crew. Classification of alien life was her call, and... she'd get to name it! Her pulse quickened, but the initial elation morphed to anxiety. Such a discovery could bring fame and attention that would make decisions about her future even more problematic.

"Why aren't they green?" Lyra said.

"They're blacker than Jonas," Doc said.

Li's face registered displeasure. "Don't be rude, Karl."

Lyra turned a scowl toward Li. Cassie wondered why Li put up with the jealousy.

Jonas smiled. "No offence taken. It is weird, everything being black. Adam, can you pan up a little?"

The angle shifted, and a lake appeared just beyond the plants. Its calm surface reflected an elongated image of Teegarden's Star. The red dwarf hung like a large orange ball a few degrees above the horizon. The black silhouette beneath the star certainly appeared to be vegetation—branchless stems and rounded tops suggested a patch of giant mushrooms. Nothing moved. No wind blew.

"A black forest," whispered Li.

"Continue panning, Adam," Max said. "I want to see aft." The image changed to a barren plain of black sand and a trail of crumbled rock suggestive of a dry river bed. The plain stretched for kilometers, unbroken by water or vegetation.

"The life forms do not extend more than one hundred eight meters from the water," Adam said.

"Possibly related to their metabolism," Cassie said. "I'll need to get samples. Adam, activate Robbie and start inflating the lab."

"Patience, Clearwater," Max said. "We need a name for this planet. Any ideas?"

"Obsidian," Cassie said, fingering the totem. Grandfather had carved the thunderbird from ebony using a black obsidian knife. The planet seemed likely to carve them a place in history.

"Daiyu," Li said. "It means black jade."

"I like Daiyu," Lyra said.

"Me, too," Doc said, smiling at Li, oblivious of Lyra's glowering face. Anger seemed to be the engineer's natural state.

"Any objections to Daiyu?" Max asked. Cassie stoically accepted Li's popularity.

"I like Obsidian," JJ said.

Silence fell. Each second seemed longer than the one before. JJ seemed relaxed, the captain looked amused, but Cassie felt strain building in everyone else.

Li spoke, her face stiff as a mask at a masquerade ball. "Obsidian is... appropriate. Volcanic glass. Often black."

Lyra raised her arms in protest. "Don't let him push you—"

Cassie couldn't see the look Li gave to the engineer, but Lyra's mouth abruptly closed. Doc's head swiveled from Li to JJ. He cleared his throat. "Obsidian's fine with me."

"So be it," said Max. "Adam, notify Earth that we landed on planet SO 02530... hell, give 'em the official designation and say we named it Obsidian."

Chapter 3

Ship Time: Day 13. 1300 hours.

The ground shifted and tugged at Cassie's boots like desert sand, but it looked more like the north Atlantic on a moonless night—endless blackness broken only by an occasional pale whitecap, the tips of rocks large enough to reach the surface. An alien sun the color of burning embers squatted above the horizon. Despite appearing twice as large as Earth's sun, it cast barely enough light to bleach the sky a sullen yellow. A hundred meters ahead, the mass of domed plants formed a stark silhouette against the pallid sky. She strained to see details, but the black plants, shadows, and soil merged seamlessly together. It was as though all color had been sucked out of this world.

Cassie glanced back at the lab, now a hundred meters behind them. Its bulging yellow walls and anchoring ropes made it look like a rubber raft floating beside the massive hull of the *Far Traveler*. The silvery disk of the starship reflected a distorted image of the orange sun, making it look as if the ship were ablaze and might soon join the black ash of the planet.

Disturbed by the image, she looked away and spied a moving orange suit—Li on her trek toward a large rock outcrop. The geologist slogged through ankle-deep dust with none of the grace she'd shown in zero gravity.

"Something wrong?" asked JJ. His voice carried a hint of concern, but no sign of exertion.

"Nope," Cassie managed to say without panting. Why hadn't fate provided a planet with gravity twenty percent *less* than

Earth's? The walk from the ship left her drenched in sweat, despite the idyllic ambient temperature. The biosuits didn't come with climate control. She could have worn a full spacesuit, which included a dehumidifier, but those suits weighed four times more than the biosuits.

JJ searched the sky opposite the sun, where several stars dotted the twilight. He pointed to the brightest. "Sol. Home. Twelve light years away." His gloved hand took hers.

She waited for him to say something more. When he didn't, she tore her gaze from the sky, let go his hand, and resumed her march to the plants. Still breathing hard, she focused on making it to the grove. Only ninety meters away now.

"Hitch a ride on Robbie," Jonas said. "I'll call him back."

Although Robbie was an extension of Adam, everyone found it convenient to refer to the robotic cart by a separate name. The mechanical arms, tank treads, sonar, ground penetrating radar, and drawers of tools and storage containers marked him as a vital member of the exploratory team.

"No, let him finish scouting. I want advance warning of any hungry, alien version of a T-Rex." Robbie disappeared into the mushroom jungle.

Jonas walked a few steps ahead of her. "We haven't seen so much as an insect."

"Let's play it safe." Cassie wondered if walking in the compressed tread marks would be easier. It was. She fast-walked past Jonas. "See? I'm fine."

"You're panting," JJ said. "You should have spent preflight mornings in the gym instead of in bed."

She flipped him the finger. He laughed.

The uniform blackness of the soil and life-forms made observation difficult until they actually entered the grove. Cassie confirmed her initial impression of the life-form's external anatomical similarity to mushrooms. The plants differed in size but seemed nearly identical. The smallest stood a few centimeters high with stalks about two centimeters thick, topped by rounded caps approximately five centimeters wide. Most plants, numbering in the hundreds, ranged from one to two meters in height, with proportionally-sized caps. The tallest plants exceeded three meters, with meter-thick stalks supporting caps as broad as beach umbrellas. Pale to medium gray undersides provided a welcome contrast to the uniform blackness.

"All we need are fairies and leprechauns sitting on these giant mushrooms," JJ said.

"Don't tell Captain Kaz, he'll come looking for the pot of gold."

"I heard that, Clearwater." Cassie jumped as the captain's gruff voice filled her helmet. "But that's Sullivan's myth, not mine."

Cassie laughed. "Forgot we were public."

"No big deal," Jonas said. "Not yet, anyway."

"Robbie, status report."

Adam responded immediately. "No movement detected other than crew. No sounds other than crew. No animal tracks, no feces, no nests or burrows to indicate animal life, Dr. Clearwater."

"Good. Join us. I could use more light and some high-res photos to accompany my observations."

Robbie emerged from the thicket and rolled to them, swerving occasionally to avoid crushing plants beneath its treads. Cassie smiled in approval and took similar care walking through the grove. Each dome tilted slightly toward the sun—except for one, a fifty-centimeter-tall plant whose undersized dome pointed *away* from the sun, leaving it entirely in shadow.

Cassie moved on, dictating initial impressions. "Plants smaller than a meter, presumably immature, have smooth caps. The caps of taller ones are covered with a dense mat of short narrow leaves, like pine needles. Jonas, help me up." She climbed atop Robbie for a better view—not to rest her legs—and performed a slow visual scan of the grove. "No apparent order to the placement of the plants. No buildings or constructed artifacts." Yet something seemed off. She scanned the grove again. "That's interesting."

"What?" asked Jonas.

"The plants seem to be randomly positioned, but as far as I can tell, each dome has unimpeded sunlight. Not a single dome is in shadow." *Except for the genetic misfit sitting in its own shadow.*

Ready for hands-on examination, Cassie stepped off the cart, clapped her hands loudly near a plant, and then poked a finger against its dome. "No reaction to sound or touch." She knelt beside a smaller plant with a finger-thick stem, grasped it firmly, and wiggled it back and forth, trying to work it free of the ground. It snapped, firecracker loud in the eerily silent grove.

"Damn! I didn't want to break it." A gray fibrous cord connected the upper and lower portions. Amber sap oozed from the broken ends.

Cassie pulled the lower half out of the loose soil, careful not to break the connective fiber. Three silver-gray roots emerged, attached symmetrically to the base of the stem. Thousands of tiny scales covered each root, giving it a snake-skin appearance. The scales sparkled in the light. Cassie touched a root. Flexible, almost prehensile. It squirmed; she yelped and nearly dropped it.

"Cassie?"

"I'm all right." She stared at the roots more closely. A new, alien life form meant anything was possible. Classifications like "plant" and "animal" might not apply.

The roots hadn't moved, merely swayed in her trembling hand. She'd spooked herself with old superstitions. She could hear Grandfather say, "The Great Spirit is within all things, Cassie. The trees, the grass, the rivers, the mountains, the animals that walk the earth, or swim the water, or soar the sky." She remembered one of the prayers he'd taught her. *Great Spirit, let me learn the lessons you have hidden within each rock and leaf. Help me remember I am sister to all that is.*

"What did you say?"

"Nothing," she said, hiding embarrassment.

"Thinking of your grandfather?"

"Science trumps superstition." She tried to snap off one of the roots. Unlike the rigid but brittle stem, the scaled, flexible root resisted all attempts to break. It finally yielded to the laser scalpel, and she dropped the severed tip into a sample bag. She placed the broken plant on the ground. "Jonas, check out those really tall plants." When he turned away, Cassie fitted the ends of the plant together and heaped soil around its remaining roots. Probably too late to do any good, but she'd check on it tomorrow.

Cassie moved to the nearest mid-sized plant, a one-and-a-half meter-high specimen with a particularly thick dome. She knelt as Robbie illuminated the underside. Hundreds of soft gray ribs radiated from the center, much like gills on a typical mushroom. A faint haze at the junction of the stem and cap caught her attention. She reached into the haze. A layer of extremely fine black powder clung to her glove as if statically charged.

"Could be spores. Get this on video." Robbie extended a camera from its bay and began filming. Cassie clapped her hands to knock off the dust before continuing her examination. The larger stem proved to be as rigid as the smaller one, and very strong. She pushed against the stem, wondering how well the roots anchored it.

The whole thing tipped as a root popped from the ground. She let go; the plant swayed but didn't topple. The dome swelled and shrank as if filled with liquid. She brushed her glove across the mat of leaves. Softer than pine needles but firmer than grass. She pressed down, felt the give of fluid beneath the resilient surface. Definitely a bladder.

The leaves stopped at the edge of the cap, leaving a narrow bald ring around the periphery. Puckered lips spaced evenly around the rim opened and closed rapidly.

"Numerous small orifices penetrate the ring like holes in a belt. They seem to be expelling puffs of gas. Possibly a respiratory system. Robbie, take an air sample."

"You sound excited," Jonas said. He leaned against a tall mushroom. In his orange biosuit, he looked like a caterpillar.

"This is *awesome*." She waved her arms and grinned so hard she could barely talk. "The first multi-cellular extraterrestrial life ever discovered. And I get to study it!" She rummaged through Robbie's compartments, found a syringe and large bore needle, and extracted a sample from a mushroom cap. Thick, golden fluid filled the vial.

"You get to name it, too. You'll be famous."

She tried not to think about that.

A double beep sounded, and they shifted frequency to channel two. Li chattered excitedly in Mandarin, or was it Cantonese? Some kind of Chinese, interspersed with the words "diamonds" and "rich." Jonas waved to Li, who stood on a boulder, arm raised high like the Statue of Liberty, though she held a softball-sized rock instead of a torch.

Cassie's anxiety eased. The mission of the *Far Traveler*— exploration—came with the expectation of discovering wealth. If Li's prediction of vast diamond deposits were correct, the limelight would shine on her, not on the discoverer of a grove of alien mushrooms.

"Jealous?" JJ said. "She doesn't get to name diamonds. They belong to the company." His smile nearly filled the faceplate. She smiled back. *I should tell him.*

He knelt to help her remove soil from the base of a small plant, a specimen half a meter high. She held open a transparent sample bag while he carefully placed the plant inside and added a few scoops of soil. Still on his knees, he took her hand. Jonas twisted a dial on his helmet and held up three fingers.

Cassie's heart fluttered. Before she could change channels, Li screamed.

Cassie and Jonas turned toward the rock outcropping. Li sat on a boulder gripping her left leg. "Help! I think I have broken my leg!"

Jonas sprinted toward the injured woman. Cassie followed. Doc's voice came over the radio. "Li, is your suit punctured?"

"I do not think so."

"Good. Jonas, when you get to her, verify suit integrity. Cassie, proceed to the lab. Clear a table on the hot side. If Li's been exposed to the alien environment, I'll examine her there."

"Roger," answered Cassie. "Robbie, go help Li."

She backtracked to the sealed sample bag and heaved it over her shoulder, silently cursing the gravity of this planet. She slogged the hundred and fifty meters to the lab, watching Jonas scoop Li into his arms and set her gently atop Robbie. When Li put her arms around JJ's neck, Cassie looked away. Anger soured her stomach, and puking inside a biosuit was even worse than doing so in zero-G. She definitely needed stronger pills. Or a better mood.

Chapter 4

Ship Time: Day 13. 1400 hours.

Cassie entered the "hot" side of the lab and sealed the Velcro door behind her. The flat, rigid floor provided a welcome change from dry drifts of sand. She surveyed the arrangement of tables and equipment, pleased that Robbie complied with her requested floor plan.

A transparent airtight wall ran through the centerline of the lab, isolating the potentially dangerous half from the pristine safe half. Four sets of long rubber gloves penetrated the wall, allowing people on the clean side to manipulate samples on the other side safely and relatively easily. An airlock-decon station combo in the center of the wall permitted safe movement between the halves. Biosuits were required in the airlock and on the hot side at all times.

Cassie placed the plant samples on a stainless-steel work table next to one set of gloves. She then cleared supplies from a second table to let it serve as an examination table for Doc. By the time she finished, her biosuit felt like a sauna. Trickles of sweat became rivulets.

She squeezed into the decon-airlock, endured five seconds of UV sterilizing light and a dowsing of antiseptic spray. She waited another ten seconds for the air to cycle before the lock clicked and allowed her to step into the clean side of the lab. She stripped off her suit. The cool, dry air tingled delightfully.

JJ's voice came over the lab speakers. "No suit punctures. I'll take her to the ship."

Doc answered. "I'll be waiting in sickbay."

The main airlock of the *Far Traveler* had the same decon setup as the lab. Cassie tried not to think about Jonas removing Li's biosuit and carrying her to the elevator and then to sickbay, no doubt with Li's arms clinging seductively to JJ's neck.

Cassie pulled up a stool and stuck both hands into airtight gloves dangling above her plant sample. Following the United Nations recommended protocols, she tested for intelligence. The plant showed no meaningful response to integer progressions using sound beeps or light flashes, each repeated over a range of frequencies. The result wasn't surprising, since she saw no external evidence of eyes or ears. Mild UV light produced a whitish secretion from the dome of the plant, but the response lacked any pattern indicative of intelligence.

She poked at the dome in the same integer sequence, again with no response from the plant. Satisfied that the alien species wasn't sentient, she laid out scalpels, forceps, and other instruments for dissection. She took pictures with the portable X-ray machine to guide the cutting, but the indistinct results provided no help. She hated to open the plant without at least a vague idea of its internal structure.

She called Doc on the lab's intercom. "How's Li?"

"No broken bones. Probably a mild sprain. Wrapped the ankle and gave her naproxen for the pain."

"Glad to hear it. When you're done, can you bring the sonogram equipment out to the lab?"

A pause. "Ah, why?"

"To use on a plant specimen. The X-rays lack contrast."

"Oh." Doc chuckled. "Sure. Be right there."

Cassie busied herself extracting biopsies from the dome to use in the DNA sequencer, gas chromatograph, and microscopes. She took stem samples using a laser scalpel to slice off small wedges for analysis. She tried to biopsy the roots, but the hard protective scales bent the needles. She reached for the laser scalpel, and noticed the stem samples were gone.

No, not gone. Turned to piles of black dust.

The hot-side entrance flap peeled open. Doc, with help from Robbie's mechanical arm, wheeled the sonogram equipment inside. He waved through the dividing window. "You know how to run this, or want me to do it?"

"Easier for you." Cassie glanced at the disintegrated sample, worried that this planet might not want to surrender its secrets. "Feed the image to Adam. I'll observe on the monitor."

Doc moved the cart to the table. "Where first, dome or stem?"

"Dome."

"Hmmm. I'll need to mow the lawn." He ran a gloved hand across the coarse straight leaves.

"There's a scalpel on the next table."

"Rather use clippers." He rummaged through a drawer on the equipment cart until he found the clippers and used it to shave the leaves from most of the dome. He squeezed a generous amount of goop from a tube, smoothing it over the dome to ensure good contact.

Doc seemed dexterous and competent, apparently unhampered by the biosuit. Cassie envied him. *I should be doing these tests.* She watched Doc place the probe against the plant.

He looked at her through the wall. "Images should be coming through now."

Blurred impressions of oddly shaped organs appeared, connected by strings—possibly fluid vessels or supporting tendons. The images shifted as Doc moved the probe over the now smooth dome, which looked uncomfortably like the swell of a pregnant belly.

Doc's hands jerked back. "What the hell!"

The plant's dome ruptured in several places. Amber fluid oozed from some of the holes. Clear, thin fluids poured from other holes, dripped to the table, and began to smoke.

"Get back!" Cassie plunged her arms into the gloves, swept the hemorrhaging plant into the sink, and flipped on the exhaust fan. As the dome and roots bubbled, the stem began to flake away, crumbling to dust like the earlier samples. She flushed all of it down the drain. An alarm sounded as the pH meter of the holding tank swung wildly from acidic to alkaline before settling to a neutral seven.

A second alarm sounded—the air filtration system. "Adam?"

The alarm silenced. "Yes, Dr. Clearwater. The exhaust HEPA filters on the hot side of the lab have been damaged. The input filters are functioning properly. The air supply to the clean side was not affected."

She looked at Doc and then the sonogram machine. "It destroyed my specimen."

"Must have hit a resonant frequency."

"Without X-rays or ultrasound, how am I supposed to figure out its anatomy?"

"Dissection." Doc began rinsing the probe.

"You saw what happened. The thing is filled with corrosives."

"Make small cuts and flush generously with water."

"It'll take forever." She sighed with frustration. "What did you and Tobias talk about?" The question came out of her mouth before she could stop it. Doc said nothing. Sweat beaded on his forehead, clearly visible through the face mask of the biosuit. Cassie doubted it came from the humidity.

The flap opened and JJ entered the hot lab. "Hi, Doc, Cass."

Neither Doc nor Cassie responded.

Jonas looked at Doc and then to Cassie. "Am I missing something?"

"No, nothing. I need to be going," Doc said.

Cassie wondered what he was hiding. "Please stay. We need to discuss this further." She addressed Jonas next. "My sample disintegrated. Would you and Robbie bring back two complete plants, about the same size as the first? Plus the upper third of that larger one I almost tipped over."

JJ's narrowed stare and pursed lips said he'd want an explanation later. "Sure."

"And a water sample from the lake. But let Robbie do the cutting and collecting. The decomposition products are highly corrosive. Water might be, too."

"So you do care about me. I was beginning to worry." JJ winked and left.

Doc relaxed; she saw it in the movement of his suit. He turned to face her.

Cassie said, "Back to you and Tobias."

Doc blinked. "I don't have a clue what you're talking about."

"I better call Jonas back."

Doc's eyes shifted nervously, unable to meet her gaze for more than a second. "It's nothing, really. Tobias thinks Li wants to break up your romance with Jonas."

"And you're *helping* her?" She felt the rubber gloves stretch around the knuckles as her fists clenched.

"No! He asked me to keep tabs on the situation. Tobias knows you and Jonas have something special, and he wants to preserve it." Doc's Adam's apple bobbed. "Tobias likes you. You have nothing to worry about."

Doc sucked at lying, but she didn't want to use Jonas for leverage until she understood more of the mystery. Fortunately, other levers were available. "Okay," she said. "I'll talk to Li."

Doc looked dumbfounded. "No, don't. She's... unpredictable. Temperamental. You'll make things worse. Just ride it out." He gave an unreassuring smile.

"She has you by the balls. Why?"

The speakers crackled as Adam cleared his electronic throat. "The captain has called an all-hands meeting in the mess hall for fifteen hundred hours. That's in ten minutes, folks. See you there."

Doc said, "Gotta go." He sprinted through the exit.

Chapter 5

Ship Time: Day 13. 1500 hours.

Li stood at the front of the mess hall, confident, smiling, dressed like a super model about to parade down the runway. She held a walnut-size stone in one palm, two peanut-size stones in the other. The stones were translucent pale gray.

"Diamonds?" Doc said.

"Oh, yes," Li said.

The greasy, dull stones looked worthless, but Li's expertise and excitement said otherwise. Cassie nodded toward the stones. "You should have left them outside until I could run them through the lab."

"I know diamonds," Li said. She held up her pocket brain as if the mini-computer constituted proof.

"They could harbor a biological or chemical hazard."

Li sighed like an impatient teacher with a slow student. "The airlock decon killed anything on them." The assumption irritated Cassie, though Li was almost certainly correct.

Doc said, "Cassie and I discovered some powerful corrosive chemicals in the plants."

"Rocks," Lyra said. "Solid, inert, rocks. What's the big deal?"

Jonas entered and sat beside Cassie. The captain frowned. "You're late, Jefferson."

"I was in the middle of collecting samples. Better to finish than have to start over." He leaned toward Cassie. "They're in the lab in an empty aquarium tank."

Max grunted and turned to Li. "What are they worth?"

Li glanced at her pocket brain. "In their current state, perhaps five million dollars. Cut and polished, perhaps thirty million."

Doc whistled. "Not bad for an hour's work."

"Adam," said Max, "compute gross value if six people worked eight hours a day for ten days."

He's going to work us the entire duration of the mission, thought Cassie. Absurd. She needed time for science. She cast a side-long glance at Jonas. He seemed to be absorbed in his own thoughts. Was the son like the father? She hoped not.

The computer said, "Using Li's estimate for 'as is' condition, and assuming the same rate of acquiring the stones, gross would be two point four billion dollars, plus or minus ten million."

Max licked his lips in a quick, lizard-like flick. "The cost of the mission?"

Jonas answered before Adam. "Rounded off, about five hundred million."

"Leaving a net of one point nine billion dollars," Adam said. "The one percent profit sharing gives each member of the crew, except Doctor Unger, nineteen million dollars."

Lyra looked perplexed. "Why not Doc?"

"It's in my contract," Doc said, "which is why I'm not digging. I'll work in the lab analyzing the plants."

Cassie felt torn by fear and desire. She could avoid publicity by letting Doc have all the credit for studying the alien species... but she desperately wanted to do it.

Max scowled. "Doc's the first ever 'Prime Directive Enforcer.' Tobias thought it would be great for public relations. So, to keep him honest, Doc gets no share of the profits."

"Why did you come, then?" asked Lyra. "Who gives up twenty-four years of Earth time for nothing?"

Jonas said, "He's altruistic. Dad donated twenty million dollars to *Doctors Without Planets*, in Doc's name, before the ship lifted off. No strings attached."

Doc looked at the floor. He muttered something about wishing he'd stayed anonymous.

Cassie reached a decision. "It's *my* job to analyze alien life. I'm not digging until I finish."

Max said, "Your job is to do what I tell you to do. Check your contract."

Cassie shook her head. "Doc isn't qualified as an exobiologist. He can't make his call until I do the analysis. Doc can help me."

"She's right," Jonas said. The captain's face darkened.

Lyra swore. "Doc's not digging. Cassie's not digging. What about you, flyboy?"

"Enough, Sullivan." The captain drummed his fingers. "Doc, I can't make you dig, but you *could* do minor maintenance on the lab and the ship. And map out the local terrain. That will free Robbie up for digging." When Doc didn't respond, Max added, "We'll each toss a million to your favorite charity."

Lyra cried, "What?"

JJ smiled. Cassie kept her face neutral; she knew where Max was going.

"Do the math," Max said. "Without him we get fifteen million apiece. Tossing him a bone gets us eighteen million each with no extra work." He looked at Jonas. "Company makes more profit, too."

Jonas said, "I'm just the pilot."

Max chuckled. Cassie suspected he could calculate odds and percentages fast as a computer. Doc would still get less than anyone else, but five million dollars was a bone with meat on it.

Doc looked reluctant until Li gave a barely perceptible nod. He said, "Fine. I'm in."

Max turned to Cassie. So did everyone else. He said, "How long for your report?"

"Well, I could have a preliminary report tomorrow morning. I don't know about the final. Until then, no digging within twenty meters of the plants."

Li said, "That will become a problem. The best place to mine with minimal effort is the alluvial deposits along the dry river bed that runs through the grove."

Lyra said, "We can start a hundred meters upstream and work our way down. Cass should be done with her study by the time we get close to the mushrooms."

Cassie gave a noncommittal shrug. "Should be."

"Adam," Max said, "prepare a work schedule. Eight-hour shifts, ten-minute breaks every hour. Thirty-minute meals."

"Yes, Captain. Start time?"

"Now. Give Dr. Clearwater the rest of today off. Put her to work at 0900 tomorrow." Max looked at Cassie, then at Jonas. "Any objections?"

"None yet," Cassie said.

"Pass out the shovels," Max said. His face seemed to fracture. She'd never seen him reveal a genuine smile.

Chapter 6

Ship Time: Day 13. 1545 hours.

Cassie returned to the lab, this time staying on the hot side in her biosuit. The new sample bag, the one that should have held the top third of a mid-sized plant, looked like an inflated balloon. Cassie carefully lifted the bag by the neck, suspending it over the sink for inspection.

Nothing remained of the stem and dome structure. Damp, black powder filled the bottom fourth of the bag, covered by a layer of gray sludge. A thin layer of amber liquid floated on top. She set the bag in the sink before moving on to check plants in the glass tank.

Neither of the intact plants showed signs of deterioration. She sighed with relief.

The door flap peeled open and Jonas entered, shovel in hand. He set it down by the door, took a step toward her, and paused. "What's wrong?"

Cassie pointed to the sink. "The partial decomposed."

JJ whistled. "Not much of a shelf life."

She glanced at the clock. "Less than half an hour."

Cassie turned away and began arranging test tubes and Petrie dishes. "I need to find out what happened. I'm going to be busy for awhile. Shouldn't you be digging?"

"I started with my ten-minute break. There's something I need to say." He tapped his helmet and they switched to channel three for privacy.

"I'm listening," Cassie said.

"Let's move to the clean side and take off these suits."

"Jonas, this isn't the place for a quickie."

His face registered surprise before breaking into a grin. "Extremely tempting, but I'm thinking longer term."

She tried to swallow with a mouth gone suddenly dry. *No. I'm not ready.* But she couldn't think of an excuse to put him off. Besides, he needed to know. Except he didn't. Why ruin his dreams, too? Inwardly cringing, she took his hand and led him to the airlock.

Their helmets beeped, followed by an announcement from Adam. "The captain has ordered everyone to stay on channel one. I will be monitoring all channels and broadcasting reminders."

Jonas frowned. "What's a guy got to do for some privacy around here?"

Adam said, "Shall I assume that is a rhetorical question?"

Cassie patted JJ's arm. "Hey, we'll have these suits off in a minute."

The airlock hissed open, but before they could step inside, the lab door peeled back and Li entered. She limped toward them.

"I am sorry to intrude, but my leg is not holding up in this higher gravity. May I have your assistance in getting to the dig site? I would ride on Robbie, but he is already loaded with tools and containers."

"I thought Doc was your flunky," Cassie said.

Jonas patted her hand. "Tonight." He walked to Li and extended an arm. "Lean on me."

Li said, "Cassie is so fortunate to have such a strong, helpful man in her life."

Cassie glared. Li smiled.

The Velcro closed, leaving Cassie alone. She cut open the distended sample bag, venting some of the gas into the chromatograph, some to sample canisters, and the rest to the exhaust stack.

The machine chirped and a yellow light began to flash. Odd. Poisonous compounds would flash red. "Adam, what's the problem?"

"The chromatograph has used all its working memory," said the computer. "Over three hundred thousand specific chemical compounds have been identified."

So many! "How do they breakdown?"

"Organic compounds, including proteins, genetic material, and sugars, primarily glucose. A variant of Chlorophyll. A large amount of carbon in the form of fullerenes. There are an unusually large number of terpenes, phenols, and alkaloids. Some are poisonous but are present only in harmless trace amounts."

"I imagine they'd make quite a stink."

"Many of these would have familiar smells. Many would have new smells or would be undetectable by humans."

The next several hours became a blur of increasingly complex analyses to understand Obsidian's life. The organic breakdown had destroyed whatever cell structure and DNA the plant may have had. Internal anatomy had to wait for more samples, if she could find a way to preserve them.

She eventually analyzed the sample of lake water. It tested pure with a few dissolved trace minerals and organic compounds matching those given off by the plant. A single species of bacteria inhabited the water. Oddly, she found no microbes in the soil or in the atmospheric samples. It left her perplexed. Life didn't evolve in isolation. It required an ecosystem, and two species didn't provide the necessary level of diversity.

The mystery deepened when she mapped the bacteria's genome and found it to be incapable of reproducing. It simply existed, apparently not aging as it fed on trace organic compounds. With no natural enemies, the bacteria might be millions of years old. It might be immortal. Shaking her head, Cassie returned to the surviving plants.

She sliced a small wedge of stem and placed it in a test tube before it crumbled to dust. The Carbon-14 analyzer pegged the sample at seventy-one thousand years old. Probably an error since the planet had so much carbon with isotopic proportions different than on Earth. But if the bacteria lived forever, why not the plants? She'd recalibrate the machine tomorrow.

She yawned. The remaining tests would run for hours. Before returning to the ship, she detoured to the mushroom grove hoping to find the small plant she'd unintentionally broken. She couldn't find it, implying it died and disintegrated. How ironic. In a world of eternal twilight where plants might survive for millennia, a seedling had vanished without a sign it had ever lived. The unmoving, unblinking sun cast a judgment dark as the black-on-black shadows. Cassie shuddered and pushed those thoughts away with a better one—getting a few hours sleep. The test results would be ready when she woke up, in time to deliver her initial report over breakfast.

In her cabin she found a love note from JJ asking her to come over. She showered, put on a lacy nightgown, wrapped herself in a robe, and stepped into the hall. Jonas needed to know. The decision should be theirs, not only hers. Halfway to his room, her stomach rumbled. She'd worked through dinner and felt ravenous. She turned and headed for the mess hall.

She devoured a sandwich then prowled around for desert. The walk-in freezer held a gallon of fudge ripple, but delight turned to frustration as the ice-cream scoop barely scratched the rock-hard surface. Cassie considered going to sickbay to grab a scalpel to attack the frozen mass.

Frozen. Scalpel. Hunger and fatigue vanished. The lab had liquid nitrogen. Freezing one of the plants should stop decomposition, allowing her to do a proper dissection. She licked the scoop, ran to the airlock, donned her biosuit, and rushed to the lab.

She hoped the surge of adrenaline would last the night.

Chapter 7

Ship Time: Day 14. 0800 hours.

Hair still damp from a hurried shower, Cassie stood in the mess hall to deliver her report to the crew. Her eyes burned from lack of sleep but she barely noticed. The information gained in the past few hours made her giddy. This was cutting-edge science, and she was doing the cutting.

The captain sat at the far end of the table, head bowed, absently doing his three-finger tap. Cassie cleared her throat. Every face turned to her, although Li's gaze kept drifting toward Jonas. Annoyance helped Cassie ignore the butterflies hovering in her stomach.

"This is really exciting stuff. I'll summarize the high points and answer questions. Adam has my full report, including diagrams, photographs, and test data, for anyone who wants to see the details. I want to stress that this is still a preliminary report. The final will include results from tests that are running now, plus any new discoveries that arise.

"My report is divided into five sections. External anatomy, internal anatomy, cellular and genetic structure, stimulus response tests, and finally, summary and conclusions. Let's jump straight to the summary. Adam, image one, please." A semi-transparent hologram of a plant appeared next to Cassie. "Although the plants look like mushrooms, they are definitely plants, not fungi." She tilted the image to show the top. "The leaves and the skin of the dome contain Chlorophyll, which is a plant characteristic."

"I thought Chlorophyll made leaves green," Lyra said.

"Usually. This is a variant that absorbs a very large range of light frequencies, which makes it appear black." The captain resumed tapping. Cassie spoke faster, describing the plant's external structure, and then moving the holographic image to illustrate features such as the gills and lips on the dome, the dust-generating collar at the top of the stem, and the three prehensile roots.

"The cross section of stem looks like growth rings on a tree," Doc said.

"I concur, although it's puzzling because the planet doesn't have seasons."

Max said, "Is there a bottom line somewhere?"

"Yes." She took a breath and let it out slowly. The data pointed to a conclusion that nobody wanted. "I think the Prime Directive applies."

Doc straightened in his chair. "The plants are intelligent? They passed the tests?"

"If you look at their genetic make-up—"

"They're goddamn *plants*, Clearwater," Max said.

"Yes, but..." She didn't understand the hostility surrounding her. Even Jonas didn't look happy, but at least he seemed grimly thoughtful. "The facts—"

Li interrupted in her haughtiest voice. "You would jeopardize all our fortunes for some mushrooms. Ridiculous."

Lyra asked, "Where's your proof?"

Max nodded. "Proof. It better be good." He glanced at the clock. "And quick."

Jonas gave an encouraging nod. Cassie resumed the briefing. "Two facts are relevant. First, the DNA of the plants is extremely efficient. There's not one molecule wasted. No 'junk DNA' that clutters the genetic codes of every Earth species. That type of perfection doesn't evolve naturally. These plants were genetically engineered."

"Engineered," Doc said, "as in designed by an intelligent life form?"

"Yes."

"But conceivably the plants could have evolved naturally to this state."

She shook her head. "Evolution requires Darwinian influences. Life forms competing for resources, adapting in a kind of biological arms race. Which brings me to the second fact: there is only one other life form on Obsidian. It's a species of bacteria that doesn't age, doesn't reproduce, whose only apparent function is to maintain perfect ecological balance with the plants."

"Balance?" asked Jonas.

"Primarily to keep the oxygen and carbon dioxide levels stable. The plants absorb carbon dioxide and give off oxygen. The bacteria do the opposite."

"Your logic is flawed," Lyra said. "You claim the plants were created by intelligent aliens, and then you say there are no aliens on the planet."

"Good point," Doc agreed. "Does seem to be a hole."

Cassie sighed. "Imagine you are exploring a cave, and discover paintings on the walls. There is no doubt the paintings were done by one or more intelligent beings. The DNA of these plants and microbes paints that picture."

Max said, "Using the same analogy, there is no way to tell if the creators are still around. They could all be dead, maybe for thousands of years."

"Possibly. But for all we know, this is their garden. They could come back at any time, and based on the genetic perfection of their creations, their science is far ahead of ours."

"Pure conjecture," Max replied.

Jonas said, "How long do the plants live? How do they reproduce? That might give clues as to how often the alien gardener stops by."

"The plants have sexual organs at the junction of stem to roots."

Doc said, "Show me your pistil, I'll show you my stamen." He seemed as eager as the captain for the presentation to end, but winning over the doctor was a must.

"The plants seem to be hermaphroditic," she said calmly. "Details of the structural arrangement make me think they can't self-pollinate. Also, one of the trace chemicals in the soil is a powerful plant contraceptive."

Jonas asked, "Why did the samples disintegrate?"

Cassie called up a projection showing the horizontal cross section of the plant's stem. As she zoomed in, hundreds of concentric circular ridges appeared, looking like the tight spiral groove of an ancient, black, vinyl phonograph record.

"Each ring is composed of tens of thousands of layers, with each layer holding billions of C-60 fullerene molecules, better known as bucky-balls." She paused at the blank looks from the crew. "Carbon atoms arranged in a soccer ball shape. Named after Buckminster Fuller, the architect and inventor who studied that shape extensively. Never mind. The layers come from the dust released from a collar-like organ at the junction of the stem and cap."

Doc showed a modicum of curiosity. "What's that gray area in the center?"

"The rings surround a central nerve cord—"

Lyra rose from her seat. "Those frigging plants have *brains*?"

"The structure is too simple to be an actual brain, but it is possible the plants have a sensory system that may help them survive."

Doc scratched his head. "Since there's no evidence of animal life, why would the plants need a survival mechanism?"

"That's one of many unanswered questions. Let me finish answering Jonas. Those trillions of bucky-balls in the stem are held in place by a small electric charge generated by the nerve stem and millions of branching nerves. When the plant dies or the bucky-balls lose contact with the charge, they fall off. Think of a bunch of iron filings clinging to an electromagnet. Turn off the magnet and the filings drop."

"What about the mushroom caps and the roots?" Doc said. "They aren't bucky-puckies."

"The structures contain hundreds of acid and alkaline bladders. They're normally closed, but they open when the electric charge fades. The organic parts of the plant quickly dissolve. It's a very efficient recycling mechanism."

"Is that what produces the gas?" asked Jonas. "The sample bag looked ready to pop."

"Some of it came from gas molecules trapped inside the bucky-balls. The loss of charge seems to open the balls."

JJ's mouth curled in doubt. "Looked like a *lot* of gas."

"Most came from reactions between the acids, alkalis, and other chemicals in the dome. Hundred of thousands of distinct gaseous compounds formed."

"Study time's over," Max said. "You'll be digging with the rest of us."

Cassie felt stunned. "Sir? These plants are a unique scientific discovery. They *must* be studied. And since intelligent life designed the plants, the Prime Directive applies."

"The plants are not intelligent."

"No, but—"

Max lifted his hand for silence. "Doctor Unger?"

"At best the plants seem to imply an external intentionality of design, but they are not themselves intelligent." Doc kept his eyes on the captain. "The Prime Directive doesn't apply."

Max turned to Cassie with his *I dare you to cross me* smile. "Grab a shovel."

"Captain?" Jonas said.

Max turned with obvious annoyance. "What?"

"I'm thinking Cassie should continue to study the plants. She raised some interesting questions, and we're near the border as far as the Prime Directive goes."

"The safe side of the border."

"She makes a compelling argument that the plants are artifacts of an alien intelligence. I'm concerned about public opinion if we deny our scientist the opportunity to study them further."

Max raised an eyebrow. "My goal is maximizing profits. What's yours?"

"The same. The government's been looking for an excuse to rein in MicroWeight Corporation for decades. Don't give them one."

Max stared at Jonas. Hard.

JJ shrugged. "Call Dad. See what he says."

A second passed. "That won't be necessary. Clearwater, finish the damn analyses. The rest of you, start digging." Everyone shambled to the door.

Cassie said, "My analysis might go faster if I could consult with specialists on Earth. I'd like to have some ansible time."

"Denied," Max said.

"The sooner I'm free to dig, the more money you make."

The crew stopped moving.

"I said no. This matter stays in-house. The ansible is off limits."

Cassie considered arguing, but she lacked the leverage Jonas possessed. She turned to JJ, certain he'd see the plea on her face.

"Captain's right, Cass." He turned to the others. "Let's go play in the dirt, people."

Li asked, "Do we need to wear those stupid suits?"

Why didn't he back me on the ansible request? Cassie abruptly became aware of the expectant stares. *What did I miss?* Oh yeah, Li whining about the suits again. "Weren't you listening? The plants are living chemical factories. They can synthesize almost any organic molecule, including poisons. So yes, suit up and shut up."

Li's eyes widened. Lyra growled and rose to her feet with fists clenched. Max stepped forward, blocking the path to Cassie. He pointed to the door. It looked as if the engineer would take a swing at Max, but something in the captain's stance or his face must have given her pause. She lowered her arms. Everyone filed out as Lyra cast death-ray eyes at Cassie.

Jonas lingered until the rest of the crew left. "Pull an all-nighter?"

Cassie nodded.

"Be really, really sure of your facts."

"Why didn't you back me for time on the ansible?"

"If word gets out about the plants, there'll be enormous political pressure to halt mining activity."

"Some things are more important than money." *Or fame.*

"Not to Dad." He kissed her. "Lighten up. Work on your Nobel prize. And leave a little time for me. Okay?" He winked and sauntered away.

A Nobel was the last thing she wanted, but it might be inevitable.

Chapter 8

Ship Time: Day 14. 1700 hours.

Cassie watered the remaining plant while wondering what intelligence created the species and for what purpose. An entire day of tests yielded only incremental gains in information. She returned to the ship and went through the decon shower and UV lamps, wondering if she might as well cancel the Biohazard protocols. With Adam's help she'd analyzed ninety percent of the gases expelled by the plants. None were harmful in the small quantities being produced. Her favorite lab rat, Mr. Jones, had shown no adverse effects from exposure to the gases or to the sap she'd fed to him. In fact, he seemed to enjoy it.

Animated voices came from the mess hall. Cassie realized she was famished as well as exhausted. When she stepped inside, conversation stopped. Every face—even JJ's—looked up with irritation.

"What's going on?" Cassie asked.

Lyra said, "You don't dig. Apparently you don't cook either."

Shit. It was my turn to cook dinner.

"Tending to mushrooms is such hard work," Li said.

"They're important! The first and only extraterrestrial life ever—"

"Did you finish the tox screens?" Max asked. "The biosuits slow us down."

"Almost." She lifted her arms, palms up. "Hey, everyone. I'm sorry."

Doc grimaced. "The suits weren't designed for extended periods of strenuous work. I'm concerned that another day of this might trigger heat exhaustion."

"You're wasting our time, Cassie," Lyra said. "By not helping the team, you're costing us millions of dollars."

Li nodded sagely. "The wearing of suits should be the doctor's call, not hers. Just as it is his decision regarding the Prime Directive."

Cassie saw JJ mouth the words, *let it go,* but she'd had enough. "I'm not going to be bullied into falsifying an official report."

"Nobody's talking about falsifying anything," Max said. "Just don't make claims you can't substantiate."

"What I put into the report will be the truth, the whole truth."

Doc raised a hand as if swearing an oath. "And nothing but the truth, so help me, Great Spirit in the sky."

Before she could launch a retort, Max stood. "Clearwater, my cabin." He brushed by her and barked orders over his shoulder. "Jefferson, heat some soup. Sullivan, make sandwiches."

More reasons for people to hate me. Cassie stomped out of the room, her footfalls echoing off the corridor walls as she followed the captain to his cabin. Max eased into a huge chair behind a desk. He gestured to a small, unpadded chair. "Close the door and sit down, Clearwater."

Unlike the pneumatic doors on every other room of the ship, a manually operated oak door guarded this cabin. Cassie kicked it closed. "I prefer to stand. This shouldn't take long."

"Suit yourself. You're a company flunky, and need to learn to do what you're told."

"I'm science officer on this ship."

"I'm captain. So what? We're both cogs on the big wheel. But you're trying to jam up the whole works. That hurts all of us."

"I'm doing what's right."

Max leaned back in his chair and put his hands behind his head. "You know why you're on this crew?"

"I'm the most qualified exobiologist in the company."

"You know better than that. Why were you picked?"

Cassie felt her face grow warm. *Where was he going with this?* "I'm the best."

"Lying makes you look stupid, and it makes me angry."

"I'm not lying," she said coldly.

The captain started his damn tapping. It frayed her composure like constant, torturous water drops to the forehead, but it did kick-start her thinking. "You think JJ pulled strings."

"Better. But who pulled his?"

She blinked in surprise. "I don't understand."

He leaned forward. "On the surface, we're all here as explorers and prospectors, hoping to make a fortune in diamonds for ourselves and the company. But we each have other, more compelling reasons. Personal reasons. Tobias most of all, because he's pulling the strings. You think he'd jeopardize billions so his son can bring a bit of fluff?"

The burning sensation spread to her ears. "Jonas loves me, and we both wanted to go on this mission. But I'm here because I'm the best, and I wanted this assignment more than anything in my whole life."

Max laughed. Cassie felt suddenly vulnerable, as if she'd been swept overboard by a rogue wave into an unknown sea.

"Let me tell you a little story," Max said. "When Tobias found that a strong enough inertia dampening field could create a new 'ghost phase' of matter, he tried to keep the discovery secret. Being able to pass through any solid barrier would be an irresistible lure to every nation, not to mention every criminal entity. No one would be safe from surveillance, theft, even assassination. Nations would kill for that technology. So Tobias moved his labs and assembly plants to secret asteroid bases.

"He knew the secret would come out eventually, and he wanted to control that moment. Creation of the first starship was a dream that most of humanity could get behind. If, and it was a damn big if, he could convince people that his project was altruistic."

She shook her head. "He *is* altruistic. He's charming. He's caring, like Jonas."

A smirk spread across the captain's face. "This flight was planned more than a year in advance. I was in from the beginning. Funny thing is, about three months before launch Tobias tells me to train a new pilot and science officer, and to keep it under wraps. You and Jonas weren't supposed to come."

"I don't believe you." Tobias wouldn't have denied Jonas the chance to fulfill his ultimate dream. And Jonas would never have allowed her to be scratched from the crew. She willed her face to become stone, her body to stand tall, and her voice to be strong.

"Jonas chose me with Tobias's blessing. Neither of us would have dropped out."

"You aren't here because of Jonas. You're here because Tobias wants you here." Max relaxed back into his chair. "Sure enough, word leaked about the new ghost technology, and former allies turned hostile. They threatened to nationalize the company. Industrial rivals offered Sullivan millions to switch sides."

"What's that have to do with me? With any of us?"

"Jesus, Clearwater. Have you ever even looked at the crew? We're all stereotypes. Asian Wu, Irish Sullivan, German Unger, Afro-American Jefferson, me—the mad Russian, and you, Miss Native American. The perfect blended team, representing the major races and countries of the world."

"Coincidence," she said without conviction. "We're the best in our fields."

He shook his head. "Reverse political correctness. A blatant appeal to the sensibilities of the masses instead of the intelligencia. People identify with us. Twelve billion people see us as heroes and Tobias as a herald of a golden age of discovery and prosperity. Even the mightiest governments dare not oppose the tsunami of public opinion. They watch as Tobias rides the wave and they hope he drowns in it." His words ended with a trace of envy.

She refused to concede the argument. "I'm a world class biochemist. An exobiologist. Multiple PhDs."

"Yeah, yeah, that's a factor, but not the only factor, and not the most important. Tobias put you back on the team for another reason. All of us are important, but you in particular, a Native American in tune with nature and animal spirits, deliver the kind of crap that charms the romantic fantasies of the public."

"Then Tobias screwed up. I'm a scientist, first and foremost."

"Exactly," Max said. "Layers within layers. Even the diamonds. I'll bet most of them will end up as bribes and payoffs. The *technology* is what Tobias needs to keep monopolized. It's worth trillions. Nothing is more important to him."

The floor seemed to drop away as the realization hit, clicking into place like the last piece of a jigsaw puzzle. The company would make her their poster child, using her skill as a scientist and heritage as a Native American to keep opponents of interstellar mining and colonization at bay. And it wasn't only her being played by Tobias. The entire crew were corporate pawns.

Max grinned, a wide, toothy smile reminiscent of a shark. "Tobias is a grandmaster. He understands strategy as he plays country against country. He understands tactics as well, forking and pinning key individuals to ensure his victory. That ansible call to Doc—yeah, I know about it—was a reminder of who's really calling the shots in case we found life here. Which we did."

The truth didn't matter, especially with the company filtering communication through the ansible. What mattered was politics, which meant public opinion, which meant the company would use her heritage to proclaim Obsidian free of intelligent life, then claim the planet as part of the MicroWeight empire.

The captain was right. She was a flunky, a cog in the wheel. They all were.

The glint in his eye said he knew she understood. There were powers that determined the really big events, powers beyond her control. Beyond even JJ's control. It shook her faith in humanity.

Adam's voice blared from the ceiling speakers. "There has been a containment failure in the lab. The hot side is venting to the atmosphere through a hole in the outer wall. I believe an animal is attempting to get inside."

Chapter 9

Ship Time: Day 14. 1730 hours.

Cassie and Jonas donned biosuits and rushed to the lab as quickly as the powdery black sand allowed. Jonas held a shovel like a club as he approached the gaping, ground-level hole. Cassie pulled him back.

"Acid did that. Don't get too close." They struggled to open the Velcro door, which had warped as the hot side of the lab partially deflated.

Cassie surveyed the damage inside. A work table tilted precariously. One of its legs, now a smoldering stub, dripped like a wax candle severed by a blowtorch. The terrarium containing the plant specimen had slid to the table's edge but not fallen over. The rat cage hadn't been so lucky. It lay on the floor, partially dissolved. Mr. Jones writhed and squealed in pain, much of his fur gone. Bleeding ulcers covered his body.

An open gash in the floor extended from the hole in the wall to the base of the table, exposing the ubiquitous black sand. The lab offered no place for a creature to hide. Whatever caused the damage had left.

Cassie scooped up the rat with a pair of tongs, rinsed him in the sink, and patted him dry. Its injuries were critical. She placed Mr. Jones in the terrarium and moved it to another table. She searched for the vial of Somulose. She didn't want to prolong the poor rat's suffering.

"What do you think happened?" Jonas said, still wielding the shovel.

She loaded a syringe with the poison. "Probably a herbivore trying to eat the plant." She lifted Mr. Jones. Frowned. The lethal sores were gone. Healthy pink skin covered the rat.

She looked in the terrarium. A bit of plant sap pooled at the bottom of the shallow depression where Mr. Jones had been. She placed the rat there again.

Jonas knelt beside the opening in the floor. "The sand is too disturbed to make out its tracks. If it even makes any."

Cassie nodded absently, her mind on Jones and the sap. "Too bad," she said. "Be good to know what it looks like and how it got in here."

"Perhaps I can help," Adam said. "I have it on video."

***

The crew gathered in the mess hall to view the recording. The holoclip showed a small hole appear near the bottom of the lab wall, followed by insertion of a flexible black tube reminiscent of an elephant's trunk, though much smaller. The tube terminated in three triangular flaps, which opened and closed at regular intervals, suggestive of breathing. The tube leaned and twisted in various directions, stopping when it faced the specimen table. The tube jerked and strained toward the plant, but could not get its body through the hole.

"At this point the pressure drop activated the alarm, and I notified the crew," Adam said.

The hole in the lab began to smoke and enlarge as the plastic melted and dripped to the floor. The creature pushed through. Cassie estimated its total mass at three to four kilograms, about that of a rabbit. Black iridescent scales covered an oval, streamlined body. The tube jutted from the top, much like a periscope or a snorkel, with tiny flaps on the tip opening and closing rapidly. The creature lurched forward on three pairs of paddle-shaped legs extending outward and down like oars on a Viking long boat. The legs slipped, unable to gain traction on the plastic floor.

The snorkel swung in a low, tight arc, spraying a clear liquid. The heavy plastic floor smoked and liquefied. The creature's legs moved rapidly, churning sand as it sank into the newly exposed soil. Soon only the snorkel remained visible. It surged in a direct line toward the table with the plant.

The periscope/snorkel bumped into a table leg, stopped for a few seconds, then sprayed acid on the leg. The spray seemed less forceful than before and ended in a dribble.

"At this point," Adam said, "Dr. Clearwater and Mr. Jefferson reached the lab entrance, while Robbie and Dr. Sullivan approached the breach from the outside."

The creature retreated through the hole, sinking completely into the soil as it moved. The video ended. "Robbie didn't see the creature as it left."

"I didn't either," Lyra said. "Maybe that's a good thing."

Cassie looked across the room at the captain. His face was a tornado of dark, swirling energy bent on destruction. She wanted to run for cover as it approached.

"Why didn't you find it sooner, Clearwater?"

"The thing's adapted for underground movement. It probably eats the plants and was after a meal."

"*Probably*? I want facts, not guesses. Your report claimed only plant life was here. You screwed up, and that embarrasses me. I've already told the company there's no animal life, and that we've begun mining."

"Sir, that was my preliminary report. I'm working on the final, and it will include details on the animal. After we capture and study it."

"Let Robbie catch it," Lyra said. "The thing spits acid."

Cassie dreaded what she had to say next. "Mining activities will need to be suspended until I can evaluate the creature. A hush settled over the room. A palpably unhappy hush.

Max roared and kicked a chair, sending it crashing against a wall. "That thing is *not* intelligent!" he shouted and turned to Doc, who paled and said nothing.

Cassie said, "Intelligent or not, the animal is potentially deadly."

"Clearwater, kill that damn thing. That's at order." Max stormed from the room. Doc followed like a kicked dog who follows its master because there's nowhere else to go.

Cassie shook her head. "Doc is the PDE, but..."

Jonas finished her thought. "He'll cave even if the critter has a brain."

"The captain is merely ensuring that proper decisions be made," Li said.

"Doc has a duty," Cassie insisted. Like Don Quixote, she tilted at windmills. The captain's earlier lecture had made that clear. But she felt compelled to do what's right.

Lyra snorted. "I'll patch your pup tent. Go catch that oversize mole."

"Leave the hole until morning," Cassie said. "I'll put a trap there in case it comes back."

JJ put his arm on Cassie's shoulder. "I'll help."

His hand felt good. Cassie wrapped her arm around his waist. "We'll work with Robbie to rig a trap. Something remotely operated so we're not exposed to the acid."

"Good idea."

"We need a backup plan, too," Cassie said.

JJ smiled. "You think Murphy's law applies?"

"Especially here."

Adam said, "Dr. Clearwater, during the past hour, solar activity has increased by nine point three percent in the infrared and visible ranges, twelve percent in the ultra-violet."

"Is it dangerous?" asked JJ.

"No," Adam said. "But if the increase continues at the current rate, in twenty-two hours UV radiation will be capable of inflicting serious burns to exposed skin."

JJ said, "Hope you all packed sunscreen."

Chapter 10

Ship Time: Day 14. 2000 hours.

Cassie and Jonas sat on the floor of the ship's open airlock, their boots resting on the powdery black sand. The location gave an excellent view of the trap they'd set outside the lab, yet kept them safely away from any potential acid spray.

Cassie felt uncomfortable with Jonas sitting close to her, in part because she wanted to strip off his biosuit and wrap her body around his. Anxiety played a bigger part of the discomfort. She expected Jonas to pop the question, the terrifying question that she didn't know how to answer. They had planned to fly across the universe on a voyage of discovery, leaving the turmoil and political intrigue of Earth far behind. Pregnancy threatened that dream while offering something equally precious.

Jonas said, "Notice anything odd in there?"

Ahh. Small talk. "Other than the captain throwing a tantrum?"

"He's always wound up about something. No, what I found interesting is that Doc said nothing."

She drew up her knees and wrapped her arms around her legs. "His ass is on the line, same as mine. If the creature's intelligent, we all lose millions."

He clapped her on the back. "And you'll go down in history as the scientist who discovered the first intelligent alien life." He grew serious. "No, Doc's had something on his mind since before liftoff."

"He's been on the ansible with Tobias. Could your dad be sick?"

He swiveled until his helmet faced hers.

She drew a deep breath. "I overheard Li and Doc talking about the call."

"Dad's fine." Jonas tapped his helmet and made a cutting motion across his neck. Cassie turned off her radio. He touched his helmet to hers. His voice, muffled but understandable, carried through the metal and plastic. "What did Li and Doc say?"

"Li wanted to know about the call, but Doc wouldn't tell. Then Li tried seducing him." Cassie tried to keep a straight face.

"The woman has some good moves."

Cassie blinked in shock. Jonas laughed before adding, "Not that I'd know." He patted her arm affectionately. "Dad's up to something. Don't worry, there's not much he can do from long distance." He tapped his helmet again and pulled away. She flipped on her radio and his voice came through with sudden clarity. "The animal must use its snorkel to locate plants by smell."

She'd lost another chance to tell him. If she decided to tell him. "The grove would have a thousand times more odors than a single plant. Plus, my sample was isolated inside the lab."

"The hot-side filter is still compromised. Maybe the creature prefers stragglers."

"You make it sound like predator and prey rather than herbivore and plant."

JJ shrugged. "Different world, different rules."

"Things still need to make sense." She pondered the situation, trying to open her mind to possibilities.

JJ said, "The presence of the animal might explain the incident with the sonogram. The plant's defense mechanism was triggered by the probe. It self-destructed with a burst of corrosives intended to kill the animal and protect the rest of the grove."

"That contradicts your speculation that it goes after stragglers."

"You got me. In fact, how could the animal eat the plant at all? What doesn't dissolve turns into a pile of dust."

Cassie latched onto an intriguing thought. "Remember my conjecture that the grove is a garden of engineered plants created by advanced beings?"

"Yes," JJ said warily.

"What if the creature is also genetically engineered? Not to eat the plants but to keep the garden neat. Contained. It destroys the strays."

"Some people might call that idea a bit far-fetched."

"What about you?"

"I think you're certifiably insane."

Cassie punched his arm. "You're lucky I love you."

"I am indeed." He stood and extended a hand. "I don't think it's coming back tonight."

She accepted his help to stand. "Robbie can snare the thing if it does." The trap was a net of acid-resistant titanium wires buried just outside the hole in the lab, half a meter deep. Titanium cables led from the net's corners to Robbie's mini-crane. Lyra had spring-loaded the mechanism for extremely fast response.

"Sounds good," Jonas said. "Let's go to bed."

"I'm not sleepy."

"Neither am I."

Chapter 11

Ship Time: Day 15. 0900 hours.

In the morning, Cassie sent Jonas to dig up another small plant—she didn't want to risk damage to her control specimen. Lyra fashioned long-handled "butterfly nets" of titanium, which in theory could scoop the animal from the powdery soil if opportunity presented itself, but the animal didn't show during the collection of the fresh bait.

Cassie positioned the plant inside a glass terrarium and turned it on its side with the open end aligned with the hole in the lab. Robbie took a position to one side, ready to spring the trap. She waited with JJ, both of them drenched in sweat. The increase in solar activity had increased temperature to 27° Celsius. The lighter sky bleached out most stars, and a slight haze limited visibility over the broad plains.

At 1100 hours, an impatient captain asked if it were safe to resume digging in the area farthest from the grove. Cassie reluctantly agreed. "I'll stay in the lab, continuing experiments, and ready to execute 'Plan B.'"

"Plan B?" Max asked.

"If it avoids the trap, I'll chase it down and scoop it up."

Max grunted his approval. The crew collected their shovels and buckets and trudged the dig site. Cassie killed time by performing more atmospheric and plant analyses. Hours passed.

Adam's voice came through the radio. "I have detected a snorkel moving from the grove toward the lab. It is somewhat more visible in the infrared spectrum. It just submerged."

"All diggers to the ship," ordered the captain. "Adam, we'll gather in the Observation Deck. Can you provide a hologram projection there?"

"Yes, Captain."

Cassie scanned the barren land but saw nothing, even when she set her helmet for infrared enhancement. She spotted what looked like a periscope, glowing green in her faceplate HUD. The periscope cut through the black soil, leaving a permanent wake like a furrow from a plow. The wake ended as the creature vanished into the ground again.

"Adam, how long until it reaches the trap?"

"Actually, it seems to be heading toward the ship. About five minutes to contact."

"Double-time, everybody!" ordered the captain. The crew reached the ship and crowded into the airlock. The animal surfaced a dozen meters closer to the ship. It submerged.

"This isn't right," Cassie said. "It's supposed to go after the bait." She grabbed the long-handled net and exited the lab.

"We're watching from the Observation Deck, Clearwater," Max said. "Adam patched us into your com link. Jonas is standing by in the airlock if you need assistance."

"Roger," Cassie said.

"The animal is green," Li said. "At last, something that is not black."

"The thing's black as pitch, like everything else," Doc said. "Adam applied an infrared filter for enhanced visibility. The warmer the object, the brighter the green."

Warm blooded meant a faster metabolism. Cassie wondered how fast it could move. Most of all, she wondered why was it attracted to the ship. She caught sight of the snorkel. The animal slowed and stopped. The snorkel angled toward the lab and began moving toward the trap.

Cassie sighed with relief. The animal may have needed time to pick up the scent. "Take the bait," she whispered. She glanced at Robbie, waiting next the trap. Actually, the robot was the trap. A quick lift would suspend the creature helplessly in the air and allow Robbie to lower it into a waiting glass cage.

Li said, "What if it sprays acid on the cage? It will escape."

"Glass is resistant to most acids," Cassie said.

The periscope stopped a meter from the trap. It rotated one hundred eighty degrees in each direction.

"Cautious little devil," Doc said.

"It can't be smart," Lyra said. "Please, God, don't let it be smart."

Cassie frowned. "Jonas, you were supposed to put the plant in the back of the cage, farthest from the opening."

"I did."

"The plant's moving!" Cassie said. The soil in the bottom of the glass box swelled and sagged as the plant's roots shifted beneath it. The plant flailed, wobbled precariously, and then righted itself, gaining a centimeter or two or progress. It had reached the center of the box.

The animal circled the trap and for a few seconds remained out of sight behind Robbie. Cassie grew worried, but the periscope reappeared and made its way to the opening. The snorkel swayed like a cobra. The plant lurched forward another centimeter.

Why move toward the animal? It should move *away* from danger.

The snorkel pointed directly at the plant. The animal moved closer.

She gave a start as JJ appeared beside her and said, "It's in position."

"Almost," Cassie said. "Adam, let it take another step, then spring it."

"Acknowledged, Dr. Clearwater."

The snorkel bumped the side of the box and slid along its surface like a blind person feeling its way. It found the opening and reached inside. The tip nearly reached the plant.

"Cassie..." Jonas said, urgency in his voice.

A root poked free of the soil. The snorkel touched it. The animal began to back out of the cage, dragging the plant with it.

"It stuck to the root," Jonas said. "Like glue."

"Now, Robbie!" shouted Cassie.

The robotic arm jerked skyward; the net enveloped the animal and pulled it from the ground. It swung suspended a meter in the air, struggling and spraying liquid. Some landed on Robbie's metal surfaces, which began to smoke.

The bait plant fell to the ground, condition unknown.

"Robbie, place the animal in the terrarium and close the lid." As Robbie complied, Cassie checked on the fallen plant. Jonas followed.

The plant had snapped in two. Its dome had already begun to dissolve. Cassie left it on the ground to finish the disintegration process. A rapping sound drew her attention to the animal, which struggled violently. The cage rocked as its body rammed against the walls. The snorkel slapped and sprayed the walls with acid, leaving streaks that etched the glass.

"Angry critter," JJ said. "Can it burn its way out?"

"Eventually. But once inside the lab I'll douse it with a neutralizer. Robbie, bring it to the entrance."

The robotic arm lifted the cage with the creature. An ugly grinding sound came from the robot, followed by a metallic whine. "I'm sorry, Dr. Clearwater. My treads are damaged. Robbie is immobile."

They walked around the machine, noting the half-dissolved treads.

"Intelligence?" asked Jonas. Angry mutterings came over the radio speakers.

"Too soon to tell," Cassie said, though she had definite suspicions. "Robbie, hand Jonas the terrarium." The arm swiveled and placed the cage onto JJ's hands. His grunt of exertion made her smile. "I'll carry the bait tank." It weighed half as much.

"Yes, Miss Cassie," he said in mock submission.

Adam said, "A second creature has surfaced and is approaching the ship."

Chapter 12

Ship Time: Day 15. 1305 hours.

Jonas set the cage on the ground. "I'm going after it."

"Let's focus on this one," Cassie said. "I don't want you getting burned."

"The range of its spray is less than a meter." He picked up the scoop, emphasizing the one-and-a-half-meter handle. "Doc, help Cassie get another tank ready." He slogged toward the ship.

"Jonas!"

He waved without turning around. "I'll have it bagged in a minute. You need a control animal. Or a spare if it disintegrates like the plants."

Doc appeared and they carried the terrarium with the animal inside the lab. The thrashing animal nearly shook the box out of their hands. They set it on the table. Doc grinned at Cassie. "Stick a bow on it."

Their helmet speakers crackled. "It's under the ship," JJ said. "Adam, turn on the landing lights. I can't see a damn thing."

"And he's the pilot?" Doc said.

Cassie smacked his helmet.

"There it is!" shouted JJ. "Almost... damn! The thing's fast."

Cassie said, "Careful, JJ. The acid..."

"Don't worry. I'm safe as a mongoose playing with a cobra."

"That supposed to make me feel better?"

Jonas laughed.

The cockiness, the adrenaline high so audible in his laugh, worried her, but she focused on the task at hand. She fastened air intake and exhaust hoses to the tank. The animal appeared to be an oxygen breather, and she didn't want it to suffocate. "Doc, prep that second tank with soil."

JJ yelped. Cassie momentarily froze, then rushed outside with Doc close behind.

The landing lights surrounded the ship in an inverted halo, but JJ wasn't underneath or anywhere within the glow. Cassie scanned the landscape. His orange suit should have popped against the black backdrop and the bright sunshine.

"Jonas? Where are you?"

"I fell into some sort of a mud pit. Pretty deep. Over my head."

"You all right? Suit intact? No acid burns?"

"I'm fine. But I'll need help getting out of here. Can you see the net?"

They stared at the bleak terrain. "Don't that just smooch the pooch," Doc said. Then Cassie saw it, a loop of Titanium waving slowly a few centimeters above the ground.

"We see it."

Li emerged from the ship. "Where is Jonas?"

Cassie pointed.

"We'll need the shovels," Cassie said. "And rope." She sped toward the ship.

"Captain, we have a situation," Doc said. "JJ fell into quicksand. Have Lyra bring rope to the airlock. I think there's some in the aft cabinet of storage room two."

"Something's happening," JJ said, his voice wavering but not panicked. "The mud is thickening. Like tar." He gave a nervous twitter. "Maybe it is a tar pit. I suggest you speed up the rescue. I don't relish being fossilized like a dinosaur."

"Stop whining," Lyra said. "Your tank has four hours of oxygen."

"Just get the damn rope," Cassie yelled. They charged up the ramp and piled into the airlock. Cassie closed the outer door and the UV lights flashed. Disinfectant sprayed and the air cycled. She cursed each second of delay. Decon finally complete, they stripped off the biosuits.

"Everyone grab a shovel and double-time back here." She reached for the button to open the inner door, but stopped as the ship shuddered. Concern plastered every face. A groan of tortured metal filled the air.

"Brace! Brace! Brace!" yelled Adam as the floor dropped like an express elevator. Cassie tumbled off walls and people as the ship lurched. The floor stopped abruptly. Cassie belly-flopped onto it. A deep boom reverberated through the ship as the lights failed, leaving them in blackness.

Chapter 13

Ship Time: Day 15. 1315 hours.

Emergency lights flickered to life, casting odd shadows in unfamiliar directions. Multiple alarms blared in a discordant symphony. Doc and Li lay across Cassie's legs and lower back, pinning her like a tackled quarterback.

"Is everyone all right?" asked Adam.

Am I? Cassie thought. She didn't seem to have any broken bones, but her stomach hurt. No, lower. A dull ache in her abdomen. Nothing serious. She hoped. "I'm okay. Just shook up."

JJ's voice crackled over the radio. "What's going on? I hear alarms."

The alarms stopped. "Landing struts one and three failed," Adam said simultaneously on radio and intercom. "It caused a serious list to port. Hull integrity has been lost. I have increased internal air pressure to compensate." Adam's radio voice ended with a slight click as his local voice continued. "You may notice a pressure or popping in your ears."

"All hands to the Bridge," boomed the captain's voice.

Cassie wiggled free of the others and thumbed the intercom. "Max, Jonas is out there. We need to rescue him."

JJ yelled. "Something touched my suit. It poked me." His baritone voice sounded an octave higher.

"Okay," Max said. "Clearwater, Doc, and Li rescue Jefferson. Lyra, get to the Bridge. I need damage and repair assessments ASAP."

Cassie opened the inner airlock door. It squealed and jerked but didn't jam. "Li, get the rope, then meet us outside." Li grasped a handrail and moved gingerly down the corridor, which tilted like a path made by mountain goats. Cassie and Doc headed for the equipment locker, where each grabbed a shovel and flashlight.

The ship's speakers crackled and JJ's voice filled the air. "Something's grabbed the net." He grunted and then cursed. "Damn. I couldn't hold on to it."

"We're coming, Jonas." Cassie kept her voice calm, though she felt far from it. "You'll be out in a few minutes."

Like the inner airlock door, the outer one moved in fits and starts accompanied by metallic wails. The exit ramp had buckled and torn away from the ship, forcing them to make a small jump over exposed metal edges. Cassie felt no relief when she reached the ground. The only task that mattered was saving Jonas.

The hoop and handle of the net was gone, but Cassie followed the impressions of human boot prints and the single furrow made by the creature's snorkel, oblivious to everything else. Doc tugged on her sleeve. "Slow down, Cassie. We don't want to join Jonas."

She shook off his hand. "As long as we see his prints, the ground's okay." Then JJ's prints abruptly stopped, as if he'd been plucked from the ground like a rabbit by a hawk. The snorkel's furrow-track ended at the same place. She took Doc's arm and moved one foot cautiously forward. The ground felt solid, and the flashlight revealed typical fine-grain black sand. It didn't give way or ooze as she put weight on it.

She released Doc's arm. "Let's dig." They dug.

"I can hear you digging," JJ said. "But it's muffled."

"Good!" Cassie said between gasps for air. "We'll have you out in no time."

"Fuck!" yelled Jonas.

Cassie stopped digging. "What's wrong?"

"Something wrapped around me like a damn tentacle."

Cassie felt a ground tremor.

"I'm moving! It's pulling me!"

"Where?"

"Help!"

Cassie scanned the ground, looking for a tell-tale disturbance in the sand to indicate where Jonas was being dragged. An almost imperceptible swell moved toward the grove, only a few meters away. She followed it, Doc close behind, heading directly toward a thicket of several medium-sized plants. Cassie ran around them, but didn't see the ground swell reappear.

"Doc, get the laser cutter. He's under these plants. Jonas, you all right?"

Jonas groaned. "Hurts everywhere. Hard to breathe with this thing wrapped around my chest."

Cassie shoved against one of the plants, but it resisted her efforts to knock it over. Doc arrived with the laser cutter, but Cassie hesitated. "We need to clear these plants away, but I'm worried about the surge of corrosives. Jonas could be burned. Let's try uprooting them, which should postpone or even eliminate the disintegration process."

They pushed and pulled for ten minutes, but these plants refused to be dislodged. JJ urged them to use the laser. Cassie reluctantly agreed, and the cutting beam made short work of clearing the obstructions. The crew moved the severed stems and domes several meters away to let them disintegrate harmlessly. Cassie dug while Doc cut and discarded intervening roots. The laser cauterized the cuts, and Cassie scooped out what little goop formed in the deepening hole.

Another mild tremor shook the ground and Jonas yelled. "Something big has me, Cass. It's reeling me in like a fish!" His voice cracked on the edge of hysteria.

Li ran up, panting, holding a coil of rope. Cassie swatted it away and scanned the ground for movement. There. No there. No, it was... everywhere, as if thousands of giant moles burrowed in different directions. Tears welled up. She began to tremble. Doc draped an arm on her shoulder.

The ground stopped shifting. She sniffed back her tears and shrugged off Doc's arm. "Jonas, make a noise. Move around. I need a sign."

"I can't move. I'm wrapped up."

"Wiggle loose. You need to help us find you."

"Tell that to the fucking alien!"

"We need to know where you are."

"Then find out, damn it." A faint beeping sounded with JJ's words. "I suggest you hurry. My suit just sprang a leak."

Chapter 14

Ship Time: Day 15. 1400 hours.

The four crew members squeezed side-by-side on the starboard side of the Mess Hall table, bellies pressed against the edge of the tabletop, waiting for the captain. The ship tilted too much to sit on the port side without sliding off. Cassie sandwiched between Doc and Lyra, with Li on Lyra's other side. *We're wasting time*, Cassie fumed. *We should be digging for Jonas.*

Doc wrapped an arm around her shoulder. She turned to glare, but his smile showed only concern. "Let me give you something to calm your nerves."

"He's been out there an hour."

Max entered and leaned casually against the wall.

"Our fearless leader arrives," Doc said.

Is he developing a backbone? Cassie wondered. It hardly mattered. "Based on his last tank charge, Jonas has about two and a half hours of air left. Maybe less since his biosuit has lost integrity. We need to rescue Jonas *now.*"

JJ's voice came over the speakers. "I second that, Captain. The big tentacle let go, but smaller ones have my arms and legs. I'm trapped and being poked by a lot of small sticks. Fingers. Tentacles. *Something.* Get me out of here, okay?"

Doc said, "From one animal, or several?"

"How the hell should I know? I'm buried in blackness."

Max said, "We're planning the rescue now. Stand-by." He looked up at the camera, and ran a finger across his neck.

"Radio transmission and reception has been cut, Captain," Adam said.

"Turn it back on," Cassie said.

"He doesn't need to hear us kick around ideas," Max said.

"The hell he doesn't."

Max cocked his head, giving her a *don't be stupid* look. She swallowed hard, realizing that the options including abandoning Jonas. "No. You can't be serious."

"We'll get to Jefferson in a moment. Sullivan, update on ship repairs?"

"At least two days to rebuild the landing struts. Another day to patch the hull. External sensors," Lyra shrugged. "A day or two. Maybe more."

"With Robbie helping?" Max asked.

Lyra shook her head. "The treads are mush. It'll take four or five hours to replace them."

"We don't have time for this," Cassie said. "We need to concentrate on rescue."

Doc said, "Do we have any weapons?"

The question surprised Cassie. "The laser cutter."

"No, bigger. Grenades? Rocket launcher?"

Lyra laughed. Max didn't. He asked why.

Doc said, "An animal of the size we captured isn't capable of towing a person through sand, and its snorkel wasn't nearly as large as what JJ said wrapped around his waist."

Lyra's humor vanished. "The intelligent creatures Cassie predicted?"

Doc nodded. "Maybe. Or the animal we caught is only a baby."

Color drained from Lyra's face. "It could be the size of a house. Of the ship."

"What if it is a carnivore?" Li said.

"Don't even think it," Cassie said. But the thought took root in her mind. A huge, squid-like monster with a gaping mouth lurked under the sand, poised to swallow Jonas. She closed her eyes and pulled up a happier image from memory. Grandfather. Twinkling stars. The last Thunderbird flying into the night.

"Sullivan, activate the IDF and get the ship on an even keel."

"Sir, the stresses won't be balanced."

"I didn't say take it all the way. Get the ship's weight down under a ton so you can prop up the port side until the struts are repaired." Max turned to Cassie. "Now, how do you propose to rescue Jefferson?"

"First we need to find him," Cassie said. "We don't have the ship's sensors, but we can use Robbie's sonar and radar."

Lyra frowned. "He's immobile."

"We'll yank the radar unit out and carry it ourselves."

Adam said, "Sorry, Dr. Clearwater. Both the radar and sonar units are integrated with the cart. They are not designed to be portable."

"Make them portable," Cassie said. "Reprogram it. Li can help with her pocket brain."

"The problem is not with the software," Adam said. "The physical alterations to make it portable will take at least twelve hours."

Cassie held back the urge to scream.

"Maybe if we jump up and down?" Li said.

Cassie clenched her fists. Doc barked a laugh.

"I am serious. If we jump, maybe Jonas hears us, and tells us when it gets louder and loudest. We dig there."

Cassie studied the Asian's face. Li wasn't being sarcastic. "Okay, I get your idea. Everyone get a shovel from the lab. We'll smack shovels on the ground." Cassie smiled at Li. "It's more controlled than jumping, and we'll get better sound transmission through the soil." She looked at Max. "Captain, the radio?"

He nodded. "Resume transmission."

Cassie briefed Jonas on the plan. Afterward, Max, Doc, and Li grabbed shovels and followed Cassie outside while Lyra and Adam worked to level the ship.

Cassie reached the spot where they lost Jonas. She raised a shovel high and whacked it hard against the ground.

"I heard it," shouted JJ. "A faint thud. I can't tell what direction."

Everyone raised their shovels. At the count of three, the four smacked the sandy soil.

"That was a louder," JJ said. "I think you're on my right."

Cassie led them closer to the lake, and struck again.

"I don't know. It's muffled. Maybe you moved too far left."

"Concentrate, Jonas." They moved a meter toward the right, putting them amidst the three largest plants. They hit the ground again.

JJ yelped. "The big tentacle's back. Shit."

"Jonas! Was our sound louder or softer?"

He screamed. "Fuck, fuck, my skin's on fire!"

"Jonas, we're going to hit again. You have to tell us if we're louder." They moved left.

"Water," moaned JJ. "Mud. Getting into the suit." Bursts of static accompanied the transmission.

"Adam, clean up the transmission," Cassie said.

"The problem is at his end," Adam said. "I believe his microphone is damaged."

Jonas screamed again, a howl of incoherent pain ending in a gurgle.

"JJ! JJ! Answer me."

Static came through the speakers.

A finger of panic tickled Cassie's brain. Stay clam. He has air. His microphone is broken, but maybe he can hear us. Don't give up.

"Back to the ship," Max said.

Cassie objected. "No, we have to dig."

"Dig where, Clearwater? You don't know where he is and he isn't talking anymore."

"We can't give up!" Cassie said. She heard the edge of panic in her voice. The captain heard it, too. She saw it in his eyes. She took a breath, forced the fear into a cold resolve. "You're right. We're wasting time. Let's come up with a real plan." She led the way back to the ship.

Chapter 15

Ship Time: Day 15. 1445 hours.

The crew sat around the mess table—on both sides, now that the ship was level. Doc and Li stared at the walls, Max and Lyra at the bare table. A slow oscillating tone with an accompanying hiss came from the radio monitor. It hadn't changed in minutes. Lyra turned off the sound.

"Put it back on," Cassie said.

"Face it, Cassie."

Cassie reached for the volume control, but Li placed a delicate hand on hers.

"I miss him, too. There is nothing we can do for Jonas. Why torture ourselves?"

Cassie jerked her hand away and turned on the sound. "I won't let him die here."

Lyra reached for the knob again. Cassie balled her fists. *If she wants a fight, I'll rip her head off. Li's too. And Doc's. To hell with all of them.*

"Leave it on," Max said. "If Clearwater wants to listen, fine. Jefferson was a fine crew member, like family." The words lacked emotion. His face remained deadpan. Typical Captain.

"He's not dead. Don't talk like he is."

"He's dead," Lyra said. "Adam, give us the probability."

"Dr. Sullivan, I have insufficient data on which to perform a statistical analysis of Mr. Jefferson's condition. However, the microphone was the least rugged component of the communication system. The carrier signal proves the radio and transmitter remain functional."

Doc looked thoughtful. "What about his helmet speakers?"

"The status of his other equipment is unknown, Dr. Unger."

Doc placed a hand on Cassie's shoulder. "Talk to him. In case he can hear you. Give him something to take his mind off the pain." Doc stared at her. Everyone stared at her.

"What should I say?"

"You're his lover. Think of something."

Cassie fingered the totem on her neck. "Okay. Adam, transmit." She hesitated. "I love you, Jonas."

Doc motioned for her to continue.

"We can't hear your transmission, but don't worry. We're working on a plan to get you back. You won't be in pain much longer."

Lyra rolled her eyes.

Doc whispered, "Pink elephants, Cassie. You can't stop thinking about something by naming it. Distract him. Take him somewhere else."

"How am I supposed to do that?" She suppressed the urge to punch Doc's face.

"Tell him a story. Something about you. Something he doesn't know."

She took a couple slow breaths. "Jonas." Her voice quavered. She took another breath. She had to be strong. "I've been in the dark before. When I was eighteen, just out of high school. I went on a spirit quest."

Cassie closed her eyes, remembering her eighteen-year-old self standing before Grandfather, pleading. "But I have to," she said. "Everyone thinks I'm a child. A vision quest will change that."

"The guide you seek is not waiting for you in the swamp or the forest," said Grandfather.

"You don't know that. Even Crazy Eddie found a spirit guide."

"The gods take pity on fools. You are no fool."

"I'm no coward, either, but that's how people look at me."

He smiled. "You haven't cared what others think of you for some time."

"What's wrong with that?"

"Nothing, if you care about yourself."

"I do."

He chuckled. "You don't know yourself. How can you care about yourself? You think a vision quest will give clarity to your life, bring respect from others, provide a purpose and a path for your life, a path away from the drudgery of your life on the reservation."

Cassie shifted weight from one foot to another, head down. "Is it wrong to want to explore the bigger world?"

"You don't want to explore. You want to escape."

"Whatever."

"You are a ship without rudder or compass, without control of where you go, without knowledge of where you are."

"You don't think I'm ready."

Grandfather looked tired. "Your spirit guide is not."

"The spirits are always ready. They are everywhere, all the time. You told me so."

"You are special. The future will demand much of you, it will strain body and soul like a bow bent to the breaking point. A powerful spirit will help you, but it is far away and hidden from me."

"I'll find it."

"Your father was impatient, much as you are. He would not listen to my counsel. His spirit guide refused to come. Joseph found a different guide in a bottle."

"I am not my father."

"Sometimes a child strives so hard to be unlike a parent that she becomes the opposite, not realizing that the same problems remain, but now come from the other direction. The grown child and the parent become two sides of the same coin, when what is needed is a different coin."

"I need your blessing. Why won't you give it?"

Grandfather closed his eyes. "You will go blind and deaf into a world you do not understand. You will invite a spirit to come into you yet will not open yourself to it. You will ask for wisdom and refuse to hear it. Nothing is louder than your desire." He opened his eyes, which looked ancient. He opened his arms and she accepted his embrace. He whispered, "You choose a hard path, child. You have my blessing. And my pity."

Cassie walked alone into the swamp, alert for alligators, panthers, pythons and water moccasins. The sun bore down with unrelenting heat, a ball of white-hot fury constantly poking at her through a canopy of Cyprus and Cedar. She paused beside three tall, branchless, dead trees to smear sunscreen on her exposed skin. Insects buzzed around her head. She waved them off and applied repellent before they could feast on her body.

That night a million stars dotted the black sky, all of which ignored Cassie. A tiny human on a tiny planet for a tiny interval of time lacked any significance to the rest of the universe. Cassie aimed her flashlight at every noise and wished she'd remembered to bring a lighter to start a fire.

The second day brought rain, which alternated between drizzle and torrential downpours as roiling gray clouds fought for dominion of the sky with spears of lightning and roars of thunder. Finding a dry patch was like smoking a pipe without tobacco—a lot of puffing with no satisfaction. Hunger made sleep impossible. At least she had plenty of water.

The third day brought the sun again. It hurt her eyes, burned her skin, and raised a stink from clinging, damp clothes. She prayed to the Great Spirit to send guidance. None came. No friendly animal approached, and no particular plant attracted her. The elementals of rock, water, and air gave no whisper of advice. She began to hallucinate, and even the delusions were devoid of guidance.

The Great Spirit shunned her. It ignored her urgent begging and her earnest promises. It paid no heed as Cassie raged at the darkness when the batteries of the flashlight died. Croaking frogs mocked her sobs and the subsequent whimpers that punctuated a tortured sleep.

A nudge in her side brought Cassie to the present. "Something *hopeful*," Doc said.

Cassie nodded. "It was my darkest hour, Jonas, but I got through it. I found my way back to the reservation. The monsters didn't harm me, and they won't harm you. Hang on, help is coming."

She didn't mention that at dawn of the fourth day, she had slunk back to the reservation, packed a suitcase, and took the first bus to Miami. She left a short note but told no one goodbye.

"You're crying," Doc said.

"Happy tears," she lied. "I left the reservation to start college. Graduated cum laude with a biology major. Went back to share my accomplishment with Grandfather. I didn't know what to expect, a lecture probably, but he was happy for me."

"He ask about your spirit guide?"

"Not much of what he said made sense." *Like saying my quest hadn't started.* She fingered her totem. The quest had taught her something valuable. Shamanism and religion couldn't be trusted. Only science offered a clear, reliable basis for making decisions. "Captain, Jonas has less than two hours of air. We need to find him, right now."

"You want to dig holes at random? Jefferson could be anywhere in a hundred square meters. You'll never find the right spot in time."

"Don't forget the animals," Doc said. "You could get sprayed by acid or pulled into the sand like Jonas."

"If we were on Earth," Li said, "we could find him by GPS."

"You need satellites for that," Doc said.

"Maybe Li has something," Lyra said.

Max frowned. "We didn't place any satellites."

Lyra's face held both concentration and excitement. "The principle of triangulation still applies. We position ourselves around the grove, and use suit radios to relay JJ's signals to the ship. Each signal will have a slightly different transit time. Adam can use those differences to compute JJ's position."

Adam said, "The differences will be very slight, Dr. Sullivan. If the major sources of error are corrected, the remaining margin of error will result in a circle two meters in diameter."

"Good enough!" Cassie said. "Let's go!" She jumped up, forgetting her reduced weight. Her head hit the ceiling and she fell flat across the table. No one laughed as Doc helped her up.

Lyra asked, "Adam, what are the sources of error?"

"The two main factors are position and time. I need the distance and direction of each suit radio relative to the ship, to within one millimeter, and the relay response time for each suit radio to the nearest nanosecond."

Cassie walked carefully to the doorway. "You can get that information, right?"

The excitement drained from Lyra's face. "The laser survey equipment is accurate enough. In theory. I can calibrate the radios to get an accurate response time."

"Great."

"It'll take two or three hours."

"Lyra! He'll be dead by then!"

Max cleared his voice. "Clearwater, this is a long shot. You know that."

"You're a gambler, Captain. Any way you can help the odds? A lucky charm, maybe? To add to mine?" She pinched the totem between her fingers.

Max grinned, and for once it looked genuine. "You and Doc set up the survey equipment. Sullivan, work on the radios. Wu, interface your pocket gizmo with Adam. It'll nearly double his computing ability. I want everything done in ninety minutes. Go!"

Chapter 16

Ship Time: Day 15. 1615 hours.

Cassie knew to expect a wave of nausea when she walked through the boundary of the inertia field, but it seemed particularly intense. She staggered as her mass ballooned from less than ten kilograms to over fifty. Doc grabbed her arm before she could fall. She pulled away when he was slow to let go.

She took a step toward the grove and froze. The plants were different. Every dome and stem looked shiny white, as if dipped in paint. They glistened under a brighter sun, although a hazy sky helped attenuate the glare. She recalled the white secretion of the sample plant when exposed to UV light. The reaction probably indicated a protective adaptation to a periodic increase in solar activity. Oddly, the largest plant remained black, but there wasn't time to speculate. JJ had only minutes of air left.

Adam required three points for triangulation. Li, Doc, and Cassie formed an equilateral triangle fifty meters to a side, with near certainty that Jonas lay somewhere inside the perimeter. Max and Lyra worked on Robbie's treads, assisted by Robbie himself, who still had full use of his mechanical arm. The repair team used a separate channel so as not to interfere with the search team. Adam processed millions of split-second triangulations of JJ's radio signal. In minutes they'd have his location pin-pointed. Cassie tried not to think of JJ suffocating before they could free him, but her thoughts circled around that idea like a moon circles a planet. She choked back a fresh wave of nausea.

"At least his transmitter is still—" Lyra said. A crackle of static swallowed the last word.

"It is hot out here. I find the sweat unpleasant," Li said with disgust.

"No hotter then Florida in July," muttered Cassie. The manifestation of the worsening solar activity had to be ignored. "Jonas, we're coming. Hang on."

"Dr. Clearwater, Mr. Jefferson—" another crackle of static, and then "—transmitting."

"Is there still a carrier signal?"

"No, Dr. Clearwater—[crackle]—or damaged."

"Tell us his location," Cassie said. The crackling worsened, eating some of her words.

"To with...[crackle] four-meter diam—" Adam said.

Doc's voice interrupted. "Adam, what's up with the radios?"

"The equipment is [crackle] properly, doctor … interference from solar flares. Suggest [crackle] to channel 4."

"Switch to channel 4, people," Cassie said. "Doc, grab some long metal rods from the shop. We'll poke for his position. Li, grab the shovels. Adam, guide me to the center of the circle."

Adam directed Cassie several meters toward the lake. "This is Mr. Jefferson's most likely location, plus or minus two meters in any direction. Dr. Clearwater, ambient temperature has increased another four degrees in the past hour. Solar radiation shows a matching upward trend."

"Dangerous?"

"At the current rate of increase, heat exhaustion will become a serious factor. A few minutes after that, radiation sickness will become unavoidable."

"Look at the sun," Li said. The disc had brightened to yellow, with remnants of orange that swirled like lava in a cauldron.

Doc, halfway to the ship, stopped and pointed to the horizon. "Holy moly. Look at that." A roiling black wall-cloud loomed hundreds, if not thousands, of meters high. It stretched along the polar-side horizon as far they could see. Lightning pulsed within the cloud. Thunder rumbled.

Cassie stared in rage and horror. Was the whole damn planet trying to murder Jonas?

"What is that?" Li said.

"Visual analysis is consistent with a large sandstorm," Adam said. "I suggest you take shelter inside the ship. The storm will reach here in six minutes, seventeen seconds."

"To the ship," ordered the captain.

"No! We have six minutes," Cassie said. "Dig."

"To the ship," Max repeated. "Now."

"We have to dig!" Cassie plunged her shovel into the ground and flung the soil away. She dug with ferocity, creating a fountain of black sand. Water welled up into the hole, creating a black slurry. "Jonas talked about mud! This is the spot!"

Doc and Lyra grabbed her arms. Cassie fought like a bear protecting its cubs.

"Use your head, girl," Doc said. "There's nothing we can do."

Lying coward. As they dragged her through the IDF, Cassie leveraged their reduced weight to jerk loose. She ran three steps toward the hole before Lyra tackled her. Cassie nearly kicked free but Doc and Max joined forces to pull her into the airlock. She stared as the door closed like a coffin lid. Stunned disbelief left her unable to move, to scream, to weep.

The spray of the decon process snapped her back to life. She jabbed her finger on the captain's chest. "We need to go back out."

"Too dangerous. Robbie, can you continue rescue operations?"

"The treads are not yet operational," Adam said. "I am unable to repair them until parts are provided."

"Let me go," Cassie said. "Just me. I can get to him with a rope."

"No." The captain's tone left no room for argument.

She refused to step out of the airlock. "I won't let him die."

Max said, "Adam, disable the main airlock until further notice."

Cassie banged on the unresponsive button. "Don't do this, Captain. Please, let me go."

Max glanced at his watch. "His air just ran out."

She glared at his granite-hard face. She turned to Lyra for support, but the engineer couldn't maintain eye contact. Li stared at the floor. Doc mumbled an apology.

Max said, "Doc, stand guard at the emergency airlock. No one leaves the ship." His eyes locked onto Cassie. "Understood?"

Doc headed down the passage to the emergency airlock. Max led the others to the bridge. Cassie followed. She had nowhere else to go.

They took their seats. Max said, "Time until the storm hits?"

"Three minutes, eighteen seconds," Adam said.

"Wind speed?"

"Sixty-one kilometers per hour in the storm, Captain. Current wind at our position is two kilometers per hour."

"Sullivan, can we maintain position?"

"We're too light. I can't keep the ship stable in that much wind. Shall I put her down on the bubbles?" In emergencies, the weight of the ship could be supported by the three "bubbles" protruding from the hull: the main airlock, the lower observation dome, and the radar-sonar dome.

"Yes," Cassie said, clinging to hope. "The ship will form a windbreak. We can resume digging."

The captain's lips compressed to a thin line while his fingers tap-danced on the armrest.

"Sir?" asked Lyra.

He ignored her. "Adam, is the ship space worthy?"

Cassie spun. "You can't leave him here!" *In the dark, alone, air running out.* Her own lungs struggled to draw a breath.

"Negative, Captain. Hull leaks have not been patched."

Lyra said, "We should turn off the IDF, set the ship's full weight on the bubbles, and wait out the storm."

The damn three-finger tap continued. "Clearwater, what's the composition of the soil?"

"Land the ship. There's time. There's still time."

His face held ten percent sympathy, ninety percent stubbornness. "Composition of the soil?"

"Carbon, asshole. Fractured bucky-balls, some graphite, some anthracite, some diamond."

Max nodded. "Sullivan, how long can the hull withstand diamond sandblasting?"

It just keeps getting worse. Cassie looked at Lyra, whose eyes went wide. They both turned to the captain. Neither spoke.

Max said, "That's what I thought. Engineer, prepare to take the IDF to maximum."

Li looked up from her console, as if just realizing the seriousness of the storm. "Ghost phase? On the ground? That is crazy. We will explode."

Max said, "Not if the wind blows fast enough."

Realization dawned on Cassie. "We'll need to wait until the storm hits."

Lyra nodded in agreement, her face pale. The engineer scanned the IDF console.

Max said, "Adam, report wind speed every ten seconds."

"Yes, Captain. Current speed four point five kilometers per hour."

Li looked lost. "Tell me what is happening. Are we going to die?"

Lyra placed a hand on Li's shoulder. "If the wind is fast enough, over fifteen kilometers per hour, then we can enter ghost phase safely. The wind will blow through the entire ship fast enough to prevent anything from shifting into our phase."

"And if the wind slows?"

Lyra didn't answer. Cassie said, "Then we die with Jonas."

Max growled. "That's enough, Clearwater."

"Wind speed eight point two kilometers per hour," Adam said.

The ship swayed. Worry lines creased Lyra's face. "I don't think the temporary supports are going to hold."

Li's voice turned shrill. "How do we get back into normal phase?"

"One problem at a time," Max said. "Prepare for impact with the storm." Blackness covered the port side of the transparent nose of the ship.

"Wind speed twelve kilometers per hour."

Darkness descended abruptly as the dust storm blotted out the sun. A raspy hiss assaulted their ears as grit scoured the hull, nose, and domes of the ship. The ship shimmied, whipping about like a flag in a hurricane. The wind howled louder and faster, a locomotive racing directly toward them.

"Wind speed twenty-eight point three kilometers per hour," Adam said with an amplified voice. Metal groaned as the ship jerked violently and began to topple.

"Now!" Max said as Lyra shouted, "Brace for impact!"

Cassie clutched the arms of her chair.

The crash didn't come.

Abrupt quiet seemed to ring in their ears. A faint, translucent implosion of soil rushed harmlessly through them before being swept away by the equally translucent and immaterial sandstorm. The ship, now rock-steady, no longer groaned. Dust-laden wind passed through them as if they had become ghosts.

"Adam, take us up two meters and hover," Max ordered.

That would have been JJ's job. But Jonas was buried, buried in a dark, forsaken place far from home. Cassie unbuckled, floated upright, and turned to study each face. She saw determination, fear, relief, and hope—but no grief. They disgusted her. "I'll be in my cabin."

She went to her room and levitated a few centimeters above her bunk. Jonas might still be alive. He had to be alive. But now that she was a ghost, she couldn't reach him even if she tried. Or could she? An insanely dangerous plan coalesced in her mind. She thumbed the ship com link. "Adam, is Doc still at the emergency airlock?"

"Yes, Dr. Clearwater. Shall I patch you through?"

"Not yet. Can you remotely operate the airlock in the lab?"

"Yes. But I do not understand the relevance of the question. The lab cannot be reached during this storm."

"Please set it to vacuum."

"Done, Dr. Clearwater."

"Thank you. Put Doc on the line."

He answered immediately. "Cassie, what can I do for you?"

"I'm not feeling well. Can you get me something to calm me down? I'm in my cabin."

"You bet. Be right there."

She felt no guilt at the deception, only giddiness as she slipped into the corridor and floated to the farthest stairwell. She descended to the lower deck, rounded the corner, and peeked toward the emergency airlock. Deserted.

The manual airlock couldn't be disabled electronically or by electrical failure. Cassie launched her body to it and sealed herself inside. She donned a full space suit, grabbed a coil of wire rope, and cranked open the outside door. The ship hovered two meters off the ground. She pushed off and floated weightless in the air, still within the IDF, which negated almost all gravitational effects.

The storm passed harmlessly through her weightless body. *This is the dumbest thing I've ever done.* One mistake and she'd end up with a billion particles of carbon sand permeating her body. But this was the only chance of saving Jonas.

She used the jet pack of the suit to maneuver and pointed herself toward the lab. Phase shift took six seconds, which left no room for error, and the count would start the instant she moved outside the IDF of the ship. She opened the throttle of the jet pack and rocketed to the lab, passing ghost-like through its walls. She braked, oriented herself, and oozed through the airlock walls. She gave a short air blast to stop moving, and pulled her arms and legs in tight.

She floated another half second, then landed hard on the airlock floor. Alive, and none of her body parts embedded in a wall. She exited the airlock and entered the hot side of the lab. The plastic walls vibrated, pummeled by the wind. Holes would form soon, deflating the lab, but that didn't matter. She opened the Velcro flap and stepped outside.

Wind slammed her into the ground. A black cloud engulfed her, jostling like an angry mob. The sound penetrated her suit without need of microphone. Beyond a howl, whistle, or roar, the storm spoke with the harsh whine of an enormous grinder sanding down a granite mountain. It would grind her down, too—if she let it. She staggered to her feet.

The wind blew in the direction she wanted to go. The spacesuit protected her from the carbon grit eager to abrade flesh and bone. The suit wasn't designed for such abuse, but it only had to last long enough to rescue Jonas.

Air tanks always had a reserve, often several minutes worth. A person in excellent health, like Jonas, could stretch that even further. She tried to forget that he'd said his suit was leaking. She tried not to think about how much air he expended by screaming.

She tried jogging to stay upright. In a few steps, her boots sank too deep and she pitched forward into the dirt. She struggled to her knees and then to her feet, leaning back against the wind. She couldn't see the plants, the ship, or the sun. She couldn't see her glove in front of her face without pressing it against the glass. Every direction showed unrelenting black. The wind became her compass.

"JJ, answer me," she shouted into the helmet microphone. "Jonas! Tell me you're alive!"

She stumbled into Robbie. She tied one end of her rope to the rover then looped the other end around her waist. Now she had an anchor.

She dove ahead in the direction where JJ vanished, knowing she would never find the exact spot. The wind knocked her down again. It raised tiny waves in the plastic suit that rippled along at her back. She inched forward, blind, straining against the evil alliance of gravity and wind. She bumped into an occasional plant. Every few seconds she called for Jonas.

Her hand plunged into mud. *This is the place.* She swiveled around and lowered her legs into the muck. The rope went taut, completely played out. She moved her legs, hoping to touch Jonas, but found nothing. She tried to climb out, but the full force of the dust-laden wind pushed like the stream of a fire hose, making progress impossible. Unable to move forward or backward, she tried to summon an inner strength, but found herself drained of energy and will. Jonas was dead. Soon she'd join him. *But not only me.*

The dust and sand formed a wall at her head and shoulders. Maybe it would form a dune over her body, a burial mound. She tried to lift her arms, but they were stuck, already inches deep. *The baby. I have to save our baby.* She worked one arm free, and then the other. She climbed from the mud pit and stood leaning steeply forward like a skier racing down the slope. Maybe they could open a black snow ski lodge, if the damn planet had any mountains. Cassie laughed, too shrill and fast to hold any humor. She'd never make it back. She forced one foot forward anyway.

A gloved hand gripped her arm. A faceplate pressed against hers.

"Hang on," Doc said. He had a rope of his own and looped a coil around her waist. "Robbie, reel us in." The ropes grew taut as Robbie pulled them away from the mud pit. "Next step is the hardest," Doc said. "We're going to hang by these ropes while Robbie suspends us in the air. Adam will maneuver the ship to get us inside the field. Once we phase shift, we'll fly to the airlock. Adam's keeping it at vacuum."

Cassie felt the rope tighten further, drawing her upward and pressing her against Doc. Their feet left the ground. The wind tugged viciously, the rope going nearly horizontal as if the two humans were bait seized by a giant, invisible fish. On cue, a huge, semi-transparent shape approached with open, glowing mouth. Cassie screamed.

"*Cassie!*" shouted Doc. "Hang on. Almost there. Another couple seconds."

Waves of nausea announced the phase shift. She felt weightless again. The monstrous shape became the solid hull of the ship. The rope linking them to Robbie severed at the boundary of the IDF. The loose end trailed from them like a tail. Robbie, at ground level, could no longer be seen in the swirling dust. Doc used his jet pack to move them toward a square of glowing white in an endless sea of black.

He removed the rope holding them together. "Into the airlock! Move it!"

Exhausted and numb, Cassie tried to climb inside, but kept missing the handholds. Doc shoved her forward, then clambered in beside her.

In the light, Cassie saw sand and rain blowing through her. *I'm a ghost again.* The airlock door slid shut. She endured the UV lamps, the liquid disinfectant spray, the push and tug of sterile dry air. Doc took off his helmet and then hers.

Cassie felt neither joy nor relief. "You should have let me die."

"You're welcome," Doc replied.

Chapter 17

Ship Time: Day 15. 1700 hours.

Doc pressed the cold stethoscope against Cassie's chest. "Lungs sound okay."

Cassie buttoned her blouse, annoyed that Doc watched as if her chest were a ship sailing out of sight. His gaze rose to her eyes. Surprisingly, the look wasn't lecherous.

"That's a lovely figurine," he said. "Did you make it?"

Her fingers touched the polished wood. "A gift from my grandfather."

She remembered that day, the same day she'd first met Jonas. "This may help you find your way," Grandfather had whispered from his hospital bed. He pressed something into her hand. An inch-long, intricately carved wooden head of a thunderbird. Black as the darkest night, with an open mouth that seemed to talk to her. A leather thong threaded snake-like through holes in its ears and eyes.

"Blind and deaf?" she asked, unable to hold back a hint of sarcasm. Nonetheless, the smooth, warm wood felt good in her hand, full of peace and power.

"When darkness comes, we do not walk by sight. We walk by faith."

"You know I don't believe in this any more."

"Do you remember the story I told you about reality?"

"You told lots of stories."

"This story has been passed down for many generations. The Creator gathers all the animals and says: 'I want to hide something from humans until they are ready for it—the realization that they create their own reality.'

'Give it to me. I'll fly it to the moon,' says the Eagle.

'No, one day soon they will go there and find it.'

'How about the bottom of the ocean?' asks the salmon.

'No, they will find it there too.'

'I will bury it in the great plains,' says the buffalo.

'They will soon dig and find it there.'

'Put it inside them,' says the wise grandmother mole.

'Done,' says the Creator. 'It is the last place they will look.'"

Cassie forced a smile. "Yes, it's a lovely story." Science was the only reality. It saved her from foolish superstitions, but she wouldn't argue the point. Not with Grandfather.

He smiled and closed his eyes. Cassie slipped the totem into her vest pocket and kissed his forehead. She was halfway down the corridor when someone called.

"Hey, miss!"

She turned as a young black man walked up to her. "You dropped this."

He placed the totem in her hand. She touched her pocket. Empty. "Thank you."

His charming smile matched his voice. "Nice workmanship. Did you get it from the man in twelve?"

"My grandfather."

"He has great stories, doesn't he? Excuse me, I'm Jonas." He extended a hand. "Friends call me JJ."

She ignored the hand. "How do you know about his stories?"

He looked sheepish. "I wanted to find out more about you. He had some stories to tell."

"Are you stalking me? Look, Mister… Jonas, neither my grandfather nor I have any money, nor any interest in you. Thanks for returning this." She started back down the hall.

He said, "Your grandfather said I should ask you out."

She stopped, then turned. "He what?"

"Surprised me, too. Interracial blind dates arranged by a ninety-year-old shaman never seem to work out."

A smile bent her lips despite an effort to fight it. "My name's Cassie. You really talked with my grandfather?"

JJ nodded. "He's an amazing man."

"Yes." She found neither condescension nor deception in his voice or manner. He was handsome, witty, and had a gorgeous smile. "I could use a cup of coffee."

"There's a great coffee shop across the street. Pretty good sandwiches, too." The hospital corridor faded away.

"Cassie?" Doc's face held genuine concern. "You zoned out."

She tried to tell him she was fine, but the tears gushed out, and her throat tightened until only sobs emerged. Grandfather had died that day, and now Jonas was gone, too. Doc reached for her, and she needed to be held. She buried her face in his chest and let his arms surround her.

He leaned back, lifted her chin and smiled. The smile wasn't JJ's, but she knew it was the best the doctor could manage. She tried to smile back, unsure if it made it to her face.

His face filled with something more than sympathy. "The two of you had it all. Sometimes bad things happen to good people. I'm sorry."

She tried to identify the "something more." Guilt, maybe? "It's not your fault."

Doc winced. "I need to get a blood sample. Make a fist." He forced a smile to his lips, but the pain in his eyes remained.

Cassie winced at the poke of the needle. The vial filled slowly with red. "Does Tobias know? About Jonas?"

"Captain says the storm's causing too much interference for the ansible."

"He needs to know."

"Of course. Tell me, Cassie, why did you sign up for this trip? To be with Jonas?"

She thought about it. "I didn't even know who Jonas was the first time we met. He didn't tell me he was the son of Tobias, and even though I worked for MicroWeight, I never suspected a thing. I told him I'd volunteered and been accepted for a top secret, first ever starship flight. Jonas said the company needed an exobiologist and an all-round scientist. He said he would volunteer, too. Thought he had a shot at being the pilot." Cassie laughed. "I still didn't know who he was. When I finally met the rest of the crew and saw how deferentially they treated Jonas, realization came to me in a flash. God, I felt so embarrassed. But the truth is that I *am* an excellent scientist, and Jonas was right to make sure I loved him and not his money."

Tears welled up. She wiped them away. "What about you? Why did you volunteer?"

"I was a surgeon. Damn good one." He held out a hand, palm down. The hand quivered. "Essential tremors. Medication helps, a little, but it ended my career." He lowered his hand, withdrew the needle from Cassie's arm, and sprayed on a bandage. "I signed up because the time dilation effects." He ran a hand through his hair. An anxious smile made a brief appearance. "They'll have a cure by the time we get home. Tobias promised."

Doc floated away and returned with two squeeze bottles of amber liquid. "Speaking of medication." He handed one to her. "Brandy. Purely medicinal."

She took the proffered bottle and squeezed a bit into her mouth. She savored the burn. Losing herself in alcohol seemed a viable solution. Her stomach disagreed. "What I need is something stronger for nausea. I'm queasy almost every day."

"Space sickness. You got a bad case is all." His face abruptly contorted. He hurled the bottle across the room. It ricocheted off a bulkhead and tumbled out of sight. "Who am I kidding? Cassie, there's more going on than you know. Tobias—"

The door to sickbay slid open and Li rushed in. "Doctor! I am in severe pain. My ankle, see? It is swollen and purple. I require immediate tests, diagnosis, and treatment." She glanced at Cassie. "Leave us, so that the doctor may perform his duties."

Cassie felt too drained to fight. She left, but paused in the hallway as the door *whooshed* shut. She pressed an ear to the door.

Li said, "Do not be an idiot."

"It's over, Li. Don't you see that?"

"In silence is your salvation. What is the phrase? Do not rock the boat."

The conversation continued but Cassie didn't care. She returned to her cabin. Captain Kazakov waited inside.

"Get out of my room."

"You could have killed us all, Clearwater."

"Well, I didn't. Cuss me out tomorrow."

"You disobeyed my orders. I can't trust you."

Cassie bristled. "You abandoned JJ. That doesn't inspire trust."

"I've instructed Adam to ignore any future commands from you that are outside your assigned duties. He'll also track your whereabouts."

"You can't do that."

"You're damn lucky I'm not confining you to quarters. I don't care if you are—were—JJ's girl. Don't screw up again." He launched himself toward the door, forcing her to dodge as he flew into the hallway. He hooked a handrail to execute a hard right turn before vanishing down the corridor.

She closed the pneumatic door, wishing she could slam it. Her stomach heaved and she rushed to the trash bin, managing to capture most of the puke before it could float away. A slip of paper, the note JJ had left two nights before, drifted by, stained with bile. She wiped it clean with reverent carefulness. Her preoccupation with science had cost her a precious night with him, and now there would be no more nights together. She glided through the corridor to his cabin, put on one of his shirts, and crawled into his bed. She fastened herself in with a bungee cord. Eventually, she fell into an exhausted sleep.

Chapter 18

Ship Time: Day 16. 0600 hours.

"Dr. Clearwater, the captain requests all hands assemble on the bridge."

Cassie felt like a satellite after a meteor shower: pitted, pummeled, and pulverized. "Leave me alone." The cabin lights turned on and brightened; Adam wasn't being fair. Cassie pulled the blanket over her head.

"Request was a poor word choice on my part. The captain has ordered all hands to the bridge."

"Fuck him."

"Regulations specify that all positions be staffed prior to flight operations, except in an emergency. Do you have an emergency, Dr. Clearwater?"

Cassie lowered the blanket. "Flight ops?"

"Dr. Sullivan worked through the night shift to make the necessary repairs."

"We can't leave." Cassie unfastened the bungee cord and smoothed out some of the larger wrinkles in her clothes. She didn't have time to change or even shower. She had to stop this nonsense now.

Two minutes later Cassie entered the bridge and found everyone at their stations. She floated up to the captain. "We can't leave."

"Take your station, Clearwater. Liftoff in five minutes."

"We need..." *He's dead. He's really dead.* "...to retrieve his body."

Max ignored her. "Adam, you'll be taking us up."

"Acknowledged, Captain."

Cassie placed her hands on her hips, a pose she realized appeared less defiant than intended since her body floated perpendicular to the captain. "Does Tobias know what's happened? What you're doing?"

"What do you think I'm doing? Taking the ship out for a leisurely cruise on a Sunday afternoon? You're the science officer. Think it through."

Cassie blinked. What was she missing? Outside, the storm still raged, but they were safe in ghost phase. Eventually they would need to go into space, where vacuum allowed a safe return to normal material existence. So why the urgency?

Because the storm could end at any time. Even a brief lull in the wind could be dangerous. Six seconds later, they'd all be dead.

Max nodded as if reading her mind. "Buckle in and keep your head clear."

Cassie drifted to her station and strapped in. Her attention kept wandering from her console to the empty seat in front of her.

Doc whispered, "Max is still pissed at your stunt. He'll get over it."

She whispered back, "I doubt it."

Max said, "Engineer, transfer IDF control to the computer. Adam, take us up."

"Yes, Captain. Climbing at five hundred kilometers per hour."

The bridge brightened as the ship cleared the dust storm, only to dim minutes later as they rose above the atmosphere into black space. "Elevation two hundred kilometers," Adam said. "Low orbit achieved, Captain."

Doc cleared his throat. "What now? Back to Earth?"

Cassie spun. "No!"

Lyra said, "Repairs will be easier there. No telling how much additional damage we sustained before the phase shift. We were damn lucky, and I don't want to press it."

Li nodded. "The monster that took Jonas is still there, lurking unseen and unheard beneath the sand." She shuddered. "Diamonds are not worth my life."

Lyra added, "I don't want to leave Robbie behind. We should—"

"It's Jonas we can't leave behind!" Cassie shouted. She lowered her voice. "We need to retrieve his body."

"If it's still there," Doc said.

"What's that supposed to mean?"

"Nothing." He lowered his gaze toward his console.

"Don't you dare look away. What did you mean, 'if he's still there?'"

A second passed, then another. Without looking up, he said, "Corrosives. They were already dissolving his suit."

Cassie shook her head. "No. It wasn't acid. His radio was still transmitting. He's still there."

"The planet is cursed," Li said. "We should go home, now."

"Soon," Lyra said. "When the storm clears, we'll grab Robbie and head home."

Cassie felt as abandoned as Jonas. "We have to bring him home."

"Clearwater, map the storm and give me a forecast," Max said. "Sullivan, work with Wu to design a seismic detector. If anything moves through the sand, I want to know where it is, where it's going, and how fast it's moving. Doc, think up some ways to kill the thing."

Cassie turned to her console, feeling marginally better until her gaze again fell on the empty pilot's seat. Every ache in her body felt magnified. "Captain, has Tobias been notified?"

He looked grim. "Yes."

"I think I should have been the one to tell him."

He shook his head. "My crew. My job."

***

Cassie, assisted by Adam, pulled up a weather simulation program and plugged in the variables relevant to this planet. The project provided a welcome distraction from the ache of her failed rescue attempt. Obsidian was tidally locked like Earth's moon—the same hemisphere of the planet always faced the sun. The eternally dark side stayed in perpetual deep freeze with very little variation in weather. The daylight side had concentric climate zones like the rings of a target. The bulls-eye, closest to the sun, was a desert where temperatures hovered around ninety-five degrees Celsius. Air rose from the desert and flowed outward toward the boundary of the dark side, where it cooled, sank, and blew back to the desert, repeating the cycle.

Cassie factored in the impact of solar flares from Teegarden's Star, and then let the simulation run. During the lull, she approached the captain.

"Max, when you spoke with Tobias..."

Max lifted his brow. "What?"

"Did he order us to go home? I don't think we should leave without at least trying to retrieve JJ's body."

He stared at her, long and hard enough for Cassie to feel uncomfortable. She said, "Maybe I should talk to him. He's practically my father-in-law." *Or would have been.*

His eyes narrowed and his fingers began their three-finger tap dance. "No need. He agrees with you."

A beep signaled that the simulation had finished, and Max motioned for her to get back to work. As expected, the solar flares rapidly warmed the planet, increasing the amount of water vapor in the atmosphere and dramatically accelerating the normally slow convective air currents. This produced planetary-wide sandstorms, followed by rain, a fairly rapid cooling, and a return to clear, stable conditions.

Cassie compared the behavior of the actual storm to the values predicted by the simulation. They matched perfectly.

"Captain, the sandstorm has shifted to rain, which should end in thirty-six to forty-eight hours. Solar radiation is decreasing but won't be safe for extended exposure for another twenty-four hours."

"You said extended. How long can we work outside the ship?"

"Lyra should be able to fix the landing strut just fine. She'll be in the ship's shadow."

"That wasn't my question."

Cassie didn't need to ponder the purpose of the question. She knew what motivated Max. "Half an hour, maybe an hour. Doc could give a better estimate."

"Another day lost." He stared at the consoles with a look of disgust, then seemed to remember Cassie. His countenance shifted into a semblance of sympathy. "Before we can retrieve Jefferson," he added.

Chapter 19

Ship Time: Day 17. 1600 hours.

As predicted, solar radiation decreased to safe levels in twenty-four hours. Telemetry from Robbie indicated the winds had slowed to ten kilometers per hour. Rain had replaced the dust, although near-blackout conditions remained due to heavy cloud cover.

Adam took the ship out of ghost phase and piloted it back to the landing site. The *Far Traveler* set down on the bubbles as gently as a leaf settles to the ground. Cassie refused to admit the computer flew the ship as well as Jonas, but couldn't deny that the straight-line descent and minimal G-forces kept her space-sickness from flaring. *Be honest. It's morning sickness.*

The landing had been instrument only, for nothing was visible through the nose of the ship. Adam created a holographic view of the surrounding terrain based on radar. The exterior view of the lab showed only a large mound of damp soil. One the of lab's interior cameras had survived and showed a large puncture in the windward wall. A few centimeters of black dust covered the floor and table tops, but there appeared to be little actual damage. The ceiling sagged from deflation and an overburden of sand, but the roof could be cleared and the walls re-inflated.

Adam's panoramic view shifted. Twenty meters from the ship, Robbie sat buried to the top of its treads in the damp soil. Sand-pitted exposed metal on one side of the rover prompted Doc to suggest renaming it "Scarface."

Max said, "Sullivan, keep the ship's mass at the minimum necessary for stability and safety. Adam, keep the propulsion system at hot standby in case we need to leave in a hurry."

"Acknowledged, Captain."

"Sullivan, have you figured out how to track underground movement?"

"I'll modify Robbie's sonar and ground penetrating radar, if it hasn't been damaged by the storm. Reorienting it from vertical to horizontal shouldn't be hard. I'll boost the signal. Should give us a range of a hundred meters."

"Good. After you make those mods, repair his treads so he can help you repair the landing gear."

Lyra nodded but Max had already turned to Doc. "You figure out a way to kill those animals and its mother?"

"Kind of difficult without a test specimen."

"Maybe the one we caught is still alive. Work with Clearwater to patch the lab. The two of you need to come up with something absolutely lethal to those things."

Cassie said, "Before Robbie starts working on the landing struts, he should locate Jonas so we can retrieve his body."

The words temporarily immobilized everyone. Then Max said, "Of course. Whatever is left, we'll gather and bring home."

Cassie swallowed. "We should have a memorial service, too."

"We will. Later. Survival first." Max turned to Li. "Wu, you and I will resume mining."

Li balked. "You are crazy to think I am going out there knowing there is a creature lurking, ready to pull me under the sand and..." She cast a quick look at Cassie.

Lyra agreed. "No one should leave the ship until I've fixed Robbie and we have some kind of weapon to protect ourselves."

Max's lips twisted into a grin. "Wu's safer with me than anywhere else." His hand dipped into a pocket and came out holding a gun.

Li gasped. Doc said, "Aren't you just full of surprises."

Cassie stared at the weapon, feeling that no good would come of this. Intelligence always provides better solutions than brute force. "Adam, color code your display for depth of the sand."

Lyra cocked her head. "What are you looking for?"

"A large sub-surface creature needs deep, loose soil, not the shallows beneath the ship. Mapping other shallows might give us pathways of relative safety."

Max nodded. "Good thinking, Clearwater." The gun disappeared into his pocket.

"I believe you're in luck, Dr. Clearwater," Adam said. "The layer of bedrock under the ship extends to the lab and also to the initial mining area, where it breaches the surface."

Another thought came to her mind. "Adam, can the radar find... JJ's body?"

"Unfortunately, the resolution is too poor to distinguish between rock, roots, or human remains."

She sighed. "Doc and I can patch the lab."

Lyra studied the floating image. "Robbie's stuck over one of the deeper spots. Sucks."

"I'll go with you," Max said. "Wu can start digging on her own."

Li's inscrutable face managed to express severe annoyance.

Max added a jab. "Too bad you have to carry your own shovel and bucket."

Cassie hid her smile. "Adam, enhance for low light and show the plant grove."

The image zoomed outward. The plants appeared to be white, although they might actually be pale gray. The tallest plant appeared to be badly weathered, with a severely scarred stem and a bald, ulcerated dome that oozed sap. It was one of two surviving giants. The other appeared to be in good shape, coated, like the rest of the grove, in a white glaze. Cassie remembered there being three giants, but no trace remained of the third. *The storm took more than my Jonas.*

Max said, "Okay, let's go."

The crew suited up, crowded into the airlock, and marched into the rain. Visibility had improved only marginally since the blackout. The Observation Room poured out light like an upside-down lighthouse, but the oppressive gloom clung tenaciously to the landscape. The grove, two hundred meters away, appeared as a milky smudge. Surprisingly, Cassie found herself missing the clear, eternal twilight.

At the current IDF setting, Cassie's mass came to only a few kilograms, which made walking in the heat and humidity of the biosuit less onerous. The relief was short-lived. Six seconds after passing beyond the field's boundary, she stumbled as her weight ballooned forty-fold. Doc extended a hand. Cassie ignored it.

The lab proved difficult to enter. The wrinkled plastic walls bowed and stretched rather than let the Velcro strips of the door flap release their grip. Eventually Cassie obtained a decent grip on the wall as Doc peeled back the door.

They stoop-walked under the sagging ceiling and found the damage to be more extensive than the video feed had suggested. The external wall suffered at least four punctures. Blowing dust or rain had infiltrated the airlock controls, rendering it inoperable.

The animal and the two plants were alive. Cassie surmised the animal survived the radiation by burrowing under the layer of soil in its terrarium. The plants were almost certainly protected by the glistening white film—probably an organic sunblock—coating their caps and stems. One lab rat, Mr. Jones, also survived, although he showed hair loss and other signs of radiation sickness that had killed his siblings.

Cassie spoke into her suit mike. "Captain, the lab will take at least a couple days to repair and clean. I'd like to relocate my specimens and equipment to under the ship."

Lyra said, "I'll be working on the landing gear. Put your makeshift lab somewhere else."

"The ship will provide shelter from the rain, and the airlock will provide a decon station," Cassie explained.

Max said, "Permission granted. Just stay out of Sullivan's way."

"Thanks, Captain." Cassie turned to Doc. "You take the plants. I'll take the animal and Mr. Jones. Next trip we'll start hauling the equipment."

Doc gave a mock groan. "Couldn't we wait for Robbie's new shoes? He could do it all in one trip."

"Sooner we get back to the ship, sooner we get this weight off."

"Good point. I'm not the athlete that Jonas... sorry."

"It's okay." They walked to the ship, and Cassie's gaze wandered to the grove again. Tomorrow she might risk going out there to discover why one giant plant died and another hadn't made the protective coating. She would need to talk Max into letting Robbie go with her. A tentacled monster might prowl under the deeper sand like a giant squid, and she didn't trust her legs to slog over sand as fast as the monster could swim through it.

On the second trip, Cassie noticed a "low memory" alarm blinking on the mass spectrometer. It had been left on during the storm and dutifully analyzed a sample of laboratory air every few seconds until its memory was full. Most of the results would need to be deleted, being duplicate samples of background air. She clicked through a few screens of data to verify her suspicion. One flurry of aromatic chemicals, thousands of them, corresponded to when she and Doc first carried the creature inside. Not surprising. The animal and plants generated an enormous number of chemicals, and the close proximity of the two species probably stimulated even more production.

Doc pushed the portable X-ray machine to the ship, which proved to be a tedious undertaking as the wheels became mired in the wet sand. Cassie began deleting mass spec results to free up the memory. Unlike the X-ray, the mass spec gas chromatograph wasn't designed to be portable. It would take both of them, or maybe three people, to move it to the ship. While waiting for Doc to return, she deleted a few duplicate graphs from the machine's memory. There were thousands; it would be quicker to do a complete wipe, but she wanted to save a few representative graphs. She began skimming the files.

She stopped, belatedly noticing something odd about the graphs. She undeleted the previous two files and opened them sequentially as if running a slide show. She stared open-mouthed at the result. The spikes in one of the short-lived aromatic chemicals could have been overlooked easily, especially in isolation. The specific chemical didn't matter—it was the timing and grouping of its release.

Spike ... spike, spike ... spike, spike, spike ... spike, spike, spike, spike. The simple integer progression continued to six. After a long pause, the spikes repeated the cycle.

Intelligence.

Cassie's excitement surged, and then faded. She couldn't tell anyone, not yet. Rejection and ridicule would follow just as before, unless she provided absolute, irrefutable proof.

"Cassie? You all right?"

She jumped at Doc's hand on her shoulder. She faked a laugh and turned off the display. "Just daydreaming. Let's get the rest of this stuff moved."

Chapter 20

Ship Time: Day 17. 1800 hours.

Doc and Max sat across from Cassie at the mess table. She studied their faces as she spoke. "I'm convinced that the animals communicate with each other through smell. We could use this to our advantage by laying down a chemical perimeter, warning them to stay away from the ship."

Max frowned. "Proof?"

"Working on it. Right now there's strong circumstantial evidence. If I'm right, warning them off is a better, safer solution than extermination."

Max rubbed his chin. "Doc?"

Doc shrugged. "Might work. Many species use scents and pheromones to influence behavior. Let her give it a try before testing poisons that present long-term problems for colonization."

"Killing it is unconscionable," Cassie said.

"That *thing* isn't a person," Max said to both of them. "It's a hostile alien life form that killed Jefferson. If you can tell those things to keep their distance, fine. But that's not your priority. We *must* be able to kill them."

Arguing with Max was like trying to push a mountain out of the way. She needed her own mountain, a mountain of proof.

"Something else, Clearwater?"

"I need borrow Li's pocket brain. I need it to interface with the gas chromatograph and my intelligence protocol software."

Doc snorted. "Fat chance. Li doesn't give up her toys."

Max said, "Adam, have Wu report to the mess hall."

Doc looked incredulous. "You're really going to do it?"

Li glided into the room and paused as if waiting for them to rise. When they didn't, she dipped her head in acknowledgement of their presence. "Captain, how may I be of service?"

Max tilted his head to Cassie, who said, "I need your help to determine how the animals communicate. Your pocket brain has nearly as much computing power as Adam. It could analyze the thousands of smells and billions of combinations to find the patterns and decipher their language."

"Language?" Doc said.

"Rudimentary," Cassie said quickly. "Equivalent to the barks and growls of a wolf pack or the way pheromones control the behavior of bees in a hive."

Li rolled her eyes. "You can not be serious." She turned to go.

"Wu!" Max barked. "You haven't been dismissed."

She turned, eyes narrowed. "The pocket brain is my personal property, a treasured gift from my government. I will not insult the givers by exposing the device to the odors of alien beasts."

The captain's face went hard, as if turned to stone by Medusa. The transmutation, instead of rendering him immobile and helpless, gave Max the fearsome countenance of a living gargoyle. Li met his gaze for only a few seconds before lowering her head.

"I do this under protest."

"Duly noted," Max said.

Cassie didn't want Li as an enemy. "Li, I would be honored if you would work with me on this project. In fact, your assistance is vital to success. Perhaps Doc could replace you as the Captain's digging partner for the next day or two?"

Li may have smiled; Cassie wasn't sure. Doc didn't look pleased, but he didn't bring up the contractual issue.

Max stood. "It's settled, then. Clearwater, you have until tomorrow afternoon to figure out what makes that thing tick." He left the room, motioning for Doc to follow.

***

Working in her open-air lab beneath the ship, Cassie labored to link the gas chromatograph to Li's pocket brain. She also rigged an aerosol dispenser to give puffs of various chemicals in whatever sequence and combination she desired. If smells were the creature's alphabet, Cassie had only a dozen letters out of their hundred thousand, but basic math didn't require spelling or grammar.

While Li calibrated her PB to its new task, Cassie used acid-resistant tongs to position the animal while she studied its anatomy, took biopsies, and snapped X-rays. The results showed a simple layout. Multi-chambered heart. Muscles with tendons connecting flippers to anchor points on the inside of the exoskeleton. A brain stem ran the length of the body. A bladder-like organ, purpose unknown, connected to the flippers. She found no sign of a digestive system.

She didn't dare perform an ultrasound, fearing it would rupture the creature's internals as it had done to her earlier plant specimen. Freezing and dissection were out of the question, regardless of what Max and Doc expected. An intelligent species shouldn't harm another intelligent species, the history of human civilization notwithstanding.

"Li, I left the laser scalpel in the lab. Would you mind getting it for me? I'm in the middle of analyzing this biopsy, and the material will evaporate before I can get there and back."

Li sighed as if the greatest of burdens had settled upon her shoulder, but nonetheless left to fetch the laser.

Cassie placed the animal back in its cage and tapped it with a glass rod. Tap... tap, tap... tap, tap, tap. The snorkel rose slowly and sniffed at the rod. Small puffs came from the tip. Cassie didn't need the chromatograph to see that the puffs were delivered in the same integer sequence. A glance at the pocket brain confirmed that the wireless data input worked properly.

Cassie tapped the pattern again, but the creature seemed listless. The snorkel puffed four times then settled to the bottom of the cage and lay still. Probably hungry. She didn't want it to starve, but she didn't have any monster kibble handy. Or maybe she did.

She grabbed a pair of tongs and used it to tease the plant free of the soil in the terrarium. She cautiously opened the lid of the animal's cage, placed the plant inside, and closed the lid. She wondered how the creature fed without a digestive system. It even lacked an excretory sphincter. Would it totally dissolve the plant and directly absorb the liquid nutrients?

The mass spec displayed a flurry of fresh chemicals. Hundreds, if not thousands, of spikes filled the screen, rising and falling in apparent chaos. Within the cage, the flaps at the tip of the animal's snorkel fluttered but made no move toward the plant.

She'd give it time. Meanwhile, she studied the biopsies. Puzzling. The animal's DNA and cellular structure were virtually identical to the DNA of the plants. Only a few genes were different, probably those relating to physical structure and organ placement. No junk DNA, no wasted space, only precise, efficient, stable coding. More evidence of an intelligent creator at work on this planet.

The scales covering the animal matched the scales on the plant roots—diamond coated to withstand abrasion from the soil. Beneath the scales was a rigid, streamlined body consisting of carbon bucky-balls identical to the stems of the plants. The flexible snorkel consisted of muscular fibers and airway with a vascular connection to an acid bladder.

The animal lacked a photosynthetic surface and a root system. It did have a nodule on its central nerve cord that probably served as a rudimentary brain. It had lungs and breathed oxygen. A sample of fluid from the mysterious bladder turned out to be residue from the chemical breakdown of a sugar similar to fructose.

The device still displayed a busy exchange of trace gasses. Cassie used a musical keyboard as the input control for the odor dispenser. Li claimed it had come from Doc, who apparently enjoyed practicing music as well as medicine.

Cassie pressed a key, sending a puff of scent into the cage. She paused, pressed the key twice in rapid succession, paused and then pressed it three times. She looked at the display.

She saw her spikes. The myriad scents of the animal dwindled to nothing. Then came an answering puff... puff, puff... puff, puff, puff. *Using exactly the same chemical she had used.*

She gripped the table, head spinning. *I just exchanged messages with an alien being.* The giddiness made it hard to think, hard to be a scientist. She forced herself to be the devil's advocate. This might be an instinctive copy-cat reaction. Could she prove otherwise?

She hit the key once. Short pause. Two hits. Long pause. Four hits. Short pause. Five hits.

She waited. The animal puffed three times.

"Yes!" Cassie shouted. The creature could identify a missing element in a sequence.

Her helmet speaker crackled. "Are you all right, Dr. Clearwater?" Adam said.

"Yes, yes. Fine. Leave me alone."

The display cleared, then began a new sequence. Two puffs. Then three. Five. Seven. Eleven puffs.

Cassie stared at the screen. *Prime numbers*. The animal comprehended prime numbers! She rapidly hit her key thirteen times, paused and hit it seventeen more, to let it know she understood.

Instead of an answer, another flurry of myriad scents erupted. She looked at the cage. The snorkel lay quiescent on the bottom. The creature's breathing seemed labored. *Damn*. Her alien genius was starving. Why didn't it eat the plant? What was she missing?

She called Doc. "Do you have any glucose in your medical supplies?"

"Blood sugar low?"

"I need it right now."

"Okay. I'm due for a break. Meet me in sickbay. Can't open your suit to swallow."

"Bring it to me in an IV."

After a brief pause, Doc said, "What's going on, Cassie?"

"You'll see."

Minutes later he arrived with an IV bag, needle, and tube. She looked at the needle, shook her head, and replaced it with the longer needle she'd used to take samples. She pulled up the X-rays and took a moment to orient the needle. Holding the animal's snorkel down with the tongs, she carefully reached forward and poked the needle into the what she hoped was the sugar bladder.

Doc grinned. "Pet needs a feeding?"

"Something like that."

It took only a few minutes to empty the bag. She withdrew the needle and closed the lid. The effect came immediately. The animal stirred and lifted its snorkel. The mass-spec display showed another flurry of scents. The screen cleared, and then showed one puff. Then another single puff. Two puffs. Three. Five. Eight. Thirteen.

"You call that counting?" Doc said.

Cassie grinned. "It's the beginning of the Fibonacci sequence. It's a pattern often found in nature and art. The animal may be smarter than you, Karl."

He grimaced and started up the ramp to the ship, pausing as Robbie rolled past on its way to the dig site. "For your sake, I hope you're wrong."

He disappeared into the airlock before she could think of a reply. She didn't dwell on it. This discovery was too important, too exciting to allow distractions. She began the intelligence test protocols. As expected, the animal scored sufficiently high on the math portion to justify classification as an intelligent species. The non-math tests were inconclusive, and fortunately, unnecessary.

She also had to show the animal wasn't hostile. Glass rod in gloved hand, she opened the lid again, but instead of tapping the animal, she gently stroked its body. The creature skittered away. Cassie stroked it again. The snorkel rose and sniffed at the rod then puffed on it but did not spray acid.

The mass-spec recorded flurries of smells. *If only I knew what they mean.* It might take hours, even days for the pocket brain to translate the language. Maybe years, if humans and aliens lacked enough shared concepts. Cassie touched the rod to the dome of the plant. The animal scurried next to it, snorkel bobbing and swaying until it found the rod and tried to push it away.

Interesting. She touched the animal again using slow, gentle strokes. Then she touched the dome using the same light touch. The animal tensed, snorkel high and rigid, but it didn't interfere. Good. This might prove easier than expected.

She told Adam to analyze the scents for language patterns. She felt happy, almost buoyant. Hungry, too. No nausea today. She couldn't wait to share the discovery with Jonas.

The happy house of cards collapsed. She blinked to clear the tears. Maybe she'd name the animal species after him. *Jonas Sapiens.* She still hated the idea of personal fame, but her dreams of flying among the stars had died with Jonas. *I carry our child, dear one.*

Li, laser in hand, trudged toward the ship. Her gait grew graceful a few seconds after entering the dampening field. Cassie took the scalpel and set it on the work table. "Thanks, Li. Let's eat. It's the captain's turn to cook supper."

The rain finally stopped. The grove appeared more clearly now, pale white toadstools starkly outlined against the black dirt. None appeared to be damaged save for one giant with a chunk missing from its dome. Something bright caught her attention. The orange sun peaked out from a break in the clouds. A good omen. If only she believed in omens.

The beef stroganoff surprised everyone. Max usually cooked hamburgers. "Doc and I mined sixty pounds of diamond," he explained. "Tomorrow will bring sixty more. Then we'll all go on shift and we'll make some *serious* money." He laughed. Doc, Lyra, and Li joined in. Cassie couldn't.

"Any updates from Tobias?"

The jocularity faded. "I spoke with him last night," Max said. "He's distraught, of course. But there's nothing he can do, and says we should proceed with the mission."

Li made a choking sound. She lifted a napkin to her mouth. She stared at the captain.

Lyra said, "He must be overwhelmed with grief."

Doc said, "We ought to take a moment to... have that memorial service Cass suggested."

"Fine," Max said. "Jefferson will be missed. Although none of us is indispensible, the loss does leave a hole, an empty feeling which is slow to fill. May whatever God or gods exist welcome his spirit, and grant comfort to those of us left behind." He looked around. "Anyone have something to add?"

Add? That was it? A twenty-second service? This wasn't a memorial, it was a chore on the captain's checklist that he'd just marked as complete. Li dabbed at tearless eyes with a silk handkerchief. Doc and Lyra stared at the table as if embarrassed.

Cassie gave a start as Max placed his hand over hers. In a surprisingly soft voice, he said, "I share your grief, but we can't afford to wallow in it. This is a hostile planet. A deadly planet. We need to be vigilant. We need to do our jobs. Don't let me down."

She pulled her hand away and left the table, heading for the makeshift lab. She stopped at sickbay on the way, where she grabbed a fresh supply of anti-nausea pills from the cabinet and an IV bag of glucose from the refrigerator. The glass rod and other necessary tools were outside. Carrot and stick. She hoped the principle was universal.

Obsidian had no mornings, afternoons, or nights, but the urgency of her work didn't need artificial measures of time. She had to prove the animal was intelligent and non-hostile in order to save the species and their habitat. Otherwise the diamonds and Earth-like conditions would draw people here and magnify human greed to insane proportions. She had to prevent that future, which meant convincing Doc to invoke the Prime Directive. Then she could find JJ's remains and go home, sharing his last ride through the starry sky.

Chapter 21

Ship Time: Day 18. 0800 hours.

For the second time in a week, Cassie worked through the night shift. Every test confirmed intelligence and non-hostile behavior, but the facts were dry and technical. She needed something dramatic. She needed full, two-way communication.

"I consulted with Dr. Wu," Adam said. "She hypothesized that each scent has an innate meaning, like Chinese characters. These scents combine with additional scents to form increasingly complex ideas. Unfortunately, I lack the ability to synthesize more than a few dozen aromatic chemicals. Without the ability to initiate or respond appropriately, my progress has been limited."

"How many chemical compounds do they use?" asked Cassie.

"I have detected 196,455 distinct chemical compounds."

Cassie sighed. "So many. We'll never manage to translate it."

"On the contrary. I now recognize the names and naming convention for their numbers and numeric operations. I have the chemical compounds needed to specify any number, and the operations of addition, subtraction and square roots. They utilize a base three system."

Base three made sense. The animal had three flippers on each side. The plants had three roots. The creators of these life forms probably had three digits. A knot formed in her stomach. The alien super-intelligence had bestowed a level of intelligence on the animals. What if the plants were similarly endowed? She'd killed some of them. A lot of them. The knot tightened, churning. Luckily she hadn't eaten breakfast.

Reason prevailed—the plants weren't conscious, because she'd done the test protocols and the plants didn't respond. Anatomy showed they didn't have well-developed brains, something necessary for rational thought and memory. The knot in her gut eased.

She still needed to prove the *animals* were intelligent and not hostile to humans. She could do both in a convincing demonstration, one that would sway the captain and force Doc to declare the planet protected from exploitation and colonization.

Lyra approached, wiping gloved hands on a rag. "Strut's fixed. You need any help packing up here?"

"I'm not finished."

"'Fraid so. Captain wants you digging with me on first shift. We have thirty minutes."

Robbie returned from the dig site, lowered a basket of diamonds to the side of the ramp, and rolled next to them. "Shall I transfer equipment back to the lab, Dr. Clearwater?"

"Lab's a wreck."

"Incorrect. I cleared the roof, patched the walls, and re-inflated the walls. Doctor Unger cleaned the interior. Dr. Sullivan repaired the airlock."

"Pack up," Lyra said.

"No. I have a demonstration for everyone. Adam, ask the rest of the crew to join us."

A few seconds passed. "They are on the way."

Li emerged from the airlock and stood next to Lyra. "Has our Dr. Doolittle learned to speak with the animals?"

Lyra smirked. Cassie mentally rehearsed the presentation.

Max and Doc arrived together from the mining area. Rivulets of sweat, visible through the helmet faceplates, trickled down their foreheads. Even more visible was the captain's frown. Doc's attention returned to the grove. Pointing, he said, "Another switch-a-rooney."

They turned to see the last few dollops of white goop fall from the plants. The grove had returned to uniform blackness.

Max grunted and turned to Cassie. "You got something to show us?"

"Yes sir. The animal is both intelligent and non-hostile. I can prove it."

"Proceed." He didn't sound happy. No matter. Facts spoke for themselves.

She stood at the keyboard. "The animal communicates through smell. Li, Adam, and I constructed a means to send and receive smells. For now, we can understand and convey number sequences, addition, and subtraction. Eventually we'll be able to build a full repertoire of language to go with the mathematics."

Doc said, "I saw a horse in a carnival that could count. Could add, subtract, even multiply."

"This isn't a trick, Karl."

"The mind sees what it wants to see."

"You saw the spikes on the mass spectrometer. The animal can count."

"Adam," Max said, "can you verify these spikes?"

"Dr. Clearwater's data is accurate, Captain. The integer progression is unambiguous."

"The animals killed Jonas," Li said. "They are hostile and deserve to be wiped out."

"She has a point, Clearwater. We can defend ourselves from hostile life forms, intelligent or not."

"Jonas fell into a mud pit and died when his air ran out." Cassie was surprised at the calm in her voice. "There is no basis for classifying the life here as hostile."

Li waved a hand dismissively. "He was dragged away when we tried to rescue him."

Lyra said, "I believe you, Cassie. The animals are intelligent. They laid a trap and murdered Jonas."

Cassie's excitement morphed into exasperation. "I can't believe you would exterminate an entire species for a few dollars."

Max's brows rose. "Not a few dollars. Billions of dollars."

"Money doesn't matter. The animal is intelligent and non-hostile. We're something new in its environment, and it was checking us out." She turned to Doc. "Care to compare this creature's ability to that of the horse you mentioned?"

Doc said, "Seventeen minus five."

Cassie pressed the keys. "The creature uses base three. A graph of the raw chemical signals shows on the left monitor. Blue for my inputs, red for the response. Adam will convert these signals to base ten and display it on the right-hand monitor."

Jagged gray peaks appeared on the left, with a few blue spikes. "17 - 5 =" appeared on the right screen.

"Slow thinker?" asked Doc. "The horse would have it by now."

"What are the gray spikes?" asked Lyra.

"Background smells. Adam, is there a malfunction?" asked Cassie.

"No, Dr. Clearwater. The creature is not responding to the question."

A twinge of apprehension came like the first cloud in her blue sky of confidence. "Try another problem, Doc."

"Five plus four plus three."

Cassie typed the keys. New spikes appeared on the left screen, including red, but no translation appeared on the right.

"Your critter's angry," Lyra said.

The animal had surfaced near the plant, and its snorkel struck the stem several times before backing away.

Cassie said, "Two plus two." No response came.

The creature lunged forward and wrapped its snorkel around the plant stem, and then shook it like a terrier playing with a stick. The plant's dome wobbled and threatened to tear loose. A root pulled free, spraying liquid, which bubbled and smoked where it landed on the animal's body.

"Robbie!" Cassie said. "Move the animal to the tank." She separated the specimens using tongs and the glass rod to avoid the acid. Robbie's mechanical arm lifted the animal from the terrarium, placed it inside a glass tank, and closed the lid.

"Does your pet have a name?" Li asked.

Doc laughed. "How about Boxer? That thing's a fighter."

Cassie stared at the mocking faces. "Adam, please play the videos of our tests." The screen flickered and showed Cassie pressing keys and the screen displaying numbers. Voices emerged from the laptop speaker, Adam and Cassie documenting the tests. The tinny audio couldn't hide the growing excitement in her voice as the creature scored perfectly on every math question.

Max looked impatient. "You'll have plenty of time to work on it during the trip home."

Cassie cocked her head. "Once we release the specimens, there won't be any fresh inputs. We'll don't have enough to decipher the language with what we've recorded so far."

Max gave the "you're being stupid" look.

"You want to bring the specimens to Earth?"

"What made you think we wouldn't?"

"They are living, thinking beings," Cassie said, arms rising and falling for emphasis. "We can't keep them imprisoned." She looked at Doc. "The Prime Directive is very clear on that."

He seemed to study the settings on the chromatograph. "Intelligence hasn't been proven."

How could he betray her? "You saw it count. Saw the Fibonacci sequence."

"What matters is your live demo, which totally flopped." Doc finally met her eyes. "Suppose they are intelligent. The problem is even worse, because they *are* hostile. We need to know our enemies. That means capture and study, so we know how to kill them."

Cassie blinked in horror. She looked around for support that wasn't there.

"You'll deliver the specimens to the lunar bio-research lab," Max said. His tone held finality. "Don't worry, you still get to name them. You'll be famous."

A flash flood of anger wash through her, but before she could hurl a suitable retort, Doc took her hand.

"Let it go, Cassie."

She shook off his hand. JJ would have said that. The words didn't sound right coming from Doc. "They are *not* hostile."

She opened the lid and tapped the glass rod on the animal's left side. She knew it would move left. It would move in whichever direction she tapped. She'd spent hours conditioning it, awarding proper decisions with glucose injections, and improper ones with sharp, though harmless, raps across its back. The animal was an extremely fast learner.

Only it didn't move left. The snorkel angled around and sprayed acid on the rod. Some splashed on the arm of her biosuit, which began to smoke. She stared at it, not believing what happened, until the burn on her skin snapped her mind to reality.

Doc helped her up the ramp and into the airlock. They peeled off her suit and poured water over the bloody red sore on her forearm. Doc had the decency to say nothing as he led her to sickbay. Today was ruined, to say nothing of her career. And the animals, the poor animals. The captain would want them killed for sure.

***

Doc applied ointment and bandaged her arm. He seemed lost in his own world, which suited Cassie's mood. She didn't want sympathy. She could lick her own wounds.

Doc said something.

Cassie looked up. "Sorry. What did you say?"

"The blood sample I drew a couple days ago. I ran some tests on it."

When Doc seemed reluctant to say more, anxiety accented Cassie's frustration and embarrassment. "So? I have an infection?"

"No, nothing like that." His gaze slid away from hers.

Her pulse quickened. *He finally knows what I know.* "I'm pregnant."

Doc's head cocked in apparent puzzlement. "You know?"

"I've never suffered from space sickness before. The frequent nausea bothered me enough to run a test. Came up positive."

"A pregnancy test?"

"I *am* a biologist."

"You should have come to me right away," he said harshly.

"The company doctor? So Jonas and Tobias would know whether I wanted them to or not?"

Doc's sternness withered under her gaze. "Cassie... I'm sorry."

He seemed about to say more, but didn't. She did. "It should have been impossible. I was on oral contraceptives. Jonas wore condoms."

Doc blinked. "I didn't know."

She raised a brow.

Doc continued, talking rapidly. "I mean, this is one of those one-in-a-million accidents. Defective rubber and a hormonal glitch at the same time." His hands shook.

"Is there something you aren't telling me?"

"No! I mean, now that you have confirmation, you must start prenatal care."

"Based on my cycle, I'm about seven weeks."

"We'll do an ultrasound, if you like. Should be able to pick up a heartbeat, too."

She nodded. *Life. Oh Jonas, why did you have to leave me?*

Part Two:

REACTION

Chapter 22

Grove time: Reign of Tarragon. Ring 2,241. Layer 61,980.

Pepper extended her roots through the powdery soil until they reached the reservoir a few yards away. She probed its walls, checking for cracks and patching them as necessary. She did the same with the top, which often cracked, being essentially just a crust to prevent evaporation. Her thorough, methodical work guaranteed no one would die from a dam failure. Most of the grove believed she always volunteered for this job because her parents died in such a failure. The truth was simpler. The solo task didn't require much concentration, leaving her mind free for more important pursuits.

Unfortunately, numerous distractions came from above ground—the piercing, peppermint laughter of pre-school seedlings playing hide-and-find, the lavender longing of students wanting to join in the play, the Frankincense frustration of the teacher trying to keep the class's attention on chemistry and genetics. Children weren't the only distraction. The entire community bustled with a million smells forming a thousand conversations, a hundred or so too compelling to ignore. The chief instigator was Myrtle, not because she was pungent (which she was), but because the old lady made Pepper laugh with outrageous allegations of who were surreptitiously touching roots, and which seedlings didn't smell like their fathers.

The voices faded as Pepper closed her olfactory gills. Now she could point her dome away from the sun and begin making biochemical adjustments to her body. She'd spent a long time, nearly a hundred rings, experimenting to identify what specific changes were needed and how to make those changes most efficiently. That knowledge might have come faster if her memory contained other voices, but no had died since the dam collapse that claimed her parents and a dozen others. So many memories were lost. *Mom and Dad.* Pepper silenced her few precious memories of them. She had work to do.

In less than a layer of time, she increased the sensitivity of her dome until faint points of light in the sky revealed themselves through minute, almost infinitesimal increases in the rate of photosynthesis. She shifted the angle of her dome by the tiniest arc to measure and map these lights. Eventually she would present her theory of alien worlds to the elders, but first she needed to solve the riddle of why the distant suns shifted position in the sky in a slow circular pattern, while their own sun remained a fixed point in the sky.

Her study contained an element of danger. More than once she'd shifted her dome too high while triangulating a light's position. Even a sliver of sunlight, magnified a million-fold, caused blisters not soon forgotten.

Everyone thought her crazy. Everybody but Narcissus. *He* claimed she provided inspiration for his poetry and prose. She took pride in that, dampened only a little by his artistic license, which discarded the science she'd worked so hard to include as support for her theory. She couldn't complain, though. After all, Narcissus had multiple voices and was therefore wiser. She was fortunate to have him as a confidant and lover.

Well, almost lover. Pepper didn't have the energy for sex. Her roots stayed dry when he touched her, barely even tingling. Her child-thin dome held less than a pint of sap—she never faced the sun long enough to build up a reserve. In contrast, Narcissus's broad dome held more than a gallon.

A stranger's root bumped hers. Pepper nearly jerked upright, which would have been disastrous in her current state. A thin crescent of her dome stung.

Moisture oozed from the unwelcome root and resolved into words. *"Pepper, stop pointing your dome where the sun doesn't shine."* She recognized the scent: Sage, using root talk to keep the conversation private and simple.

"Go away. I'm working." Pepper pulled her root away. Sage always seemed to be stalking her, but she had nothing to say to this spoiled son of an elder.

His root found her again. *"There's something I need to tell you. Something I should have said a long time ago."*

Pepper squirted acid on the offending appendage. It jerked away and a moment later came his yelp of pain, the smell clear and sharp even through her closed gills. Gratifying.

Unfortunately, others in the grove smelled it, too. His cry included her name, punctuated by a few unsavory adjectives. Pepper opened her gills a bit and immediately caught the teacher's whiff of irritation.

"Pepper! You are disturbing my class."

She puffed a quick apology. *"Sorry, Valerian."* She couldn't afford to alienate the teacher, one of the few plants not openly hostile to her ideas.

Conversations hung in the air as everyone stopped to sniff the exchange. Arguments were rare in the grove. Deliberate infliction of pain even rarer. Valerian puffed again, evidently trying to turn the event into a teaching moment. *"Truth comes from past memories, interpreted through consensus reached by debate. Fights indicate one or both parties hold an opinion based on emotional conviction rather than truth. Do you agree, Pepper?"*

Pepper remained silent. Her belief—that truth should emerge from verifiable facts and rigorous logic, without regard for consensus, conviction, or voices of the past—stank of heresy.

Sage said, *"Teacher, you're right, but it's my fault. I apologize."*

Valerian puffed a perfunctory acknowledgment and resumed his lesson on proteins and genetic expression. Fresh conversations filled the air. Pepper caught her name in several.

She lacked the concentration to resume searching for lights in the sky. Her thoughts kept returning to Sage. What had he wanted to tell her? Why did he take the blame?

A slight vibration signaled an approaching root, probably Sage stalking her again. She waited, ready to give him another sting, but his root didn't come. Her gills fluttered at a faint whiff of a disgusting odor, one she didn't recognize. It stank of something once organic and alive, dead now for millions of rings and totally devoid of memories.

A waft of agony from a nearby student grabbed Pepper's attention. Lily, a shy seedling who never bothered anyone, screamed at full puff, drowning out everything else. The heady odor of evaporating sap indicated a serious injury. Pepper restored her dome to normal sensitivity and shifted upright, gills wide open, sniffing out Lily's exact location. She shoved a root in that direction, knowing the girl might die if not mended quickly.

The ground vibrated as if something heavy slammed against the surface repeatedly. It felt big as an elder's root, yet moved fast as the wind, fast enough to stir old memories from the ground. The sunlight dimmed briefly as the shadow of something huge passed.

Valerian shouted, *"Who's there? Stop pushing me!"* The unknown ruffian ignored the strong coffee-scent command. *"Ouch! My sap! Stop it!"* Hints of vinegar soured the coffee aroma. Fear. From Valerian. It scarcely seemed possible.

Lily moaned, her smells almost lost in the growing commotion. Pepper fought to remain calm as she reached for the girl. The damp ground didn't bode well, not with the honey-sweet scent of evaporating sap. Pepper called for help, giving each blast of aerosol as much volume and height as possible, worried that her call wouldn't be noticed in the bedlam. The whole grove huffed and puffed now, millions of scents swirling into an incoherent stink.

Lily's trunk was broken, snapped all the way to the brain stem, yet curiously the break lay underground. Pepper slipped a root tip into the crack and pumped in sap, trying to keep up with the hemorrhage, but Pepper's dome emptied within a few layers. Lily's moans faded. The girl was dying and Pepper couldn't stop it. Help hadn't come. She blanketed Lily with soothing perfumes, and then formulated a painkiller that would let the girl expire in peace.

"Relax, Lily. The hurt will stop soon."

Then Sage's root slid over Pepper's root and into the girl, pumping life-sustaining sap.

"I got her," Sage said. *"Good work, Pepper. Partially buried, she'll last until the doctors take over."*

"I didn't bury her."

Sage gave a surprised puff, which mixed well with Pepper's puzzlement.

A fresh scream came from another seedling. Holly, a friend of Lily and not much older. Pepper thought at first the scream might be in sympathy for her friend, but the scent spiked sharper and thicker than the cries of the other seedlings and saplings.

Holly wailed, *"I'm being pulled up!"* Her scream grew ripe with panic, then abruptly stalled, lingering in the air as if she'd been plucked from existence in mid-puff.

Chapter 23

Grove time: Reign of Tarragon. Ring 2,241. Layer 61,995.

The elders halted the panic by spraying a cloud of deodorant to smother all conversations. As it gradually dispersed, Tarragon, the eldest, decreed that everyone should hold their questions and speculations. Only plants with direct knowledge had permission to speak.

Pepper said, "*Lily is seriously injured.*" It felt strange, her words drifting alone in the air.

Sage said, "*Her stem is broken, and she's missing a root.*"

Pepper caught scent of the parents' gasps, laced with concern. The ground shifted as their roots approached, but a much larger root arrived first.

"*I have her,*" said Elder Marjoram. "*What happened to you, child?*"

"*Someone grabbed me and broke me,*" Lily said, the words steeped in pain.

"*Who?*" asked Marjoram.

"*I don't know. They didn't smell.*"

"*Whoever pushed me didn't smell, either,*" said Valerian, "*and wouldn't answer me.*" An idea formed in Pepper's mind. A wild, wonderful, wistful idea.

Camellia's worried scent popped up. "*Holly? Answer me, dear.*"

"*A rogue wind,*" said Elder Nasturtium, "a *dust devil, struck Lily and then Valerian.*"

"*Did anyone else feel the wind?*" Valerian asked. No one had. The teacher continued, "*Winds don't focus on single plants. Furthermore, it pressed only my stem, not my dome. Strong as an elder's root, it was, and nearly tipped me over.*"

"*Ghosts,*" said Myrtle.

In the background, Cryptomeria, chief scientist and Camellia's mate, exhaled forcefully, "*Holly, answer your mother. Are your hurt?*"

"*Myrtle, you've been sniffing too many of Narcissus's stories,*" snorted Valerian. "*There's no such thing as ghosts. Something* real *poked a hole in my dome and sucked out some sap. It sure as sunshine wasn't the wind.*"

"*Perhaps an adolescent was playing pranks,*" puffed Elder Nasturtium. "*A misguided misfit starving for sap.*" He didn't need to mention Pepper's name; it popped up in whispers all around.

Pepper ignored it, enthralled that the facts fit her theory. It really could happen this way. No, not could. It *was* happening this way.

"*It wasn't Pepper, father,*" objected Sage. "*She and I were root talking.*"

"*Don't be led astray by your feelings,*" Nasturtium said.

"*Lily is healed,*" Marjoram announced. "*I moved her closer to me and found the break to be clean and easily mended. The root has regrown as well.*"

"*Elder,*" said Cryptomeria. "*My daughter, Holly... I can't smell her.*"

Odors swelled as dozens of plants shouted for Holly, not realizing the situation called for sniffing, not spraying. The plants not searching for Holly began arguing about wind, ghosts, and unruly adolescents. Pepper gave a disgusted puff. So did Sage.

The surge of smells threatened a return to chaos. Tarragon loosed a mighty blast of ammonia that stung the gills and returned everyone to shocked silence.

Tarragon said, "*If anyone knows where Holly is, let them speak.*"

A few puffs passed. The elder's words faded from the air, and still no one spoke. Then Myrtle said, "*She's gone.*"

"*If she were dead, we would know it,*" Nasturtium said.

"*I didn't say dead. I said gone.*"

"*Buried, perhaps,*" said Marjoram. "*Nothing like this has happened in all my memories.*"

Pepper guessed those memories extended back a hundred thousand rings. Trepidation made her pause to gather courage before exhaling, "*She was taken.*"

"*Taken?*" Nasturtium said. "*By whom?*"

"*Alien beings from a different world.*"

Nasturtium's question and her response hovered in the air and produced a silence every bit as profound as Tarragon's preceding blast. The quiet lasted several puffs, almost an entire layer, before erupting into assorted jeers—some amused, some irritated, a few angry.

Sage's root touched hers and whispered, "*Recant, Pepper. Say it was a bad joke.*"

"*I can't. Everyone needs to know the truth.*" Publicly she said, "*I've spent years studying the sky. There are other suns out there, far, far, away. So why not worlds paired with those suns? And why not life on those worlds? I think we are being visited by these alien beings.*"

Elder Nasturtium scoffed. "*Why cobble together a set of nearly impossible events and proclaim it to the world as truth? You should have consulted a scientist instead of a story-teller.*" He targeted a puff toward Narcissus. "*No offence intended to you.*"

"*None taken,*" said Narcissus. "*Pepper does have quite an imagination.*"

Pepper couldn't believe her gills. Narcissus's sublime olfactory skills could turn doubters into believers. Instead, her soon-to-be mate refused to offer even a token defense on her behalf.

Elder Marjoram said, "*Pepper, have you considered the practical obstacles to what you suggest? Even if other suns exist, they are in the sky and must be millions of times farther away than our sun. How would beings from there get here? They would need to fly, and flying takes more energy than photosynthesis can provide over long distances, even if they altered their bodies into a perfect aerodynamic shape.*"

"*Perhaps they know more than we do,*" Pepper said stubbornly.

Tarragon's words gently, but irresistibly, filled the air. "*We will not embrace fringe theories while mundane answers suffice.*

The most likely explanation is a rogue wind, a dust-devil, which hit Lily and Valerian—"

Valerian started to object, but the scent barely registered before being overwhelmed by Tarragon's continuation. *"—and hurled a stone or a sliver of diamond which penetrated Valerian's dome and allowed sap to leak. That same rogue wind buried Holly, leaving her unable to communicate. So, everyone will now sweep their roots in a slow, methodical manner until we find her."*

The search had just begun when an incoherent burst of odors descended on the grove. A million shards of shattered, jumbled memories—mired in confusion, pain, and death—was unmistakably Holly.

Camellia wailed. Cryptomeria cursed. The majority of the grove made not a whiff, as if playing hide-and-find, but the occasional escaping puffs held no excitement, no joy. Only fear.

"Ghosts," repeated Myrtle. This time, no one argued.

Chapter 24

Grove time: Reign of Tarragon. Ring 2,241. Layer 61,994.

Pepper snaked a root beneath the grove, guided by scent and memory toward Narcissus. Fortunately she didn't bump anyone along the way. In her present mood, she'd either spit acid or seep like a seedling. She touched one of his roots, but he didn't respond.

"*Narcissus?*"

"*Wait.*"

Narcissus smelled preoccupied and Pepper realized he was root-talking with someone else. The other plant withdrew before Pepper could identify the individual.

"*I've been expecting you,*" said Narcissus, the words mildly caustic.

Annoyance seeped into her own words, so she added a dash of sweetness for balance. "*I could have used your support.*"

If they were physically close, a tiny puff of a hundred nuanced odors would tell him precisely how she felt. But he stood many yards away. Root talk would have to do. Better, in fact. Bluntness felt more honest than subtlety.

Disdain coated his words. "*You proposed a fringe theory in the midst of a calamity.*"

Pepper stopped adding sweetness. "*You sound like Elder Nasturtium.*"

"*You'd do well to emulate him.*"

"*You're supposed to support me, not jerk my roots around.*"

"*Don't be childish.*"

"You spew out made-up stories that contain no knowledge, no insight, no redeeming value whatsoever. You don't study, you don't work, you just distract the people who are working. THAT'S what children do, Narcissus. That's what YOU do."

"I use imagination to metaphorically interpret reality. But I know the difference."

"And I don't? That stinks, Narcissus."

"You need help. Trust me when I tell you—"

"That I'm an orphan with a twisted mind, unable to tell truth from fantasy?"

"Pepper..."

"If I'm right, there will be more bizarre incidents, more tragedies. We need to establish contact with the alien. We need to learn about each other."

"You force me to distance myself from your rants, lest the grove think I'm crazy, too."

"Truth doesn't have to make sense."

"You know nothing."

In a culture that valued knowledge above all else, no greater insult existed. She pulled her root away, wounded beyond the power of sap to heal.

She reached for the lake. Plants rarely sent roots here. Bacteria thrived in the water, and they smelled terrible when absorbed through the roots. Yet here she could move without bumping into someone and being drawn into trivial conversations. She closed her gills to block out the grove, trying to forget pathetic Sage, stubborn elders, and her stink-wad of a paramour. The memory of their argument clung to the outer layer of her stem, triggering faint replays in her mind. Tired, irritated, and hungry, she pointed her dome to the sun and basked in the warmth.

She fanned a root slowly through the soggy bottom, stirring up sludge. Sometimes a bit of trapped gas would break free, bringing a word or touch or some other tiny flash of memory to life. What little remained of her parents lay here. When the reservoir collapsed, rushing water tipped them enough for the storm wind to catch their domes. They died instantly of decapitation. With everyone's gills sealed against the abrasive sand, the killer wind blew her parents' memories away. All but a few grains, which fell into the lake.

She longed for their scent, but received only anonymous fragments of thoughts and fears carried by small bubbles that burst and died. Perhaps this was fitting. Some plants got mired in the past. Some worried incessantly about the future.

The tingle of sunlight on her leaves, the quickening of newly formed sap, the soothing swell of a refilling dome, all graced an eternal *now*. She opened her gills and the perfume of ten thousand conversations lulled Pepper into a rare moment of enjoying the present, unhaunted by the past and undaunted by the future.

A malodorous scream jolted Pepper from the reverie. She recognized the scent of Daphne, who screamed again, and then shouted, "*Narcissus, help me!*"

"*Let go of me!*" Narcissus said before cursing in cloying blasts of formaldehyde.

A chorus of "*What's wrong? What's happening?*" from the grove nearly smothered additional shouts from Narcissus and Daphne, reeking yelps of shock and terror that they were being pulled from the ground.

Pepper retracted her root and thrust it toward Narcissus, worried she would be too late to do anything and terrified there would be nothing anyone *could* do. She felt the ground shake. Her roots vibrated as something hidden—completely scentless— brushed against her dome. For a moment the warmth of the sun stopped, just like when Lily was attacked.

The ground trembled again, and the sun returned. Fresh screams stopped while Daphne's old ones lingered, exactly as Holly's had done. A few puffs later, Narcissus's fresh cries stopped as well.

Pepper's root reached the spot where Narcissus should be, but it swept though empty soil. She stretched to Daphne's space and found it empty as well. They were gone, completely gone. Every plant began to shout; the scent of fear escalated until it smothered the grove.

Valerian's scream pierced the din, louder than anything Pepper had ever smelled. His pain swirled with terror, saturating the air with the scent of sulfur and vinegar. His screams abruptly stopped, but unlike Daphne and Holly, Valerian's personal scent didn't simply fade—it mingled with something worse. The scent of fresh cut grass. The scent of death.

Chapter 25

Grove time: Reign of Tarragon. Ring 2,241. Layer 62,010.

Fear fed on fear, growing on itself. The sun lost warmth, the ground lost solidity. Pepper's mind swirled as the lake bottom had swirled, and like the lake, her thoughts came in jumbled fragments.

A part of her—an emotional, irrational part—insisted that she was responsible for these disasters, that by thinking about aliens she somehow had brought them to life. Had her fight with Narcissus caused him to be taken? Logic didn't matter. Emotion generated its own truth.

Nasturtium bellowed, *"Calm! Everyone calm!"* When the air partially cleared, he continued, *"This is another instance of that new atmospheric phenomena. Our scientists are studying it and will soon put an end to the disturbances."*

He had to be lying, although Pepper caught no scent of deception. It didn't matter. *"We have to rescue Narcissus!"* she shouted. *"Daphne, too."*

"They've been blown away," Nasturtium said. *"A tragic loss, and one we can do nothing about."*

Before Pepper could respond, Sage said, *"Wind doesn't shake the ground, father. I felt vibrations from the surface, before and after the abductions."*

"You talk as if these accidents were intentional." The elder's words dripped with sweet condescension that turned bitter inside the gills. *"You've been sniffing Pepper far too much."*

"I felt the vibrations," blurted Pepper. *"And I felt them before, when Holly...when she vanished. They come and go to the same place. I can find them."*

"Ignore her," Nasturtium said. *"She's insane."*

The words stung, and not just from the caustic chemicals specifically targeted for her DNA. An elder, one of the very wise, had publicly declared not only that she was wrong, but that she was flawed. He'd destroyed her credibility forever.

Tarragon discharged a mighty blast of ammonia. When the air cleared, he said, *"Put aside your fears, doubts, and squabbles. Valerian's memories are about to be set free."*

"I feel tingly," Lily said. *"I'm dropping a lot of dust."* Pepper felt it, too.

"That's your body's response to the smell of death," Sage said. *"My father told me to expect it."* Although Sage puffed to the seedling, Pepper felt his root touch hers. She lacked the will to pull away.

"Absorb," commanded Tarragon.

Without Valerian's brain to generate the stabilizing electrical charge, his stem returned to powder a layer at a time, releasing the memories of his life in reverse order. Pepper knew this from school, but had never witnessed death directly.

A second reality formed in her mind, filled with thoughts, emotions, and memories not her own. She smelled Valerian as he had smelled himself, flavored by his individual perception of life, beginning with his final conscious thought, an anguished *why?*

***

The question implodes. Pain slashes through his stem. Incoherent screams spray from every orifice as panic triggers involuntary contractions of the scent glands. Panic laced with fear, doused with denial. *It's happening again.* Fear. Concern for Narcissus and Daphne.

Irritation and a hint of fear stems from Myrtle's second sulfurous utterance of *"Ghosts."* The soothing, loving touch of Iris's roots. Relief that it wasn't him. Horror and revulsion at Holly's shattered, mashed-up memories.

Dust devils and diamonds be damned. He prepared to argue with Tarragon over the endorsement of Nasturtium's explanation of the inexplicable. The rejection of Pepper's rant about alien invaders. Irritation at Myrtle's ridiculous claim of ghosts. Arguing with Nasturtium's assertion that mere wind had tipped him.

The curiously embarrassing sensation of sap being sucked out of his dome. A brief stabbing pain in his dome. Leaves rippling without wind. A blast for *"Help!"* Tipping, struggling for balance. A root pulls free of the ground. Fear. A mighty force pushing against his stem. *"Who's there?"* Anxiety. *Why can't I smell who it is?* Startled at a light touch on his collar. Concern at Lily's screams. Irritation at Pepper and Sage disturbing the class. Pride in this class of students. The children answer his questions, demonstrating understanding of mathematics, chemistry, and basic genetics. He wants a child of his own someday—not that he's eager for anyone to die and provide an opening.

His thoughts turn to Iris and his plans to surprise her with the sap he has saved in preparation for asking her to be his life-mate. A mixture of anticipation and anxiety percolated along his brainstem while fantasizing of sex.

***

Pepper caught a whiff of dismay and grief from Iris, quickly and kindly neutralized by the elders. The tingling in her collar had moved down to her stem as it absorbed, stored, and integrated Valerian's memories. Pepper hadn't known what to expect at her first death ceremony; the new memories whispered, shared, and advised just like her own, but in Valerian's smell and personality. The commotion within her brain felt dizzying.

Her roots trembled. She had been less than three yards from Valerian when he died. It could have been her. In a way, it *was* her, with Valerian's mind now a part of her. She forced the thought away to focus on the next layer of his memories.

***

Valerian is content as a teacher. He enjoys the curiosity of young minds, the reckless abandon with which they expend energy. He respects both knowledge and tradition, and unlike many others doesn't see the qualities as synonymous.

His joy and pride swell at being selected as the teacher for the generation of seedlings now grown to saplings. He absorbs the congratulations from friends and family. He eagerly accepts the responsibilities inherent with the appointment, although the acceptance is tempered by sadness, knowing that each young life fills a niche left by death. The necessity of balance in an ecosystem is an early and vital lesson.

Time spins ever backward. His memories reach a thousand rings into the past, spanning an eon of post-graduate research, an accumulation of facts and dogma common to all plants. And then...sex. All plants learned about sex in school and from their parents, but knowing the mechanics is far different from having your roots entangled with another, the build-up of emotional and physical pressures that urge both the release and the reception of reproductive proteins. The exquisite point of no return when one partner ejaculates, triggering the other partner to absorb the seminal fluid and bear the seed.

***

Pepper almost giggled at the memory of Valerian's first encounter. He'd been a late bloomer—his leaves didn't sprout until his five-hundred-tenth ring. He was so eager, so overwhelmed by the sensations that his protein secreted at the first touch of his paramour's root. Neither had intended the foreplay to culminate in release, and fortunately, no pregnancy occurred. Their roots had met in a denser area of the grove where no deaths had occurred for hundreds of rings, so the contraceptive level in the soil was high. Nevertheless, the embarrassment convinced Valerian to adopt a life of chastity.

Until I met Iris.

Valerian's voice in her mind shocked Pepper. The voice continued, *Breathe deep my life.*

Ring after ring of Valerian's stem released its memories and fell away. The smell of pride wafts strong as he celebrated graduation from school, mingled with the remembered smell of friends and family congratulating him. His anxiety at starting school. The jumbled, frantic memory of his bald dome blistering in an unexpected solar flare, his father's sacrifice lifting and extending a mighty root, shading and spraying healing sap while the mother taught Valerian to adjust his biochemistry to reject the sunlight and secrete a protective coating.

Pepper noted with surprise how much time had passed. Her stem had grown several new layers. Valerian's stem must be very thin now, his final public oratory nearly finished. His memory is that of a mere seedling, eager to explore and heedless of risks, believing deep down he is immortal. A penultimate memory of warmth from the sky bathes his dome, bringing the first rush of photosynthesis. Then a final flash, his very first memory, yet not his alone—a wash of vanilla bubbling with peppermint—the scent of his parents' love and joy at the moment of his birth.

The air drifted pure and scentless through the grove. Valerian was gone, his stem returned to the dust from which it came.

Tradition held that the Eldest would be first to speak, but many puffs passed before Tarragon broke the stillness. *"Valerian's voice and memories are now part of us. Uniqueness becomes ubiquity."*

"Uniqueness becomes ubiquity," repeated the grove again and again until the air grew redolent with the scent.

Tarragon invited Iris to send her roots to the spot where Valerian died, to absorb Valerian's sap before it evaporated.

I had over a gallon. Pepper shed a couple leaves in surprise. The subtle scent of Valerian inside her mind would take some getting used to. One of Myrtle's sayings suddenly made sense: you never really know someone until they die, and then they're part of you forever.

Tarragon exuded puzzlement. The soil shifted as his massive root swept under the surface. *"There is no sap, and only enough organic residue to account for his roots."*

"I don't understand," said Iris.

"When Valerian died, his dome vanished. Sap, leaves, olfactories. Everything."

"How?"

Pepper wondered the same thing. Her theory predicted conundrums like this. She knew it was poor etiquette to interrupt, but tiny whiffs of ammonia and popcorn already betrayed her excitement. *"Valerian was killed by an alien life form."*

The words hung in the air, blending with remnants of 'uniqueness' and 'ubiquity' to form a strange prophetic emphasis.

Iris released a caustic aerosol chemically tailored to hurt Pepper. Tarragon sighed, neutralizing the insult before it did more than sting Pepper's leaves.

"We don't know what killed Valerian," Tarragon said. *"But ignorance is not justification to embrace a fringe theory. There are more plausible explanations."*

"A decapitating wind?" asked Pepper. She kept her words bland, knowing the question itself invited a disciplinary response. She'd take that risk if it got them to smell the truth.

Nasturtium responded. *"The simplest explanation is that a rogue lightning bolt stuck Valerian's dome, vaporizing it."*

"Lightning would be instantaneous. Valerian was conscious during his... end." Everyone knew it. Valerian was a part of everyone now.

"Easy, Pepper," warned Sage with a drop of musty oil from his root.

"All we know," said Elder Nasturtium in sickly-sweet irritation, *"is that he asked 'why' an instant before his death. The pain preceding that moment came from the buildup of static charge just prior to the lightning strike, not the strike itself."*

He's wrong. Keep talking, Valerian said in silent encouragement. Pepper took his advice. *"If I'm right, more inexplicable things will happen."*

"Everything has an explanation," said Elder Nasturtium with unmistakable finality.

"Explanations can wait," replied Pepper. *"We need to act now to rescue Narcissus. And Daphne."*

A not-so-subtle scent of irritation spread from the elders, but a much stronger odor emanated from the rest of the grove. With Valerian's pain fresh on their minds, they wanted action. They wanted action *now*.

"Enough!" Tarragon said. *"The elders will decide what is to be done."* A blast of deodorant cleared the air. Pepper kept her frustration to herself, not that it mattered. The elders were like unchanging boulders. Narcissus was good as dead.

Chapter 26

Grove time: Reign of Tarragon. Ring 2,241. Layer 62,012

If not for the deodorant and subsequent quiet, the grove might have missed the faint strands of conversation.

"*I'm scared,*" Daphne said.

"*Me, too,*" Narcissus replied.

"*Where are we?*"

Their scent came from at least a hundred yards away, further than an elder's root could stretch. The entire grove strained with open gills to catch every word. Pepper called out, "*Narcissus! Narcissus and Daphne, we smell you!*" The rest of the grove joined her call until the air grew saturated with their names. Everyone waited for the response.

"*...surrounded by walls. I don't know what material. It feels odd,*" said Narcissus.

"*The sun is too high,*" said Daphne. "*How can the monster move the sun?*"

Narcissus said nothing. Daphne started screaming his name.

"*What?*"

Relief diluted Daphne's anxiety. "*I thought the monster took you.*"

"*It took both of us.*"

Pepper wondered why they didn't answer the grove. Surely they smelled the shouts. It saturated the air.

"*I'm not going anywhere. I don't think either of us are,*" said Narcissus.

"*Are we going to die?*"

"*I don't think so. Whatever has us could have killed us already.*"

"*How did we get here? One moment I'm fine, the next moment my roots are in the air. Magic, like one of your stories.*"

"*I wish it were magic.*"

"*I want to go home.*"

Narcissus yelped. "*Something stabbed me! It stuck my dome!*" His words grew frantic with sharp bites of alcohol and vinegar. "*Uh, Uh. It's pulling the sap out of me! Stop! Stop!*"

I know just how he feels, thought Valerian.

"*Stop hurting him!*" shouted Daphne. "*Stop!*"

Narcissus's screams softened to whimpers. "*It's out. It's gone.*"

"*I didn't smell anyone. Why can't I smell whoever's doing this?*"

Narcissus groaned, but it smelled off to Pepper, who knew him well. Narcissus was exaggerating.

"*How can I help?*" murmured Daphne with words of cinnamon sugar.

"*Remember before all this craziness started?*" he answered. "*What we didn't get to finish.*" A waft of vanilla laced his words with erotic overtones.

Sage touched Pepper's root and said, "*Close your gills. You don't need to smell this.*"

Chocolate. Orange. Spearmint. Pepper could almost feel their roots twining. Valerian agreed. *Yes. That's how it feels*. How could Narcissus do this? Publicly, without so much as the modesty of root talk.

"*Narcissus, your root feels so good. Yes...oh, yes. Almost— Oh! Something touched my dome.*"

"*Daphne, don't stop...*"

She yelped. "*It cut me. Ouch! It stings. I don't know how it happened. I don't smell acid. It was all so fast. How can anything make a hole that fast?*"

Narcissus moaned, and not in pain. *Approaching the point of no return*, Valerian said.

Daphne screamed, flooding the air with alcohol, sulfur, and ammonia. The stench swallowed up their words for several puffs. Whimpers emerged as the scream faded.

"Please don't kill me. I promise to be good. I do. I do. Don't kill me," Daphne begged. *"Please. Why don't you answer me? Why don't you say something? Answer me! Answer me!"* Her pleas burst into shouts. *"It's lifting me! I'm in the air again!"*

"Let go!" huffed Narcissus. *"You're dragging me with you!"*

"It might take us home!"

"Don't be an idiot! Let go I say!" Acid tinged his words.

Daphne must have let go, but the girl's hope turned to terror. *"No!"* she shouted, the odor nearly smothering Narcissus's sigh of relief.

"Daphne? What's it doing?"

"It's cold, Narcissus. Terrible cold. I can't move my roots. I can't—"

Daphne's scent faded to nothing. Narcissus's scent faded as well, but Pepper caught a whiff of fear leaking past a smothering wall of deodorant. Narcissus never was very good at playing Hide and Find. Now, when his life might depend on it, he did no better. Pepper didn't care anymore. He'd given her one more hurt, one more insult to endure.

A deeper hurt came from being wrong. She had expected the alien to be curious and benevolent. Maybe there'd be a few misunderstandings, a few accidents as the species got to know each other, but she expected a being smart and powerful enough to travel between worlds to be wise and wonderful.

This monster didn't ask any questions or make any demands. It gave no scent yet let the grove smell the tortured screams of its captives. It kept those captives from smelling anything beyond their prison. Cruelty defined its essential nature.

Reality proved to be worse than any story Narcissus had ever told. The lack of reason and morality made Pepper want to scream.

Daphne's mother did scream. She screamed as fast and hard as her lips could blow.

Chapter 27

Grove time: Reign of Tarragon. Ring 2,241. Layer 62,015

Tarragon loosed another blast of ammonia, silencing the grove. *"Grave danger is upon us."*

Myrtle muttered that some of it came from the elders, claiming you couldn't swing a root without raising a cloud of ammonia that stung for hours. Pepper knew the old plant exaggerated, but there really had been a lot of blasts lately.

"Ghosts," Myrtle puffed loudly. *"Spawn of the dead."*

"Not ghosts," Tarragon said. *"Not wind and lightning."*

"Then what?" shouted someone.

"It killed my daughter," cried Cryptomeria. *"Whatever it is, kill it."*

"It still has Narcissus," Pepper said. *"We need to rescue him."*

Tarragon exhaled a demand for quiet. *"We need facts to guide our decisions. Marjoram, please summarize what we know."*

"Precious little," said Elder Marjoram. *"These events are not accidental, nor pranks, nor the result of natural phenomena. The kidnappings and murder occurred extremely fast. A vibration in the ground preceded and followed the events. Some witnesses felt a slight wind or something brush against their domes. The attacker is otherwise undetectable. No scent at all."*

"What do you conclude from this?" asked Tarragon.

"That we have been attacked by a physical being able to move above ground at great speed and able to conceal itself perfectly."

"I concur," Nasturtium said.

"Where do they come from?" asked Sage.

"From another grove, of course," said his father. *"We don't know yet which one."*

"Why would another grove attack us?" asked Pepper.

"Does it matter?" huffed Nasturtium. *"We must defend ourselves."*

"Any other anomalies, Marjoram?" Tarragon asked.

Marjoram hesitated. *"Lily's injury."*

"A broken stem?"

"The missing root. It had a perfectly flat stub that didn't seep. No pitting from acid. No jagged edges from tearing. No abrasions."

"How were these precisely shaped wounds inflicted?"

"I do not know, Eldest."

Pepper couldn't stay odorless. *"Perhaps by an alien creature with a more advanced technology."*

Sage said, *"Pepper, this isn't the time."*

"This is exactly the time! We need to learn more about it, try to communicate with it, and convince it to release the captives."

"Communicate with a murderer? We need to kill it!" demanded Cryptomeria. Murmurs of assent grew to a heady incense.

"Yes, but how?" asked Nasturtium. *"We know almost nothing about the creature."*

Marjoram agreed. *"How can we study what we can't detect?"*

"Its vibrations," blurted Pepper. *"They'll let us know when and where it's moving."*

"It moves too fast," Nasturtium said. *"We know from Narcissus's scent that it nests at least a hundred yards away. Too far to reach, too far to send a cloud of acid or poison, especially with the wind against us."*

"We need a scout," Tarragon said. *"A volunteer. Someone willing to undergo bio-genetic alterations that will shift its metabolism to an oxygen basis for energy and alter body structure for speed and stealth."* Uncomfortable odors wafted from the grove. Tarragon added, *"All changes will be temporary, of course."*

Healing was one thing, biological reengineering quite another. A deep aversion to biological alteration permeated their society, although the specific memories from which the reluctance germinated had never been identified. Nevertheless, knowledge of the critical steps of genetic manipulation were sequestered and divided among the elders of each grove so that only by unanimous agreement and sharing could major alterations be made at the genetic level.

"*Is this really necessary?*" Marjoram asked. "*Such a sharing has not happened in all my memories.*"

"*Yes,*" answered Tarragon and Nasturtium in unison.

"*No one will volunteer for such a mission. The risks are enormous.*"

"*Oh, I think one might be found,*" Nasturtium said.

"*I'll do it,*" Pepper said.

"*No, you won't,*" Sage said. "*It's too dangerous.*"

"*I'm a good observer. Level headed. Open minded.*"

"*Pepper—*"

"*I'm not afraid,*" she said.

You should be, thought Valerian. She ignored his voice. "*If I get the chance, I'll try communicating with them. Mathematics. That's the key. I'm sure of it.*"

"*No!*" Nasturtium said. "*Avoid all contact with the creature.*"

"*Observe and report back,*" Marjoram said. "*Nothing more.*"

"*Correct,*" Tarragon said. "*We cannot risk you being captured or killed. Knowledge is the only thing that will save us. You must obtain that knowledge and bring it to us.*" He paused, then added, "*Besides, your new body will have very limited ability to communicate.*"

An open discussion followed, which identified the requirements of the mission, the functions necessary to meet those requirements, and the specific design aspects of the new body that would provide those functions.

Elder Marjoram argued for a speedy body, to which Nasturtium replied, "*Stealth is more vital than speed.*" Tarragon agreed, and the three elders finished the final design within a dozen layers. Pepper was surprised at such speedy deliberations, and more surprised when she learned implementation would take only three dozen more layers.

"*Pepper, are you sure you want to do this?*" asked Tarragon.

"*Yes, Elder.*" She filled her response with confidence, grateful he couldn't feel her roots quivering. Then his root touched hers, and a gasp of embarrassment leaked out.

"*It's all right to be nervous,*" Tarragon said in root talk. Something warm and bitter soaked into her roots. "*I'm numbing your brain stem. You're going to feel quite odd when you regain consciousness. Parts of you will be missing. Don't worry about it. Do you job, and be quick. Your new body will carry only a few ounces of stored sugar. Your acid stores will be limited, too. Memories will be internal, wrapped around an oversize brainstem, limiting your ability to create more.*"

"*How many more?*"

"*A few hundred layers. More than enough for the mission. Find out as much as you can about the creature, then hurry back. If you die like this, you'll be lost forever.*"

Like my parents. Pepper hadn't known that. She should be worried, and wondered why she wasn't. Then she wondered why the grove had blurred to a sweet perfume that faded, faded, faded....

Chapter 28

Grove time: Reign of Tarragon. Ring 2,241. Layer 62,064.

Pepper inhaled slowly while twisting her snorkel to get a bearing on Narcissus. His scent was faint, only a few parts per billion, but she doubted that his attempt to hide would fool the alien. She submerged and burrowed in his direction, surfacing every few yards to make small course corrections. While surfacing for the fifth time, a flexible but impenetrable surface blocked the way. Pepper froze, afraid she'd encountered the alien, but the object didn't move and gave no indication of being alive.

She backed away until she found the outer edge of the material, and then raised her snorkel an inch above the surface. She caught Narcissus's muffled scent but nothing else. No heavy vibration disturbed the ground, and no mysterious breeze disturbed the air. She wiggled to the surface and ran her snorkel along the barrier.

The obstacle didn't merely lay flat atop the ground—it bent at a right angle, changing orientation from horizontal to vertical. It formed a wall higher than she could reach. Surprised, Pepper submerged and paddled through the soil to trace the outline of the alien artifact.

She struck something small buried in the soil and became entangled in long, thin roots connecting the object to the wall. She dove deep, thrashing madly and squirting acid on the alien tendrils. Finally freed, she stopped moving and waited attentively for the alien vibrations to know which way to flee.

No vibrations came. Pepper desperately needed to breathe. Hating this limitation of her modified body, she shoved her snorkel to the surface and sucked air. The odor of dissolved metal and organic polymers surrounded her. Metal was rare in the environment but not extremely so. The polymers, being totally unfamiliar, bothered Pepper more. She noted their exact chemical composition, then extrapolated the tendency of those molecules to form a tough, highly plastic film. It explained the behavior of the barrier wall. These were real, physical materials, not magic or supernatural manifestations. With renewed caution, she continued her survey.

The wall had a rectangular base measuring twelve feet by twenty-four. Near the end of one long side she found a strip of porous material which sucked in air as if taking a never-ending breath. She backed away, alarmed by the thought that the wall was alive, with a snorkel as large as her body and a body a thousand times larger still.

Reason and logic turned fear to embarrassment. She hadn't smelled any genetic material. Plastic and metal were great for hidden enclosures, but they were untenable materials for a life form. Therefore the barrier had to be an artifact, something created by an alien of vast intelligence and virtually unlimited power over the elements.

The thought rekindled hope that the alien's purpose was benign, probably to study and gather information. So why did it torture and kill? Pepper couldn't fathom the motives of the alien, but hoped the root cause of its actions was a simple misunderstanding. Perhaps Narcissus's close personal contact with the alien could provide a clue to solving the mystery.

Pepper realized from the changing direction of her paramour's scent that Narcissus was a prisoner atop the object, several feet above the ground. There was no way to get to him, and even if she could, her current body lacked puffers to communicate properly— the flippers allowed only the most rudimentary root-talk.

Maybe Narcissus *wasn't* on top. The flexibility of the barrier suggested it served more as a bladder than a monolith. The yielding walls might enclose a hollow space where Narcissus lay trapped, his cries drifting out an opening at the top. But if the only way in and out was through the top...

Pepper's new heart fluttered. The alien would have to be a giant, with enormous roots able to pluck a plant from the ground and lift it several yards into the air. Or maybe it could fly, regardless of what Marjoram said. Pepper's mind filled with the image of an invisible alien, hovering in the air, ready to sniff out unwary plants, then swoop down and snatch them away to this lair. She froze, afraid to move.

She again forced her mind to reason through the situation. There hadn't been any vibration or unexplained wind, so the creature wasn't nearby. Narcissus's sustained hiding lacked the urgency of imminent danger, so the alien wasn't currently inside the structure. Where was it? Impossible to say. Conjecture? The creature had to be tall, heavy, strong, and mobile. Probably too heavy to fly, regardless of how much energy and strength it could muster. Pepper speculated that it moved entirely above the ground, not through it, though her theory failed to explain how such a massive being could maintain balance without roots for anchors. She again wondered where the creature was now. Could a creature as large as a giant play Hide and Find perfectly?

She felt a vibration. Not the rhythmic thumps she expected, but a continuous low rumble. She submerged, hiding while the vibration increased, peaked, and diminished. Cautiously, she extended her snorkel and caught a whiff of petrochemicals. She recognized it from before— the stink of organic residue of plants dead for millennia, devoid of memory. She shuddered, wondering if Myrtle was right, that a ghost had returned to haunt the grove for unknown transgressions.

But a ghost wouldn't need metal and plastic. Pepper followed the scent of oil for about thirty yards, where the vibration lessened and soon stopped. The trace scent vanished as if snatched away into a separate reality. Pepper proceeded slowly, not wanting to enter a place from which escape might be impossible.

She bumped into something hard, broad, and smooth. She sprinkled a bit of acid to analyze it. Metal, like the roots on the barrier—only much, much larger, and somewhat resistant to acid. Metal veins and nuggets sometimes hid inside bedrock, but never in such quantity or as an alloy like this, nor with such a perfectly smooth surface. Pepper couldn't remember ever touching a surface so perfectly smooth and pure. The inability wasn't due to missing memories. She retained enough knowledge of mathematics, geology, and chemistry to realize perfection didn't occur in the real world.

Yet here it was. The wide, flat metal plank angled upward from the ground. Perhaps it formed a ramp to the sky, a wondrous path to the stars, but one impossible to follow in her current body. She stroked the surface with her snorkel, reluctant to leave.

Eventually she moved past the ramp, sniffing and feeling her way. She encountered metal with an even more unusual shape, a flat circular pad about two feet in diameter that supported a huge cylinder stretching to unknown heights. Pepper continued exploring and found two more identical metal pillars. The three formed the vertices of an equilateral triangle, similar to the roots of a plant, but grotesquely larger. The triangle formed by these cylinders measured more than twenty feet on each side. Pepper shivered, and then realized she hadn't felt the warmth of the sun since passing the ramp. The pillars supported something so enormous that it blocked the sun.

It triggered a memory of a story Narcissus once told about a giant who threatened to wipe out a grove. It was a fairy tale of course, but touching the pillar with her snorkel, Pepper feared the horrible tale had come true. She couldn't remember how the story ended. She couldn't remember the end to any of his stories, only the wonderful, exciting beginnings, overlaid with her admiration of Narcissus and the warmth of their budding love.

The inability to remember frightened her and gave greater incentive to complete the mission and be restored to her former body and memories.

She moved to the middle of the triangle, trying not to think of what would happen if the giant decided to sit down. She surfaced, lifted the front of her body from the ground and stretched as high as she could with the snorkel. She touched a hard surface. More metal. She felt a vibration in the metal, a deep steady hum. Metal conducted vibration better than soil; she could make out individual sources of vibration with different frequencies and locations inside the giant. Panic surged, as if she'd lost her balance and was falling. There wasn't *one* alien, there were several, all nesting in the giant metal pod.

Pepper sank into the ground and paddled away, anxious to be out from under the monstrosity, eager to get back to the grove.

The scent of fresh sorrow wafted past. Narcissus had given up on Hide and Find. Pepper couldn't leave without trying to save him. She returned to the plastic wall and sprayed acid at the base.

The stench of dissolving plastic faded quickly as sterile air gushed from the hole. She discovered a second plastic wall behind the first, and sprayed it. A gentle flow of air emerged from the interior, carrying the clear shouts of an excited Narcissus.

Pepper pushed through the hole, cutting a path to Narcissus with acid. She bumped into a metal pillar, provoking the thought that aliens must *love* metal. She smelled Narcissus almost directly above her. She drenched the pillar, intending to bring it down, praying that the fall wouldn't crack his stem. He could ride on her back as she carried him to safety.

The acid stream petered out as her bladder ran dry. The pillar didn't collapse. The ground shook with the approach of aliens. With a silent scream of frustration, Pepper sank deep into the soil and paddled toward home.

Chapter 29

Grove time: Reign of Tarragon. Ring 2,241. Layer 62,065.

Pepper made her way directly to Tarragon, but before she could secrete a word, he commanded that she follow his root to the outskirts of the grove and beyond. There she felt roots from Nasturtium and Marjoram, yards beyond the reach of any other plant.

"*Your report?*" asked Tarragon.

"*In root talk?*" Pepper said. Blunt words weren't adequate for such strange and important revelations.

"*For now,*" said Marjoram. "*Later perhaps, we may ask you to elaborate.*"

A tinge of anxiety marred the tingling awe at being touched by all three elders. She hadn't realized that elders might keep secret counsel among themselves. It seemed wrong somehow. Dangerous. She wished she were in her original body and had Valerian's voice back. She could use his several hundred rings of perspective and memories.

Pepper gave her report. The facts were complete and accurate, though some details, such as the composition of the plastic and the metal alloys, couldn't be expressed in root talk.

"*Four of them,*" said Marjoram. Dismay soured her words.

"*At least four, Elder,*" Pepper said. "*And at least two different species. Three if the giant pod is alive, although I think it isn't.*"

"*Narcissus is alive, at least.*"

"*A prisoner.*" Frustration dribbled out. "*I couldn't get to him. He didn't even know I was there.*"

"No whiff of Daphne?"

"No, Elder. Not a trace, not a memory."

"The metal giant... you're sure of the dimensions," asked Nasturtium.

"Yes, Elder."

"Huge. But since it never moved and the vibrations of the other creatures came from inside, I concur with your assessment that it is nothing more than home to the monsters."

"It elevates and protects them from many dangers," Tarragon said, *"but how could they enter and leave?"*

"The nest must move up and down as needed," Nasturtium said, his uneasiness seeping into the soil. Moving something so large would require humongous energy and a technical sophistication beyond anything ever contemplated by the grove.

"Will you change me back now? I'm tired and hungry. I need sunshine."

Tarragon's root patted her back sympathetically. *"Not yet. Marjoram will restore your energy reserves while we decide our course of action."*

The ground moistened as Marjoram secreted a generous amount of sap and sugar water. Pepper's six flippers sucked up the stored energy as fast as it came out. The boost left her jumpy and restless. She lifted her snorkel and smelled the distant elders calling various scientists to extend their roots. Chemists, mathematicians, and biologists communed with the elders, their root talks hidden from Pepper and the other plants. The mood of the grove grew anxious, even fearful. Fear rebounded as anger. Vaporous calls for revenge gained strength, thickening like dust at the start of a storm. Tension grew in the elders as well. The number of questions grew, but the number of answers did not.

***

Tarragon closed his gills to the mutterings of the grove, the better to listen to the millions of voices in his memories. He sought answers to paradoxes. The voices agreed that ideal geometric forms didn't exist in the real world—except they did. Pepper had found rectangles, cylinders, triangles, all precise to the limits of her ability to measure. She'd even discovered perfectly flat solids.

The thousands of voices within him said it wasn't possible. Nature works in fractals and approximations, not absolutes. *Reality is not perfect*, they said. *Even the surface of the lake, the closest physical representation of a mathematical plane, has ripples easily felt by root tips.*

The matter of exotic materials also bothered him. The monsters used organic polymers and metal alloys, materials that neither occurred in nature nor could be produced by any means known to science. How did they exist? To this question his voices provided no insight.

Did the monsters draw power from magic, like creatures from one of Narcissus's imaginary tales? Were the beings ghosts, as Myrtle suggested? He extended a root and asked her.

"What I believe is that we don't know a snort of dust about the creatures," she replied. *"They are powerful, dangerous, and undetectable. That's all we know, and we're unlikely to learn more. It takes a ghost to know a ghost, Eldest. And we aren't ghosts."*

Tarragon withdrew his root, no closer to understanding the monsters' abilities.

Understanding their motivation would make understanding their ability less of an issue, said Valerian. Tarragon encouraged the inner voice. Why did they attack? Why kill, maim, and abduct members of the grove? If they wanted information, they need only ask, but they stayed silent. Their silence intensifies our fear. Is that what they want? To impress us with their power and random acts of cruelty?

The Enemy could have killed everyone in the grove. They hadn't. Therefore, they must want something from us. Something we wouldn't willingly give up. What? Every grove on the planet had the same natural resources.

Clearly, the grove lacked key information. Pepper's reconnaissance, though helpful, was woefully inadequate for answering the most important questions. How could the grove possibly study these scentless, fast-moving beings?

Those two advantages must be neutralized, said Valerian. *Capture one,* said a voice from an ancient elder. *In a scentless trap,* said another. *Render it immobile,* said still another. These voices were nearly smothered by the majority, which cautioned against angering beings of unimaginable powers. Tarragon listened carefully to all the dead voices, but consensus proved elusive. He conferred with the other elders in root talk.

Nasturtium supported immediate, decisive action. *"For reasons unknown, another grove has declared war upon us. They may think us weak, and they may think us cowards. We are neither! We will show them our power and make them regret their impudent attacks."*

Marjoram took an opposing stance. *"As you observed, Eldest, the monsters could have killed all of us. They still can. Our best option is to wait them out. Eventually they will tire of these horrible antics, and they will leave, returning to their home or moving on to some other hapless—"*

A startled burst of vinegar vapor interrupted her speech. Wisteria, a plant not much older than Pepper, wailed that something had touched her dome. Pepper started paddling in that direction, but Tarragon wrapped a root around her flipper.

Wisteria's shock turned to terror. *"It's pulling me from the ground! The monster has me! Sage, help! Save me!"*

Pepper strained to get free.

"Let her go, Pepper," Tarragon said in root talk.

"Eldest!" she protested.

"Your time will come."

Wisteria's fresh cries ended as had those of previous victims. The old cries hung in the air until supplanted by the panicked sputtering of the grove.

Tarragon's words billowed. *"Enough! We will no longer meekly accept capture, torture, and death. We face a serious and immediate danger. Action must be taken to protect the grove and, if possible, to rescue Narcissus and Wisteria."* He paused, letting the gravity of the situation saturate their memories. It was scarcely necessary. Fear, anger, and frustration seethed everywhere.

A rich odor wafted from the grove, a mix of shock, fear, relief, excitement, and resolve. The elders puffed for calm and quiet, and eventually it came. Into the clear air, Myrtle aired her two scents. *"It's silly to wage war with the solar flares coming soon. And besides, how do you intend to fight ghosts?"*

Tarragon said, *"We will capture one. We will learn their weaknesses and use that knowledge to destroy them."* His words brought a swirl of apprehension.

Pepper rubbed a flipper along his root. *"You left me like this for a reason."*

So smart for someone so young. *"I intend to use you for bait."* He felt her mixed emotions, and gave what comfort he could. She knew the grove was in danger, especially Narcissus. Tarragon knew she would accept this mission, even though the danger was greater than before.

Sage's words filled the air unexpectedly. *"Elders, Pepper has risked her life once already. Someone else should take this risk. Someone without an emotional involvement with Narcissus."*

Pepper blurted, *"Stay out of this, Sage!"* but her root words only reached Tarragon.

"Son, let's talk privately," exhaled Elder Nasturtium.

Pepper pulled free from Tarragon's root, and he let her. She needed rest and time to think. Tarragon extended a root to Sage. *"I also will have words with you."*

Chapter 30

Grove time: Reign of Tarragon. Ring 2,241. Layer 63,003.

Pepper followed the vibration of Tarragon's retreating root straight to Sage. Good. The Eldest would put an end to the son-of-an-elder's foolishness. Pepper wanted the mission and was better prepared for it than anyone else.

Snorkel raised, she eased closer to Sage, which also meant closer to Nasturtium. Pepper's body gave no odor. It felt oddly exciting to be as undetectable as the aliens. She liked spying—not for malicious reasons, but because she could learn directly, without censorship or flavoring, exactly what others thought of her.

Her flippers brushed the roots of Sage and Tarragon. She pulled away quickly, feigning accidental, anonymous contact, but stayed close enough to pickup most of their root talk.

"It is a dangerous mission you want to undertake, Sage. It will take all the strength and courage you have. Your father will urge you to turn from this path, for he loves you, and knows the chance of death is very high."

"We all die, Eldest. Our memories remain."

"Why do you want to do this?"

"It needs to be done."

"The voices of the dead speak only the truth," Tarragon said. *"They cannot deceive, they cannot cajole, they cannot extrapolate. Death strips away everything extraneous. Only truth remains, embedded in memories covering every moment of their lives: the good choices and the bad, the joys and the hurts, the highest accomplishments and worst embarrassments, all unedited, all*

open. The dead are content, having left their legacy of memories to the living, to return their physical bodies to the environment. The living are content, for grief is tempered by the new yet familiar voice in their minds. The dead often release memories of thoughts never expressed during life. Secrets that give insight and understanding to the living. The voice of every soul is remembered back to the dawn of our species. Would you have future generations remember you with pride, or with shame?"

"I must speak with my father."

"Remember my words, Sage." Tarragon's root withdrew.

Pepper pulled back, disappointed that Tarragon hadn't rebuked Sage and vetoed his participation. However, Elder Nasturtium surely wouldn't allow his son to undertake such a dangerous mission. Like Tarragon, Nasturtium chose root talk to discuss matters with Sage, and Pepper couldn't resist spying.

"Don't be a fool. You are not going on this mission." Nasturtium's words stung even though Pepper was inches away. The ground remained perfectly still, and she wondered how Sage managed not to flinch.

"Pepper was right all along," Sage said. *"These are aliens, beings we have never encountered. We need her fresh ideas, her insights, if we are to comprehend the monsters. We shouldn't risk her."*

"Don't mistake novelty for truth. I speak with the wisdom of a million voices. Pepper has but her own and Valerian's, and he was an idiot."

"What if this is a new type of threat? Doesn't that demand new solutions?"

"Nothing is new. It only appears new because of your limited memory. That's what I'm trying to get through your thick dome."

"Your voices... they have experienced this type of attack before?"

"Of course. A very long time ago, with voices very faint. Perhaps even Tarragon can't smell them anymore, but I can." Pepper edged a flipper an inch closer. Something didn't smell right, but root words couldn't express the nuance.

"I'm sorry for doubting you, father."

"Good, then it's settled."

"I'm volunteering for the mission."

The acid level of the soil spiked. *"I forbid it."*

"You cannot prevent me from offering my services. At best you can try convincing the other elders to deny my request. I doubt you would succeed." Pepper hadn't thought Sage capable of standing up to his father. Had she misjudged him?

"It's Pepper. You care for her."

Pepper would have laughed at the magnitude of the elder's misconception if not for the caustic tension permeating the soil.

"You're twice the fool I thought you were," Nasturtium seethed. *"Let her sacrifice herself and improve the gene pool."*

"You are cruel and think only of yourself. An elder should think first of the grove."

"Tarragon's platitudes cling to your roots. You had best keep your allegiance with me. War is coming, and I'd not lose you in our first strike."

"We all die, but our memories endure."

"Sterile imprints. What matters is now. Only in the present do we have power and freedom. Only while alive can we set goals, work to achieve them, and enjoy our success. Survival of the grove depends on bold action, terrible action that will offend most sensibilities. Fate has given me long life, and with it, the power and authority of an elder. I shall not hide that power under my dome; I shall wield it until the entire grove reeks of me, until they cannot tell where their scent ends and mine begins, and all will think my thoughts their own."

"I have smelled quite enough, father. I mean no disrespect, but this is something I must do, if for no other reason than preserving our family honor after you die."

"The sweet aroma of my son has become a stench I cannot stand. Do what you will."

The soil shifted and freshened as the elder's root withdrew. Pepper felt her own chance for heroism and adventure fade and crawled to the outskirts of the grove to be alone. It seemed to be her natural state.

Chapter 31

Grove time: Reign of Tarragon. Ring 2,241. Layer 63,010

Sometime later, Pepper jerked in surprise when Sage touched her flipper. He'd snuck up to her, scent masked until the actual touch. His root felt different. Misshaped.

"They changed you," she said. More anger went into the words than she intended, but she did not apologize. *"You saw a chance to be a hero and you took it."*

"That's not how it went."

"I was already modified and ready to go. Your vanity wasted precious time. I don't need a partner."

"I'm not your partner. You're not going."

Pepper squirted nervously. *"Of course I am."*

"You've done your part and done it well. I'm proud of you."

"Tarragon kept me in this form and restored my energy supply. He wouldn't have done so unless I'm needed."

"What you did was incredibly brave. But this mission is far more dangerous. Let someone else handle it."

"I'm the best qualified!"

"Narcissus wouldn't want you to go, either. Not if he loves you."

His words implied jealously, even if she didn't smell it. *"He's out there, trapped and alone. Let me save him. That's what love's about."*

"You're right." A hint of vanilla and chocolate escaped with his words.

"No! You can't love me. I have Narcissus. And Wisteria has a crush on you."

Sage said nothing, and Elder Tarragon discouraged further conversation as his massive root found them. *"Time to go, Sage. Stay underground. Follow Pepper's trail. You know the plan."*

"Yes, Eldest. Disable the metal creature first, then attack the nest."

"Pepper will remain here, in reserve should you be captured or killed."

The flat delivery of the elder's words brought a new level of understanding to Pepper. Tarragon spoke of Sage and Pepper as if they were things, not plants—distancing himself from the guilt that he was sending one of them, perhaps both, to death without release.

Elder Nasturtium withheld his aromas as Sage burrowed away. To Pepper, the father's emotions seemed barren as a rock uncovered by the wind.

The air freshened as conversation ceased and everyone sniffed, hoping for a whiff of the heroic son of an elder, even though they knew Sage couldn't gill talk. Pepper, with her more sensitive and directional snorkel, caught scent of acid on metal. She touched Tarragon's root. *"He's partially dissolved the metal creature."*

Tarragon relayed the information to the grove.

Pepper caught another scent, which sent a tingle along her body. *"Wisteria is outside the plastic wall! She's calling for help!"*

"Wisteria has escaped," said Elder Marjoram.

"Don't be a fool," huffed Nasturtium. *"It's a trap."*

"Nasturtium is right," Tarragon said.

A chant began, sandwiched in warning waves of ammonia and sulfur. *"Trap! Trap!"* But Sage had been engineered for speed. He'd wouldn't get the warning in time.

"My son knows it's a trap. He will complete the mission," Nasturtium said.

Pepper felt certain Sage would turn aside to help Wisteria. It was what she would have done. But here, removed from the action, she saw that decision for what it was—a mistake.

She plunged forward, burrowing into the ground, following the same path Sage took. His scent, overlaid with hers, produced a heady mix laden with sexual overtones. Anger fueled her muscles as she paddled faster. She didn't want Sage to make her feel good. She'd promised herself to Narcissus.

Pepper paused, lifted her snorkel, and sniffed. As expected, Sage had veered toward the captive plant. Wisteria shouted, "*Sage, don't let go of me!*" A short, intense scream followed.

Pepper lunged in that direction, but caught scent of the grove's earlier chant. *Trap. Trap.*

With a forceful, frustrated exhalation, Pepper turned to the nesting place of the monsters. She reached its first leg and sprayed acid where the grove's scientists had calculated the most vulnerable stress point to be located. She caught the scent of cut grass and hoped it wasn't Sage. Guilt followed, for wasn't that the same as wishing Wisteria had died?

The ground shook with heavy rhythmic vibrations. She dashed to the second leg, but had only a moment to spray before the vibration intensified, forcing her to turn back toward the grove. The vibration quickened: something heavy kept smashing into the ground, over and over, closer and closer. She smelled the bitter vinegar of her own fear.

She paddled as fast as she could, following the path memorized at Tarragon's insistence. The alien defied physical limitations, pulling ever closer despite Pepper moving faster than anything that ever lived on this planet.

She wanted to dive under the surface and change direction, leaving her pursuer with no scent to chase. However, the elders' instructions had been quite clear: keep your snorkel up, exposing enough scent to lure the creature to the reservoir.

The creature would catch her before then. She dumped all her stored sugar into the muscles of her six paddles. She sucked air so fast it burned the lining of her snorkel. The gritty soil stung as friction abraded the protective shell of her body. It wore through at several points. Sand dug into raw muscle fibers. Sap oozed from the wounds.

Something brushed her snorkel—thin strands of metal roots trying to snag her like those of the mysterious wall she'd encountered before. She angled her snorkel and shook off the strands. She'd never make it to the reservoir. A fatalistic corner of her mind appreciated the irony of dying so near the reservoir where her parents had died.

She cornered sharply left and skittered across the top of the reservoir. Irony morphed to hope. The surface bowed but held— she'd done too good a job maintaining it. She dumped all her remaining acid and kept moving. The creature pursued, now mere inches away.

The upper crust collapsed. Pepper paddled desperately, but the bog pulled inexorably downward. Her snorkel dropped below the surface. Oxygen became the immediate and only need, but water and mud filled her lungs as the alien tumbled atop her.

The world faded to scentlessness.

Chapter 32

Grove time: Reign of Tarragon. Ring 2,241. Layer 63,012.

Tarragon's roots shifted constantly through the soil, issuing orders designed to secure the creature without unleashing a flood. Marjoram softened the reservoir walls, Nasturtium thrust a root inside and bound the creature tightly, while Myrtle's surprisingly long roots also slipped inside and expertly gelled the reservoir's water. The odorless medium would facilitate study of the monster.

Tarragon recovered Pepper's body and revived her with oxygen and sap. He ordered her original body restored and full memories returned as soon as was practical.

The grove worked quickly and smoothly, but the aliens proved to be devilishly clever and unbelievably fast. The monsters reached the reservoir and attempted to rescue their comrade. Nasturtium dragged the monster to a new inspection site beneath a group of adolescents.

Once again, the monsters sniffed out the location of their missing member. *How can they do the impossible?* thought Tarragon. The captive emitted no odor; the miniscule amount of scent shed by Pepper could not have reached the surface through the intervening absorbent ground. The odorless wrath of the aliens came with terrible speed, delivering death and destruction.

They aren't tracking by smell, said a few of his oldest voices. He pondered their wisdom and reached the only possible conclusion: The monsters used touch—vibration—for determining location. Tarragon exhaled new orders to the grove. "*Everyone not otherwise engaged: sweep your roots through the soil.*"

Under the cover of the shifting sand, he gathered the monster closer to himself. He ordered all scientists and doctors within reach of the creature to extend their roots and begin a comprehensive examination. He then turned his attention to the grove.

The smell of the wounded, the dying, and the dead made normal communication impossible. He tried in vain to conduct ceremonies for the dead, but with three plants simultaneously shedding memory rings, the dead voices became jumbled, mixed, and incoherent. The chant "Uniqueness becomes ubiquity" lacked joy and respect; it became a mournful dirge with a chorus of pain. Many memories were lost.

Nasturtium expressed his impatience in root talk. *"There isn't time for ceremonies. The sun's getting hotter. A storm comes soon. The creature must be studied before then."*

"We will not abandon tradition in troubled times, nor will we rush the examination of the life form that threatens us," answered Tarragon. *"We need to understand this creature in detail."*

"Eldest," said Marjoram softly. *"Nasturtium's son is out there. Please hurry."*

"It will take whatever time it takes," Tarragon wafted. *"And cost whatever it costs."* He sympathized with the grove and shared their anger and fear. Many wanted the creature killed immediately, expecting its memories to provide answers. Others wanted the creature released in hopes of avoiding more attacks from its brethren. His own voices warred within, unable to come to agreement, yet knowing the matter was too important to drop.

Nasturtium complained bitterly. *"We all know their technology is beyond anything we possess. We will never understand it in time to defend ourselves."*

"Other groves exist," Tarragon said. *"We know this from foreign memories blown here by storms. Somewhere, a grove has found a new technology, and invented new biological forms with great strength, speed, and stealth. They are not yet sure of their capability, and are using us to test their weapons."*

"There hasn't been war for as long as I can remember," said Marjoram. *"I suspect there has never been a war except as a theoretical concept. What possible motive could they have?"*

"I don't know and don't care," Nasturtium said. *"Our immediate goal is to survive. We must find a way to neutralize the monsters. Once that is done, then we can find out which grove is*

responsible. They will be held accountable by every grove in the world, and punished for these murders."

"*Punishment is not enough,*" Tarragon said. The words reeked with odors strong enough to singe nearby gills. "*Whatever grove is responsible for this must be killed and their memories obliterated. The secret of creating monsters of pure destruction must be erased. Even elders are not wise enough to control such power.*"

Shock welled up from the other elders and the scientists, emphasized a puff later by the rest of the grove. Tarragon's reputation for kindness, diplomacy, and mercy was rooted in more than two thousand rings of consistent behavior. Stating that Nasturtium's proposal was not sufficiently harsh seemed so out of character that it quieted the entire grove. Even Myrtle, bless her sweet dome, said nothing, but she kept her gills wide open.

Chapter 33

Grove time: Reign of Tarragon. Ring 2,241. Layer 63,015.

Pepper swished a root through the soil, trying to recapture the sensations of speed and mobility. Having her memories restored and getting Valerian's voice back couldn't compare with being a muscle-powered, oxygen-breathing *animal*. The only consolation was being treated with respect by the grove. Heroism had perks, not that she considered herself a real hero. But she had helped to capture the monster that took Sage and Narcissus.

"*Stop swishing your root and pay attention,*" Tarragon said.

Pepper stilled her roots as a scientist explained genetic modification, immune response suppression, and splicing of nerve tissue. Valerian's voice whispered, *Your job isn't done.* It made the lecture smell ominous. Pepper suddenly realized Tarragon's plan and gave an involuntary squirt of surprise. The Eldest secreted a calming lotion.

"*The mission is to stop the monsters, to forever end their ability to attack us,*" Tarragon said. "*The most obvious way is to kill them, which is in itself quite risky, but killing them is not enough. We need to know where the creatures come from, who sent them, and why. The only way to get that information is to become one of them. Whoever takes the mission cannot afford to be obvious. If it is you, you must learn their secrets while waiting in perfect concealment for opportunities to kill. If the monsters discover your presence, they will kill you and the host.*"

"*I'm not afraid,*" Pepper said.

Tarragon sighed the briefest hint of sadness, and she knew he'd caught her in a lie. Her first. She prayed the scientists were right about the monsters being poor sniffers. Deception was a skill she lacked.

"Pepper, no one will force you to take this mission. But if no one takes it, the attacks will continue, and the plants held captive will certainly die."

"I'll do it."

"If you fail, everyone you know will die. Every voice back to the dawn of time will be silenced forever."

"I will not fail."

"The operation is irreversible. You can never be a plant again, never mate with Narcissus, even if you free him."

"I'll do it," she repeated. She knew Tarragon smelled her fear, sadness, and resolve.

"The grove will never forget your bravery and your sacrifice."

"If I don't succeed, there will be no one to remember anything."

"Pepper," Tarragon said. *"You need to select what memories you want to take with you."* He smelled apologetic. With the wind picking up she had to concentrate on absorbing his meaning before it dispersed.

"Eldest, I don't understand."

"Your body will be altered drastically. Most likely there will not be space for more than a hundred rings."

"Will I get the other memories back if I succeed?"

Tarragon did not respond, and her courage faltered. *"Eldest?"*

"You won't be able to add many new memories. Not that you'll need to." Tarragon gave a whiff of embarrassment. *"Sorry. That was callous."*

"You don't expect me to survive."

"Whether you succeed or fail, your death is certain."

Pepper pondered this. *"I'm to become one of them. Therefore I'm to die with them."*

"There is no other way, Pepper."

She'd do what she had to do when the time came, but refused to think about it before then. *"What will happen to the memories I do not keep?"*

"They will be released at your funeral. Select your memories quickly. Your surgery begins soon."

Choosing which memories to keep and which to release proved to be difficult. Pepper wanted to hold on to the happy thoughts—praise from her parents, playing with friends, the aromas of Narcissus's stories, the touch of his roots, the tingle of sunlight on her leaves. But what would that leave for the grove to remember her by? Arguments with Narcissus, frustration with the elders, annoyance with Sage? If she took the best, the grove would remember her as an angry, morose, loner. If she carried the worst memories to her death, she would become that bitter hero, hating herself and others even as she died for the good of the grove. Neither option gave a complete picture. Neither was totally true nor totally false.

"*I don't know how to chose.*"

"*Why are you a going on this mission?*" Tarragon asked.

"*To save the grove by killing the demons after discovering their secrets, and if possible, rescuing Narcissus and Sage.*"

"*Yes. Remember the priority. Even though you care for Narcissus, there are greater stakes.*"

"*Yes, Eldest.*"

"*We cannot restore your body afterward. The mission will sacrifice your life.*"

"*I know.*"

"*Your scent will be remembered to the end of time.*"

"*I don't understand.*"

"*I think you do.*"

She did, but the finality terrified her. She huffed a cloud of bravado, but Tarragon seemed to read her mind.

"*Death comes to us all, child. But memories endure. What words will you leave to inspire future generations? What words will comfort Narcissus when your body is no more?*"

Pepper's roots moistened the ground. "*I wish I were wise like you.*"

"*Being an elder doesn't guarantee wisdom,*" Tarragon said. "*It's not age that makes a person wise, nor how many voices speak within. Wisdom is realizing that mortality makes life precious. It means making decisions that will benefit the most lives, including those of future generations, even if those decisions come at great personal cost.*"

***

"There is no time to implement your plan," Nasturtium said. *"The storm is nearly here."*

Tarragon didn't waver. *"We will have the Ceremony of Ubiquity for Pepper, and we'll analyze the monster afterward."*

"Omit the ceremony," Nasturtium fumed. *"Although even then our scientists will have barely enough time to analyze and report before the storm sends us all to sleep."*

"We will not abandon our most sacred tradition." Tarragon transplanted Pepper to the upwind edge of the grove, hoping to ameliorate the disruptive effect of the storm. He then expelled a blast of ammonia, overwhelming all other odors in order to claim full attention of the grove. *"Smell this, all of you! Pepper's bravery and sacrifice deserve the highest honor. Pepper gives up more than her life. She gives up her body, to take on the shape of a monster. She gives up civilized behavior to adopt the savagery of beasts. She must become a killer of killers to make safe our grove, knowing that she will not survive to savor the victory. I give you the memories of Pepper. Absorb them with respect."*

With great care, the doctors neutralized her electrical charge at precise locations, letting certain memories evaporate while others were quickly severed and moved to Tarragon's base. A network of his roots produced a charge to hold her memories together while awaiting implantation into the captured beast.

Pepper experienced the most peculiar sensation, impossible to put into smells, as memories left her brain by one route or the other, putting her consciousness in perpetual backward motion.

Helping other plants. Doing maintenance. Searching for proof of other worlds. Wondering if other life forms existed and what they would be like. Touching roots with Narcissus. Sharing ideas with him.

Her life unwound, each memory perfectly clear and then completely gone. She tried in vain to hold them as they slipped like wind through her leaves, leaving a sense of loss without knowing why or for what.

Laughing at Myrtle's gossip. Meeting Narcissus—finally someone who was interested in her idea that other worlds existed. Working hard as a student. Grief at her parents' death. Her parents' pride as she started school. Playing games with other preschoolers. Her birth.

Pepper sobbed, her roots draining into the soil, leaving palpable emptiness. The air stung her exposed brainstem. For a moment she knew some memories would return when the doctors grafted her brain onto that of the monster. Then that realization vanished, leaving her abandoned by every memory she ever had, cast into a void without hope or fear, right or wrong, past or future. Even her name drifted away, and she floated alone without even herself for company.

Chapter 34

Grove time: Reign of Tarragon. Ring 2,241. Layer 63,018.

Pepper awoke to a curious lack of sensation. She could think, but had no feeling of root, stem, or dome. The rhythmic pulse of respiratory puffs was missing. Had the implantation process failed?

"It has not yet fully begun," Tarragon said. *"Your brain is connected to mine via modified roots. You can communicate through me. We are about to hear the reports of the scientists."*

Roots of the elders and a dozen scientists often grazed Tarragon's roots, leaving Pepper snippets of tantalizing discoveries. She felt out of place around so much secrecy and seniority, but the elders knew best, and Tarragon himself had placed her here. The grove's endless gossip filled the air, most of it totally wrong. The scientists didn't try to correct it. Tarragon had sworn them to secrecy.

"I can't emphasize enough how dangerous this creature is," said the first scientist. *"It has an outer shell which renders it scentless. It has bilateral articulated upper limbs. The limbs terminate in five short tentacles, each jointed and terminating with a hardened, blade-like surface. The design seems suited for reaching, grasping, tearing, and gouging."*

"Alarming," Marjoram declared.

"Grotesque," Nasturtium opined.

The scientist continued. *"The creature is designed for speed. It does not utilize photosynthesis at all. Instead, cellular metabolism is based on oxidation of dissolved nutrients, which provides a much higher sustainable energy output. Stored chemical energy powers contractions in muscular tissue at will, similar to our roots. Thick bands of this muscle tissue are connected to end points of a rigid but articulated support structure. This overall structure is bipedal, approximately two yards high. It's capable of bursts of speeds in excess of 800 feet per layer. Nearly 35 inches per puff. Far too fast to track."*

Marjoram gasped and Nasturtium grunted at the phenomenal number, faster than anything other than a windstorm. Marjoram asked, *"How can a bipedal structure move through soil that fast?"*

"The creature moves above the soil, not through it."

Tarragon asked, *"How does it obtain nutrients?"*

The scientist accented his words with odors of vinegar and rotten cabbage, revealing a level of fear and disgust Pepper had never before smelled from a scientist. *"A single large and roughly spherical appendage at the top of the main body has an orifice lined with hard, sharp projections which are designed for tearing into the flesh of other living beings. The flesh is ingested and moved along an internal canal where it is dissolved in acid. The desired nutrients are absorbed through porous linings, and unneeded remains are excreted through another orifice at the end of the canal."*

"Disgusting," Nasturtium said.

"Sickening," agreed Marjoram. *"How can such a being exist?"*

"It could not have evolved naturally," said the scientist. *"It was designed for a single purpose—to hunt down and destroy other living things. Then eat them."*

"Pepper, it that also your opinion?" Tarragon asked.

Pepper felt as if her roots had snagged. The elders never asked for her opinion in an open meeting. Just the opposite, in fact.

"Pepper?"

"Surely my opinion is of no concern to the wise and powerful," she answered.

"No one but you dreamt of worlds beyond ours, or of beings so unlike us," Tarragon said. *"It seems to me that your concept of reality smells more like truth than ours."*

Nasturtium said, *"I am not yet convinced this is an alien from some hypothetical planet. Practical considerations strongly suggest another grove has engineered this monster."*

"I want Pepper's opinion," Tarragon said.

Pepper hesitated. Should she be respectful or say what she really believed? Could she manage both? *"I think perhaps the creature could have evolved naturally,"* she puffed gently.

A scientist started to argue, but Tarragon hushed him. *"Continue, Pepper."*

"Imagine another world, populated with not just one species, but thousands, each competing for space and nutrients, each trying to reproduce. Under those conditions, each species would evolve abilities and attributes to enhance survival. In such a world, violence and cannibalism could be an option adopted by some life forms."

"That theory was dismissed millennia ago," said the scientist. *"If you had more memories to draw on, you'd know that such an ecosystem is unstable. Hundreds of monsters of all shapes and sizes, in a frenzy of feeding, reproducing, and trying to avoid being eaten—it's a hell too terrible to exist. It would inevitably collapse."*

"Yet isn't that what the creature is?" asked Tarragon. *"A real, living monster?"* When the scientist didn't answer, Tarragon continued, *"An object was found with the creature."*

A different scientist answered. *"Yes, Elder."*

"Describe it."

"The object was grasped in one of the creature's tentacled appendages. The object has no smell. It is a long metal tube with a large open loop at one end. One hundred long and very thin metal filaments connect at opposite ends along the circumference of the loop. It is my opinion that the object is a tool."

Tool. It was a new word, like *plastic*, which the scientists had adopted as if they invented the substance. But *tool* didn't smell only of substance; it smelled of work and of something touching yet external to the body.

"Explain 'tool' to us," Tarragon said.

"Suppose a storm toppled a seedling near a large rock. If you dig to free the child, there is danger that the rock will fall and crush the child, so you secrete a binder to solidify an oblong area of soil under the rock. The solidified soil is a lever to allow safe removal of the rock. A tool is an inanimate object created to perform or assist in a particular task."

"Granted there may be rare instances where a tool would be useful, but on a routine basis? Why make tools when it's so much easier to use your own roots?"

The scientist smelled uncomfortable. *"In theory, sir, having tools can multiply the effectiveness of certain activities. Tools could make a person faster and stronger, or give him control over certain events from a great distance, or greater precision at very small distances."*

Pepper thought of the perfect cylinders and rectangles. The plastic enclosure. The metal hive. Could these all be tools?

The next scientist presented a particularly distressing report. *"The creature was given every opportunity to communicate, but remained silent. It thrashed its limbs violently, and we needed to restrain it. I focused on the outer shell of the creature, which renders it odorless. The creature does have a distinct odor when not enclosed by the shell. The flexible shell consisted primarily of plastic, but it included metallic devices of intricate design and a self-contained system of tubes and tanks with a mixture of nitrogen, oxygen, argon, and some trace gases."*

"Air," Nasturtium said.

The scientist dribbled a bit of nervousness. *"Not precisely, Elder. The proportions were different than found in our atmosphere."*

Pepper's excitement created a cloud of memory dust from Tarragon. At last hard evidence had been found to support her theory; it made sense that other planets would have different atmospheres. *"Easy, child!"* said the voice of the Eldest in her mind. *"I'm sharing new memories with you, but I can ill afford to be distracted."*

Tarragon asked the scientist, *"What is the purpose of the metal devices you found?"*

"I... we... have no idea what purpose they served. We know very little about the shell proper. A physical examination found no connection points between the shell and the rest of the creature. Unfortunately, the shell was destroyed in the search for memories and the mapping of internal anatomy. We have no idea how the creature grew the shell. Recreating it is beyond our technology."

"Let's proceed to the report on the anatomy," Nasturtium said. *"What makes the monster so powerful?"*

A fresh root wiggled in and oozed out information. *"The creature has no memories. We know this because we dissolved the outer shell, then a half-inch of its body proper. No memories were released, even though the creature died. We performed a gross anatomical study—"*

"*The creature died?*" Marjoram asked.

"*And was reanimated,*" Nasturtium said impatiently. "*Continue, scientist Ancho.*"

"*We discovered a very large brain, also without memories,*" said the scientist. "*We believe the size is due to embedded instincts and instructions. At no time did it attempt to communicate, which surprised us until we found the thing has no olfaction gland. It's mute and has only limited ability to detect smells.*"

"*A preprogrammed warrior without memories cannot reveal information to the enemy,*" mused Nasturtium.

"*What is the condition of the creature now?*" asked Tarragon.

"*We repaired the structural damage and reversed the cellular damage. It responds well to sap, which restored all its organs, including those whose purpose we don't yet understand.*"

"*Tell us more about these mystery organs,*" Marjoram said.

"*There are several, most of them on the round 'head' at the upper extremity, which houses its bulbous brain. Two sets of external interface organs are particularly noteworthy. The first is a pair of small orbs filled with gel, set into the head and close together. The second is a pair of semi-rigid flaps set on opposite sides of the head. The flaps surround a narrow, shallow hole. On the interior side of each hole is a delicate network of hard and soft tissue connected to nerves.*"

"*What makes these organs noteworthy?*"

"*Having a backup for each organ suggests they are important. This supposition is further supported by the location of the organs so near the brain. Close proximity shortens the time for nerve signals to reach the brain, so these organs are sending priority signals. Not surprisingly, the olfactory detection organ is also located nearby.*"

"*Do you have a theory on the purpose of the mystery organs?*"

"*Not even a guess, Elder Marjoram.*"

"*The beings communicate somehow. Perhaps the mystery organs are for telepathy? That would explain how they can remain silent, yet act in concert.*"

"*That's as good a guess as any, Elder.*"

"It isn't enough to have a fast, strong, undetectable monster. Let's imbue it with supernatural abilities." Nasturtium's sarcasm soaked the soil. *"You take Narcissus and Myrtle too seriously."*

A bit of the elder's words reached the surface and escaped. Through Tarragon, Pepper sensed the resultant surge of anxiety in the grove. The elders had always spoken as if they were a single entity with complementary voices. The smell of discord didn't bode well.

The scientist continued. *"The creature does have some drawbacks, Elder Nasturtium."*

"Let us hope so. What are they?"

"It needs a constant supply of oxygen to survive."

"There's plenty of it."

"The creature has no chlorophyll. None at all. To live, it must find, kill, and eat other beings."

Marjoram said, *"Haven't we smelled enough obscenities?"*

"My point, Elders, is that the monster doesn't live very long. Its cellular structure is not robust; the cells wear out and need to replicate themselves, but each replication contains minute flaws which accumulate until the organism can't sustain life. As it lacks the ability to produce sap, we estimate its life span at less than two hundred rings."

Marjoram gasped. *"The thing is an infant?"*

"We believe the creature is an adult. Their strength and speed come from an extremely fast metabolism. It makes them age rapidly. An entire life compressed into a few hundred thousand layers."

"More than enough time to kill everyone in the grove," Nasturtium said. *"What if it escapes?"*

"We lowered the oxygen level in the gas we provide to its respiratory system. The creature's brain is not capable of deliberate muscular control under such conditions."

"You said it died during examination," said Marjoram. *"How difficult would it be to kill this creature again if it broke free?"*

The scientist pondered the question. *"A wide range of chemical agents would kill it, as would gross physical damage to any of its major organs. However, if the creature were loose, I can't think of a way to deliver poisons or inflict damage to something this fast, especially if it acquires another invisibility shell. I am sorry, Elders. This is the ultimate weapon."*

A new scientist thrust in his root into the conversation. *"Killing it could be a very big mistake."*

"Why?" asked the elders in unison.

"While studying its cellular structure and genetic design, I discovered the presence of microorganisms inside the creature's digestive organs. The billions of bacteria would ultimately decompose the dead creature. But they would not stop there. The bacteria are not sterile; they are fast-growing and capable of mutation. They could have infected the grove and killed many of us before we realized the cause. Fortunately, the creature is underground, which severely limited the bacterial spread. I identified and exterminated the few million microorganisms that escaped. With the body alive and sealed in skin, the danger is minimal."

"The creature was designed to spring a final trap on us," Nasturtium said. *"What more proof do you need? The enemy is more dangerous than we thought. They need to be wiped out before they destroy us."*

What happened next frightened Pepper more than any of the reports from the scientists. Tarragon said, *"Nasturtium, Marjoram, withdraw your roots. I will receive the remaining reports alone."* Such a thing had never happened before. Elders kept no secrets from one another. Pepper had trouble believing it was happening now.

Apparently Nasturtium did too, for he refused to leave until Tarragon threatened to have the grove soak him in acid. The stench of Nasturtium's anger lingered after his roots retreated. There would be repercussions from Tarragon's action. Pepper hoped the Eldest restored calm soon. Perhaps he was doing so now... she felt sleepy, so sleepy, and drifted away.

Chapter 35

Grove time: Reign of Tarragon. Ring 2,241. Layer 63,020

"You're planning a symbiont," Nasturtium said.

"Yes," Tarragon said, lacing the word with the sad smell of wind without moisture.

"Oh dear, oh dear," said Marjoram. *"My oldest voices shudder at the thought."*

"Pepper is neither brave enough nor ruthless enough," Nasturtium said. *"We need someone who won't hesitate to kill these monsters."* He puffed a sigh. *"If only my son had not been captured."*

"We need someone exactly like Pepper," Tarragon said. *"A symbiont of this magnitude carries an inherent danger. It could be used beyond its defensive purpose to subjugate other groves or dominate this one. Pepper is not capable of turning on us."*

"We don't even know if we can make a symbiont," said Marjoram. *"The process has never been tried."*

"A weapon needs to function reliably," insisted Nasturtium. *"Pepper is too gentle. She can't do it."*

Tarragon exuded sadness laced with inevitability. *"She will do exactly what needs to be done."*

"You can't be sure. We need a contingency plan if she fails."

"She will not fail. She's hurt by Narcissus's infidelity yet feels guilt over his capture. She's confused by Sage's affection. She's addicted to mobility. She's eager to find proof of her theories. These are the openings through which I shall turn Pepper into her opposite, replacing gentleness with harshness, openness with

secrecy, kindness with murder. The changes cannot be undone; she can never return to the grove. It is a cruel thing I do.”

Tarragon felt Marjoram touch roots with him. *“You're a good plant, Tarragon. If you say it can be done, and must be done, I know it is for the good of the grove.”*

“The good of the grove,” echoed Nasturtium.

Tarragon let the words of the others linger. In the last hundred thousand rings, every decision by the elders of this grove had been unanimous. It would not do to break that tradition now, in the midst of so much fear and mourning. Every plant had to smell the solidarity of their leadership. *“The good of the grove,”* he sighed.

“And yet,” Nasturtium stated bluntly, *“there isn't time to complete the surgery. The storm will put us all to sleep, the monster will be forgotten and will die. Irretrievably. Perhaps if you share your knowledge, we will be able to grow a fresh monster after the storm.”*

“The creature will neither die nor be forgotten if I stay awake.”

A rare scent of surprise wafted from Nasturtium. *“You intend to do the surgery yourself.”*

“Yes.”

“I can help,” Nasturtium said. *“The surgery will go faster and with higher chance of success if we work together.”*

“The knowledge must die with me. It is far too dangerous for anyone to know and must never be passed on to others.”

“Your plan is flawed,” puffed Marjoram. *“It's impossible to make memories during a storm.”*

“Not impossible, merely suicidal.”

“It's a waste of valuable knowledge,” Nasturtium said. *“It goes against tradition.”*

“Enough! The decision is made.” Tarragon's words saturated the ground. *“Nasturtium, Pepper will make regular reports. Once the monsters are dead, use the information to find the grove that created them. Wipe them out. Allow no memory to survive. Erase them from history.”*

“It shall be done, Eldest.”

***

Pepper awoke to a bath of Tarragon's strong, confident aroma. *“Pepper, smell deep and true. You'll eventually share a single consciousness, similar to Valerian's voice in your mind. Perhaps you'll be a voice in the monster's mind, too, although the scientists believe you will operate below the level of its consciousness... if it has one. Learn to control the host quickly. Find out where they come from and then kill the monsters as soon as you are able. If possible, kill all of them at once."*

"Because once the aliens discover my existence..."

"They will kill you."

"I'm not afraid," Pepper said. As before, she couldn't quite make the words smell like the truth.

"After you, they will kill all of us."

Although she currently lacked a body, she felt her missing gills flutter with the odor of responsibility.

"Don't let their microbes escape, either," added Marjoram. *"Keep their digestive track contained. We can ill afford a planetary epidemic."*

"The grove will issue three blasts of ammonia, 80 layers apart. Each blast marks a third of your allotted time," Tarragon said.

"I have a time limit?"

"When the final blast sounds, the monster's mind will be only a dozen layers away from full integration with yours. We do not know how the new whole will behave. Therefore, you must ensure all the monsters are dead by the third blast. Your own life ends three layers later."

Pepper had suspected as much. *"For the good of the grove,"* she said.

Tarragon's aroma changed and took the edge off Pepper's fears, leaving her relaxed but not sleepy. Each of the Elder's words smelled crisp. *"I'll make minor enhancements to the monster's body. These will not alter its shape or its smell. The alterations may give you an advantage. You won't need to eat flesh, but I encourage you to try, if that is their normal behavior."*

"Thank you, Eldest."

"Do not thank me! I send you to your death."

Tarragon's aroma faded, replaced by the scent of Nasturtium. *"Tarragon has advised you to kill them all at the same time. Perhaps with a poison gas."*

"That would kill me, too. But if that method is foolproof, and I can leave the information for you to retrieve, I will do it."

"Don't. None of us know with certainty how quickly their bodies will succumb to poisons, nor what actions they might take in a final fit of rage and frustration. They could kill Sage."

"And Narcissus," Pepper said.

"Yes, of course."

"What do you suggest, then?"

"Kill one at a time, ensuring no witnesses—use plenty of deodorant. If possible, make each death seem accidental. If that isn't practical, leave a trace of a different monster's scent to divert suspicion from you. I have no doubt the monsters fight among themselves."

Pepper wondered if Nasturtium might have been a better choice for the mission but kept the thought to herself. *"Thank you, Elder."*

Marjoram covered Pepper with a gentle, soothing perfume. *"Our thoughts and prayers go with you. Your parents would be proud, as are we."*

Chapter 36

Grove Time: Reign of Tarragon. Ring 2,241. Layer: N/A

The body of the monster hovered in neutrally buoyant antiseptic mud surrounded by a hundred tendrils of Tarragon's roots. One tendril currently filled the creature's mouth and extended into its lungs, providing an oxygen-nitrogen mixture laced with additives to keep it alive but unconscious.

Pepper's brain floated in a bubble of life-sustaining sap while Tarragon connected the two brains with an intricate network of conductive fibers compatible with both biologies. He next inserted her memories. The process—replacing the monster's skeletal tissue with layers of carbon balls holding her memories—although simple in theory, proved difficult in execution. Proper functioning required perfect placement, and a constant electric charge was needed to prevent spontaneous breakdown. The composite brain would take over that task once the memories were connected. He also established a process for storing new memories.

Tarragon labored long and alone. The wind carried no conversations. The thick coating of sunscreen that shielded other plants from burns and abrasions also shut down their memory production and photosynthesis, inducing a state of disjointed, unremembered dreams. Tarragon couldn't afford the luxury of sunscreen. He needed full awareness and all his chemical reservoirs to manufacture the proteins and related compounds necessary for the surgery.

Fierce UV light withered his leaves. Some broke and blew away. Ulcers formed on the bald patches. Sap could keep his dome intact for awhile, but he needed most of the sap to keep Pepper and the monster alive through the operation.

He precisely executed thousands of fundamental alterations at the organic, cellular, and genetic levels, none of which could be allowed to change the creature's smell or external shape. He had much to do and only a few hundred layers to do it. Worse, he lacked an accurate way to pace himself as the wind tore away layers as fast as they formed. Memory loss became problematic as well, but he compensated by dumping prodigious quantities of memory dust on the leeward side of his stem.

He snaked a tendril into the creature's nasal passage and spent considerable time expanding and redesigning the olfactory bulb to allow recognition of several hundred thousand distinct odors. He modified salivary glands to allow production of several thousand distinct chemicals necessary for communication—and to create poisons Pepper might need to perform her mission.

He worked quickly and diligently on the other modifications required for the harmonious integration of the two species. The sunlight ceased to burn. He could not remember a more absolute lack of sunlight. The wind raged with unrelenting fury.

He held Pepper's naked brainstem in his roots, reluctant to close the cranial cavity. It felt wrong to place this innocent, naïve child inside the body of a monster; to join her brain to one that knew only a lust for violence; to force her to adopt its obscene, murderous behavior. Regret seemed too weak a scent to describe his emotion. Obligation had never smelled more bitter.

He had no desire to live with such a burden of guilt or to pass that memory on to others. Fortunately, the storm would take his life. When sunlight returned, it would not be to Tarragon's 2,242nd ring as Eldest, but to Nasturtium's first ring as reigning elder. And Pepper, alas, would wake into a living nightmare.

At the back of the creature's sinus cavity, he added an inch-wide bladder filled with a fast-acting neurotoxin. The bladder would rupture in 243 layers. Pepper wouldn't want to live as a monster, but she might not have the strength of will to take her own life after her brain fused completely with that of the monster. This gift would spare her from such a curse.

A final change remained: converting the monster's lymphatic system to a more robust regenerative system based on sap, which Tarragon supplied by emptying his dome. Now the monster—no, it had become a symbiont, their hope of salvation—could live many layers without oxygen. It would sleep until the storm passed.

Tarragon knew he would not live to experience that moment. The end came quickly, as the sandstorm turned his unhealed sores into gaping holes and tore away ever larger chunks of his dome. A thousand tiny reservoirs of acid and alkali ruptured and added to the destruction.

He let the wind claim his memories.

***

Nasturtium endured the pain. Sustained levels of above-normal UV radiation produced a semi-autonomous secretion of protective lotion that would harden and eventually flake off. Nasturtium let the thick fluid flow over his dome, but exhaled vigorously to keep his stem clear. The excess lotion sprinkled the ground, and he stirred it into a paste. The paste formed large clumps, which he pushed into place. In this way he built two walls.

He risked losing his memories, possibly his life, if the wind intensified before he finished. Help was out of the question. Other plants were already asleep in their shells, dreaming dreams they would not remember. Only the Eldest remained naked and awake, forcing Nasturtium to work in stealth, creating as little disturbance as possible. Fate was kind to have positioned his birth downwind of Tarragon.

The first wall would divert the wind so that instead of the Eldest's memories blowing by out of reach, they would be channeled to Nasturtium. Unfortunately, storm winds blew too fast to allow memories to be captured. Worse, the abrasive wind would eat away his unprotected stem.

Nasturtium designed the second wall to prevent that. It formed a semi-circular enclosure to slow the wind enough for heavier abrasive particles to drop out yet allow memory dust to remain suspended—and swirling close enough to absorb.

The storm would erode the walls quickly, but they only needed to last long enough to capture the memories of Tarragon's outer ring. After that, Nasturtium would cover his stem sunscreen and join the others in hibernation.

He finished the walls. Eddies of wind tugged at his dome as a thousand internal voices begged him to tear the walls down. He ignored the ancient warnings and waited for Tarragon to die.

***

"*Eldest, are you all right?*" asked Marjoram.

Nasturtium felt the last drop of protective shell peel and drop away. "*Yes, I'm fine,*" he lied. His plans had nearly come undone when an unexpected blast of sand and pebbles gouged out a chunk of his dome. Before he could heal the breach, the wind burrowed beneath the sunscreen shell, creating a vortex above his dome that ripped away most of his leaves and siphoned off much sap.

None of that mattered. Sunshine would replenish sap and heal wounds. What mattered was that he now had the secret memories of the creature's genetic code. Let the enemy grove beware— Nasturtium could grow monsters, too.

"*Has everyone survived the storm?*" he asked, and then answered his own question by sniffing deeply, identifying each individual in the grove. As expected, only Tarragon had perished. The melancholy scent of charcoal and cut grass clung to the air, refusing to drift away.

"*We miss Tarragon,*" Nasturtium said. "*His sacrifice will not be in vain. The symbiont will soon awake, and it will rid our land of monsters. As your new Eldest, I pledge to—*"

His speech was interrupted by popcorn and peppermint excitement as the grove picked up a familiar aroma. One of the missing plants.

"*I can smell you!*" shouted Narcissus. "*But you're far away!*"

Nasturtium puffed out a response, and the grove chanted his words in unison. "*Narcissus, are you hurt? Have you smelled Sage?*"

Almost two layers passed before the answer came. "*Yes and yes. In fact, I have managed to establish contact with the creatures. As I suspected, they communicate with mathematics.*"

"*Do not cooperate with the enemy,*" Nasturtium said. "*Our counter-attack is about to start.*"

"*Finally! I'm ready to be rescued.*"

"*How is Sage?*"

"Oh, he's here with me, trapped inside scentless, impenetrable walls. He wants me to maintain contact with the creatures. He says more communication is needed, not less."

"Tell him there will be NO further contact," commanded Nasturtium.

Narcissus's scent diminished, but the grove could still make out anger-scented words. *"I'm just following orders. Stop hitting me! I swear, I'll spray the monster if you touch me again."*

Nasturtium prepared to shout a reminder to his son about duty and obedience. Before he could puff the words, Marjoram spoke.

"The symbiont is awake."

Part Three:

INTERACTION

Chapter 37

Ship Time: Day 18. 0900 hours.

Jonas rose from oblivion into awareness of a massive, hostile presence. He tried to rouse himself from the nightmare, but the presence controlled him. He couldn't move, couldn't see, couldn't hear. Helpless as a puppet, all he could do was think. The presence tried to control even this, plucking at his memories like the strings of a guitar.

A fish struggled feebly on the utility table next to the dock.

"Gut it," said his father, pressing the handle of a knife into JJ's twelve-year-old hand. "It will make you feel better. Then we'll cook it for lunch."

Jonas usually enjoyed fishing with his father, but not that day. Jonas didn't want to kill the fish. He wanted his mother back. He missed her voice, her touch, her smell. He had dropped the knife, ran back to the mansion, and barricaded himself in his room.

This time, he couldn't drop the knife.

"Redeem yourself," said Tobias in a voice that smelled like potpourri.

Jonas clutched the knife more tightly, trying desperately to throw it away.

"It's all right," said a female voice. *"I'm with you."* The voice smelled gentle and firm like his mother, but Mom was dead, *dead*, and killing a stupid fish wasn't going to make him feel better. He fought for control, to make his fingers loosen, but the voice said, *you must*. It seemed to come from inside his own head.

Jonas's free hand reached out to steady the fish. The knife hand hesitated, then stabbed the fish and cut a clean line down its front.

The fish stared up with black, unblinking eyes. The female voice in his head smelled pleased.

Jonas screamed and awoke from one nightmare into another. A million shards of glass pierced his eyes and gouged furrows under the lids. The pain set off false sparkles of light in a world of blackness, a world that abraded every square inch of skin as if he'd been wrapped in sandpaper. Liquid rushed into his open mouth, sent tributaries into his nostrils, and proceeded to drown him.

He jerked, more by instinct than deliberate thought, expecting restraints but finding none. He kicked his legs and paddled his arms through the syrupy mud, hoping that he headed toward the surface, hoping he wasn't too deep, hoping most of all that the tentacles wouldn't return to drag him back to a hell of eternal darkness and invisible fire.

His arms thrust into open air, into freedom and coolness. His head cleared the surface. He coughed out black bile then sucked in air with wheezing, shuddering gasps. The burning eased in his lungs. He pulled himself from the pit and rolled onto his back. The beautiful orange sun made his skin tingle. He stared at it in amazement. He blinked and sat up, aware his eyes no longer hurt. His skin didn't burn either, though it looked darker. He was naked. *Jesus Christ, what happened to me?*

The place smelled different. Of course it did. He'd always worn a biosuit with its own air supply. He reached out to a mound of loose soil, felt the dampness at its base, and scooped up a handful. He sniffed several times, the elusive fragrance swirling up a childhood memory. The gardener, off-track in his mowing, had cut down the flowers lining the walkway to the mansion. Jonas had picked one up and sniffed, but its fragrance was lost in the thick aroma of cut grass.

He dropped the dirt and began to sob. *Shock. I'm in shock.*

The surrounding mushroom-like plants made him uneasy and kindled a sense of urgency that drove away the shock. *I need Cassie.* He staggered upright, fighting vertigo, and looked for the ship. The *Far Traveler* beckoned from a hundred yards away. He took a step toward it. Wobbled. Took another. The vertigo receded. The soil felt delicious beneath his bare feet.

***

Cassie sat on the edge of her bed wondering how Tobias would take the news of her pregnancy so soon after his son's death. Hell, she wasn't yet sure how she felt about it.

"Excuse the interruption," Adam said on the ship-wide page. "But Mr. Jefferson is approaching the ship."

"If this is a joke, I will personally amputate your humor circuits."

"No joke, Dr. Clearwater. My facial recognition subroutine is one hundred percent confident that it is Jonas Jefferson."

Cassie dashed to the airlock and suited up. She opened the door and stepped outside. A hundred meters away stood Jonas. Her heart raced to him, but her body stood paralyzed as the joy of this miracle fried every nerve of her body.

Doc appeared beside her. "Knock me down and call me shorty."

His words broke the paralysis, or maybe it was seeing Jonas stumble. She started toward him. Max blocked her way.

"Clearwater."

"Don't Clearwater me. Move."

"You want to help him. So do I. But we do it by the book."

She held both fists tight against her thigh. "Get out of my way."

"Explain it to her, Doc."

"She knows already. She has blinders on."

"Know what?" Cassie said. Why weren't they helping Jonas?

"Contamination protocol," Doc said. "He needs to be quarantined."

"Oh, come on! It's Jonas."

"I know, I know. But what's happened to him?" Doc asked. "He could've picked up a microbe. The bacteria you identified. We can't let him aboard until we know he's clean."

"And sane," said the captain. "He was buried alive for three days."

"He can't stay outside. He needs food, clothes." She stared pointedly at the doctor. "Medical attention."

Max nodded. "Put a cot on the hot side of the lab. He stays there until Doc says he's clean."

"Fine. I'll take him there now."

The captain looked at her for a second, and then stepped aside.

She ran to Jonas. The ground, damp and firm from the recent rain, no longer tried to pull the boots from her feet. It was as though the planet knew JJ belonged to her and had returned him to her. She'd figure out later what happened to his biosuit. In fact... she unfastened her helmet and tossed it aside.

A thousand smells assaulted her nose as if a spice bomb had exploded inside a florist shop. Strong smells, subtle smells, some familiar and many strange, every one alive and potent, seemed out of context with the black, sterile landscape. She pushed the observation to the back of her mind.

She wrapped her arms around Jonas. She laughed, cried, kissed his face. He flinched, but she couldn't let go, couldn't stop blubbering. His arms gathered her in, tentative at first, and then tightly. They kissed. They kissed a long time, and every second she prayed that this wasn't a dream; or, if it was, that she'd never wake up.

Eventually—reluctantly—she pulled back, took his hands, and looked into his eyes. They were full of tears, even as he smiled and squeezed. She grinned as matching tears ran down her cheeks. She led him to the lab. Everything would be fine now. Everything.

***

He let Cassie support him as they walked, her shoulder under his, putting the top of her head near his nose. The scent of her hair comforted him with familiar memories of basking in the afterglow of lovemaking.

The lab was a bright yellow that bothered his eyes. It wasn't pain but a sense of strangeness, as if he were seeing the lab for the first time and trying to make sense of it. The Velcro made a ripping noise as Cassie pulled open the flap. Jonas squinted against the LED ceiling panels that glowed so much brighter than the twilight sun. The captain's voice boomed from hidden speakers.

"Cassie, that was stupid."

"Helping JJ?"

"Now you're both in quarantine. Stupid."

"The air is harmless."

"You'd better hope so. How's Jonas?"

"I'm fine, Captain," Jonas said.

"You're both barred from the ship until Doc proves you aren't infected with something. Then I'll think about letting you back inside."

"Do what you need to do, Captain," Cassie said. "I need to look after Jonas." She jabbed a button on a wall panel. "There. We have privacy now."

JJ looked around while drawing a slow, deep breath. The plastic walls of the lab didn't smell. It felt sterile, dead except for the two of them. He took another breath. Something was missing, something important, but he wanted to linger on Cassie's scent, complex and layered with mysteries and revelations. "You're not invisible anymore."

Cassie cocked her head. "What an odd thing to say."

"I'm waxing poetic after a near-death experience." He took another breath and tried to focus. Stale odors came to him, familiar smells he didn't recognize. Smells that should be much stronger. The faintness made him uneasy.

"What, do I have BO?"

"Where are they?"

"Everybody's on the ship, Jonas."

Her intense gaze made him feel like one of her lab rats. His pulse quickened and his palms sweated as if hiding a secret. He smelled his own fear.

"Jonas, do you feel okay?"

"Yeah."

An uncertain smile flickered on her face. The smell of her fear merged with his own and the rational part of his mind realized the craziness of it all. He made a sweeping bow. "Jonas Jefferson. Lover, pilot, poet, billionaire. At your service."

Her tension seemed to ease. "Says the naked man."

"You smell like perfume. I bet you taste like..." the words stopped, his throat suddenly paralyzed with disgust. He regained control and tried to pass it off as a trailing suggestive thought.

She handed him a biosuit. "Put this on. I'll have someone get clothes from your cabin later."

He slipped into the orange jumpsuit, skipping the boots, gloves, and helmet. Cassie sat on the undamaged table. Jonas sat on a stool. They held hands, hers warm and gentle, his alternately tentative and squeezing. She looked down at his hands. The palms were as black as the rest of his body. Her smile faltered. "What happened to you, Jonas?"

"My skin? I don't know." *Vision is an amazing sense.*

"You've been buried three days." She lifted his chin and stared into his eyes. "Your body has changed. We need to know how and why. Tell me what happened."

Memories flashed by: gasping for breath as the air tank went dry... hundreds of worms burrowing into the suit, tickling his body, then burning... the terrible burning as they ate his flesh.

"Jonas?"

"I don't remember."

The door flap opened and Robbie rolled in, piled high with lab equipment and the plant and animal specimens. "Welcome back, Mr. Jefferson. Dr. Clearwater, the captain orders you to turn on the video and audio surveillance and leave it on."

"Thanks, Adam," Cassie said. She made no move toward the intercom.

Jonas pulled free of her hands and walked to Robbie. He lifted the lid to the caged plant and animal, barely noticing Cassie's shout of warning.

There was the missing smell. A tickle in his throat made him cough, and an odd odor wafted from his mouth. Smells poured out of the open plant box. Disturbing images leaped into his mind, images without shape or form but full of pain, anger, and frustration.

Cassie pushed him away and dropped the lid into place. "Don't do that again! They're dangerous."

"Sorry." She was right, of course, but he forced a smile to hide the fear. It wasn't the plant or the animal that frightened him. It was her.

Chapter 38

Ship Time: Day 18. 1000 hours.

Cassie's computer displayed the live image of the crew gathered in the Mess Hall. Their unsmiling faces stared at the camera—at her—with occasional uneasy glances to one another. Cassie kept her voice light. "I don't see the necessity of being quarantined. I've finished analyzing the air, water, and soil. Nothing is toxic. The bacterial species is not infectious." She glanced at Jonas, napping on the cot that she'd jury-rigged. "Think of what he's been through."

Max said, "I am. I don't think you are."

"What's that supposed to mean?"

He nodded toward Doc, who said, "Three days with no food, water, or air. Intense solar radiation. He could not have survived."

"Well, he's tough." Cassie spread her arms, gesturing vaguely at the world. "Maybe it's something in the soil or the plants. Something beneficial." She thought of how quickly Mr. Jones had healed. "The important thing is that he's not contagious. I've run tests. He's cleaner than we are. Even intestinal microbes are way down."

Doc nodded, though his mouth was set in a frown. "Another surprise I'm not totally comfortable with. Make sure he eats yogurt with live culture."

Lyra said, "Maybe he was dead. The monsters killed him, sucked out his brains, and brought him back to life as a zombie."

Cassie started to laugh, saw Lyra was serious, and the humor escalated from funny to ridiculous to hysterical. The laugh shook her belly for half a minute before she brought it under control. "Lyra, it's JJ, not some doppelganger."

Lyra opened her mouth but Li placed her hand on the engineer's. "Lyra, it is wrong to keep Jonas caged like an animal. He should come back aboard the ship."

Cassie welcomed the unexpected ally, but Li's wiles didn't sway the captain.

"Contagious or not, we don't know what happened to Jefferson. He stays in the lab."

"Get serious, Captain," Cassie said. "You planning to leave him here when we take off?"

Doc said, "There's his old man to consider."

Max drummed his fingers. Tap, tap...tap. "Give him a complete physical. If he gets a clean bill of health, I'll consider letting him come aboard."

Lyra protested. Doc lifted his hands in mollification. "I'll do a DNA test to make sure he's human. Plus X-rays, blood work, et cetera. But some results won't be ready until morning."

"This planet does not have mornings," Li said. "Or nights, either."

"Ship's time," Doc said.

"Put him in handcuffs," Lyra said. "Constant video surveillance. I don't want him changing me into a pod person while I sleep." Her face filled the laptop's screen. "You swear it's really Jonas? You know for sure with all your heart and brain?"

Cassie felt a lump form in her throat. She swallowed. "It's JJ."

"Why the hesitation?" Lyra asked.

"It's Jonas, it really is. But there have been a couple changes."

Lyra's right hand formed a fist that slapped repeatedly into her left. "Like what?" Everyone leaned closer.

"Minor, cosmetic. Nothing significant."

Max growled. "Clearwater."

"Really, Captain. Just minor stuff. His skin is darker than before. Probably a reaction to the soil."

"What else?" Doc asked. "Be specific."

"His navel is gone. No belly button." Her anxiety rose as the crew exchanged worried glances.

"He's a clone," Lyra said.

Doc grimaced. "Anything else?"

Cassie hesitated again, knowing it hurt their chances of getting back aboard ship, but Doc would find out during the physical. "His foreskin grew back. He's no longer circumcised."

For a moment no one reacted. Then a smile began at the edge of the captain's mouth and kept growing until he burst out laughing. Lyra scowled. Doc chuckled, and then asked, "Did you make sure everything still works properly?"

Li, totally serious, said, "Perhaps we should abort the mission and take Jonas back to Earth immediately. He may need medical attention. Such changes... are not natural."

Cassie hoped Li remained an ally. "She's right, Captain. Doc should do a physical, but there might be subtle changes that we don't have the equipment to find. In two weeks, Jonas could be in the best hospital on Earth."

"No."

"Captain..."

"No. One, we find out exactly what's been changed in Jefferson. We are NOT going to allow him aboard if there's the slightest chance he's contagious or otherwise dangerous. Two, we're here to mine for diamonds and the hold is less than a quarter full. Three, we evaluate the suitability of the planet for colonization and mining. Future humans won't take kindly to underground, acid-spitting monsters."

Cassie blinked. "But the animals are intelligent. Numbers. Language."

"So you say. But you haven't provided proof."

"I need time—"

The look on the captain's face killed her request.

Doc cleared his throat. "Just thought of a problem. I'll need to take X-rays, but the one in sickbay isn't portable, and the one in the lab is too small."

"I can help," Lyra said. Every turned to her with surprise. "Hey, I don't trust him, but I want the facts. I'll modify the ground penetrating radar on Robbie to use on Jonas."

"Without killing him?" asked Cassie.

"Until we have to." Lyra's smile was anything but reassuring.

***

Jonas stretched out on the cot, interlaced his fingers behind his head, and stared at the ceiling of the lab. He was tired and ached all over, but feared if he fell asleep he'd wake up buried in the ground. Knowing the fear was irrational didn't help. Fortunately, music did. The soothing rhythms absorbed his mind and gave fear less places to take root.

Subtle aromas from the plant and the animal also seemed to have a rhythm, a complex pattern that shifted and flowed between the cages. He wondered if he was part of the pattern; he could smell his own body odor wax, wane, and change. Like music, the aromatic patterns felt comforting, and he let his eyes close.

"*Something just happened,*" Pepper said.

"*What?*" asked Narcissus.

"*I can't see anymore.*"

"*What is 'see'?*"

"*I can't hear either.*"

"*Pepper, you're not making sense.*"

"*I need to get the eyes open. There.*" The host body stared at the ceiling again. She tried to sit up, but managed only a few spastic tics. She had lost motor control. The host mind was unresponsive; jumbled snippets of sights and sounds, tinged with emotions, mostly fear and pain.

The snippets came from an unsuspected part of the human mind, one that lurked in the depths of its brain, bigger and more powerful than the conscious mind. This *subconscious* mind was a juggernaut, a massive internal construct that the scientists had missed.

Pepper braced for battle, but the new mind ignored her. The bits of sensory data seemed random and imaginary. Furthermore, the host brain had disconnected control of the voluntary muscles. She plumbed the memories—a tedious process without help from the host's consciousness—and learned about sleep and dreams.

A natural process, one that she could use to her advantage. The monsters would be easier to kill while they slept once she gained entry to their nest.

It would be many hours before she mastered control of this body without participation of its consciousness. *Hours.* What a confusing and artificial unit. Time should be measured in natural biological units, like puffs, layers, and rings. But these were aliens with alien concepts. For now, Pepper tried to relax and experience the dreams, even the dark and terrifying ones, pretending they were entertainment, much like Narcissus's stories.

The snippets coalesced into a nightmare of plants dying and burning. The smell was pervasive, terrifying, and growing stronger. Something shook him and he screamed. He jerked upright, completely awake, colliding with a startled Cassie.

On the table beside her sat a tray of steaming vegetables and sliced meat. He doubled over with dry heaves.

Chapter 39

Ship Time: Day 18. 1200 hours.

The lab's flap opened and a figure in an orange biosuit stepped inside, carrying a small black bag. The figure turned toward Jonas and waved its free hand. "Welcome back, slacker."

Jonas recognized Doc's face inside the helmet. He smiled without putting much warmth into it.

"He's not contagious," Cassie said.

JJ found it reassuring that she wore no protective gear. Her jeans, t-shirt, and sandals helped him pretend things were normal.

"Maybe you should wait outside, Cassie," Doc said.

"When everyone thinks JJ's a monster? No. I'll stay right here."

"Suit yourself." Doc sat on a chair and faced Jonas. "I need to examine you to see if there are any adverse effects from your recent, ah, incident."

JJ sniffed, swallowed hard, and fought down his nervousness. There was nothing to be nervous about. He'd known Doc for over a year. "Go ahead."

Doc opened his bag and set various instruments on a nearby table top. He picked up a tiny flashlight and had JJ follow the light with his eyes. Then Doc shone the light into each of JJ's eyes. "This would be so much easier and faster in sickbay, but Captain Bligh says I need to do house calls." Doc proceeded to check JJ's ears, mouth, throat, temperature, pulse, blood pressure, and reflexes. Vision and hearing tests followed. Then he said, "Okay, strip."

Jonas stood and removed the coveralls. The anxiety spiked to the point of panic. *What if they find out?*

"You okay, Jonas?" asked Cassie.

The voice in his head was gone. Residual shock? "Yeah. Fine."

Doc touched JJ's abdomen, the spot where his navel used to be. Doc pressed then leaned back, frowning.

"What's wrong?" asked Cassie. Her face showed more than a hint of concern.

"These gloves don't allow enough tactile sensation." The look on Doc's face was like that of a child on a diving board for the first time. "I sure hope we're right about him not being contagious." He took off his helmet and peeled off the suit and gloves.

He donned a pair of surgical gloves then placed both hands on JJ's abdomen. He pressed. "Any pain?"

"No." Jonas hesitated, then blurted, "How did I survive?"

"That's the million-dollar question. Two hundred thousand after taxes." Doc inspected the skin on JJ's arms and hands. "You're black as the plants, Jonas. Like someone left you in the oven too long. Add to that the missing navel and regrown foreskin, and you have a serious creep factor. Turn your face to the left." Doc gripped his testicles. "Cough."

Jonas did, and then said, "I should have suffocated."

Cassie, back turned from this portion of the exam, said, "My theory is that the liquid surrounding you contained a high percentage of dissolved oxygen. Like the perfluorocarbon used by deep sea divers."

"Hmmm. Interesting idea," Doc said. "Get a sample of that fluid. Showing how Jonas survived will help ease the tension in some of the crew."

The lab flap opened and two more orange-dressed people entered. Cassie moved to block their view.

Doc frowned. "Well, if it isn't the Wit sisters. Dim and Nit. Don't you know better than to interrupt a doctor when he's with a patient?"

Lyra flipped up her middle finger. "Robbie's ready. It's too crowded in here, so we set up outside."

Li held a shirt and pair of jeans in her hands, both neatly folded. She tried to slip around Cassie, but didn't make it. "I'll take those, Li. Thanks."

Doc grunted. "Fine. We'll be out in a few minutes. Jonas, you can get dressed."

"Did I pass?" asked JJ. He sniffed. Something strange permeated the air.

Doc looked puzzled. "You catching a cold?"

"Smelled something." He slipped on the clothes Cassie handed to him.

"My cologne. It drives Li wild." Doc winked. "I need to take urine, blood, and tissue samples. Then we'll go outside for the X-rays." He collected the samples and repacked his bag. "Have you experienced any new or unusual pain? Changes in eating or sleeping patterns?"

JJ felt torn between a desire to open up to the doctor and a sharp feeling of dread—a premonition that something bad would happen if he talked.

"He's been sniffing a lot," Cassie said.

"I noticed. Probably an allergy to the dust. Does it hurt? Any burning? Shortness of breath?"

Don't say anything. JJ gave a start at the voice in his head and wondered if he was becoming schizophrenic. This wasn't a time for secrets. "Sometimes there are thoughts in my head, only they're not like voices. They're smells. The weird thing is that I understand them. Sometimes as words. Sometimes feelings or images."

Doc raised an eyebrow. "Worried you're going crazy?"

JJ nodded. "When I smell things, I get more images, more clarity. Better vibes."

"It is called synesthesia. The senses get cross-wired."

"I can smell things I couldn't smell before." The odor came from Doc's pores. JJ put a hand on Doc's arm. "Traces of things intended to be secret."

Doc pulled away. "Synesthesia expressed as smells is very rare, but not dangerous."

"Is it permanent?" Chemistry had never been interesting to JJ, but thoughts of molecular patterns, valences, neuron receptors, and metabolic by-products spun through his mind like NASCAR racers. That smell came from the breakdown of a drug. He didn't know the name but knew it affected signal transmission in nerves.

"I'm not a specialist in the field. Anything else?"

"Sorry. What did you say?"

Doc raised an eyebrow. "I asked if anything else is bothering you."

"No."

"He won't eat," Cassie said. She pointed to the untouched plate.

A wave of nausea rippled through JJ's stomach. He turned away. "I don't want to eat."

Doc said, "I made dinner tonight, Jonas. My cooking is superb. Better than getting your food through an IV or a feeding tube."

JJ forced a smile. *Fit in.* "Okay, I'll eat."

"Good. Now, let's get the X-ray before the prima donna and the Amazon warrior get their panties in a bunch."

Jonas said, "Cassie, let Li and Lyra know we'll be out in a minute."

Cassie looked at him, eyes slightly narrowed, but she turned and left.

"What's on your mind, Jonas?" asked Doc.

"You need some help. I can provide it."

"What are you talking about?"

"The drug you're taking. I think there's a better variant."

Doc scowled. "What did Tobias tell you?"

Jonas leaned back. "Dad? Nothing."

"I don't care what you know or think you know. My medications are not your concern."

"I'm trying to help."

A muscle twitched in Doc's cheek. "Without a clean bill of health, you don't get back on the ship. You'll be marooned here. Got it?" Doc turned and walked out, leaving a trail of fear and adrenaline. Jonas reluctantly followed.

Lyra had built a small ramp to a platform suspended half a meter above the ground. Robbie waited atop the platform. The space underneath was open, and a plastic tarp was spread on the ground. "Okay pod-man," Lyra said. "Crawl underneath."

"Face up or down?"

Doc snapped, "Doesn't matter. Down."

Jonas took a deep breath. He stiffened in surprise. Voices came from the grove. Mysterious voices in a silent tongue.

"Jonas?" Cassie said.

"Can we do this without Lyra and Li here?"

Lyra looked at Li, who showed no signs of leaving.

"My patient wants privacy," Doc said. "Thanks for setting up the X-ray. I'll take it from here."

Lyra looked ready to fight, but Li stroked Lyra's arm and led her back to the ship. Doc watched them go. "I didn't know you were modest, Jonas."

"Just scared," JJ said. "Out here, it's like the plants are talking. I can almost understand them. But it's all in smells."

"Must stink."

"You know how in a crowd you can pick out separate threads of conversation? It's something like that. Only different, more persistent." JJ struggled to find the right explanation. "Think of watching the financial feeds, each stock scrolling by in a band with its own font and size and color, moving at its own speed. Now imagine there are dozens of these bands, even hundreds, and instead of numbers, it's words that scroll by. Some of the bands converse with one another. Sometimes words jump from one band to another, sometimes they loop around and repeat."

Cassie asked, "What are they saying?"

Doc said, "It's a manifestation of the synesthesia."

Jonas looked thoughtful. "But it feels like words, a foreign language."

"Gibberish is what it is," Doc said. "Crawl under the stand so we can get the X-ray." Doc stepped on top the ramp to stare at the display screen. Cassie sat cross-legged on the ground and watched Jonas.

"The resolution stinks. It's made to map underground rocks and minerals, not human organs and bones."

"Can you make out anything?" asked JJ.

"Ah... no. Li might be able to enhance the resolution. I'll let you know in the morning. I'll let everyone know in the morning, before breakfast." Doc hopped off the platform, but his knees buckled and he fell to the ground. "Damn gravity." He rose, using the platform for support. "The lab results will be finished. If the results are benign, we'll all dance a jig and sing hallelujah."

"You saw something on the X-ray," Cassie said.

"You can come out now, Jonas," Doc said. "Robbie, turn off audio surveillance. And don't record this yourself, either. This is doctor-patient stuff."

"Surveillance and recording are off, Doctor Unger. Wave when you're ready for me to resume."

"Cassie, you better go, too."

JJ objected. "Whatever you have to say, we both want to hear it." He sat beside Cassie and gripped her hand.

The Doctor's face grew grim. "I'm pretty sure you have a tumor."

JJ felt Cassie's hand tighten. She sucked in a noisy breath.

Doc continued. "Plum size mass, deep, far side of the sinus cavities. Possibly extending to the thalamus."

"Why didn't you catch it before we left Earth?" Jonas asked.

Doc pursed his lips. "It wasn't there before we left. I checked your X-rays two days before lift-off."

Jonas smelled no hint of deception. "How long do I have?"

"I don't know whether it's benign or malignant."

"Oh, come on. Nothing good grows that fast."

"I'm sorry, Jonas. Maybe the enhanced X-rays will show I'm wrong. The lab tests include protein markers for cancer. If they're negative, well, that will be good."

"The synesthesia. Could the tumor be causing that?"

Doc rubbed his chin. "Maybe. Probably."

"If it is cancer... can you operate?"

Doc touched his shoulder with surprising gentleness. "We don't have the facilities for major surgery, especially so close to the brain. But chances are it's benign. I'll have results at oh-seven hundred. Assuming they're normal, you can eat breakfast in the mess with the rest of us. Even if the mass is cancerous, we're only a couple weeks from Earth, ship time." He lay a reassuring hand on JJ's shoulder, then turned away and waved. "Come on, Robbie."

The cart rolled off the ramp and followed Doc to the ship.

Cassie pointed at a star. "Home. Right where we left it." Jonas didn't reply, though he recognized his words from days ago being parroted back to him. His gaze fell to the bleak terrain and his thoughts fell to dark outcomes.

Chapter 40

Ship Time: Day 18. 1300 hours.

"You want what?" Cassie said. Max had to be joking. Maybe the intercom was malfunctioning.

"You ought to be happy, Clearwater. This is a chance to prove Jefferson is still a healthy, productive member of the crew."

"By having him dig for diamonds? Think what he's been through. Doc won't allow it."

"He already did. There's nothing preventing Jefferson from having moderate physical activity. The two of you can work as a team, and if you see him getting winded, take a ten-minute break."

"You're an asshole."

He laughed. "I've been called worse. Look on the bright side. Without the biosuits, it will be easier to move around, not to mention cooler. We can make up for lost time."

"Money, that's all you think about." Cassie paused. "What about the animals? They're still a threat."

"The shallows are mapped. Nothing bad can get to us, and no pits to fall into."

Cassie couldn't think of a reason to refuse, at least, none that would convince the captain. "Fine. We'll be ready in ten." She turned to Jonas.

"I heard," he said. "Actually, it might be a good idea to get out. I'm going stir crazy."

"It's only been a few hours."

"Funny how brains are wired for time. Seconds, minutes, hours, days, weeks, months. Night and day. Even when night and day don't exist, we make them exist, programming the lights to dim and brighten to match our biological rhythm."

She rarely heard Jonas talk that way about time. "Worried about the results of the tests?"

"No, not that."

"Then what?"

He shrugged. "Come on, let's go. It'll feel good to be in the sun."

Robbie had stuck small colored flags into the soil to mark the boundary of the safe area. Cassie and Jonas made their way to the ship, where the others had already assembled. Li looked ridiculous in a blue silk kimono. Doc and Max wore jeans and t-shirts. Lyra wore a full biosuit.

The work proceeded without small talk, but Cassie felt the eyes of the crew on her and Jonas. If he felt it, he gave no sign. JJ worked hard, filling his bucket faster than anyone else, and passing it to Doc, whose job had returned to being a beast of burden. Robbie patrolled the perimeter, monitoring sonar and radar arrays, but nothing prowled beneath the black sand sea.

Six hours later, Max called an end to the work and announced that Lyra would cook an Irish stew for supper.

"An old family recipe," Lyra said. "From Dinty McMoore."

Jonas and Cassie headed for the lab while the others walked toward the ship. Jonas opened the flap and entered, but before Cassie could follow, a shadow loomed next to hers on the lab's wall.

Li sidled up to her. "Cassie, we must talk."

"I'm really tired. Later, okay?"

"This cannot wait."

Cassie sighed in annoyance. She called through the flap, telling JJ she'd be a moment, then followed Li halfway around the lab and out of sight from the ship.

Li straightened her robe, pursed her lips, and narrowed her eyes. "Have you told him?"

Cassie's annoyance vanished, replaced by suspicion. "Told him what?"

"Do not play coy. Your recent nausea has not gone unnoticed. Your affection for Jonas is obvious. Nature had taken its course."

Why am I bothering to discuss the matter at all? "It's not your concern."

"I am your friend. I am here to help."

"I don't need help." Cassie turned her back on the pushy woman.

"If you love him, you will listen to my advice."

"Li, stay out of this." She stepped away.

"Do not tell him you are pregnant."

Cassie halted. *Don't tell him?* What was Li's angle?

Li's voice rose. "Ask yourself what it is that Jonas most wants. It is not you. It is not a child. Yet, being an honorable man, he would sacrifice what he truly desires in order to care for a family."

Cassie spun and in two steps stood nose to nose with Asian. "What is it, Li? What do you think he loves more than me?"

A sad smile appeared on Li's face. "He loves what you love. What you will be giving up. Look up, Cassie. Tell me what truly calls to your heart." Li's eyes glanced upward.

Points of distant lights beckoned like the call of sirens, beautiful and irresistible.

"The stars," Cassie whispered. When she lowered her gaze, Li was gone. Cassie walked around to the entrance as troubled thoughts filled her head. She understood Li's point all too well, but Jonas had a right to know. Furthermore, Cassie's inclination was to do the opposite of whatever Li suggested.

She resolved to tell Jonas immediately, but when she entered the lab, he was pacing next to the plant and the animal cages, his behavior changing chameleon-like from restlessness to fear to anger. The timing wasn't right for a life-changing announcement. Instead, she soothed his inner beast by convincing him to watch a video on the computer, a movie about early spaceships and the building of the first Mars colony.

She watched his hands unconsciously manipulate invisible controls as the rockets took flight on the screen. He found peace in that ideal world, and she couldn't bring herself to disrupt the calm. Not tonight, not now, not so soon after the miracle of getting him back.

Chapter 41

Ship Time: Day 19. 0630 hours.

She spent the night curled on the lab floor next to Jonas. When she woke at six-thirty, he was already awake. She asked how he'd slept.

"Nightmares."

"Want to talk about them?"

He shook his head.

She kissed him. "You've been through a lot but you're fine now."

"Yeah. Everything's perfect."

Cassie raised a brow. It wasn't like Jonas to be morose, especially having gone to bed happy. He seemed to sense her concern and flashed a reassuring smile.

"Jonas, I need to go to the ship. You can use the decon shower to wash. You have clean clothes on the table."

"I'm lucky to have you, Cassie."

"Don't forget it!" she said before ducking through the flap. The outside air smelled particularly foul, and her stomach lurched in complaint, reminding her that she hadn't told Jonas about the baby. Tonight she'd fix JJ a candle-lit dinner, if she could find candles and privacy.

The thought of food pushed her nausea over the top and she bent over to throw up. Why did this planet stink so bad? Hoping no one watched on the surveillance monitors, she kicked loose soil over the regurgitated remains of last night's supper. She'd used all her anti-nausea pills and would need to ask Doc for more. No need to be shy. Doc knew it was morning sickness.

She entered the ship's airlock and closed her eyes for the UV flash. The planet's foul air flushed away, and she gratefully inhaled the ship's filtered air. She stopped at her cabin to shower, brush, and change clothes before heading to the mess hall.

The rest of the crew were already there. The captain did his three-finger tap on the table. "About time, Clearwater."

"Sorry sir."

"Okay. Doc, your report."

Karl stood and cleared his throat. "Lots of good news, folks. Jonas is in almost perfect physical health. Faster reflexes, excellent muscle tone, perfect vision and hearing. Urine is normal. He is alert and responsive."

"What about his penis?" asked Lyra.

"Normal. In some ways Jonas is even better than normal. His skin is remarkably smooth and resilient, more like the skin of a child than an adult. No scar tissue, and no calluses, even on his feet. Even his tooth fillings are gone. The former cavities are now healthy, hard enamel."

"How... odd," Li said.

Lyra shook her head. "He isn't human."

"No, it's Jonas Jefferson," Doc said. "DNA is a match. Blood type is a match."

Cassie asked, "Then it's okay to let him on board?"

Doc scratched his chin and grimaced. "There are a few anomalies."

"I knew it," Lyra said.

"Shut your mouth before I shut it for you," Cassie said.

Lyra glared and snarled. She shook off Li's restraining arm and took a step toward Cassie.

The captain turned his head. "Sullivan, do as the Science Officer said."

The scowl stayed on Lyra's face, but she stopped moving.

Doc continued, "Yes, well, in addition to the healing, his skin is darker than before, nearly black, but not from melanin. I took a skin sample and examined it under high magnification. There are normally a few hundred mitochondria in a skin cell, but his cells have thousands, and their structure looks odd. I haven't figured out how they differ from normal mitochondria."

Cassie thought of the plant cells she had studied from the dome of the frozen specimen. Its cells had similar internal structures. They were biological powerhouses where chlorophyll converted sunlight to chemical energy. She kept quiet.

"He has some kind of infection," Lyra said.

"Well, it's an anomaly, but not necessarily an infection in the strict sense. The structures exist only in his skin and hair cells, they are not multiplying the way a virus would, and they don't appear to have any adverse effects. They just make his black skin blacker."

Max twirled a finger in the air.

"On the negative side, Jonas has a tumor. It's too near his brain for a biopsy, so I can't tell with certainty whether it's benign or malignant, but the proteins in his urine and blood don't show any markers for cancer. It's probably benign, though the rapid growth worries me. Determination must wait until we're back on Earth."

"Anything else?" Max asked.

"A couple things. His bones look odd on the X-ray. It doesn't impair his mobility, but I want to get a better picture from the unit in sickbay. Also, the DNA test showed something unusual."

Lyra growled.

Doc gave a single nervous laugh. "Easy girl! It's human DNA. No doubt about it. Some sequences that are normally dormant were turned on, and a few look like they've been modified. Maybe by exposure to the radiation. But the really interesting thing is the telomeres."

The fine hairs on Cassie's neck went erect.

"Telo what?" asked Li.

Doc pursed his lips. "It's a bit complicated. Cassie's a biochemist. She can explain it better, or at least simpler."

Cassie didn't want to talk, but four sets of eyes compelled her. "Simple. Okay. You all know that your body is composed of cells. During your life, each cell in your body reproduces many times by splitting into a duplicate. The split is controlled by proteins which are controlled by chromosomes, which are portions of your DNA. Unfortunately, the splitting process damages the two ends of the chromosome. If the damaged portion contains genetic information, the cell will not function properly and may even die. To delay this from happening, evolution has placed caps of repetitive DNA at those end points. Each cell division still damages the end, but there is enough redundancy to allow several divisions before the damage reaches the critical part of the genetic code. These protective end caps are called telomeres."

"Thank you, Cassie," Doc said. "The telomeres on JJ's chromosomes are smaller than normal, which implies his cells should die off faster. But they don't. They can die from damage, but they don't die from old age."

"Bottom line," Max said. "Does he present a danger to us in any way?"

The doctor smiled at Cassie. "No. He's not contagious, and he's not crazy. He's our ever-loving Jonas Jefferson."

She felt indebted to Doc. He hadn't mentioned the synesthesia or the voices Jonas was hearing. The only sound in the mess hall was the three-finger tap of the captain's fingers on the table.

Max stood. "Clearwater, tell Jefferson he's cleared for duty. He gets a daily check-up with Doc. Any unusual behavior or any sign of infection, he gets booted off the ship. Let's meet here in an hour to go over work schedules."

Lyra rose, kicked her chair across the room, and stomped out.

Doc nodded toward the door. "Li, maybe you should stick your finger in the dyke before it bursts."

Li left without comment. Cassie turned to Doc. "Did you escape her leash?"

He winked. "I'll pay for it later." His expression grew serious. "I need to talk with you. Soon."

"After I tell Jonas the good news." Cassie hurried to the airlock, smiling. They'd finally gotten through the worst of things.

Chapter 42

Ship Time: Day 19. 0715 hours.

At the sound of the flap opening, Jonas closed the lids of the cages and pretended to study a report displayed on Cassie's computer. He hated subterfuge but felt compelled to keep his affinity for the plant and animal a secret.

Cassie bounded inside. "Great news! Quarantine's over!" Her arms pulled him close for a kiss. She backed off, giggling. "Whew, BO *and* morning breath. Didn't you shower?"

"I got interested in your report. Lost track of time."

"Well, come on. You can shower on the ship."

With a last look at the captives, he followed Cassie outside. She seemed to skip across the ground, oblivious of the higher gravity. His morose mood melted under the onslaught of her exuberance, but it didn't completely evaporate. The grove smelled ominous.

They entered the ship's airlock. While they waited for the decon sequence and air flush, Cassie again pulled his face close. Their eyes closed and lips locked as the UV lamps flashed. He yelped and jerked away. His ears, hands, and back of the neck stung as if pelted by a rain of needles. Pain bit his face and he raised an arm to shield his eyes.

"What's wrong?"

"Nothing." The pain eased.

"Don't lie. Let me see your face." He dropped his arm and let her study his face and hands. She pushed up the sleeve of his coverall. "You have blisters on your exposed skin."

"Must have developed sensitivity to ultra-violet light."

"Doc said there's something unusual about your skin cells. He wants to run more tests."

He grimaced. "I'm sick of tests. I'll grab some sun block from the pharmacy."

The inner door slid open and they hurried down the corridor to his cabin. They stripped and showered, which lifted his mood and prompted Cassie to joke about his body being happy to see her. He suggested they make love, but she said the crew was waiting for him in the mess hall. He brushed his teeth, reluctantly applied deodorant, and dressed.

She inspected him. "The blisters are healed. Wow." She handed him a bottle of cologne. "Put on a splash."

He dabbed a bit on his face, sneezed, and set the bottle on the shelf. He washed his hands and complained, "It covers too much without saying a thing."

Cassie gave him a quizzical look, which he ignored. He didn't understand his own words and refused to dwell on it. She pulled him into the corridor. Jokes and laughter spilled from the mess hall into the corridor, but so did odors which triggered another bout of anxiety. The word *monsters* popped into his mind.

"You're hurting my hand," Cassie said.

"Sorry." He loosened his grip and stopped at the entrance. The smells were very strong. Bacon, eggs, coffee, juice. A wave of nausea washed over him.

Cassie pulled her hand loose and gave him a shove. "You're not contagious. Go on."

Three heads turned his way. Doc raised a glass of juice as if proposing a toast. "The prodigal son returns."

"Jefferson! Welcome back," Max said.

Li, seated next to the captain, patted the open seat next to her. JJ accepted the offer, forcing Cassie to sit on the other side of the table next to Doc. JJ noticed her irritation, but it couldn't be helped. He felt safer sitting near the exit.

"You must be starving," said Li. "You did not eat anything in the lab, and you were buried for days."

He watched anger build on Cassie's face as Li heaped scrambled eggs on his plate and added half a dozen strips of bacon. Smell drew his eyes to the plate, to the embryonic proteins destroyed by heat and the strips of animal flesh fried to a crisp.

"You look pale," Doc said. "Not easy for a black man."

They eat flesh, nothing but flesh. "I'd like some water." He averted his eyes from the food.

Tap, tap ...tap. Tap, tap ...tap. The captain's hands drew JJ's attention. Max's eyes were sharp as a raptor evaluating potential prey.

"You need coffee," Li said and poured a cup. "Black, no sugar. Correct?"

The aroma came with images of helpless seeds being roasted, crushed, and drowned. Jonas slammed the cup onto the table, shattering the ceramic mug and splashing coffee everywhere. He lurched to his feet, catching the edge of his plate and spilling eggs and bacon onto the table. He fled from the torture chamber and the ritual of digestive carnage.

***

Cassie stared with the others as JJ stomped off. "Could this be caused by the tumor?"

Doc shrugged and slurped his coffee. "Is this yesterday's swill? No wonder he left."

She stood. "I better check on him."

Doc placed a hand on her arm. "Give him a few minutes. I think it's PTSD."

"How dangerous?" Li asked.

"Post traumatic shock disorder," he said, "can be quite serious. It's like waking up and finding Lyra in bed with you."

Cassie began cleaning up the mess. "He had nightmares. He wouldn't talk about them."

"With love and patience, he'll come around. I have some medication that can help with the panic attacks. Try getting him to eat. It will help restart peristalsis."

Li said, "Perry what?"

"Not over breakfast, darling. Come by my cabin later and I'll explain."

Lyra entered the room. "Stop hitting on her. She's not interested." Lyra nodded to Cassie and Max. "Sorry I lost my temper before. What's for breakfast?"

"Eggs, if you pick the shrapnel out of them," Doc said.

Lyra frowned. "Jonas?"

Cassie finished wiping the table and put down a clean plate and utensils for the engineer. "He has a touch of PTSD. Doc says it will pass."

Lyra shook her head. "It's going to get worse."

Li said, "Should we not show compassion for someone who came so close to death? Should we not rejoice that our comrade has returned?"

"Nope." Lyra took the seat vacated by Jonas. "First off, the changes in him aren't natural. Second, he's a jackass, just like all his kind."

Max said, "What kind is that, Sullivan?" He smiled like an alligator—too many teeth, too little humor.

Lyra met his gaze. "The rich. The arrogant. People who keep you under their thumb."

Max held her stare until Lyra looked away. Then he stood. "Time for work. In pairs. Doc, you're with Jefferson. Yeah, yeah, you don't dig. Just watch him, okay? Li, it's you and Lyra, as usual. Clearwater, you're with me."

"There's lab work I need to finish. It's important."

"It always is. Tough shit. You're digging for the next eight hours. After that, if you want to hang out in the lab, fine. Same goes for tomorrow. Work before play."

Chapter 43

Ship Time: Day 19. 0800 hours.

Since none of the ship's cabins could be locked from the outside, Jonas easily slipped inside Doc's room. Drawn by scent to the desk, he pulled open a drawer and removed a prescription bottle of Propranolol. The label had several warnings.

He dumped the yellow tablets onto his palm. Their complex smell set his mind and pulse racing. He wasn't a chemist, yet knew the chemical structure of the medication, the binders, even the dyes used in the tablet. It was all there in the smell.

One moment he was looking at the pills, the next they were in his mouth, bathed in bitter saliva. He spat them onto his hand, where they foamed like a mass of golden Ossetra caviar swimming in raw egg whites. He felt sick. Insane.

Jonas grabbed a towel and dried the pills. Surprisingly, they hadn't dissolved. He wanted to throw them away but couldn't. It took several tries to put them all back in the bottle—his hands kept trembling and dropping the pills. He returned the bottle to the drawer and ran to his room. He locked the door and collapsed on the bed, wondering why he'd just tried to kill himself.

He jumped at Adam's voice. "Mr. Jefferson, the captain says it's time to work. Please join the others outside."

Jonas took a calming breath before heading to the airlock, and he stopped at the pharmacy on the way to drench his face, arms, and hair with sunblock. A bottle of anti-nausea pills caught his attention, even though his breakfast queasiness had long passed. Cassie's breath had smelled of these pills. *One monster at a time.*

The voice spooked him. It didn't feel like an errant thought or vivid memory. PTSD? Schizophrenia? His supernatural medical knowledge apparently didn't extend to his own maladies. Anxious and jittery, he hurried to the airlock, grabbed a shovel, and stepped outside to join the others in a day of digging for diamonds.

Doc said, "You're with me, flyboy." Cassie stood next to the captain, looking unhappy. The crew listened to Li's reminders on where to dig and what to look for. Lyra warned them to stay within the safe zone. Everyone nodded, grumbled, and went to work.

Jonas worked twice as hard as anyone else. It helped to distract him from the angry odors swirling out of the grove and from Doc's nervous banter and crude jokes. He worked through the breaks and through lunch.

At 1700 the captain called a halt for the day. As they packed up the tools and collection buckets, a cloud of ammonia from the grove sent the crew into coughing fits. Jonas faked a few coughs as he helped guide those blinded by watery eyes. The decon spray in the airlock set things right. The sunblock got Jonas through the UV with nothing more than a tingle.

He skipped dinner but took an apple from the galley, claiming he would eat in his room. The fruit went under a pillow. He showered, stretched out on the bed, and stared at the ceiling. His stomach growled. A glass of water helped briefly. He resumed staring at the ceiling. Dark thoughts fouled the air. *A third of my time is gone.* He sat up. What the hell did that mean?

Hoping to escape the morose feelings, he went to Cassie's cabin. She wasn't there. He sat on her bed, looking and sniffing. It smelled nicer here than his own room—fresh, alive, green. It smelled like Cassie's favorite color.

He caught scent of Burt and went to the shelf that held the small, potted cactus. He sniffed, frowned, and sniffed again. A lump squeezed his throat. Why had he given it to her—a plant that couldn't think, couldn't talk, couldn't even move? Stranger still, why did Cassie care for it, give it water and light and good soil? He felt confused. What kind of a monster was she? What kind was he?

***

Cassie spent the evening in the lab with the surviving rat. DNA tests confirmed it was indeed Mr. Jones, though he looked younger. The tests showed altered telomeres on the chromosomes, exactly like those on Jonas. What else did they have in common?

Sniffing, but that meant nothing—Mr. Jones sniffed at everything. She made a list of tests to run. Skin biopsy to look for abnormal cell structures. Protein and enzyme tests to determine biological age. She prepared syringes and biopsy needles, calibrated the lab equipment, and dove into the work.

She remembered JJ's sensitivity to ultraviolet, and plucked Mr. Jones from his cage and held him under the UV lamp. Exposure evoked only normal squeals and squirming. Neither fur nor skin blistered. She took an X-ray of its body. To Cassie's relief, the pictures showed no tumors, no abnormality of the bones or anything else. She returned Mr. Jones to his cage and spoke to him in soothing tones, thanking him for his help. She fed him a bit of cheese and a sip of golden plant sap.

Adam spoke from the lab speakers. "Dr. Clearwater, Dr. Unger wishes to speak with you. Shall I patch him through?"

"Yes, please."

"Hi Cassie. Say, do you have a few minutes to talk?" His words held a distinct slur. Tired? Or had he been into another bottle of brandy?

"About Jonas?"

"More about you. And me."

Uh-oh. Silence stretched a few seconds while she tried to come up with words. "Karl... I don't understand."

He gave a short nervous laugh. "Oh, nothing like that. There's something I need to tell you. Something I should have told you before the trip."

A dozen time sensitive medical tests were running. "Can we talk tomorrow? After breakfast?"

A short pause followed before he said, "Sure. It's waited this long. What's another night?" A beep signaled his disconnection.

An hour later she leaned back and rubbed her eyes. The results were contradictory. Like Jonas, the rat was biologically younger and healthier. It had improved telomeres but no sensitivity to UV light. The rat's mitochondria were normal. He healed with almost supernatural speed—the biopsy holes were already covered with fresh skin. JJ's blisters had healed that way.

Why should Jonas and the rat have *anything* in common? Mr. Jones hadn't been buried for three days. Or had he? The lab had partially collapsed in the storm, which may have allowed a liquid or gaseous compound in the soil to contaminate the rat cage, a chemical with astounding healing and restorative properties.

She had stopped wearing a biosuit. Had she changed as well? She could take a DNA sample of herself, but did not want to wait all night for the results. Instead, she took a large bore needle and poked a hole in the back of her left hand. The pain was about what she expected—intense. So was the bleeding. She grabbed a gauze pad and applied pressure until the bleeding finally stopped, twenty minutes later. She spent another hour in the lab waiting for the wound to heal. It didn't, even when she stuck her hand in a soil sample. She irrigated the wound with water then with alcohol and covered it with a bandage.

Nothing made sense. Exhausted and frustrated, she trudged back to the ship and headed for her cabin. She wanted JJ but wanted sleep more.

He was in her bed, asleep. She slipped off her clothes and slid into bed. She felt the warmth of his body, the tickle of his breath on her neck, and knew with all her being that this was Jonas, the man she loved. She closed her eyes and slept.

***

Pepper considered the woman sleeping beside the host body. *Start with the hardest. If I can kill her, I can kill any of them.* It was the midpoint of their species nocturnal period, the perfect time to pick them off one by one. Closed doors wouldn't be a problem— the host's memories revealed a way to bypass the locks.

Pepper leaned forward. She drew a deep breath, saturating it with a fast, painless poison. A gentle sigh would end Cassie's life.

The scent of the woman carried a hormonal marker that made Pepper hold her breath. Realization spread to the host's awareness before Pepper could suppress it. Jonas flung himself from the bed and tried to scramble out the door as Pepper fought to regain control. She forced the host back toward Cassie.

***

Cassie jerked awake, heart thumping like a war drum. Jonas loomed beside the bed, face contorted, eyes wild, hands trembling. The muscles in his neck and arms bulged.

"I can't do it." The words came from his mouth, but the voice was of a person eaten by shame and swallowed by grief. "Nasturtium was right. I cannot do this thing."

"Jonas, honey, you're talking in your sleep."

"Everyone depends on me." His right hand snapped forward to seize her left hand. He lifted it to his face. Cassie tried to pull back, but his strength overwhelmed her. He ripped the bandage from her hand. He kissed the wound and let it go. His eyes pierced her soul.

"You're pregnant."

The room spun. She was falling, sucked into a black hole, squeezed, stretched, ripped apart, smashed together. "I was going to tell you. Oh, Jonas, Jonas."

He said nothing more. Conflicting emotions rippled across his face.

She began to cry. "I don't know how this happened. What are we going to do?"

War raged on his face before settling into a sad truce. "What kind of monsters are we?"

She took his hand. "You're not a monster. You're the kindest, most honest, most loving man I know. Our baby will be perfect."

He pulled away. "Please, say nothing more."

She searched his face but found no solace there. Was he leaving her? Staying with her? Forgiving or blaming her? The sadness in his eyes masked everything she needed to know.

Jonas swayed like a tree in the wind. The news must have rocked him deeply, for she had never known him to be at a loss for words or decisiveness. He stepped away as if to exit the cabin, but he stopped, crawled into bed, wrapped his arms around her, and shushed her tears. She tentatively touched his arms, worried about his UV burns but then remembering they had healed. So had her hand. She stared at the smooth pink skin where the scab of the biopsy hole had been. She spooned into his body, wondering where fate would lead them next. Alternately fearful and hopeful, she drew strength from his presence, from the simple sound of his breathing.

Eventually, sleep stilled her thoughts.

***

Pepper tried to ignore the warmth of Cassie's body, the fragrance of her hair, the pheromones and hormones of love. *It was a mistake to start with a ... monster... who had a close emotional attachment with Jonas. The first murder must be done with detachment. Killing would get easier with practice—if he kept suspicion off of himself.*

Chapter 44

Ship Time: Day 20. 0700 hours.

"Good morning, Dr. Clearwater," Adam said. "The captain has asked me to awaken all crew members. The time is 0700."

Cassie stretched, turned, and saw she was alone. JJ's clothes lay scattered on the floor, but he wasn't in the room or the shower. "Adam, where is Jonas?"

"Mr. Jefferson is outside the ship, as are Dr. Wu and Dr. Sullivan."

Cassie dressed and hurried outside. Li and Lyra were standing a few feet away, admiring something behind the ship. Cassie joined them and turned to see what held their interest. JJ stood on a low rise, arms uplifted, facing the sun, completely naked.

"I can see why you are attracted to him," Li said. Lyra nudged an elbow into Li's side, but the Asian ignored it. "I wondered whether the sun lingered at sunrise or sunset," Li continued. "Jonas obviously thinks it is a sun *rise*." Li giggled.

Lyra started to frown, looked at Cassie, and burst into laughter.

"Jonas!" Cassie said.

He gave a start, looked around, and smiled at women. Then his eyes widened and he looked down. "Oh, shit." He turned away.

"Nice ass, also," Li said.

"Cassie, get my pants. I must have been sleep walking."

Cassie stood rooted to the spot as shame and anger forged a bitter alliance. This was her punishment for getting pregnant. It wasn't enough to just dump her; he had to publicly display his availability to the other women. Well, she didn't play games and she was done feeling guilty. He wanted it over. Fine. It was over. Paralysis ended, she marched to her cabin and opened the lower smiley where JJ kept a change of clothes.

The drawers built into the outer walls were called smilies because their backside curved slightly to conform to the hull of the ship. Cassie didn't smile when she dumped JJ's clothes in the corridor. She cried.

She'd see Doc after breakfast. She needed an abortion pill. *No. Not that.* A life grew inside her, a sacred life created by her and Jonas. How did the damn birth control pills fail? And it *wasn't* her fault alone; Jonas must have skipped wearing a condom at least once. Love was supposed to last forever, but it was tears that went on and on.

***

Max sat behind the massive desk in his cabin, and he waved Jonas toward a small unpadded chair. "That was some exhibition, Jefferson. Might even tempt Sullivan to switch sides."

"I was sleep walking."

"Right. Claim whatever you want. I had Adam cut your flasher scene from the surveillance record." He smiled. Jefferson would know there was a copy tucked away for future use. The rich boy knew how these games were played.

"Thanks," Jonas said in underwhelming appreciation.

"What do you remember about the accident?" Apprehension flashed across JJ's face, subtle and brief—a millisecond or two—but clear as a fifty-foot, three-D advertisement. What was the kid hiding?

"Nothing. It's all a blank."

"You were screaming. Was the animal biting you? Or was some kind of acid in the soil?"

"I told you, I have no memory of it."

"Clearwater found similarities between a lab rat and you. She thinks something in the soil might affect the biology of terrestrial life forms."

"What similarities?"

"You're biologically younger, faster, stronger. Quicker to heal." He drummed his fingers on the desktop. "Like you've been dunked in the fountain of youth."

Jonas squirmed in his seat. Max liked that, liked the way the pilot looked at the door, the floor, his hands. Anywhere but his captain.

"Why so nervous, Jefferson? Got something to hide?" That seemed to get his attention. Jonas finally met his gaze. JJ's eyes were wide, shifting orbs. Rich boy was definitely spooked.

"What would I be hiding?"

Max shrugged. "Something too important or too valuable to share."

"Believe me, I have nothing you want to share."

"You can't con a con man."

"I don't remember anything. How many times do I need to repeat it?"

"You're different. Changed. Maybe it's trauma. Maybe it's something else."

"I'm Jonas Jefferson. Not some monster!"

Max leaned back in his chair. *Interesting.* "No one thinks you're a monster. Well, Sullivan does, but she's a twit."

"I'm done being interrogated." Jefferson stood. "There are things I need to do."

Max stood as well. "What things?"

"Cassie and I... need to work something out."

"What's to work out? You dumped her."

"I need to go." Jonas turned away.

"What do you see in that woman? She's pushy, short tempered, plain looking, naïve, and sure as hell doesn't have a clue how the world really—"

JJ spun, eyes narrowed. Anger drove out every trace of prior nervousness. His face shouted *drop the topic.*

Max knew his own face betrayed nothing. He'd perfected a granite poker face that made his opponents increasingly nervous until they inevitably made a mistake. He sensed Jefferson teetered on the verge of such a mistake. Already the man had revealed he really did love Pocahontas. The obvious next question was whether Jonas was the kind of man who goes all stupid with love, or the type that keeps his wits. "They say love is blind. Maybe Clearwater found a pair of glasses."

"Don't dig your hole any deeper, Captain Kazakov."

Ah. Not a mere "Captain," that would acknowledge a formal superiority which would blunt Jefferson's words. Not simply

"Kazakov," which was how one addressed subordinates, and in this context would be a direct challenge for command. Nor simply "Max," an informal avoidance of the situation. "Captain Kazakov" gave notice that JJ knew who commanded the ship—and who had put Max in that position. Jonas considered himself an equal and had given notice to take his warning seriously. Jefferson hadn't gone stupid and he wasn't a pod person, not that Sullivan's accusations were ever more than wild speculation.

"Sullivan needs help inspecting the landing struts. After breakfast, you're with her."

JJ smiled—a thin, tight curve of the lips. Genuine. "Aye, aye, *Captain.*"

They walked to the mess hall, where Jefferson sat next to Clearwater. She didn't bother looking up. Max sat across from them, wondering which star-crossed lover would crack first.

Li waltzed in, her perfect smiling face set atop a temple of robes and scarves. Jasmine perfume flowed like the silk. "Jonas, you must eat something. We are concerned for your health."

Sullivan took a seat beside the Asian. "If he doesn't want to eat, don't force him."

"Eggs, perhaps? Toast? Yogurt?"

Jonas perked up. "Yogurt."

"Some fruit, too? Do not grimace. You like fruit."

"His tastes have changed," Cassie said. Jonas reached for her hand. She pulled away.

"Cassie, we need to talk."

Max looked around. "Where's Doc?"

"Talk about what?" Cassie snapped. "You made your intentions clear."

Max frowned. "Adam, tell Doc to get down here."

"Obviously I haven't, if you think I want to break up."

"Doctor Unger is not responding, Captain. He did not respond to my wake-up call, either."

Max turned to Wu. "Go get him."

She stared intently at Jonas and Cassie. "I will go later."

"Wu." He gave her the *look.*

Wu sighed and set a bowl of yogurt in front of the pilot. "Excuse me, Jonas. I will be back as quickly as possible."

"I'm going with you," Lyra said. The pair left the room, leaving Max alone to watch the squabbling love birds.

"Cassie, let me explain," Jonas said.

"You really want to do it here, in front of the captain? Fine. You obviously appreciate having an audience."

"I was sleepwalking! I don't remember going outside."

Max said, "Another hole in your memory? Better get checked for Alzheimer's."

Cassie and Jonas turned to the captain and said in unison, "Keep out of this."

Max grinned. "You might need a referee."

Jonas said, "Cassie, let's go to the lab."

"No."

"You're cutting me off without a chance to explain."

"You know why."

"I don't want to lose you. I love you."

Max studied their faces. Cassie looked doubtful, clearly afraid of being hurt. But more than that. *Ah, she's afraid of hurting Jefferson.* Interesting. Fly Boy, on the other hand, looked pathetic. The rich, powerful Prince Charming reduced to begging.

Cassie said, "Yeah. Right."

Lyra's voice came over the speakers. "Captain, Doc's cabin is locked and he's not answering. Request you have Adam override the lock."

"Adam, unlock the Doctor's quarters."

"Done, Captain."

A moment later Lyra said, "Christ. Doc! Doc!"

Max surged to his feet. "Sullivan, report!"

Lyra said in a muffled, hurried voice, "I'll breathe. You give chest compressions." Then, louder, "Captain, we need the paddles from sickbay. I think Doc's had a heart attack."

Jonas and Cassie stood. Max said, "Let's go!"

Cassie ran with him. Jonas followed. They grabbed the defibrillator from sickbay and ran to Doc's cabin. Li's hands pressed the doctor's naked chest, while Lyra's lips covered his mouth. Probably one of Doc's fantasies, but the man was beyond fantasies now.

Max charged the paddles and shocked the doctor without success. After three more attempts, he set the paddles aside and glanced at his watch. "Adam, record in the log that I pronounced Dr. Unger dead at oh-eight fifteen ship's time." He turned to Cassie. "Clearwater, I want an autopsy done immediately."

"I'm not a doctor."

"You're what we have. The rest of you, back to work."

Cassie said, "Sir, this should wait until we return to Earth. Standard protocol..."

Her argument withered under his glare. He motioned for Jonas to help him lift the body. They carried it to sickbay and placed it on an examination table.

***

An external exam of the doctor revealed little. Slight bruising and discoloration in various locations, which wasn't surprising given the physical stresses they all had undergone. She found silk fibers around his neck, also not surprising considering that Li loved to use her scarf like a collar and leash.

Cassie fought off her squeamishness and proceeded with the internal examination, and discovered remains of two caplets in the stomach. They had only partially dissolved, which indicated Doc had swallowed them close to the time of death. Cassie wondered if the pills might be the *cause* of death. She put the pills and stomach contents into specimen jars for later analysis.

"Dr. Clearwater," Adam said. "You have a text from Dr. Unger, sent on time delay."

"Read it, please."

Cassie,

Of all the people on board this ship, I think you may be the only one able to understand why I took my life. I am in love with Li, but she doesn't love me. Each day my desire for her grows and I have reached my limit.

I have seen that type of obsessive love in your eyes. For the sake of your life and the life of your unborn child, leave Jonas! He does not love you. He loves the stars. He loves adventure. If you tie him down, he will come to hate you and the child, blaming you for becoming an anchor chained to his soul.

Leave him. Do not tell him that you are pregnant. Do not risk falling into despair and then doing what I must do to escape it.

Doctor Unger

Dumbfounded, Cassie said, "Doc didn't write that."

"The note originated from the doctor's tablet."

"When?"

"Oh-twenty-two hundred hours."

Less than an hour after he called me last night. Doc may have been drunk, but he wasn't suicidal. But if this was murder, who was responsible? And why?

She wrapped the doctor's body in plastic and squeezed it into the walk-in freezer. Making it fit required removing a few bulky ingredients. She might as well make a casserole. She'd pretty much come to terms with the nausea.

Chapter 45

Ship Time: Day 20. 1700 hours.

Jonas worked alongside Max, Lyra, and Li for the entire dayshift while Cassie performed the autopsy and prepared meals. She cooked a casserole, perhaps trying to regain favor with the crew. Jonas forced himself to eat with the others, distracting himself by listening to conversations. Cassie said the autopsy was still underway but would be finished soon.

Max grumbled. "Finish it after dinner while the rest of us dig."

Li looked up. "We have already completed a day of long labor."

"So? You got plans? With Doc and Cassie out, we're behind schedule, even with Robbie helping."

Lyra said, "The ammonia came about this time yesterday. What if it returns?"

"We'll change into suits and respirators," Max said.

Cassie scowled. "A man's dead and all you care about is the money you might lose." She stomped out of the room without finishing her dinner.

The remaining crew ate for a while in silence. Doc would have cracked a joke, but nobody seemed willing to fill his shoes. They ate in silence and went back to work. They weren't plagued by ammonia or other fumes, but the odors he smelled were far from pleasant. At the end of a two-hour shift, the crew slunk off to their cabins to shower and sleep. Jonas paced.

Yesterday's cloud had been a signal of some kind, but the meaning eluded him. The harder he concentrated, the fuzzier his thoughts became. He gave up and went to sleep.

Pepper made her way to the lab, eager to speak with Narcissus and Sage. She entered the airlock and opened the lids to the prison cages. The host would remember this as a dream, if he remembered it at all.

"Pepper, is that you?" asked Narcissus. *"Are the monsters dead?"*

"One has died. It was terrible."

Narcissus puffed dismissively. *"They're killers. Let's get out of here."*

Sage rolled on his side, lifting a flipper in the air so his root talk could evaporate enough to be noticed. *"Pepper! Are you alright?"*

"They aren't monsters. Well, yes, they are, but they think, they feel. In some ways they are not so different from us."

Sage exuded strong disagreement. *"You can't afford to identify with them! They have the power and the intent to wipe out the grove."*

"I keep thinking there might be another way. If both species understood each other, maybe mutual compassion would—"

"Compassion!" Narcissus huffed. *"Those things want to kill us! You've been inside their hive for a hundred layers and only killed one! What's wrong with you?"*

"Are they hard to kill?" asked Sage. *"Or is the human half of your brain taking over?"*

Narcissus wailed. *"She's a failure. We're all going to die."*

Pepper whacked the side of his terrarium. The box slid to the edge of the table and set Narcissus tottering and screaming. She savored the sudden waft of vinegar with grim satisfaction. *"I gave up my body and memories for you! But you couldn't wait to put your roots on Daisy."*

"We thought we were going to die, trapped and alone. She needed comforting."

"I'm glad I don't remember loving you." Pepper slammed the lid shut, refusing to let the cheating orator have the final scent.

"I'm sorry for you, Pepper," Sage said.

"I was a fool."

"Narcissus is the fool. You are a hero. How many monsters are left?"

"They aren't monsters. They are human beings."

"Whatever you call them, they need to die. How can I help?"

Killing was a terrible, irrevocable solution. Pepper wanted an alternative—for Cassie, at least.

"Pepper, focus on the mission."

She sucked in a breath and exhaled. *"There are four left. When alone, humans are easy to kill. Poison or severe trauma works best. Even acid sprayed into their respiratory system would work."* She paused as Jonas tried to regain consciousness. She found some soothing memories that lured him back to dreams. *"But humans are mobile and communicate over distances. I don't have a reliable way to kill all of them at once."*

"Then kill them one at a time, in such a manner that you are not implicated or incapacitated in the process."

Pepper nodded, and then realized Sage had no way of detecting her response. Vision and hearing were amazing new senses, yet beyond description. Only through experience could they be understood. *"Yes,"* she breathed, *"that's what your father told me. But... it's wrong."*

She heard the lab flap opened. *"A human is coming now."*

"How can you tell?" asked Sage. *"I only smell you... oh, I smell it now."*

Li entered the lab and went to the control panel, where she turned off the surveillance equipment. She moved with seductive grace toward Pepper. Jasmine perfume swirled around her, as tangible as the colored scarves that floated on the air. "Jonas, I have wanted to talk to you alone for some time."

"I'm busy, Li," Pepper said.

Li laughed. "A pilot is not busy unless he is piloting. You want to be alone to lick your wounds, for Cassie has wounded you deeply."

"Now's your chance," Sage said. *"The monster's alone."*

"What makes you think I'm upset with Cassie? Doc just died. Isn't that enough?" *"It's not that simple, Sage."*

Li's face morphed from haughtiness to sympathy. "The doctor's death is very sad. I tried to save him. His face was so pale, his body so cold." She squeezed her eyes closed, as if she could unsee the memory. She opened her eyes, fluttering the lashes. "But it is not the doctor that makes you hide here alone. A woman knows such things. You grieve for the loss of a love that was never truly there. Cassie tried to trap you by pregnancy. She has no honor."

"*It's not complicated. It's them or us, Pepper.*"

Li's words stirred something inside Jonas. Sage's comments didn't help. Pepper struggled to dampen her host's level of consciousness. "How did you know?"

"Yes, deeply wounded. I know a remedy for such hurt." She removed a scarf and draped it around his neck.

"Li..."

She pressed a finger to his lips. "No talking. I will dance for you. I am a very good dancer." Her eyes were jade green islands surrounded by pearl white seas.

"*Kill her, Pepper. Before the opportunity evaporates.*"

Li stepped away and twirled. Another scarf fell away. Jonas's body reacted in a way beyond conscious control. "Li, you should go."

She laughed as a satin blouse billowed up like a balloon then dropped to the floor. A golden bra lay nearly invisible against her bare shoulders and midriff. The breasts beneath seemed to swell, straining against confinement. An emerald glinted in her belly button. Li writhed like a serpent, sensuous and dangerous.

Pepper breathed heavily. The host's pants grew painfully tight, responding to sexual stimulus faster than she could counter it.

Sage said, "*She's releasing pheromones. So are you. Don't let the human half of your brain take control! Kill her, Pepper! It's a trap.*"

"Stop. Just stop."

Li kept moving, teasing. A hand swept out and glided across his crotch. "Your body wants more." She knelt on the floor in front of him. The bra fell away. Her breasts pressed against his thighs; the nipples like bullets pressing through the fabric. She reached for his zipper.

A piece of lab equipment beeped, loud and incessant. Pepper, momentarily freed from the spell, pushed Li away. She fell onto her butt, then rose to her feet, muttering angrily in Chinese. She trudged to the offending machine—her own pocket brain. The beeping stopped. A digital version of Li's voice said, "Basic dictionary compiled. Translation complete."

Li frowned. "Cassie cannot be right." Her fingers tapped the screen. "Recite the translation." Pepper moved behind her.

A monotone androgynous voice came from the device. "There are four left. When alone, humans are easy to kill. Poison or severe trauma works best. Even acid sprayed into their respiratory system would work." Pause. "But humans are mobile and communicate over distances. I don't have a reliable way to kill all of them at once."

A second voice said, "Then kill them one at a time, in such a manner that you are not implicated or incapacitated in the process."

"Yes, that's what your father told me. But... it's wrong." Pause. "A human is coming now."

Pepper touched Li's shoulder. The bare skin trembled. Human fear had its own scent, and it rose from Li's skin like steam from coffee. In a soothing voice, Pepper said, "The plants are intelligent, Li. They have language, society, culture. There's been a terrible misunderstanding."

Li's head bobbed in a curt nod. "Yes. Yes. Now there is proof beyond doubt to present to the captain." She removed the pocket brain from its cradle atop the mass spectrometer.

Pepper sighed. "I can smell the lie on you."

"Lyra was right. You are a monster." Li spun. The sway of her breasts distracted Jonas from Li's kick. His groin exploded in white-hot pain, dropping him to the floor. He grabbed her ankle as she darted past. She stumbled, hit her head on the table, and fell to her knees. Pepper climbed to her feet, fighting Jonas for control. The symbiont body moved jerkily to conflicting orders.

Pepper's will proved to be dominant, at least for now. She had Jonas wrap both arms around Li's chest and lift her from the floor. Pepper thought Li would be helpless with arms pinned to her sides, but the captive's feet kicked with desperate force.

"Li, I just want to talk!"

One swinging leg knocked a laptop to the floor. The other leg caught the plant tank, which gave Li enough leverage to push Jonas off balance. Li tumbled backward, landing on the floor atop Jonas. The tank shot forward and fell with a crash. Pepper hoped Narcissus wasn't injured, then realized she'd lost her grip on Li. The Asian scrambled forward on hands and knees. Pepper grabbed the ankle again, but Li thrashed like an enraged dragon and shook loose.

Pepper snorted in frustration. *"She's getting away!"* Li was fast; she'd be on her feet and out the flap in an instant. *"Sage! Spray acid up and left to block her way."*

A stream of acid arced over the lip of the open animal cage and hissed on the floor inches in front of Li. She cursed and turned away. She placed a hand on the fallen plant tank, preparing to stand. The lid had fallen off; the open top faced her.

"Narcissus! She's right next to you. 1,2,2,2-tetrafluoroethyl difluoromethyl ether."

Instead of the expected vapor cloud, a stream of acid spurted from Narcissus's raised root. Li batted at the stream, but much had already covered her face. A short scream degenerated into rapid, pain-filled gasps that ended with a loud gurgle. She collapsed face-down. The pale skin of her naked back peeked through the spill of black hair cascading from her head. Her arms and legs jerked in spasms that quickly stilled. Blood pooled under her head. Unpleasant odors reared up as bladder and sphincter relaxed.

Pepper ignored the smell and carefully rolled Li over.

Only the back of Li's skull remained intact. Gas bubbled up through the remnants of her brain, but it held no memories. Humans weren't plants. When they died, they died completely.

"I wanted her stopped, not killed! I could have convinced her to be friends."

Narcissus puffed, *"Her kind killed Daphne. I'm proud of what I did."*

"I need to put you back on the table and close the lid. I need to think of an explanation. I can barely keep control of this human."

Sage said, *"Finish the mission! Don't become one of them!"*

Pepper placed Narcissus's terrarium tank on the table. It wasn't broken, hadn't even cracked. Jonas fought for control as if trying to wake from a terrible nightmare. Pepper hid the recent memories and secreted a mild sedative into the host's bloodstream.

Pepper put the laptop computer back on the table, then searched for Li's pocket computer. She scanned the table top, the floor, the cages. The damn thing had vanished. Maybe acid had dissolved it. Pepper accessed Jonas's memories on how to turn off the mass spectrometer.

Nothing looked out of place, everything was functional. Li's death had to look like an accident. Humans were not inherently evil. They didn't deserve to die. There had to be a way out of this mess before it escalated further. When Pepper concentrated on how to accomplish that, the host broke free.

Jonas shook his head, confused and disoriented. Something lay on the floor, and he tried to make sense of it. "Dear God!" He staggered to the sink and vomited.

Chapter 46

Ship Time: Day 20. 2140 hours.

The stink of urine, excrement, and vomit filled the lab. Cassie cupped a hand over her nose, which provided only psychological relief. When her stomach threatened to heave, she took shallow breaths through her mouth.

Beneath the dark human odors, she recognized the tart, acidic smell of the animal. Had it escaped? The cage lids were closed when she left the lab earlier. Another scent caught her attention, fainter than the others, but more bothersome. Cassie lowered her hand and sniffed to be sure. Jasmine—Li's perfume.

"Li?" She scanned the floor, wary of encountering the animal. Sobbing came from near the decon-airlock. "Li?" She crept toward the sound.

Jonas sat on the floor, knees to his chest, arms hugging his legs, head bowed. His body shook with sobs. She'd seen him cry before, but never like this. "Jonas, what's wrong?"

His head rose, exposing wet, red eyes. "Cassie, get away from me."

"Jonas, what happened?"

"Go away. Head back to Earth. Now."

"Li. Where is she?"

"Cassie, it's not safe. *I'm* not safe. Get out of here."

Cassie walked cautiously to the cages and then froze. A scream turned to a squeak as her throat constricted in shock. Lustrous satin wrapped Li's slim waist and legs. Gold rings adorned fingers, toes and ankles. Naked breasts exposed beauty as pale and perfect as a marble statue of Aphrodite. But the face was gone, completely scooped away. The back half of the skull formed a bowl filled with red sauce and gray gelatin.

Cassie threw up. When her stomach finally settled, she looked at the cages. The animal was inside one with the lid closed. The plant was in the other tank. She studied the floor, looking for holes or trails. "Jonas, another animal might have broken in." Why hadn't the alarm sounded? She called out, "Adam! Sound the alarm."

The computer didn't respond.

Jonas said, "Nothing broke in. Trojan horses are invited."

Someone had turned off surveillance, including the intercom. She reached for the controls then changed her mind. She walked back to Li, found the Asian's robe and scarves, and dressed the corpse. Cassie dry-heaved when she turned the head and blood drained to the floor.

"What happened, Jonas?" Her voice rasped. Her nose and throat burned from bile.

"Cassie, listen. It's me. It must be me. I need to be locked up. Maybe sedated."

"You were..." she swallowed. It hurt to talk, and not only from the vomiting. "You were going to have sex. What went wrong?" When he said nothing, she knelt beside him and grabbed his shirt in her fists. "Jonas, tell me what happened."

"I don't know! I'm fucking sleepwalking or totally insane. I lose chunks of time. I wake up on my feet and don't know when or where I am. Smells are everywhere and it's like voices telling me to kill everyone. Cassie, I'm crazy. Crazy dangerous."

"Li wanted her hooks into you for a long time. You gave in. But this..."

"No! There's only you. Especially now."

"Enough lies. You auditioned to be a flagpole this morning."

He touched her arm, then pulled his hand back. "I'm dangerous. Not to be trusted."

"I know." She took a deep breath. "Jonas—did you kill her?"

He looked lost. "I don't know. I don't remember."

Cassie released his shirt and placed her hands on his shoulders. "Listen up. You were here waiting for me. Li came in, you talked. She opened the cage to the animal."

"Why would she?"

"Don't be dense! The thing sprayed her face, it happened so fast you couldn't do anything to help her. You sounded the alarm. I was the first one here."

He said, "Cassie..." The muscles in his shoulders tensed like a catapult being wound tight. "I have to make this right. There's too much at stake."

Jonas was clearly in shock. Maybe in a PTSD episode. She helped him to the control panel. "Adam," he said, "sound the alarm. There's been a terrible accident in the lab. Li is dead."

A claxon blared and the captain's voice said, "We're on the way, Jefferson."

Cassie turned the exhaust fans to maximum. No need to have *everyone* puking.

Lyra arrived first, belligerent and terrified. She shouted for Li, demanded to know where Li was, and punched Jonas when he tried to block her way. Max pushed past them both and demanded a report. Jonas pointed to the floor near the plant and animal table.

Lyra screamed. She rushed forward and knelt by the body, babbling incoherently. Cassie gently convinced her to step away as Max moved in for a closer look.

"The specimens are dangerous, Captain," Cassie said. "We need to turn them loose."

"How'd you get here so fast?"

"I've learned everything I can from them. The data is in the computer. We should let them go."

"I asked you a question, Clearwater."

"I was already on my way here."

"Doc's autopsy's done?"

"Yes." She swallowed. "Overdose."

"Suicide?"

Cassie nodded. "Looks that way." The lie didn't bother her as much as she wanted it to. Doc was murdered, but she lacked proof other than an obviously fabricated email. She'd ordered Adam to hide the file.

Max stared at her. She stared back. "The plants, Captain? The animal? Can I let them go?"

Jonas said, "I think we should keep them a bit longer."

Cassie spun on him. "This isn't your field."

"Jefferson is right. We keep the things here. Put a lock on the lids."

She sighed. "Two dead. Let's just go back to Earth."

Max turned his gaze to Li's body.

"What did Earth say about Doc's death?" asked Cassie. "Or do you want me to do the notification?"

Max ignored her. "Adam, what does surveillance show happened here?"

"Surveillance was turned off by Dr. Wu when she entered the lab. Surveillance was reactivated by Mr. Jefferson five minutes ago."

"What a whore," said the captain.

Lyra growled. "That's a lie."

"Face the truth, Sullivan. Your partner's been boffing the doctor for weeks, but her eye was always on Jefferson and the family fortune."

"Shut up! Shut up, shut up!"

"Jefferson, am I right?"

Jonas blinked in surprise. He gave Cassie a side-long glance. "Yeah. We started kissing. Bumped into the terrarium. It fell, Li tripped. She screamed. I put the lid back on, put the tank back on the table, but it had already sprayed Li. There..." he closed his eyes and shuddered. "There was nothing I could do."

Max turned to Cassie. "Clearwater, the reason you need to keep the specimens is so you can develop a quick and efficient means of eradicating both life forms." He shook his head in disgust. "Should have been done days ago."

"These beings could be intelligent. The Prime Directive—"

"Stop whining. Doc is dead, so I make the call. There is no conclusive evidence of intelligence and ample proof that the indigenous life is hostile and deadly."

"But—"

"I don't give a fuck. Got that, Clearwater? Find a way to wipe out these buggers so we can get on with the mining."

Had she heard him correctly? "Protocol is to terminate the mission." Cassie saw something in his face. "You're not going to tell Earth about Li. Or Doc."

His silence was answer enough. Cassie didn't argue. If they returned to Earth now, she'd never be able to prove the animal possessed intelligence. Jonas would face scandal, embarrassment, and maybe incarceration in a psychiatric facility. Doc's murder would go unsolved—Tobias would insist that suicide fit the facts.

She needed to play along until the situation improved. "Captain, the plants and animals are sensitive to ultraviolet light. I could probably rig up a death ray or sorts."

"Cassie!" shouted JJ.

She'd never seen a face so contorted by rage. He should be happy—the creatures were killers and had traumatized him to the edge of paranoia. So why did her stomach twist with a feeling she'd just done something terribly wrong?

"You have a problem, Jefferson?"

Jonas turned his rage from Cassie to the captain. "Would it do any fucking good?" He stormed past Lyra and out of the lab.

"Sullivan, give me a moment alone with the Science Officer."

"I need to stay with Li."

"Take a walk. When you come back, we'll bury Wu."

"No! Li isn't going to be buried! I'll build a pyre behind the ship. I'll use Li's clothes, God knows there's enough of them." The engineer left, making no effort to hide her tears.

Cassie shifted her weight, uneasy to be alone with the captain. He seemed to enjoy her anxiety. "What really happened?"

"You know as much as I do." She felt his eyes bore into her. "I broke up with Jonas. Li made her move. Accidents happen."

"You put me in a difficult position."

"Sir?"

"Normally I'd have you perform an autopsy on Wu. But you're involved with her death."

"I—"

"Shut up. I already know you're lying. She was naked when you showed up. Did you catch them going at it like rabbits? Yeah. Stirred up the warrior inside you. Put you in a jealous rage. Were you trying to scalp her? Did she jerk back at the last minute, or did the laser slip?"

Cassie shook her head violently. "No! It was the animal."

"Blood all over the floor, all over her neck and hair. Barely a drop on her clothes, and no acid burns, no rips."

Cassie averted her eyes. "She must have been looking down. The glass walls would have protected her clothes from the spray."

"Why are blood stains on your arms and clothes?"

His infuriating calm frightened her. "I was comforting Jonas."

"Who didn't have blood on him."

Her mind shut down under the relentless interrogation. She couldn't save Jonas. She couldn't even save herself.

"You see my problem, Clearwater? It was stupid of me to have you do Doc's autopsy. I can't trust you. I bet Doc was murdered, and I only bet on sure things. But who's the perp? You, Lyra, or Jefferson? I can't pin it down for sure. Even if I could, I think it may be justified. Temporary insanity. The father of your unborn child, fucking a stunningly beautiful woman who had the ability and desire to take him from you?"

"Does everyone on the damn ship know I'm pregnant?"

"Yeah. Jefferson was probably the last to know."

"I didn't kill Li."

He shrugged. "I'm pretty sure she blackmailed Doc to get you pregnant."

Cassie felt suddenly cold, colder than the dead doctor. "What?"

"Didn't you feel anything odd about the pre-flight medical exam? A little woozy, like he double-dosed you with anti-anxiety medicine? Feel anything warm, wet, and gooey way up inside you during the exam?"

She shook her head. "He didn't fuck me." She hated Max for even suggesting it.

"Of course not. He just had to inject some of his sperm in your womb on the day he knew you'd be fertile."

Cassie felt numb. Empty. "No."

"If the unexpected pregnancy didn't break up the two of you, a paternity test sure the hell would. That was Wu's plan." He glanced at Li's body. "For all the good it did her."

"I hate you."

He grinned. "I opened up to you, Clearwater. Now open up to me."

"I told you everything."

"You're a terrible liar. What really happened here?"

Was that why Doc wanted to talk? To confess? To warn her? And the captain *knew*. She hated him, hated Doc, Li, everyone. She was sick of the lies and the secrets.

She told Max what really happened.

Chapter 47

Ship Time: Day 21. 0045 hours.

Jonas waited until after midnight before donning a biosuit and heading into the grove. He paused by a large plant and removed the rubber stopper from the small hole he'd bored through the faceplate. He inhaled quickly then plugged the hole. This wasn't the right plant. Vision, for all its wonders, lacked the certainty of smell. He turned left, careful not to step on children or to brush against adults. The grove fumed under a smog of anxiety. He didn't want to add panic to the mix. Jonas wasn't sure how he knew their mood, or how he navigated by smell. The voice in his head knew those things, and he had no choice but to trust her.

Two more course corrections brought him to his goal. He knelt under its dome, pulled the plug from his helmet, and stayed very close to the gills. He exhaled softly. *"Hello, Myrtle."*

"Pepper! You startled me. I didn't smell you coming."

"We need to talk," Pepper said. *"Privately."*

"Pity you don't have roots."

"I'll breathe easy. You keep deodorant in the background."

"Are the monsters dead? We all smelled the odor of their burning tissue."

"I need more time."

"That, dear girl, is impossible."

"The creatures can be reasoned with. They're not weapons. They killed plants by accident. On their world plants are brainless food."

"Why tell me all this?"

"With Tarragon dead, you are the newest elder."
A dozen heartbeats passed before Myrtle responded. *"Nasturtium is Eldest. I won't intercede on your behalf. Finish the mission."*
"They aren't monsters! They're called humans. Two are dead. There is no reason for more of them to die. I'll make sure they don't kill any more plants. There can be peace, Myrtle! Think how much we can learn from each other."
Myrtle waited and even longer time to reply. *"Put your gills on one of my blowholes. I can't risk a whiff of this getting out."*
"But I won't be able to reply."
"Just listen. I'm used to doing the talking."
Jonas pressed his helmet to the rim of her dome, the opening of his faceplate surrounding an orifice.
"Don't trust Nasturtium."
The odor made Jonas gasp, but of course Myrtle couldn't smell the surprise with his faceplate sealed around a pair of her lips.
"Why, you ask? I'll tell you. Your parents were fine upstanding plants. Buckeye never cheated on your mother, nor she on him. Though with roots that long, he could have reached anyone in the grove. Thick stem, too, and gallons of stored sap. He and Camellia waited quite a while before having you. In fact—"
Jonas tapped the top of her dome.
"Don't be impatient! When the storm of Tarragon-Ring 307 hit, the one that took their lives, The surge of water from the reservoir washed away my sunscreen and woke me instantly. Once I realized what was happening, I searched for any seedlings that might have been washed away. The sun burned like hell-fire as I sniffed around. I could only check directly upwind of course, but it was enough to realize you stood at the edge of the flow. I made sure the ground around you stayed firm. It was too late to save your parents."
Please, thought Pepper. *If there's a point, get to it.*
"I put on fresh protection, but before it covered my stem, I caught whiff of Nasturtium, which was strange since he should have been covered, but I figured he was doing same as I was, making sure the young ones were all right." Jonas tapped her dome again.
"Okay, okay. I smelled your parents, too, but their memories were unwinding. I couldn't wait to absorb any of them—the

radiation burned too much and the wind snatched most of it away, leaving fragments. But I think Nasturtium waited it out. He had gallons of sap even then, you know. More even than Tarragon, I think, because Tarragon shared his whenever someone got hurt.

"Well, the thing is, when you changed into this... thing, I stayed more or less conscious during the storm by keeping a narrow strip of stem exposed on the leeward side and dumping enough memory dust to stick. I was hoping to help Tarragon, bless his memory, but he was already dead and the last of his dust blowing in the wind. Surprisingly, Nasturtium was awake, too. I smelled him clear as I do you. Well, not with you sealed up like this plastic cocoon, but you know what I mean. Nasturtium couldn't smell me. I was downwind.

"The point is that Nasturtium has Tarragon's memories! Tarragon took such steps to keep the monster genome a secret, including dying alone. Now Nasturtium knows what Tarragon knew, and our new Eldest hasn't let anyone know that he knows. That's what worries me. It's one thing to let the grove know you have secrets, it's quite another to keep secrets that no one knows about."

Jonas sighed with Pepper's disappointment. Did it matter if Nasturtium absorbed Tarragon's memories? That was the way things were supposed to happen, and would have, if the storm hadn't forced Tarragon to remain behind to meld Pepper's brain into the human. Myrtle wasn't going to help. This clandestine meeting had been a colossal waste of time. Jonas pulled away.

"Wait! I'm not finished."

He pressed his helmet against her again.

"Nasturtium knows how to create monsters. I worry that after you've killed this batch, Nasturtium will create a monster of his own and use it to find and destroy the grove that started this. And he'll learn the secret of their technology as well."

Nasturtium would unleash a needless and fruitless reign of terror. Jonas couldn't breathe. He tore off the helmet and sucked air in and out like a bellows, until he felt the world begin to spin. "No!" he shouted. "*No!*" He strode toward Nasturtium. "*The monsters don't come from another grove. They're from an entirely different planet!*"

Smells popped up from the surrounding plants, smells with voices attached. "*Pepper? Is that you? Pepper?*"

A sharp smell cut through the others, but it came from behind.

Jonas turned, saw the flap of the lab hanging open, and caught scent of Narcissus screaming. Jonas ran toward the lab, trying to watch where his feet fell. He barged through the opening and skidded to a halt.

Lyra held a high intensity UV lamp like a flame thrower, sweeping it over a frantically burrowing Sage.

Narcissus shrieked, "*Help! Help! I'm burning!*" A glance at his cage showed puddles of amber sap and white sunscreen, neither of which could set properly when mixed. The blisters didn't look critical. Sage, however, lacked the glands for sap and sunscreen while in animal form.

Jonas shouted, "Lyra, stop!"

She didn't stop, didn't even look up. A maniacal snarl exposed clenched teeth.

He grabbed the lamp and struggled with Lyra for control. It jerked and swung erratically, hitting the plant cage, which fell to the floor. The lamp went out as its bulb shattered.

Lyra dropped the lamp and pounded Jonas with her fists.

"Lyra, it was an accident. Stop hitting me!" Her strength nearly matched his own, and he worried she'd break his arms as he blocked her blows. "The plants are intelligent, they were just trying to defend themselves, it's all a huge tragic misunderstanding."

"You're one of them. Monster!"

"*Pepper! Help me,*" said Narcissus. "*I've fallen and can't get up. There's no soil here. Help!*"

"I'm Jonas Jefferson. Look at me, Lyra. You know me. We've worked together. Look at me. I'm not a monster."

The hammer fists slowed and lost strength. She didn't look at him; she crumpled against his chest, sobbing. "They killed her, Jonas. They killed my Li."

She sagged and Jonas eased her to the floor and sat beside her. He stroked her hair, and held her while she cried. He thought the worst was over, until her body went rigid.

"You're wearing a biosuit." She said it like an accusation.

"I saw a patch of mold by the lake. I thought it might be dangerous."

"Liar." She jabbed an elbow into his gut and was on her feet before he could catch his breath. She held a laser cutter. "Don't move, or I'll slice you to pieces."

She moved close to the animal cage. "I'm going to do to your friend what it did to Li."

"Lyra, please. Don't hurt Sage." He rose to his feet, palms open, non-threatening.

"How cute. You even have a name for it." She glanced up as Cassie entered. Jonas used the momentary distraction to tackle Lyra, sending both of them to the floor. The laser skidded away. She pounded his head, chest, groin, anywhere her fists could reach. He refrained from hitting back.

A shadow loomed overhead. "Lyra, if you don't stop beating the crap out of my boyfriend, I'm going to put you to sleep for about three days." Cassie stood poised with a syringe.

For a moment Lyra seemed to dare Cassie to follow through— her fists remained closed, and the scowl stayed on her face. But she stopped swinging.

"He's a monster," she said. "The plants are monsters. The animals are monsters. They killed Li. Don't you get it? It's them or us."

"Lyra, you've been through—"

"He's wearing a biosuit. Why? He's planning something, Cassie. Something bad."

Cassie frowned. "Why are you wearing a suit, Jonas?"

The voice in his head told him to lie. Lies hadn't worked so well lately. "I walked through the grove. I didn't want to frighten them, so I wore a suit."

"Why would a suit make any difference?" asked Cassie.

"See? He's a monster."

Cassie said, "And you're paranoid." She gave a slight shake of the head as if deciding what to do. "Both of you, on your feet. Jonas, take off the biosuit and go to the ship. Lyra, let's have a talk, just you and me. I don't want to stay up all night worried that you're going to destroy my lab specimens."

Jonas left the biosuit in the lab and walked to the ship, watching the grove as he moved. "I sure hope you and your friends have a plan," he said to himself. *"I share that hope,"* Pepper answered. He wrinkled his nose at a blast of ammonia from the grove. Time grew ever shorter, and hope withered.

Chapter 48

Ship Time: Day 21. 0115 hours.

Cassie sat on the ground with Lyra, the ship at their backs, which blocked all view of the plants. Cassie sat cross-legged. Lyra sat with knees bent, arms wrapped around them as if holding herself together. The posture reminded Cassie of how she'd found Jonas huddled in the lab earlier this night. A few meters ahead, the remains of Li's funeral pyre sent a thin column of smoke on a long journey across the sky.

"It ought to be dark," Lyra said. "This never-ending twilight weirds me out."

Cassie agreed. Eternal twilight formed a surreal backdrop for death, resurrection, and more death in a world of stinky mushrooms and acid-spitting beasts that do math and swim through powdered coal.

"Want to talk about what happened in there?"

Lyra grunted. "Flyboy didn't start it." Her face hardened. "Won't finish it, either."

"What happened to Li was terrible, but it was an accident."

"Yeah."

"Killing my lab specimens won't make you feel better."

Cassie felt Lyra's unspoken disagreement. Peripheral movement drew Cassie's attention upward. "A shooting star!" The trail of light arced across the sky, stirring bittersweet memories.

"My grandfather called them tears of the moon." She could almost hear his raspy voice and smell the tobacco on his clothes.

"One night, when I was seven years old, he woke me." She closed her eyes.

"Come, girl," said Grandfather. "You need to witness a sad and wondrous sight." He turned and left her room. She heard the front door open and close. She slipped on her shoes and scrambled to catch up before his fast, silent walk took him into the croaking, buzzing, blackness of the Everglades.

"Where are we going?" she asked, but Grandfather kept walking, following a path that skirted through meadow, swamp, and jungle. His steps were sure even in darkness. He never tripped on the roots that grabbed Cassie's ankles. Branches that smacked her face avoided his.

Alligators lurked in deceptively quiet pools. Pythons lay concealed in the dappled shadows of moonlit trees. Grandfather ignored the monsters, and the monsters ignored him.

They climbed a small hill, the only hill, the highest point in the glades, a sacred place for the Seminole shaman. The crescent moon smiled, surrounded by a million tiny diamonds sparkling in a black velvet sky.

"What do you know of the Thunderbirds?" Grandfather asked.

"Emissaries of the Great Spirit. Heralds of change. Immortal beings of great power, whose very touch can heal or kill."

They reached the top of the hill. "Look to the north, Cassiopeia."

She hated her name and kept it secret from kids at school. What possessed her parents to name her after some vain Greek queen whom the gods chained to the stars as punishment? But Grandfather called people by their true names, which held power. Perhaps, like medicine, power tasted bitter and that was why she didn't like her own name. Cassie didn't know which direction was north, so she faced the same way as Grandfather.

A bright light with a tail of fire appeared on the horizon. It rose slowly, majestically, gathering speed as it climbed higher, ever higher, until becoming one with the field of stars. It was the strangest, most beautiful thing Cassie had ever seen.

"The last Thunderbird, called home by the Great Spirit," Grandfather said. "Humanity has declared science is god, and will have no other gods before it." He stared at the sky for long minutes, perhaps peering into the future or pondering lessons of the past. Then he tousled her hair, and she smiled into his deep-set eyes, which twinkled as if they were stars, too. He turned her round, letting her lead the way back to the house, making an occasional grunt if she strayed from the path. She crawled into bed, exhausted, and dreamt of flying up and up and up, all the way to heaven, where she danced with the Thunderbirds above the stars.

Cassie opened her eyes. "Years later I realized I'd seen the final launch of a chemical rocket from Cape Canaveral. The IDF made rockets obsolete."

"Living your dream," Lyra said bitterly. "I was never happy on Earth. Too awkward, too plain, too thin-skinned and hot-headed. I learned to fight young, and when I couldn't fight I'd run away. I stowed away on an asteroid mining ship. Discovered I had a knack for machines."

"How'd you meet Li?"

Many seconds passed. Cassie neither welcomed nor dreaded silence. "You don't have to tell me."

"No, it's not that. It's... complicated." Lyra sighed. "Li's actually the reason I'm here. Part of the reason, anyway. Tobias offered to let me start a rival company if I agreed to go on this mission. I refused. Giving up twenty years of family and friends is a steep price. Plus, how could I ever realistically compete with MicroWeight?

"That's when Li appeared and told me she could work a deal with her government. A guaranteed multi-billion-dollar contract to supply the IDF drive—the full version with phase change—to their space ships."

"Setting off an arms race."

Lyra shook her head. "Exploration, like us. Anyway, she changed my mind. We became friends, then more than friends. I'd thought until then that only machines didn't judge, tease, or trick you." Her eyes glistened. "Poor Li, so loving, so beautiful. Fragile as a flower petal."

Cassie had many adjectives to describe Li. Fragile wasn't among them, but it wasn't Cassie's place to take off Lyra's blinders. "You were the lead engineer for the entire company. Seems odd you would step away from that to go star hopping."

"You think it was fun working for the company? You ever hear of the loyalty pill?"

Cassie shook her head.

"You every wonder how Tobias managed to keep the inner workings of the IDF secret? MicroWeight has no competitors. None."

Cassie said, "I know the housing is tamper proof. It self-destructs if the seal is broken."

"The security on the physical product is excellent. So is the cyber security on the design. Tobias doesn't have patents because he doesn't need them, and he doesn't trust the governments who issue them. But people, *people* have always been a weak link."

Lyra unwrapped her legs and swiveled to face Cassie. "He has explosive capsules embedded in the brain of every scientist and engineer who has sensitive information. Any thought of the IDF design triggers a timer. It also initiates a connection to a MicroWeight security computer. If you're still thinking design thoughts at the end of thirty seconds, the computer determines if you're working on an approved job. If so, the computer resets the timer and continues its monitoring. If not..."

"Tobias isn't that heartless."

Lyra smiled. "Li was right. You *are* naïve. Ask Adam to pull up the doctor's pre-flight medical records on me. Look at the X-rays of my head."

"Dear lord, you really have one in you?"

"Not anymore. Tobias kept his word and had it removed."

"Jonas isn't evil."

Lyra sneered. "The rich and powerful will do anything to stay that way. That's not what worries me." Lyra stood pointed at Li's ashes. "She was murdered."

"Jonas is a good man. I trust him with my life."

Lyra's eyebrows raised as if Cassie had grown a third eye and spoken in tongues. "That thing is a clone, programmed to kill us. You might be next."

Cassie shook her head. "Jonas is... Jonas. I'd know the difference." Something *was* different, but she knew he wasn't a killer.

Lyra brushed the black sand from her pants. "Love blinds you." Smoke no longer rose from the funeral pyre. "It's not safe. I can feel it in my bones. Lock your door and sleep with a knife under your pillow."

An errant swirl of ammonia sent them scurrying to the ship.

Chapter 49

Ship Time: Day 21. 0800 hours.

Jonas ate slowly from a bowl of plain yogurt, ignoring uneasy stares from Cassie and Lyra. Judging from their red, sunken eyes, the women had cried themselves to sleep. Or maybe they were caught by the ammonia fog. The captain's face showed no emotion, which wasn't unusual. Max's day often seemed to start in neutral before going downhill. Cassie ate fruit and cereal; the others chewed eggs and bacon. Jonas swallowed and tried to calm the queasiness in his gut.

Cassie was the most important thing in his life. He needed to get their relationship back to normal. Scratch that. Normal didn't exist anymore, not with a parasite commandeering his body. If it was a parasite. Parasites could be killed or removed. What if it was his own mind, his brain gone akimbo? Could he ever trust himself again?

There was the baby to consider. Had Cassie considered an abortion? God, he hoped not. He needed to talk with her, convince her to keep the child no matter what happened to their relationship. *I wish she didn't need to die.* Shut up, voice.

Lyra began clanking a fork on her plate until everyone stared at her. "I can reconfigure the ship's external floodlights to emit ultraviolet light."

Jonas slammed his spoon on the table. "That will kill them."

"That's kind of the idea." Lyra's tone and expression indicated she was ready for round two. "The circuit can be amped up a hundred times what the solar storm put out. From seven meters up it'll cut a swath ten meters wide. Like a flame thrower to incinerate the bastards."

"Sautéed mushrooms. I like it," Max said. "What about the animals?"

"They are intelligent beings," Cassie said. "It's murder."

She's right. Jonas said, "Cassie's right. We can't do it."

Lyra shook her fork at him. "Shut your mouth, freak." She turned to Max. "Without a food source, they'll starve or move on."

Max nodded. "Good enough for now. Reconfigure the lamps."

Cassie shook her head. "Captain, the animal species might be dangerous, but there's no evidence the plants are. I'm not even sure the animals eat the plants. I can't find a digestive system. I need more time to study them. Once we establish communication, we'll begin to understand them."

"Study, study, study. I'm tired of that one note song."

Jonas said, "I can prove the plants are intelligent." The words surprised him.

"They're not plants," Lyra said. "They're *aliens*. They think alien thoughts impossible for us to understand." Her hate-filled gaze settled on Jonas.

"It's the animals, not the plants, Jonas." Cassie slid her hand across the table to Lyra. "I know you miss Li. We all do. But this isn't a time to lash out." She swiveled back to the captain. "It's a Prime Directive issue. We're obligated not to harm them."

Max grunted. "I warned you before about playing the PDE card. This isn't *Star Trek*."

"Kill these creatures—whatever they are—and you'll end up in world court on charges you can't beat. With MicroWeight as co-defendant."

His eyes narrowed. "That a threat, Clearwater?"

Jonas repeated, "The plants are intelligent. I can prove it. I can translate their language." No one seemed to hear.

Cassie glared at the captain. "You can't cover up murder."

"Not murder," Lyra said, smiling. "Genocide. We'll sterilize the planet."

Max shot her a warning look. "It would take too long."

Cassie rose and planted both palms on the table. "You'd kill everything on Obsidian? Revenge won't bring Li back."

Lyra's smile turned to a snarl. "Robbie will have it done before the first colonists arrive."

"Sullivan, shut your mouth." The captain's glare seemed hot enough to blister Lyra's face. She lowered her head to stare at the table.

Cassie's face flushed. "Is that what this is about, Captain? You get a bonus for sterilizing the planet for colonization?"

"They're dangerous. Isn't that obvious?"

"No, it's—"

Jonas stood and raised his voice. "They're just trying to defend themselves!"

All faces turned to him, none of them friendly. Lyra's held anger, the captain's held suspicion, and Cassie's held apprehension. *Diplomacy*, said the inner voice. "The plants have a language," Jonas said. "We *can* communicate with one another. Come on, I'll prove it right now, in the lab."

***

Upon exiting the airlock, Jonas smelled the grove chanting, "*Kill them. Kill them.*" By the time they reached the lab, Nasturtium's scent overpowered everything else. "*I smell them with you, all unprotected. A blast of cyanide will save the grove. Do it, Pepper. Make us proud.*"

Jonas blew strongly in that direction. "*I have a better way.*"

"It stinks out here," complained Lyra. "Maybe we should put on biosuits."

"Actually, that's a good idea," Jonas said. "We're okay inside the lab and the ship, but it isn't safe to go near the grove without a suit."

"The gases given off by the plants aren't poisonous," Cassie said.

They soon will be. Jonas didn't repeat the words aloud. He led everyone to the lab, although Lyra refused to enter until Max shoved her inside. Jonas opened the lid of the plant terrarium. "*Narcissus, I have three humans with me. No one is going to harm you. We're here to talk.*"

Narcissus puffed an obscenity. "*It won't work. They have noses but cannot smell.*"

Cassie coughed. Lyra hung back near the open flap, poised to run.

"*I'll translate,*" Pepper said. Jonas turned on the computer and gas chromatograph. "You remember the tumor Doc found in my head? It's not a tumor at all. It's a new organ which can detect a huge range of smells and translate them into thoughts. And vice versa. It gives me the ability to communicate with the plants."

"You understand these things?" The captain's voice was low and mean, with a tone more feral than human. "Why didn't you tell us sooner?"

"My mind couldn't make sense of it before. Doc called it synesthesia, a crossing of sensory signals to the brain. But it isn't a crossing, it was my brain trying to interpret something entirely new."

Cassie touched his arm. "You can talk to the plants? This plant?"

He nodded. "The plants captured me so they could learn how to communicate with us. They want the killing to end."

"By killing us," Lyra said.

Max raised a hand for her silence. "Prove you can talk to the plants."

"Goddamn Dr. Doolittle," muttered Lyra. "Can't you see he's one of them? He's conning us. He killed Li!"

"Sullivan..." Max warned.

"The *animal* killed Li," Cassie said.

Jonas didn't bother to correct her. She seemed as wary as Lyra and the captain.

"Does the animal talk, too, Jefferson?"

JJ hesitated, then leaned over the animal cage and sniffed. "A little. I think they are more like pets. Less intelligent, but playful and loyal."

Lyra stepped forward, fist raised. "Playful? You fucking son-of-a-bitch."

Max's arm shot out, blocking her path. She leaned against it, her breath quick and noisy as a race horse eager to charge out the gate.

"Jefferson, prove you can talk to these things before my arm gets tired."

"They have names. The plant is Narcissus. The animal is Sage."

Lyra's gaze stayed on Jonas. "He names these monsters, personifying them. Hoping it will it make it harder for us to kill them. It won't work. We're on to your games, cross-breed."

"Jefferson?"

"Ask it a question. I'll translate, and the computer will translate their answer to English."

Chapter 50

Ship Time: Day 21. 0900 hours.

Lyra crossed her arms. "This is ridiculous."

Cassie disagreed. Jonas might be able to provide indisputable proof that life here possessed intelligence. She watched him open the top of the terrarium and stare nervously at the plant inside. She touched his arm. "Can it tell us apart?"

He nodded. "After I make introductions."

Max raised a brow. "Why can't the computer talk to them?"

Cassie answered. "The gas chromatograph can detect thousands of scents, but it can't generate any of its own."

Jonas leaned toward the tank and exhaled. Complex odors drifted in the air. A computer-generated voice said, "Jonas. Cassie. Captain Kazakov. Lyra." A second later the computer repeated the names in a different voice.

Jonas smiled. "He knows each of you, now. So does Sage, but it's more difficult for an animal to speak."

"Different organs?" Cassie said.

"The animal can only emit odors via glands on the flippers."

Lyra made a rude noise. She lifted a hand, something small clutched in her fingers. "Ask it what I'm holding."

"They can't see. But if it has an odor, he might be able to identify it."

Lyra slowly opened her hand, revealing Li's pocket brain. Cassie felt Jonas tense. Why? His reaction and the engineer's smirk worried her.

Lyra said, "Too bad. Let's try something else, then. Turn around, Jonas. Face the wall."

When he complied, Lyra cautiously approached the terrarium. Casting a defiant look at Cassie and the captain, she reached inside and yanked a leaf from the plant's dome.

A spray of vinegar and ammonia erupted from the orifices on the plant's dome. Through watering eyes, Cassie saw Jonas spin. His shout drowned out the computer's voice. "You hurt Narcissus!" He rushed forward, teeth bared. Lyra shifted into a boxing stance, fists raised. Max stepped between the two combatants.

"This your proof, Jefferson?" Max said. "You can sniff out who's hurting a plant?"

Jonas glared at Lyra, his own fists ready for the fight. But when he spoke, his voice held more passion than anger. "They have a civilization. Knowledge, art, history. We can learn from them, Captain. They can learn from us. This is huge opportunity for both species."

"He's lying," Lyra said. "They have no buildings, no tools, no artifacts. They do nothing more than bask in a twilight sun, and think black thoughts on a black world. He says they have a civilization. The facts say otherwise."

A nod from Max revealed his inclination to back Lyra. With a calm she didn't feel, Cassie said, "Civilization is a collaborative endeavor. What does Narcissus do for his society?"

Jonas exhaled noisily. Computer Voice One said, "Tell them what you do for the grove, Narcissus."

Voice Two answered, "Lyra hurt me. You said they wouldn't hurt me."

"It's a misunderstanding. One of many. Please, answer the question."

"I am a teller of stories. A poet and orator."

"Yeah?" Lyra said. "Tell me the story of how Li died."

JJ's glare faded, but the tension increased. Cassie saw it in the thin line of his lips.

"Go on, Jefferson. Have the mushroom give its version."

Voice One said, "Tell us how Li died."

Two said, "She came into the lab, drenched in a ghastly perfume that didn't hide her increasingly profuse pheromones. Yours grew, too. Pepper said humans live in a dimension impossible to describe without experiencing it firsthand. I'm starting to believe it. Time passed, and then I smelled fear. Something knocked me over. Pepper shouted that Li was getting away. Sage squirted acid, which sent Li toward me. She attacked me, clawing, jabbing. I couldn't avoid her, so I sprayed her. I had no idea how fragile you creatures are until I smelled her dissolve. She had no memories. Is that enough?"

The knuckles of Lyra's fists looked ready to burst through the skin.

"Who is Pepper?" Max asked.

"Another plant," said One. "No, an animal. She came from the grove to check on us."

Cassie eyed Jonas. No one else seemed to notice that the answer hadn't come from the plant. She decided to play along. "What do the plants want, Jonas?"

Max said, "I don't care what they want." He placed his hand on the lid of the plant terrarium and began to drum his fingers. Tap, tap... tap. Tap, tap... tap. "Tell the animal to sit up and beg."

Jonas opened the lid and leaned over the cage. Cassie cringed. If it sprayed Jonas in the face, they'd never get him to the shower in time to save his life.

Voice One said, "Sage, come toward me and raise the forward part of your body."

All eyes watched as the black crab-like creature paddled to the end of the cage nearest Jonas, then rose almost vertical, supported by two pair of rear flippers.

"Son of a bitch," Max said. "Ask it how your foreskin grow back. Why is your skin blacker?"

"They don't know."

"Really? You didn't ask him."

JJ waited an instant too long before responding. "I did before. I was curious myself."

"Ask them now, Jefferson."

Jonas leaned briefly over the cages. "They don't know."

"I didn't hear the computer translate."

Jonas sighed. "It's the sap. It has healing properties."

"Sap," Max said. "How's it work? Need to get buried for three days?"

Jonas shook his head. "Sap is stored in their domes and secreted through the roots as needed." He nodded at the captain's right hand. "Stick your hand in the soil."

The captain raised his four-fingered hand. "You think I'm going to put this in there?"

Lyra leaned close. "It's a trap."

"Might be. Stick your hand in." Max grabbed Lyra's wrist before she could pull away and pushed her hand into the dirt. She cursed and jerked, but couldn't break free.

"They won't hurt you," Jonas said.

"Liar!" Lyra finally yanked her hand free and held it in front of her face. "It's... normal."

"They're not monsters. Captain, it can make your finger grow back."

Max pulled a revolver from his pocket. Cassie gasped. Nobody moved. He leveled the gun at JJ's head. "If that thing hurts me, you're dead."

Jonas eyed the gun. "Put your hand in the soil near the base of the plant. You'll feel a burning; they need to dissolve the surface layers before the healing can begin. It will hurt."

Voice One said, "I need you to secrete sap on the captain's hand."

"I won't shoot until I pull my hand out." Max plunged his hand into the black powder. Everyone stared, barely breathing. The soil moved in a small wave as the roots moved underneath. "The thing is crawling on me. Feels like a damn snake."

"Pull your hand out," whispered Lyra.

"Not yet," Jonas said.

"Tingles. Starting to burn. Damn, really burn. My hand's on fire!"

"Keep still. Don't move your hand."

Lyra smirked. "I hope he blows your head off."

"Itching, too," Max said.

"Part of the healing. Don't move."

"Tell the fucker to hurry before my trigger finger gets itchy, too."

"Another minute. The sap creates stem cells, growth hormones, and accelerants. It takes time to assemble the proteins coded by the human DNA."

"You've been hanging out with Clearwater too much. You talk like a biologist."

"She's the smartest woman I know." Jonas glanced her way.

Sudden heat rose to her face and warmed her heart as well. Maybe she'd been too hard on him.

"The itching stopped."

Jonas didn't seem fazed by the gun barrel hovering near his face. "Pull your hand out, Captain."

Unlike Lyra, Max removed his hand slowly, as if afraid to view the result. Five complete fingers emerged. He wiggled each one before lowering the gun. "I've carried this piece ever since Bernie Big Bucks taught me a lesson about welching on a bet. When I gave him the finger, he took it. Literally." He thrust his new middle finger up and barked a laugh. "Fuck you, Bernie."

It wasn't like Max to share personal history. Cassie's concern grew, even though JJ looked like he'd just hit the winning home run, and Lyra looked like the losing team's pitcher.

"So, Captain, let's release these innocent creatures," JJ said, "and start negotiation."

Cassie nodded. "Lyra can stop working on the UV lamps. The killing's over."

"No, we aren't going to kill them," Max said, almost to himself. "They are intelligent, valuable life forms." His alligator grin appeared, sending chills rippling down Cassie's back. "But don't let these critters go just yet, Clearwater. Study the sap. I want to know everything about it." He turned and left, whistling as he walked.

Chapter 51

Ship Time: Day 21. 1000 hours.

Jonas dreaded the upcoming conversation with Lyra, but it couldn't wait. He found her under the ship, head and arms hidden in the housing for the power coupling of the external flood lamps. Robbie waited beside her, tools spread across his top surface. His mechanical arms held two flashlights, one aimed up at the engineer's work area. The second pointed down to create a comforting circle of light under the shadow of the ship.

"Don't come any closer. I've got a wrench that will lay you flat."

"We need to talk."

"More light here, Robbie." Her face brightened with reflected illumination. She grunted and applied more torque to the wrench. A relay clicked, filling the air with a high-pitched, mosquito-like hum. A burnt charcoal smell came from the ground, accompanied by a cascade of pops and snaps. Smoke rose from a circular patch of ground directly under the forward flood lamp.

Jonas shook his head in frustration. "The captain rescinded his order to reconfigure the lamps."

Lyra lowered herself and began bolting the housing back into place.

Jonas continued, "Max knows they're intelligent now. He won't let you kill them."

Lyra sneered. "And I thought Cassie was naïve."

"Revenge won't bring Li back."

Lyra's glare burned hotter than the UV lamp. "This isn't revenge. It's survival."

"The captain—"

"Is a money-grubbing asshole. Me? I'm a survivor."

Lyra's determination to kill the plants settled like a heavy weight on his chest. It didn't matter what the captain wanted; Lyra wanted revenge. *Kill her now.* No! There's been enough death. "Damn it, Lyra. You don't know what you're doing."

"Right back at 'ya, plant brain."

Lyra knew as much about the ship as he did. In her current state of mind, she might very well ignore Max's orders and go on a killing spree. Time was in short supply. Worse, his ability to prevent or minimize the damage Lyra could cause depended on the fragile alliance he'd established with Cassie and the captain. "Lyra, I want Li's computer. Her pocket brain."

Lyra finished securing the hatch cover. "Adam, turn off the forward flood." The humming stopped, followed by the pops, and finally the smell. She turned to Jonas, her hands gripping the wrench. "I wondered when you would get around to that."

"Adam, give us some privacy."

"Audio and visual surveillance suspended, Mr. Jefferson. To resume, please access Robbie's local control panel."

Lyra's grip tightened on the handle. "You'll find me harder to kill."

"Do you know what's on it?"

"Afraid it will make Max change his mind?"

You have to kill her! "The recording doesn't prove anything. It's out of context."

"The plant killed Li, but you were there. Did you fuck her before watching her die? Did you even try to help her? Maybe you held her down while your creepy-crawly friend chewed her face off." Lyra twirled the heavy wrench as if it were a mace, and she stood like an Amazon warrior preparing to charge. "Do the right thing, Jonas. Kill yourself. Save Cassie the shame of watching you be executed for murder."

"Do you have any idea how many plants we've killed? Even so, there's still a chance for peace. Give me Li's computer."

Lyra took a step toward him, face distorted by rage and shadows. Jonas retreated, unable to see a resolution to the conflict. Once out from under the shadow of the ship, he felt strength return to his body and clarity to his mind. Not hope, only clarity. He gazed at the grove and smelled their fear. No hope came from that direction, either. He took a deep breath and blew forcefully. "*The monsters can make their own solar flares, sending down death as their hive floats in the sky. I will attempt to stop them. War comes soon, if I fail to stop them.*"

Nasturtium's reply came back. "*Do not fail me. Time grows short. KILL THEM.*"

With the engineer hellbent on genocide, Pepper smelled no alternative.

***

Cassie sat on the cot in the lab, trying to convince herself to be happy. After all, she had flown between the stars, named a planet, and discovered new extra-terrestrial species. JJ had proved the plants were intelligent and convinced Max not to kill them. Life was good.

On the other hand, Doc was dead, probably murdered and then staged to look like suicide. Li was dead, killed by a plant who claimed self-defense. Jonas had died, decided he didn't like it, and came back as a diet-conscious schizophrenic. Life was so *not* good.

In which list did pregnancy belong? It topped both. She fingered the ebony token that hung on her neck. "Grandfather, I need your wisdom more than ever." His voice stayed silent.

Max wanted her to study the sap, so she drew a vial of it from the plant's dome after donning thick gloves and positioning herself near the decon shower. She wished for the ability to talk to the plant to let it know why she was collecting more samples. Jonas could have helped, but he insisted there were tempers to calm, which apparently meant arguing with Lyra and then pacing through the grove and breathing heavily.

Cassie called Lyra on the intercom. "I noticed that you have Li's pocket brain. May I borrow it again? I want to resume work on the language program. Maybe we can get an independent verification of JJ's translation."

Lyra laughed. "Tell Jonas an end run won't work." Lyra refused to answer further calls.

Cassie chose not to escalate the matter to Max. More head-butting wouldn't ease Lyra's grief. Or maybe it would. People were so damn complicated.

Cassie returned to her notes on Doc's autopsy and ran tests on the caplets found in his stomach. The medicine didn't quite match the prescription in Doc's personnel file. Or rather, it did, but had also been infused with an unknown chemical. She suspected this was the fatal poison, but very little of the pills had dissolved, and she found none of the chemical in Doc's tissue or blood.

One more mystery on a planet filled with them. Tired of questions without answers, she returned to the ship to fix dinner. She spied Lyra under the ship fiddling with equipment, probably finding solace through her love of machines. Jonas stood in the grove, looking forlorn.

She called out, "Hey guys, supper in fifteen!" Neither person responded.

She didn't see Max. He wasn't in riverbed mining diamonds. In fact, he hadn't harped on anyone about digging today. That change seemed just as inexplicable as Doc's death or JJ's transformation. The thought did not give her a warm feeling.

She fixed toasted-cheese sandwiches. Max finally appeared and sat beside Lyra. They all ate in silence, with occasional sidelong glances to Jonas, who peeled off the bread and ate the cheese. Cassie skipped the sandwich, opting instead to finish off the half-gallon of fudge ripple ice-cream.

Chapter 52

Ship Time: Day 21. 1900 hours.

Tap..tap..tap..tap. The restoration of his finger felt and sounded odd, but appropriately symbolic of change and new opportunities. Max leaned back in his chair and put his feet on the desk. The plants were valuable, more precious than diamonds, a fact no one else grasped. Their sap could cure anything. It could prolong life, maybe indefinitely. People would pay through the nose for that. Who could set a price on the fountain of youth? The potential wealth dwarfed the trillion-dollar industry of MicroWeight. His mouth watered at the thought.

Capitalizing on the golden elixir faced serious obstacles. If Tobias found out, he'd claim it all, and ruthlessly defend that claim with all the wealth and power of the mightiest company in history. The sap had to remain secret. Not merely for the short term, but forever. That meant coming up with a cover story, a damn good one, to convince Tobias that Obsidian was a complete write-off.

"Adam, secure access to the ansible. No one sends or receives messages without my personal authorization."

"Acknowledged, Captain. Ansible chamber is now locked."

The next obstacle was the plants themselves. The damn things were intelligent, and therefore dangerous. Jonas wasn't sent back to negotiate peace, he came as a spy and assassin for the plants. Hell, he must be a plant on the inside. That slip about "Pepper" proved it. There was no other animal in the lab when Wu was killed. The walls and floor of the lab had no holes other than a small spot under the body. Therefore, Jonas *was* Pepper.

There had been only two deaths. Why hadn't Mr. Trojan Horse killed everyone? Because he fears what Tobias will do if we stop broadcasting. Hell, Tobias probably had a whole fleet of starships by now. The old man would send a ship or two to investigate, which would lead to enslavement or eradication of the plants. So what if they took twelve years to get here? The plants considered long term consequences, and those consequences didn't look good for them. Did common ground exist? The plants wanted to live, and Max wanted them to as well. They were worth nothing dead. All he needed to do was convince them that he was there best and only chance for survival.

"Adam, tell Sullivan to report to my cabin."

Two minutes later a knock announced the arrival of the engineer. Max lowered his feet to the floor and adopted a more conspiratorial pose. "Come."

The heavy wooden door creaked open and the engineer entered with a stiff, almost military stride. Her bellicose attitude matched the bearing. "I'm going to kill the plants. You can't stop me."

"Of course you are." He gestured toward the empty chair. "Let's talk about how."

Caught off guard by his acquiescence, she took the proffered seat. "I thought you were backing Cassie."

"Had to do it for show." He smiled. "Adam, no surveillance for ten minutes, please."

"Acknowledged, Captain."

His eyes bored into hers. "Sullivan, you know what the problem is."

"Jonas," she hissed through clenched teeth.

He nodded. "He's not really human anymore. The plants are killers. He knows it, yet defends them... because he's one of them."

"Fucking right. But he's also the son of Tobias."

"It does present a problem." Max leaned forward and lowered his voice. "He may need to suffer a fatal accident." He kept his face deadpan and studied her reaction.

She nodded slowly. "If it looks like the plants turned on him, it will keep Cassie and Tobias off our backs."

He leaned back, satisfied. "My thoughts exactly. As for the plants, how is the weapon of mass destruction coming?"

"The UV lamps are done." A sly grin spread across her face, giving her a girlish look. "And I have a second weapon. I modified the ship's sonar probes. They can now emit ultrasonic bursts at the same frequency that shatters their domes."

"No shit? That's great."

"So... when do we wipe out the bastards?"

"Tomorrow. Right after I deal with Jefferson."

She rubbed her hands. "I can hardly wait."

When she left, he considered his next move. Jefferson wasn't really human; he hadn't lied about that. It called into question whether he could be manipulated by human reason and emotion. Max couldn't afford a miscalculation. Cassie was a sure bet—her motivations and fears were an open book, available for him to insert editorial comments. But first things first.

"Adam, tell Jefferson to report to my cabin."

When the pilot arrived, Max went straight to the heart of the matter. "Jefferson, you have a problem. Or shall I call you Pepper?" Max grinned at the look of complete shock. "Yes, I know your alter ego. You slipped up at the lab. But it doesn't matter, because I want to help you."

The black man's eyes were full of suspicion. "I'm not admitting anything... but what do you mean by help?"

"First off, I'm not blaming you or the plants for the deaths. It was all a terrible misunderstanding." A look of relief eased some of the tension visible in Jefferson's face and posture. Max continued, "I figure you—the Pepper you—came here to gather information. Well, now you have that information and it sucks."

Jonas nodded.

"It boils down to your father. You can't kill us because Tobias would send a ship to investigate. Even if you kill them, another ship will come. Eventually humans would simply sterilize the planet from space. No more plants. You lose, period."

Jonas slumped, seeming to melt into the chair.

"If you don't kill us, my past reports of diamonds and the nearly ideal environmental conditions guarantee the arrival of miners and colonists by the thousands. Again, the plants would be wiped out."

Anguish filled JJ's eyes with moisture. "But we're a peaceful, sentient species! We live, we love, we dream just like you. The planet is ours."

Max raised a brow. "Ah. Hello, Pepper. Yes, it's sad. A real tragedy. That's why I'm going to help you out of this mess. I'm going to fake a few reports to Tobias. If I can convince him the planet is both worthless and extremely dangerous, he won't bother sending more ships."

JJ shook his head. "He'll come for me. For us."

"Not if he thinks we're all dead."

Surprise struck a spark that kindled hope in the pilot's face. Max smiled in response. "There are details to work out, of course, but with you and Clearwater helping, I think we can pull it off."

"And then you and Cassie will head back to the solar system... and acquire new identities."

"You catch on quick. The diamonds we have in the hold will last the rest of our lives." Max let the cheerfulness fade. "My biggest concern is Sullivan. She's a hothead, she hates the plants, and she's a genius. She's making a weapon. You've seen her working on the UV lamps."

Jonas nodded. "She won't listen to reason."

"She won't listen to orders, either. I told her to stop and she didn't."

"You could revoke her authority, have Adam lock her out of the controls."

"Sullivan knows the ship better than anyone. She'd find a way around any lock. I read her the riot act ten minutes ago. I'm hoping it knocks some sense into that thick Irish skull. If not, I might have to confine her to quarters."

"She needs to join our conspiracy," JJ said. "The plants have to survive."

"She'll never join. At best I'm hoping she'll keep her mouth shut when we get home. Going incognito, giving up her dreams, swallowing her grief... it's a lot to ask." He cast a sympathetic look at Jonas. "Don't worry. I'll think of something." He put equal parts doubt and worry into his voice, confident that Jefferson's thoughts would turn in the proper direction.

Chapter 53

Ship Time: Day 22. 0300 hours.

At oh-three hundred, the time Pepper believed the crew to be in deepest slumber, she forced Jonas through the corridor, every movement exaggerated and jerky like a marionette. As their brains moved closer to full integration, control became increasingly difficult. The host fought her continuously. A laser scalpel, slick with sweat, required a grip so tight that the knuckles formed pale hills under his black skin. She stopped outside the engineer's cabin. Jonas tried to step away, but she locked his legs.

Thousands will die if she lives. Open the door. No. His hand trembled as he fought for control, but the arm rose and his finger depressed the access button. The button glowed red.

Aloud he whispered, "It's set for do not disturb. An override will set off an alarm." His other hand lifted the laser to the door. "Pepper, cutting a hole big enough to walk through will take forever with a scalpel. The fumes will probably wake her. The smoke alarm certainly will."

She lowered the scalpel.

"We need to trust each other. The killing must stop. All of it." He felt her uncertainty like a spark falling on dry tinder, and tried to nurse it into flame. "You're not a killer, and you don't need to be. Let's go back to my cabin and work on a plan."

The puppet master loosened the strings on his muscles, but his relief triggered a surge in Pepper's resolve. Two blasts of ammonia had come and gone. The third and final was hours away. She had promised the Eldest of living things that she would save the grove.

She would fulfill her promise, regardless of personal feelings or danger. Tarragon had sacrificed himself to save the grove. She could do no less.

"Pepper, Tarragon was wrong. Saving the grove doesn't mean killing the humans."

You know much about the ship. I'm sure to find something useful in your memories. Images of wiring diagrams and ship schematics spun by like symbols on a slot machine.

Jonas sank into frustration. He'd been so close to winning her over. If only he knew more about her, knew what events shaped her character, what motivations drove her behavior. It might provide a basis on which to build trust. On a hunch, he relinquished all control of his body and gave Pepper full access to his memories. Resistance could be worse than useless; it often became counter-productive. His consciousness drifted, open, receptive, and expectant. Myriad odors swirled in his mind, then coalesced into memories that were not his own. As she plumbed his memories, he plumbed hers.

"You've spent your whole life in a quest to prove a universe exists beyond this planet. Now that you have proof, now that you know life—intelligent life—exists in that universe, you're going to kill it."

Get out of my mind!

"Our mind, Pepper. We can paralyze this body through relentless opposition, or we can find common ground for cooperation."

As a species, your first instinct is to kill what you don't understand.

"Isn't that what you're doing?"

You killed first. We're defending ourselves.

"We were ignorant, not malicious. I won't let it happen again."

The spinning memories of ship schematics clicked into place. Pepper visualized the control relay just inside the wall at eye-level to the right of the door. She cut a triangular hole with three quick slashes, examined the exposed relay, and shorted two of its contacts. The door slid open with a barely perceptible hiss. Dim light from the corridor revealed Lyra asleep on the bunk.

Nor will I. Lyra plans to destroy the grove. If not now, then in the future. She has to die.

The symbiont stepped inside, and the door hissed shut. The laser scalpel hummed softly.

Chapter 54

Ship Time: Day 22. 0715 hours.

Cassie entered the mess hall, poured a cup of coffee, and dumped granola into a bowl. Max wolfed down eggs and bacon. Without looking up, he pushed a tray of blueberries her way. She plopped a few on the cereal. Jonas sulked at the far end of the table, listlessly stirring a spoon through a cup of yogurt.

"Clearwater, I told the company that Obsidian was uninhabitable and of no economic value."

For a moment she couldn't believe she'd heard him correctly. "But the diamonds?"

He shrugged. "We'll have to dump them."

That couldn't be Max talking. Greed surrounded him like a magnetic field, pulling him toward any accumulation of wealth. No way could he walk away from the fortune they'd mined. Altruism and the Prime Directive didn't enter into his calculations.

"Why?" she asked.

"The only way to protect this planet is to fool Tobias into thinking it's worthless. We can't very well show up with a cargo hold full of diamonds."

She frowned. "Haven't you already told him that we've struck it rich?"

"Yes, but I've amended my reports. Turns out that the diamonds are highly radioactive. Deadly. Unsellable. Already killed Unger and Wu. The rest of us have radiation poisoning."

She munched on her cereal as she digested his words. The berries tasted particularly sweet. She ate them with relish, then wondered if Jonas had spit on them. Or something worse. She pushed the bowl away. "You in on this, JJ?"

Jonas nodded. "Yeah." He managed a smile. "Prime Directive needed some backup."

His lack of enthusiasm worried her.

The captain continued. "I didn't mention the plants." He scrutinized her face like an interrogator waiting for a reaction. "You said they need to be protected. The best way is through secrecy and subterfuge."

The intensity of his stare felt as wrong as JJ's despondency. Did Max find a way to make more money than the diamonds would bring? But they were worth millions, even billions. Where else—

The explanation fell into place. Jonas must have paid Max to abandon the diamonds and falsify reports to make the planet appear worse than worthless. Wow. Dear wonderful Jonas.

Max seemed to sense her suspicions. "Some things are more important than money. Right, Jefferson?"

JJ mumbled assent without raising his head. The price must have been huge to put Jonas in such a mood.

"But there's a problem," Max said. "The engineer is hell-bent on extermination. We need to convince her that the plants should not be killed. In fact, they need to be protected. Which means she has to give up the money and keep her mouth shut. Won't be easy. But if the three of us show a united front..."

"Why not just cut her in on the money?" Cassie asked.

Jonas looked perplexed. Max scowled. "What money?"

Had she read the signs wrong? She had obviously missed *something*. "Sorry. Brain fart."

The captain's scowl eased into a smile, but the look of scrutiny in his eyes remained intense. "Then I can depend on both of you to back me up. Sullivan's a hard nut to crack." He popped more bacon into his mouth. His lips undulated as he chewed, rendering the smile far from reassuring. He wiped his mouth with his sleeve. "Adam, tell Sullivan to get her ass down here for the morning briefing."

A moment later, Adam said, "Captain, the engineer is not responding."

Cassie glanced at Jonas, who had resumed stirring his yogurt.

"Where is she?" asked Max.

"Dr. Sullivan does not show up on surveillance. Most likely she is still in her cabin."

"Clearwater, go check on her."

Cassie appreciated the chance to slip away. She wasn't sure how to deal with the reformed captain. It added complexity when she wanted simplicity. If Jonas wasn't paying him off, then what angle was Max playing? And what of Jonas himself, so moody and distant? Was he angry about the pregnancy? They needed to talk about it, bring it into the open, not act like it wasn't real. *Damn.* This whole mission, instead of fulfilling her lifelong dream, seemed destined to destroy it. It had already killed Doc and Li. Two lives lost, and for what?

Bad things often came in threes. *Lyra.* She quickened her pace.

The engineer's cabin door refused to open, apparently locked from inside. A triangle drawn on the wall caught her attention. It wasn't a drawing. Straight, narrow cuts penetrated the wall, outlining a section that fit snugly as a jigsaw puzzle piece. Only a laser made such fine lines.

"Adam, override the lock. Open Lyra's cabin."

The door slid open. The smell of excrement triggered a cough that soon had her spewing blueberry-stained granola on the floor. When she caught her breath, she shouted, "Adam, intercom. Captain! Get down here now!"

She covered her mouth and nose with the bottom of her shirt. It didn't help much as she stepped into the room. "Lyra?" The rumpled bed sheets were splattered with blood and other stains. Lyra wasn't in the shower or on the floor, though Cassie saw Li's pocket brain under the desk. She slipped it into her pocket.

A second look around the room found a bloody smear on the handle of the lower smiley. She pulled the drawer open.

The engineer's head stared up with death-clouded eyes. Sections of arms, legs, and torso surrounded the head, each precisely cut and neatly stacked within the drawer.

Cassie's stomach heaved again, adding a bitter splash of bile to the remains.

***

Max let Jonas take the lead as they dashed to the engineer's cabin. When Jonas knelt to comfort the dry-heaving science officer, Max scanned the floor and then the drawer. He pulled the gun from his pocket and pressed the barrel to the back of JJ's head.

"Clearwater, grab some cable ties from the supply locker."

"I'm sick," she said, not looking up. "Dear God, poor Lyra."

"Cassie," Jonas said, "he has a gun on me."

She lurched to her feet. "What the hell?"

"He murdered Sullivan," Max said. "It sure wasn't you or me."

She backed away, horror twisting her face. "Jonas, what have you done?"

"Plastic ties, Clearwater. Now!"

She sprinted from the room. Jonas started to rise. Max pressed the barrel harder. "Don't move. Don't stand. Don't talk. I really don't want to kill you, Jefferson."

They waited silently until Cassie returned with the ties.

"Bind his wrists." He watched as she did a decent job. "Good. Okay, Jefferson. Stand up. Slowly."

Using the gun, he prodded Jonas into the corridor and then into cargo bay one, where he made Jonas sit on the floor, back to the wall. "Clearwater, use the rest of the ties to bind his ankles." He appreciated her excellent work. No love lost there.

He handed her a rope, which she wrapped around the cable ties and then fastened to an equipment anchor set into the wall. He inspected the ties and nodded. "Good job." He slipped the gun in his pocket.

JJ said, "It's not too late for peace, Captain. Even now."

Max laughed at the sad, puppy-dog face. He glanced at Cassie and frowned. The girl still had feelings for the monster.

"Clearwater, check the engine vents, make sure they're not clogged with black grit. I want the ship ready for takeoff in a couple hours." He saw puzzlement on her face. "No, we're not going home. Yet. Just hovering."

"Why?"

"Safer."

"Go ahead, Cassie," Jonas said. "He won't kill me."

She frowned as if trying to concentrate. She turned to Max. "He's entitled to a trial—"

"Impossible, Clearwater. Think about it. Unger, Wu, now Sullivan. He's the link. He's the murderer."

She swayed, wavering.

"Check the vents, Clearwater."

She didn't move. "Are you... are you going to kill him?"

"It's within my rights as captain."

"He's tied up. Helpless. And his father—"

"Move it, Clearwater. You're the engineer now. Engines operational in two hours."

Jonas said, "Go, Cass. He won't kill me. He needs me."

When she left the compartment, Jonas said, "What did you put in the blueberries?"

Max chuckled. "Smart man, not warning her. She might live through this after all. You might, too." He hunkered down next to prisoner. "Here's what you're going to do."

***

After clearing the vents, Cassie made her way to the bridge, where she performed pre-op tests of the reactor, IDF, and engines. Each of the crew had cross-trained, so she knew what to do, yet nervous sweat oozed from her pores to crawl like ants over her skin. She used to love being alone. Now solitude equaled vulnerability. She activated the internal video monitors. One showed Jonas in the cargo bay.

"Something wrong, Clearwater?"

She jumped at the captain's voice. How did he get so close so quickly? "I can't believe he did it. I thought I knew him."

"There's something you should see." Max touched a control on a second monitor. "This is the surveillance recording of the corridor outside Sullivan's cabin. Last night, just after oh-three hundred hours." The video showed JJ walk to the cabin door, use a laser scalpel to remove a small section of the wall, and reach inside. The cabin door opened.

"Oh, no," whispered Cassie. "I saw the cuts on the wall."

Max turned off the monitor. "Too bad there are no cameras in personal quarters. Not that it matters. Jefferson came out about forty-five minutes later. No one else entered or left until you showed up this morning."

She stared at the blank screen, feeling numb, unable to think. "Why?"

"You know why. Sullivan wanted all the plants dead. The plant half of his brain couldn't ignore the threat. He had to stop her." His hand covered hers. "It's not your fault."

"It's not a brain, just an organ for translating smells and thoughts."

A look she couldn't quite read flashed across his face. "Right. That's what I meant." He looked at the monster on the monitor screen. "You want to see him, talk to him. Don't. He's dangerous. The authorities can handle things when we get back home."

She felt drained. Defeated. The girl who had failed the spirit quest had failed again. She had nowhere left to run. "I had such dreams, Max. They're all gone."

"Let's salvage what we can of the mission. I need you to collect more specimens for transport to Earth."

"Sir? We should release the ones we have. Certainly not take any more."

He placed a hand on her shoulder, then leaned down to speak softly in her ear. "These plants represent an amazing, a profound discovery. Proof we are not alone in the universe, proof that intelligent non-human life exists. The philosophical implications are staggering."

She pulled away. A toothy grin spread across his face, at odds with wary eyes. She frowned. "You said they need to be kept secret."

The smile wavered. "Exactly. For now. That's why you, and only you, will handle their education and eventual introduction to human society. There's obviously been a tragic misunderstanding. Until we achieve mutual understanding, those things are dangerous killers, just like Jefferson. What if they figure out how to build space ships? We need to know what makes them tick. It's a matter of self-defense."

"Captain, what's going on?"

"Take Robbie, collect as many as will fit in the hold. Be careful not to harm them."

Part of her wanted to argue, but she couldn't quite pin down her objections. It was simpler to do what he said and put this mess behind her. Maybe take a nap when the work was over. Or a cold shower. Something to clear the fuzziness in her head.

Chapter 55

Ship Time: Day 22. 0800 hours.

Cassie found nineteen containers suitable for transplanting small or mid-size plants. Each container could hold three or four plants. How many plants total? JJ's murderous actions had left her befuddled. She asked Adam to do the math. Between sixty and seventy-five. Seemed like a lot.

Robbie staged the containers at the base of the ramp while she concentrated on how to fetch the plants themselves. The lab had large sample bags and rolls of plastic wrap. Robbie could bag the roots and soil, and then wrap the stem and dome of each plant. If she stacked the plants horizontally, she could probably have all the specimens collected in three or four trips. She donned a biosuit after Adam reminded her of dangerous chemical emissions.

"Let's go, Robbie." She started for the lab, but the robot didn't follow. Her radio wasn't on. Where was her mind? *Click.* "Let's go."

Narcissus and Sage waited in their cages. Sage lay on his side, three flippers resting atop the black sand. It looked too cute to be sentient, but intelligence didn't imply morality. These cold, calculating creatures turned Jonas into a killer. Now it was up to her and the captain to make things right.

She touched her abdomen. She'd have to tell Tobias. No, she couldn't. Max said they had to keep everything secret. Besides, it wasn't even JJ's baby. What a fucking mess.

She jumped as something buzzed against her thigh. She peeled off the suit and fished Li's pocket brain from her pocket. A tinny voice said, "Connection reestablished. Translation in progress."

Hands trembling, she tapped the screen and projected a holographic list of files, one of which was blinking. "Play file," she said.

"One of the humans is here," said a voice.

A second voice said, *"Quiet, Sage! Don't let it smell you."*

"This is the one Pepper told us about. I don't think she intends to harm us."

"Pepper's a fool. This one tortures and kills."

"The human didn't know any better. I'm going to try communicating with her."

"It won't do any good without Pepper."

"Maybe she's taught them how to smell."

"If we were going to be freed it would have happened when I healed the branch on that foul-smelling monster. They have plans for us. Plans that don't end well."

Cassie felt rooted to the floor. Language. True communication. If only she'd had this proof before they took Jonas. The plants weren't inherently dangerous. They simply reacted to a perceived attack against them. The crisis had come from monumental misunderstandings on both sides.

Peripheral movement attracted Cassie's attention. The animal rapped its snorkel against the wall of the cage. *"Alien being... Cassie, can you understand me?"*

She couldn't answer without Jonas. Or could she? Come on, girl. *Think.* She tapped once on Sage's back. The creature went very still. The PB said, *"You and I once discussed integers. What does two plus two equal?"*

Cassie tapped four times on the creature's back.

"It's working! The human understands integers!"

"Is Pepper with her? I don't smell her."

Cassie had no way to send smells to the plants and animal. Only Jonas could do that, but he'd turned homicidal, maybe as a result of the biological tampering by the aliens. Cassie wondered why the plants referred to him as Pepper, but her thoughts kept spinning around the answer like a whirlpool above a drain.

"There's a neurological chemical affecting her brain," Sage said. *"Narcissus, spray her with a neutralizing agent."*

"I'll have nothing to do with the monster."

"Please. We need her help."

"No."

"You do remember that I'm son of an elder. In fact, I am now son of the eldest."

A few seconds passed before Narcissus answered. *"Very well. I shall bravely risk life and limb for the well being of the grove. Cassie, if you can smell me, open the lid to my prison."*

Cassie hesitated, afraid to trust the aliens. The fear made her feel ashamed. She lifted the lid to the terrarium. A gentle mist bathed her face. She thought of Li, slammed the lid, and grabbed a towel.

Nothing burned. Nothing hurt.

She returned to the PB's virtual screen and tried to open more files. All were locked and encrypted except for a translation file from two days earlier. She listened to it with growing horror. JJ's brain was half alien. Hadn't he said something about being a Trojan Horse? Jonas had tried giving her a warning, and she had ignored it. People died as a result. The monotone translation never changed pitch or speed, but Cassie's mind filled in the panic and urgency.

"She's getting away! Sage, spray acid up and left to block her way! ... Narcissus! She's right next to you. 1,2,2,2-tetrafluoroethyl difluoromethyl ether ... I wanted her stopped, not killed! I could have convinced her to be friends."

A second voice said, *"Her kind killed Daphne. I'm proud of what I did."*

"I need to put you back on the table and close the lid. I need to think of an explanation. I can barely keep control of this human."

"Finish the mission! Don't become one of them!"

The virtual monitor flashed: END OF FILE.

Poor Li. No one deserved to die like that. Lyra had been right all along. It wasn't Jonas come back from the dead, but a doppelganger to kill them all, with the plant half of his brain calling the shots while his human body kept them fooled. How could she have been so blind? Even the captain saw the truth.

Cassie's fog cleared. Fear lifted the tiny hairs on her neck. *Plant half of his brain.* Max used those exact words. They weren't a misstatement. He'd already listened to Li's PB.

Chapter 56

Ship Time: Day 22. 0830 hours.

Cassie stood outside the door to the cargo bay, finger poised above the "open" button, caught between desire for truth and fear of dealing with it. Her left hand held a laser scalpel, the closest thing to a weapon she could find. Knowing that Lyra had been butchered by the same type of tool made her want to throw it away. The same knowledge tightened her grip. Did Jonas suffer that same internal dichotomy?

She steeled herself against being sympathetic to JJ's current helplessness and felt reasonably immune to his charms. She depressed the button and walked inside. She wasn't prepared for his look of concern.

"Cassie, you shouldn't be here."

"We need to talk." She held the scalpel behind her back.

"It isn't safe. Leave. Do whatever the captain says."

She revealed the laser. "I'm not afraid of you."

The corners of his mouth bent upward. "I'm not exactly in a position to hurt you." He tugged on the rope. "Or protect you."

"I need to know the truth." She forced the question out. "Did you kill Doc and Lyra?"

The normally strong lines of his face sagged. "My mission was doomed from the start." His tone and cadence subtly shifted.

Cassie shivered. "Pepper?"

"Ah. You know."

"What are you? What happened to Jonas?"

"I am Jonas. I'm Pepper, too. I'm both and neither. Two sets of memories, two brains, though each hour, each layer, brings us closer to unity."

"So Pepper is the killer, not Jonas."

"I swore to kill all of you. The elders said it was the only way to save the grove."

"Fight it Jonas! Come back to me."

His haunted eyes met hers. "I never wanted anyone to die."

"You killed them."

Jonas opened his mouth, then shut it. He took a deep breath before answering. "What does it matter? Humans want the plants enslaved. Plants want the humans dead. It's naïve to think peace is possible."

"You talk about peace, but murder three people? Am I missing something?"

"I didn't kill anyone."

"You lie." She blurted out the painful truth. "Both your brains had motive. Doc is the father of my baby! That's why you killed him." Her hands shook as her voice wavered.

He blinked in surprise. "You carry *our* baby, Cassie. I'd know if it weren't so by the smell of your skin."

"Max said Doc impregnated me during a pre-flight physical."

His surprise morphed into thoughtfulness. "He probably did, but with my sperm. Dad insisted I leave some in cryogenic storage." His face hardened. "Dad's plan is clear now. He always wanted me to take over the company, have kids, continue the dynasty. I told him no, that I wanted to spend my life exploring the galaxy. He was pissed. Took him months to get over it. Except he didn't."

"Tobias would do that to us? To me?"

"Dad always gets what he wants. That's a big part of why I needed to get away." His gaze held unflinching honesty. "Cassie, I did not kill Doc."

She studied his face, his body language. "You altered the chemistry of his medicine."

"To cure his tremors. Pepper thought it would make him an ally in negotiating peace between the species."

Cassie's mind spun, making connections with almost audible clicks. "Li killed him."

Jonas raised a brow.

"I found silk fibers around his collar. She smothered or strangled him, then left a suicide note for me to find. Not a very good one, either."

"Motive?"

"I think Doc was going to tell me the truth about the pregnancy. That would complicate Li's plans to steal you from me. Or maybe Tobias hired her to make sure Doc kept his mouth shut."

Jonas nodded. "With Doc dead, I had to change plans. I hoped your efforts to communicate with the plants would lead to a peaceful resolution, but Narcissus killed Li and everything fell apart." JJ clenched his fists and jerked on the rope. "Max killed Lyra. Can't you smell his greed? He means to harvest the sap, but Lyra would never have allowed him to bring plants to Earth." His tone turned hard. "Play along with Max. Until I can kill him."

"We'll stop him together." Ignoring his protests, she stepped forward, intending to cut through the plastic ties on his wrists and ankles. She heard the door open behind her and peered over her shoulder.

Max leveled the pistol at her. "Clearwater, you should not have come back here."

She turned to Jonas, who strained against his bonds and said, "You're scum, Kazakov. The worst dregs of humanity." He spat to emphasize the words.

"Soon to be the richest, half-breed."

Cassie stared at the gun. The black hole of the muzzle seemed to fill the room. Her heart drummed fast and hard, the beat of a war dance. The scalpel grew slippery in her palm. She tightened her grip and took a step toward Max.

He cocked the hammer with his thumb. "You'll be dead before you can touch me."

Jonas stood, smoke rising from melting plastic ties. "You kill her, I kill you. The plants win." He joined Cassie. Neither guilt nor doubt contorted his face. She loved this man.

"You're right." Max swung the gun toward JJ.

Events took on a strobe-like intensity. Cassie threw the scalpel. The captain dodged. The gun fired. Jonas rushed forward. The men merged in a tangle of thrashing legs and hammering fists. The gun clattered on the floor.

"Cassie, get out of here!" Jonas yelled.

She watched the fight for another few seconds, unable to turn away. The scalpel glinted on the floor. She snatched it and slashed the captain's leg. He roared and rolled off Jonas—and onto the gun. Jonas scrambled to his feet and sprang to the door, pushing Cassie through with him. She hit the close button. The gun boomed. A crater appeared in the wall an instant before the door slid shut.

"Give me the scalpel," Jonas said.

Another moment of trust. She handled him the laser.

His eyes thanked her. "Keep your finger on the close button." He cut a small opening in the wall and rerouted some wires.

She stared at the hole. "That's how you got into Lyra's room."

"Let's go. This won't hold him for long."

On cue, the door slid open about a centimeter. Red lights flashed from the ceiling and a claxon blared. "The hand crank is connected to the emergency alarm. We need to get out of here."

He winced as he gave her the laser. A red stain spread across his shirt.

"We need to get you to sickbay."

He shook his head. "No. The lab."

Chapter 57

Ship Time: Day 22. 0845 hours.

Jonas nodded toward the animal cage. "Take Sage. I'll get Narcissus."

"Not until I bandage that wound. Take off your shirt."

Jonas started to protest, but the way she stood with arms crossed and feet planted wide apart convinced him it'd be quicker to comply than argue. The touch of her hands on his skin made him tingle; the thought of the captain made him sweat. Time was in short supply.

"In and out," she said. "Lower left abdomen. You're lucky. It's starting to heal already, but you lost a lot of blood. Can you regenerate blood?" She wiped the wound with alcohol and taped gauze over it.

"With sunshine, water, and a few minerals." He ran his fingers over the bandage. "Thanks. We need to reach the grove." Without bothering to don his shirt, he flipped open the plant cage.

Cassie started to lift the animal cage.

"No, take him out of the box."

Cassie opened the lid, but she hesitated to reach inside.

A muffled voice came from Cassie's pocket. "*Sage, Narcissus, we're here to free you. Don't struggle.*"

JJ said, "He won't hurt you."

Cassie lifted Sage from the cage. Jonas-Pepper felt a surge of love for both beings. "Set him down as soon as we get outside. I'll have to carry Narcissus." He lifted the plant from the terrarium.

"What's the plan, Jonas?"

"I'm working on it."

"*It's about time,*" puffed Narcissus. "*We thought you abandoned us.*"

"I appreciate your gratitude," Pepper said. "*I hope you find a mate just like yourself.*"

They hurried outside. Cassie set the animal on the ground. Jonas handed her Narcissus. "Run to the grove. Hide. I'll be right behind you." "*Narcissus, Cassie will carry you home. She is an ally. Tell everyone she is not to be harmed, and they have nothing to fear from her.*"

"*She's a monster,*" said Narcissus stubbornly.

"Button your blow holes," said Jonas-Pepper. "*She's your only chance for survival. Harm her and I'll kill you myself.*"

Cassie kissed Jonas and ran. He watched for a moment before squatting next to Sage. "*I need you to dissolve the landing struts on the ship and then clog the vents.*"

"*Finally, a chance to redeem myself.*"

Jonas took a look at the ship and saw Robbie rolling toward the lab. Why wasn't it chasing them?

"*Pepper. I love you.*" Sage said before disappearing under the surface. JJ ran to the grove and hid with Cassie behind a wall of mature plants. While Pepper explained the situation to the grove, Jonas explained his plan to Cassie.

"A strut failure will tip the ship over. The vents will clog, so even if he manages to take off, he won't be able to maneuver. Nasturtium has already converted a few plants to animal form. They're being sent in to kill the captain when he comes out to do repairs."

"How about us?" Cassie said.

"What?"

"You say you love me, but you've never asked me to marry you. Now I have your baby inside me."

"You want to talk about that *now*?"

She nodded. "There might not be a later."

"There will be." He studied the ship. No sign of the captain. *Hurry, Sage. Tip the ship and get your roots back here.* Jonas leaned close to Cassie. "You're the most honorable person I know. You don't tolerate lies or deliberate distortions."

"I'm not after a character analysis."

"When this is over... I *want* to marry you. I want that with every fiber of my being."

She heard the hesitancy in his voice. "But?"

"I'm not the same me that you fell in love with. I don't know what I am."

Did she? Was he more than before? Less? "People change. Especially when they're in love."

Jonas heard a deep humming noise. "Shit." He peeked around a stem. The ship hovered several meters off the ground. Sage hadn't reached the struts in time. Max didn't rush after them because he knew the ship held strategic high ground. Above the range of acid sprays, Max could hunt them down at leisure.

"He's leaving us here to die," Cassie said.

"No. He needs me."

"As a translator? He'll just harvest the domes without you."

He shook his head. "War has come. Max has no way to collect the sap without getting the plants to surrender. I'm the only way he has to communicate threats and demands."

A loud whine filled the air, rapidly climbing in pitch until it became inaudible. The flood lights on the underside of the ship began to glow. The ship moved closer, until it was nearly overhead. Robbie rolled from the lab on an intercept course.

"He has ultrasound *and* ultraviolet," Cassie said. "Not good."

The captain's voice boomed from Robbie's speakers. "Come out, come out, wherever you are... or I'll fry every living thing here."

"I need to lure him outside the ship," Jonas said. "Cassie, give me scalpel."

"It's in the lab. All I have is Li's pocket brain."

His eyes widened. "Even better." He took the PB, opened a virtual keyboard, and typed in a series of commands. A voice said, "Comm link opened."

Jonas said, "Adam, establish a full linkage with this computer."

"Acknowledged. Link established."

Cassie asked, "What are you doing?"

"Committing mutiny. Adam, display pilot console."

The PB keyboard vanished, replaced by the familiar virtual controls of JJ's bridge station. Jonas grinned. "A barrel roll followed by a high-speed nose dive into the sand should disable the ship long enough to mount an attack."

His hands flowed through the controls. Nothing moved. The ship stayed rock steady.

Adam's voice came from the PB. "Sorry, Mr. Jefferson. Your authority to operate the controls was rescinded by the captain."

"The captain's a murderer. Restore my authority."

"I am not empowered to determine guilt or innocence, nor am I programmed to override orders due to extenuating circumstances. I am sympathetic to your plight, but cannot help."

Jonas looked at Cassie. "You try."

"I can't fly the ship."

"You have to try." He kissed her hands without breaking eye contact. "You've watched me often enough. Yaw, pitch, thrust—you know the controls. Hey, you can't mess up, because the goal is to crash."

She plunged her hands into the virtual console.

"Sorry, Dr. Clearwater. Operation of the navigation and piloting controls are restricted to Captain Kazakov and me by order of the captain."

Cassie coughed as a cloud of ammonia rose abruptly all around her.

Jonas cursed. "My time's up." He stood and exhaled heavily. "I told Myrtle to keep you safe." The ammonia seemed to dissipate. Jonas-Pepper stepped into the open and waved his arms. "It ends now."

Chapter 58

Ship Time: Day 22. 0900 hours.

Cassie crawled to a position where she could watch Jonas while remaining concealed behind a curtain of skinny stems. The nauseating smell of sulfur and vinegar forced her to take shallow, open-mouth breaths. The plants were terrified of her. The feeling was mutual.

The *Far Traveler* moved in majestic grace toward the grove. On the ground, Robbie reached a position beneath the ship. The lab's mass spectrometer perched atop the robot, and a power saw extended from one of its arms. Robbie stopped ten meters from Jonas. The ship hovered two meters above the robot.

A ten-meter-wide circle of light blazed down from the underside of the ship. Smoke swirled above crackling sand. Plants caught within the circle of death blistered and disintegrated. Even plants that had covered themselves with protective white shells perished as their domes split from ultrasonic vibration. Odors of burnt grass and charcoal overpowered the smell of fear.

When nothing remained alive beneath the ship, its ramp extended toward the robot like the hand of a mechanical giant reaching out to touch its child. Max, dressed in a full spacesuit, strutted down the ramp and stepped atop Robbie. A thin cable tethered Max to the ship—even if he fell or was knocked from the cart, Adam could lift him promptly out of danger. Max carried the handgun in his right hand.

Cassie's hopes, already dashed, sank further into despair.

The captain's voice boomed from Robbie's speakers. "Finally see the light, Jefferson? Or whatever you are."

"You didn't have to kill more plants."

"Just driving home the point, half-breed. You know what I want. Translate my orders into something these things understand. Robbie will translate the smells into English, so do try to be accurate. Each lie will cost the life of a mushroom."

"What do you want me to tell them?"

"Adam, all translations on speaker."

A noisy jumble filled the air, like a popular bar where everyone spoke at once. Individual words were recognizable, but too many voices and conversations overlapped to focus on any one thread.

"Jefferson, tell them to shut up."

JJ's voice came from the robot. *"This is Pepper. Everyone, be silent."*

The cacophony ended. One deep voice said, *"Why did you bring a human into the grove? You were supposed to kill them all."*

"Who is talking?" asked Max.

"Nasturtium," JJ said. "He's an elder, one of three. They govern the grove."

"Which one is he?"

Jonas pointed to the largest plant in the grove.

"Adam, plot a spiral path to the center of the grove, slow enough to ensure every plant is dead. Jefferson, or Pepper, or whatever you want to call yourself, tell Mr. Nasturtium what will happen unless the grove does exactly what I say."

Jonas delivered the ultimatum. Numerous voices spoke at once, expressing fear, outrage, and disbelief.

"Robbie, grab the nearest plant and cut it in two."

"No!" Jonas lunged toward the cart as it scooted ahead. The gun boomed and JJ fell to the ground clutching his knee. Blisters bubbled up on his skin. Cassie forced herself not to cry out.

Max said, "Adam, dim the lights. Keep the ultrasonics on."

The ship stayed directly over Max as he rode Robbie to the nearest living plant. Robbie seized it with a metal claw, pulled it from the ground, and swung it to the arm holding the saw. The grinding sound lasted less than a second. The bottom half of the plant fell away. The top followed as Robbie released his grip. The odor of cut grass intensified. Wails and sobs filled the air.

"Remind the plants that I ordered silence."

"Bastard."

"These things need to know I'm serious. Tell them to be quiet."

Jonas struggled to his feet, favoring his left knee. The wound in his side resumed bleeding. *"Nasturtium! Keep everyone silent or more will die."*

"You're weak, Pepper. I warned Tarragon of this. You've become one of the monsters."

"Nasturtium, you can't smell him, he exists in a different reality. But he knows where you are. He knows the location of everyone between him and the sun. He has the power to bring down radiation more powerful than the worst storm. Obey him or perish."

Max tucked the gun under a strap and clapped. "Very good, Jefferson. I like your style."

A snorkel appeared beside Robbie, out of sight from both Max and Jonas. The animal reared up, front flippers fighting for traction on Robbie's treads. It began to climb. If Max looked down, Sage was dead. He needed a diversion.

Cassie stood and strode toward Jonas.

"Ah, Clearwater. Nice of you to join the party."

"You hold all the cards, Max. The best we can hope for is for you to spare our lives."

"Which I might do, if I can figure out how to guarantee your loyalty."

Cassie nodded. "Jonas, have the plants tilt their domes away from the sun as a sign of respect. They should face the new master of the world, Captain Maxwell Kazakov."

Jonas looked incredulous.

She mouthed, *Do it.* "Make sure to give accurate directions of where he is."

Jonas nodded and exhaled forcefully. *"Everyone, point your domes toward our new master. He stands where Valerium once stood, but six feet higher."*

"Stop!" Nasturtium said. *"I am Eldest. I command, not Pepper."* Hundreds of domes quivered with indecision.

Cassie glanced at the captain. Some sixth sense must have warned him, for he stepped back onto the ship's ramp an instant before a spray of acid arced through the space where his chest had been.

Max spied Sage clinging to the treads, pulled his gun, and fired two shots. Sage fell.

"These fuckers are slow learners," Max muttered. "Adam, lamps to full intensity. Robbie, proceed on a direct path to Nasturtium. Cut it in half like you did that twig."

Robbie rolled forward, translating the screams and curses of plants being crushed beneath the treads or broiled by the ship's floodlights.

Jonas collapsed and Cassie knelt beside him. Blood saturated his pants and the bandage. Cassie pulled out the PB. "Adam, please, please, stop this. Can't you see Max is insane?"

"Sorry, Dr. Clearwater. The outcome depends on you. Admittedly, your options are rather limited. You have access only to the science console and the engineering console."

She recalled Max had added engineering to her responsibilities. "Pull up the engineering console."

The virtual controls appeared in the air above the pocket brain. She could control the fusion reactor—no help there unless she wanted to create ten-megaton thermonuclear explosion. Shutting it down would trigger an automatic switch to batteries. But she also controlled the IDF.

"Jonas, tell the plants to hang on. Have the animals burrow deep."

Her hand hovered above the virtual IDF dial. He nodded. "*Shield yourselves. Brace your roots. Burrow deep.*"

Max ignored the wakes in the sand. His gaze fixed on Nasturtium.

Cassie twisted the control to maximum. In six seconds, hell would break loose. She stared at the *Far Traveler*, praying Max wouldn't notice further weight reduction, but confident he wouldn't have noticed a hurricane. His laughter merged with the deepening whine of the power saw as black powder flew from the growing slash in Nasturtium's stem.

"*Die with me, monster!*" Nasturtium said. An enormous root emerged from the soil and swung wildly through the air, spraying acid everywhere. It missed Max but splashed Robbie. Metal plates began to smolder just as the saw broke through Nasturtium's stem. The huge dome tilted, tottered, and dropped. The ground reverberated with the massive fall.

The space ship shimmered and faded to a diaphanous state. So did the captain's head and shoulders. Fragments of domes, stems, roots, soil, and the captain's lower body jerked inward as an implosion filled the perfect vacuum. An instant later, everything rebounded in an explosion of equal proportion, scattering debris everywhere, while the *Far Traveler* floated in ghostly but temporary immunity.

Ears ringing from the grandfather of all thunderclaps, Cassie shouted, "Adam, go to orbit and await orders!"

The ghost ship ascended rapidly, dragging the still-tethered upper body of the would-be master of the world. In two heartbeats it vanished in the distance.

Jonas said, "Hang on for part two!"

Six seconds after entering ghost phase, all material that had been within the ship's IDF field returned to its normal physical state—into space already occupied. Geysers of sand erupted as small explosions cascaded on the ground. A million tiny balls of lighting flashed in the air as droplets of blood and molecules of air smashed their way back into existence. Cassie held her breath, hoping nothing appeared inside her or Jonas.

Robbie said, *"Pepper, help! Cover my father, quickly!"*

Jonas shouted to Cassie, "Wrap plastic around Nasturtium's stem. Seal him up. Hurry." She ran through the mass of damaged stems and torn domes. Jonas called to her again. "Wrap Sage with his father."

She scooped up Sage where he'd fallen and carried the wounded animal to the severed halves of the fallen elder. With plastic wrap from Robbie's supply drawer, she covered the stump and fallen top, tucking the film underneath as far and tight as she could. Black dust had already begun to fall from the outer ring as Nasturtium's memories spoke to the only person able to hear them.

Part Four:

TRANSACTION

Chapter 59

Ship Time: Day 22. 1200 hours.

Cassie sat cross-legged on the ground directly across from Sage, who remained in animal form but appeared to be bloated from absorbing his father's recent memories. Jonas sat slightly ahead and left of Cassie, with his knees drawn up and bare feet slowly swishing through the powdery ground. Robbie parked ahead and to her right, translating Sage's words. The four of them formed a circle—or a square. It was all a matter of perception.

They sat in the shade under Myrtle's dome, ostensibly negotiating the terms of peace. Elder Myrtle had removed the poison time bomb from JJ's head and healed his gunshot wounds. Marjoram, now the Eldest, had given tacit approval by not stopping the procedure. Iris, now the third elder, had also abstained from hasty judgment. Pepper's courage, sacrifices, and ultimate success in stopping the human threat had some plants, including Narcissus, calling her a hero.

Although safe within Myrtle's immediate presence, Cassie, Jonas, and Robbie were not free to move about. A ring of periscopes surrounded them, ready to spray acid at the slightest provocation. Cassie found breathing difficult in the fog of grief and anger, although Jonas said Myrtle kept the air from becoming lethal. Fortunately, plant society was not a democracy.

Jonas—who now preferred to be called JP—had forestalled the threat of Cassie being summarily executed for war crimes by explaining that the spaceship orbiting the planet remained under her control. If she died, the ship would return to Earth on autopilot. Tobias would certainly launch another ship, or an entire fleet of ships, to investigate. In twenty-five years—about ten rings—humans would return to Obsidian with the capability to destroy every living being on the planet while remaining safely immune from retaliation.

The only way to avoid that outcome was to convince Earth that this planet was both worthless and dangerous. Max had taken steps to do that, and Cassie had the scientific knowledge to ensure the message was believed.

She whole-heartedly supported JP's idea. The sticking point was how to keep her and their unborn baby alive afterward.

Pepper's heroism, plus the fact that JP had chlorophyll in his skin and could manufacture food from sunlight, made him somewhat more palatable than Cassie. JP had the option of staying on the planet, although not within smelling distance of the grove. He couldn't return to Earth, at least not openly, for his altered biology would be discovered and ultimately lead to the conquest of the plants by humans in a quest for youth and immortality.

Cassie didn't relish staying on this black and cheerless planet, but might have done so if there was a food supply. The ship could provide shelter indefinitely, but food stores would run out in six months. The plants had the ability to create a food crop suitable for humans, but refused to do so, being philosophically and morally opposed to creating brainless life forms for the sole purpose of being devoured.

"Stay here, JP. I'll return to Earth alone." The words tore at her heart, but she had the baby to consider. "I'll keep our child safe."

He took both her hands in his. "You can't go back, either."

"Sure I can. Max had a plan to set up an undocumented mine on a small asteroid. I'll scuttle the ship and fabricate a story to explain the diamonds. We'd get by. I can lie quite well when I have to."

He gave a fleeting smile. "You can't lie worth a damn. But even the best lie won't stand up against the curiosity your return would generate. Diamonds—from where? Claim jumpers will search for it. Missing ship? Any part that's found can be traced to the *Far Traveler*. Besides, there's a much bigger problem with you going to Earth." He looked at her abdomen. "Eventually our child will need a medical exam. Automatic DNA screening.

Scammers are always trying to clone the family DNA in hopes of claiming to be a long-lost bastard child entitled to a piece of the trillion-dollar fortune. Dad pays doctors across the solar system to stay alert for that. If he finds out that the child is ours, your cover is blown. If he thinks it's a scam, you and the baby will die in some unfortunate accident."

"He wouldn't."

JP gave her a look.

"What then? I'm not going to give up and die."

JP looked at the stars. "I... all of me... longs to explore, to discover new and amazing things." He looked at Cassie. "That same longing is in you. We could fly to another star system. Search for a habitable planet. Find edible food before the supplies run out."

"It's a billion to one shot," Cassie said.

"*Pepper, I don't want you to leave,*" Sage said through Robbie.

"*Part of me wants to stay here with you,*" JP answered. "*But I'm not entirely Pepper anymore. I'm a symbiont with one mind and two sets of memories. I'm different. I can't stay here.*"

"*I love you.*"

JP's face withered in anguish. "I love you. And I love Cassie."

She knew JP loved them both. The issue of jealously didn't arise. "Sage, I'd invite you to come along, but we don't know where we're going. We're likely to die there, too."

JP exhaled her words.

Robbie translated Sage's reply. "*Actually, I can't stay with the grove, either.*"

"But you're a hero!" JP said.

"*My father was ruthless, I suppose like your father.*" Robbie's volume dropped to a whisper, following syntax cues from the aromatic language. "*Nasturtium witnessed Tarragon's death. He learned the secret of human genetics. Now I have that knowledge. I can create a human body. I could make an army of such beings, which he intended to do.*"

"That's very dangerous knowledge," JP said.

"*I can't risk passing those memories on. I planned to drown myself in the bog, but I find the idea of leaving with you to be preferable.*"

Cassie fingered her totem and thought, *Grandfather, I can't let my baby die.*

Then don't, came his remembered voice. An idea came into her head. She leaned over and kissed JP's cheek. "I have an idea. A wild, insane, terrifying idea."

"What—"

She cut him off. "The limiting factor is my food supply. What if I could make my own food, like you?"

His eyes went wide. "You'd need to become a symbiont."

She nodded. "Sage, would you like to learn what senses a human possesses, and what technologies we have mastered?"

JP translated and Sage responded. *"You want me to become... part human?"*

"It worked for Pepper and Jonas." Cassie stood and paced excitedly within the narrow confines of the circle. "Sage, you'll need to show JP how to do the surgery." It was her turn to look up at the stars. "There are minerals and sunlight everywhere. We can go anywhere. Two bodies, each with a conjoined mind."

JP grinned. "You might have something there."

A troubling thought snagged her enthusiasm. "Sage, what about the baby?"

JP translated, and Sage replied through Robbie. *"Nothing harmful. The genetic changes will give the child chlorophyll skin and new organs to generate and detect smells. The change will also include our healing ability. The baby will have a composite brain that will function seamlessly. It will be initially devoid of memories, unless you want some to be implanted. Genetically and biologically, you and your children will be members of the unique species of which JP is now the sole member."*

Cassie squeezed JP's hands. "I want to do this."

"So do I."

Sage said, *"There's a problem. Although I can handle the genetic and biological aspects of the change, I obviously can't do the surgery on myself. Nor can JP. It requires extreme precision not possible with human hands. We need the elders to help."* He didn't smell hopeful.

"They don't trust us," JP said.

"Because we need to earn their trust," Cassie said. "Let's ensure humans never again come to this planet. No matter what happens to us."

Chapter 60

Ship Time: Day 22. 1300 hours.

"I need to talk to Tobias," Cassie said.

JP shook his head. "Too risky. We don't know exactly what Max told Dad. Any discrepancy in your story will guarantee he sends a ship comes to investigate."

She turned to Robbie. "Did Max record any of his conversations with Tobias?"

"No," Adam said, speaking through the robot. "Furthermore, the ansible was designed for privacy. It lacks recording capability at this end."

"We're screwed," JP said.

"Not necessarily," Adam said. "Dr. Wu circumvented security and placed a small audio-video transmitter inside the chamber. Recordings of all ansible conversations are contained in her pocket brain."

"You know this how?" asked JP.

"Captain Kazakov ordered me to hack into the pocket brain and to decipher and download all its files. He also ordered me not to discuss this with anyone else, but that order expired with his death."

"You cracked her encryption," JP said.

"My algorithms were equal to the task," Adam said with as much pride as a computer could muster.

"Good," Cassie said. "We need to hear the recordings."

"I have unlocked the files on the PB," Adam said. "You may play them when ready."

She tapped the screen and selected audio-visual files created since the day they entered the Teegarden's star system. A holographic projection appeared in the center of their circle.

***

AVfile.12.2200

Dr. Unger squeezed into the dark chamber of the ansible and closed the door before pressing the blinking ACCEPT button. The doctor's face took on a pale back-lit glow from the unseen monitor.

"Well? Is it confirmed?" asked Tobias.

"Probably."

"I want proof."

"I can't very well order the test without a reason. This has to unfold naturally."

"This should have been done pre-flight. Your procrastination is costing me twenty-four years."

Doc swallowed and looked toward the floor. "Mr. Jefferson, I'm ninety percent sure. Give it time. Another week or two."

"Time, always time. It's the real enemy."

Doc sighed. "I should never have agreed to this."

"But you did, and the cure for your tremors will be waiting when you return. I kept my end of the agreement."

"Cassie deserves to know the truth. She's in love."

"Love." The old man's tone suggested a *Bah, humbug* should follow in the empty seconds that followed. Eventually Tobias said, "Goodnight, doctor."

The chamber went dark.

AVfile.17.1000

Captain Kazakov climbed into the chamber and hit the Open Channel button. A few seconds passed before the screen lit up.

"Max?" Tobias said. "Where's Jonas? This is our day."

Max winced. "Mr. Jefferson, it is with deepest sympathy that I must report your son is dead."

The silence seemed to stretch forever before Tobias asked, "How?"

"He fell into a bog and couldn't climb out. We started rescue effort immediately but had to call it off when a solar storm came, followed by a dust storm."

"You could have worn suits and continued the rescue."

"No, sir. Radiation reached lethal level and the dust here is extremely abrasive. I had to put the ship into ghost phase before take-off just to maintain hull integrity."

"How is Cassie?"

"Taking it hard, as you'd expect."

"Keep her safe, Max. How long is the storm going to last?"

"Clearwater—Cassie—is monitoring it. Probably a couple of days. Then we'll land and resume mining."

"Bring back my son's ba-body. Body. Bring back my son's body."

"I'll do my best, sir." The fading light revealed the captain's thoughtful look as he stroked his chin with three fingers.

AVfile.21.1000

Max absently drummed his fingers on the console. All four fingers. He stopped, stared at his hand, and moved it out of sight from the ansible's camera. He tapped the ACCEPT button with his other hand.

"What's going on?" demanded Tobias. "Adam stopped broadcasting telemetry reports."

"All hell's breaking loose," Max said. He glared at the screen. "Computer crashes, hull leaks, sickness. Dr. Unger and Li Wu are dead."

A momentary pause from Tobias. "Is Cassie all right?"

A millisecond of surprise flashed across Max's face. "For now. We may be contaminated or whatever."

"Disease or toxin?"

Max shrugged. "Clearwater's working on it. Might be the diamonds. They're highly radioactive. He slammed his fist against the wall. "Goddamn! How could we have missed that?"

"Return to Earth immediately."

"Preflight ops are underway. I'll get us back somehow."

"Call me when you're off planet." The fading light left the captain's face in shadow, but a toothy smile lingered like that of the Cheshire Cat.

AVfile.22.0500

Max looked extremely ill: bloodshot eyes, blood under his nostrils and on his shirt, drooping shoulders. He opened the channel and waited.

Tobias said, "Are you in route?"

Max shook his head. "Sullivan died last night. Clearwater's infected. Chances are this is my last report." He coughed and spat blood.

"Set the ship for auto-return."

"The *Far Traveler* isn't coming home, sir. Adam's malfunctioning. The hull seals leak like Swiss cheese. Repairs impossible."

"Go to ghost phase. Accelerate to maximum speed. Orbit the star. It'll essentially freeze time for you while I dispatch a rescue ship."

Max laughed and began coughing. He covered his mouth with his sleeve; the sleeve came away bloody. "Clearwater says it's the dust. Gets into everything, even our lungs. We're the walking dead, Tobias."

"Do what I said, Captain. Wait it out. You and Cassie will make it."

"Engines are shot to hell. Sorry I let you down, sir."

Seconds passed. "You did what you could. Goodbye, Captain Kazakov." Tobias sounded cold and distant.

The chamber darkened. Max muttered, "God, I need a shower."

***

Cassie sensed JP's tension and placed her hand over his. "What's wrong?"

"I'm sure that was Lyra's blood, not Max's. It was right after he killed her."

Cassie looked into his eyes. "At that point he knew he couldn't let either of us live."

JP said, "Once we were gone, he would pilot the ship to an asteroid outpost, buy a new ship with the diamonds—"

"Transfer the plants, destroy the *Far Traveler*, and start selling the fountain of youth," finished Cassie. "Just as he said—minus us." She drew a heavy sigh. "Can sap heal acid burns?"

JP cocked his head. "You know it does. Why?"

"I need to look as bad as the captain did in order to convince Tobias that Max was right in claiming the planet is worthless and dangerous."

"No need. Max did a good job."

"I need to look into his eyes. To give Tobias the opportunity to show regret."

"He might not be capable of it."

"Doesn't matter. This is about my honor, not his."

JP and Sage convinced the elders to allow Cassie to summon the ship and board it. Her anxiety, already high, spiked at the huge number of volunteers wanting to spray acid on her face and body. Myrtle insisted on doing it herself and used root tips to position small amounts in appropriate spots specified by JP. Cassie refused to cry out as patches of her skin dissolved. A fine mist burned her eyes and throat. JP led her to the ship.

She had rarely used the ansible, but had no trouble sliding into the chamber and pressing the *Open Channel* button.

"Cassie!" said Tobias. Concern underlay the veneer of surprise. "You're alive."

"Hello, Tobias." The hoarseness of her voice made the words almost unintelligible. She tried to clear it and ended up coughing up blood. "The captain's dead. Everyone is dead. I'm dying."

"Come home. Maximum speed."

"Ship is falling apart. It's the dust, Tobias. Diamond dust. Radioactive, electrostatic, and microscopic. Erodes everything. Too small to filter out. Passes from the lungs into the bloodstream and abrades every cell in the body. No cure." She coughed again, then began to wheeze. She wished she was faking it. "Hurts."

"Cassie..."

"Jonas proposed to me before he... died. I was so happy. I wish I had the chance to know you better." A cough turned into a minute-long hacking fit.

"I'm... sorry," Tobias said in a thick, strained voice.

"Goodbye... Dad. Think of us when you look at the stars." She cut the transmission and left the chamber. "Adam, cut all power to the ansible."

"Dr. Clearwater, that would permanently sever the quantum link with the ansible's Earth-side twin."

"As long as the link exists, Tobias will know part of the ship survives. I need to squash all his hopes."

"Understood." A distinct click sounded. "The ansible has been rendered useless."

Cassie coughed, this time with particular violence and persistence. The room spun and dark sparkles filled her field of vision. JP and Sage would have healing sap ready, but did she deserve to be healed after the deaths she caused? Maybe, maybe not—but she had a baby who certainly deserved to live.

Chapter 61

Ship Time: Day 22. 1400 hours.

"The elders are willing to let the operation proceed." The good news didn't mesh with the concern on JP's face.

"What's the catch?" Cassie asked.

"They still don't trust you."

"But if they're doing the operation—"

He hugged her and touched his forehead to hers. "They want to rummage through your memories during the procedure."

"Okay. I have nothing to hide."

"They will, um, mess with your mind. Create scenarios for you to solve."

"Directed dreaming?"

"More like hyper-realistic hallucinations."

"How can they do that without understanding vision and sound?"

"Experience. Mine. I'm their Rosetta Stone. It boils down to patterns of meaning. The same message can be conveyed visually in text, aurally in speech, or tactilely in Braille. Smell is simply another media of expression. The neural patterns that correspond to the meaning is similar in all cases. Once they knew where and how those senses were input, and they identified the different manner that humans process memories, the elders figured out how to put whatever they want into your mind." He drew back and stared into her eyes. "The choices you make will determine whether they fuse your mind with Sage, or..."

She hugged him. "This was my idea. It'll work out. It has to." She felt the tension in his muscles. "Hey, I heard the operation has a side benefit. No more morning sickness."

He made an attempt to smile. "Then what are you waiting for?"

The plants created another jelled-water pit and began lowering Cassie into it. JP gripped her hand and refused to let go.

"Jonas... JP... there's something you have to do."

"Anything."

"Take the ship. Visit every grove on the planet. They need to know what happened here. They need to prepare in case humans return."

His head jerked in an awkward nod. His grip tightened and his eyes took on a haunted, desperate look. "I remember the nightmares. I *died* when they did this to me."

"You came back. I will, too." She gave a final squeeze and pulled away. Thick roots looped around her waist and legs and pulled downward. Slender roots slipped into her nostrils and mouth. The sense of suffocation triggered a panicked thrashing until a fragrant mist filled her sinus, and sleep filled her mind.

***

"Cassie's right. Humans will eventually return here," JP said.

Sage answered, *"The elders will prepare. They'll ensure conditions will be similar to those she described. You'll spread the word to other groves. Explorers will find a hostile world with nothing of value."*

JP puffed skepticism. *"Your species will attract human scientists like memories to a stem."*

"The elders can create a microbe to mimic the effects of the dust Cassie described. It will kill any human quite rapidly. Visits here will be painful and short even if humans wear biosuits."

JP sighed. *"I wish our species could come together in peace."*

"Neither side is ready for that."

"I suppose you're right."

"My turn," Sage said as a root encircled him and pulled him into the water pit. JP stared into the rippling water and prayed for both their lovers.

***

The sun blazed white hot in an azure sky. Cassie closed her eyes to the brightness, though it seemed to go right through her lids. The light felt exhilarating after so many days of twilight.

A voice said, "Tell us where you are."

"I'm an astronaut on a planet twelve and a half light years from Earth." Cassie caught a whiff of peppermint, which made her smile.

"No," said the voice. "You are a spirit wandering the archives of your mind, exploring paths not taken. Open your eyes."

Cassie stood in a clearing dominated by three massive totem poles. Grandfather had scorned such things, claiming the only charm they possessed was luring money-bearing tourists to the village. She realized with a start that this was the entrance to a sacred area of the Everglades, the spot from which she started her doomed quest.

"This isn't real. I'm hallucinating."

First Totem said, "The explanations are not mutually exclusive."

Second Totem said, "This was a seminal moment in your life. After the quest, you turned from spirituality to science. Why?"

"Science is also a quest for truth. I realized it provides a more certain path." Cassie felt a sudden constriction around her chest.

"Justifications and rationalizations," said Third Totem. "Why do you avoid answering the question?"

After all these years, it still hurt to remember. She had wanted more than anything to make her grandfather proud, and she had let him down. "I failed the spirit quest. I felt ashamed, so I ran away from the reservation, from spirituality, from my grandfather. I turned to science because it offered a path to knowledge that didn't depend on my defective intuition."

Third continued, "I am not convinced that she should be allowed to proceed. The gifts we would bestow are not limited to her."

The baby. Cassie said, "I will teach my child to be respectful of all life."

"The way you showed respect to Holly? To Valerian, to Daphne, to Westeria, to the dozens of others cut down by you and your kind?"

Several animals gathered in the clearing. Cassie felt their angry stares. Foul odors filled the air. This quest might be over before it began. "I am sorry for what I did."

First said, "Who supports allowing the human to relive its memories?"

No one spoke.

"Will *anyone* speak in support of this human?" asked Second. Cassie felt the tightness in her chest intensify and realized she was about to be crushed in the real world.

Turtle lumbered forward. "She broke my stem. Then she said a prayer and put me back together." It ambled to Cassie's feet and looked up. "You smell nice. I know you didn't intend anything bad."

Cassie knelt and kissed the shell. "Thank you."

Second said, "Too long have we lived in smug superiority, thinking we knew all the secrets of the universe. Cassie, like Pepper, reminds us of our ignorance. It is a bitter smell, and the only way to clear the air is to let her proceed with the quest."

Third said, "Perhaps this is a test of us as much as it is of her." The pressure on her chest eased.

"It is settled, then," said First. "Cassiopeia, go forth and find your guide."

Three paths led from the clearing into the glades. The first path meandered through a swamp. The second passed through tall grass and stunted trees. The third path disappeared into a tangled jungle of vines, trees, and underbrush.

Cassie had faced the same choice nine years ago. She felt no affinity for any particular path. The middle path through the grass seemed quickest then, as it did now. She took a step in that direction.

"Ha!" called a voice. Cassie turned to see a crow land on a stubby arm of the shortest totem pole. The bird regarded her with unblinking eyes. "You took that path before."

"So?" Cassie said warily. Grandfather claimed crows were tricksters. They never actually lied, but they were masters at distorting the truth.

"Do you expect a different result?" asked Crow.

"Which path do you suggest?"

Crow cocked his head. "What is that trinket around your neck?"

"A gift from my grandfather."

"I will advise you, but you must give me the trinket in payment."

It's only a hallucination. Cassie started to remove the charm, then realized the bird hadn't actually promised that she'd find her spirit guide. Cassie let the totem settle back into place. "I appreciate the offer, but I'll find my own way, thank you."

Crow said, "The path is long and filled with hardship. For you." It cawed in laughter and flew away. Cassie moved into the tall grass.

The sunshine that initially delighted her now bore down with unrelenting fire. The open terrain offered no respite as her skin reddened and blistered. She trudged on, silent and resolute, searching for a sign, a clue, anything that would lead to her spiritual mentor.

A low growl from behind grabbed her attention. She spun to see a tawny panther regarding her with interest.

"I've followed you for an hour," it said. "Are you looking for your guide or taking a stroll down memory lane?" It licked a paw and slicked back the fur on its head.

Cassie considered telling the cat to stalk someone else, but decided on a different tact. Vanity. "You are a master of stealth, Panther. No one, least of all me, would detect your presence."

Panther smiled and trotted up to her. It sniffed and then rubbed against her body. "This creature is a collection of contradictions. It nurtures and it kills. It loves and it hates. It is filled with caution and acts with courage. It is surprisingly like me. Let's explore together."

Panther led her to the edge of the grassland, where a small stream meandered on its way to the great swamp. The big cat drank its fill and then splashed with delight. Cassie did the same.

"Hey, watch who you're splashing," said a new voice.

Cassie looked around. The voice came from an Aloe Vera plant.

Panther stopped playing. "The plant has healing properties. Rip off its leaves and rub the sap on your skin. It will heal your burns." The big cat watched her with great interest.

"I won't harm any living thing here," Cassie said, "even though it's a dream. There has been enough pain and death already."

"I like you," said Panther. "The sun is going down. Sleep here, and I will ensure no harm comes during the night."

Cassie slept.

In the morning, both Panther and Aloe were gone. Cassie sighed with disappointment. The grassland had offered up no guide. She followed the stream into the marsh. Crow circled high above, taunting with raucous laughter.

The sun seemed less harsh, but her bones and joints ached as if they'd been pulled out, sand-papered, and jammed back into place. Each step, each movement of any kind, rubbed raw nerves against hot coals. Cassie bore the pain without complaint. She would willingly go through what Jonas had been forced to suffer.

She froze at a slow guttural grumble a few feet ahead. *Alligator.*

It crawled up from one of the many pools dotting the swamp. His head jerked to the left to seize a piece of driftwood in its jaws. The wood shattered with a loud snap. His teeth grinned around the remaining splinters. He coughed them out and waddled toward Cassie. She tensed, ready to run.

Alligator stopped. "You killed many beings. You have... potential."

"I acted from ignorance. I've learned to be respectful of new life forms. I will teach my child to do the same."

"Bah! Hasn't science taught you about evolution? Kill or be killed. Eat or be eaten. I will show you how to be strong, for no one is stronger than I am. No one will be stronger than you will be."

"I don't want to kill."

"You kill to survive."

"On my planet, that is true. I gave thanks for the spirits of the animals and plants that sacrificed their lives so mine could continue."

"You would kill and eat me if you could," said Alligator.

"No. I would never knowingly kill a sentient creature for food."

Alligator mumbled to himself in several voices before responding. "Come, I will show you something that may help."

Alligator plunged into the swamp, and Cassie followed, never complaining of the agony in her bones. She fell a few times, but got up and forged onward. The shadows of tall cattails shortened and then lengthened as the sun tracked inexorably across the sky.

"Here," said Alligator. They stopped at a stout tree at the border between swamp and jungle. Enormous thorns protruded from the bark, covering every inch of the tree. "You need to enter the jungle, which is beyond my domain. Many dangers lurk there. Strip the bark and gird yourself in thorns. Nothing will bother you then."

"Thank you," Cassie said, "but I'll not harm this tree."

"Death waits for you in the jungle."

"Death waits for everyone. I failed before because my fear was stronger than my faith."

"Sleep here, then. It is nearly night, and the jungle is particularly dangerous then."

Alligator plopped down on the path between Cassie and the jungle. Nothing would come to her without first passing him. She reached out a hand and tentatively touched the knobby skin of the beast. "Thank you."

She slept.

In the morning, both Alligator and Thorn Tree were gone. Cassie sighed again. The marsh had offered no guide. Offer, test, abandon seemed to be the plant's pattern for the quest. Fine. The jungle offered a last chance for redemption. The path became a cave into a tangled mass of vines, trees, and underbrush. Crow circled high above, calling "Ha... ha... ha."

Cassie moved slowly into the jungle, hoping not to trip over a root or get tangled in a vine, but the more she worried about it the more it seemed to happen. The dappled light that fell from the trees concealed more than it revealed. Cut, bruised, and out of breath, she fell yet again, landing in a patch of flowering ivy.

"Beauty charms the savage breast," said Ivy. "Drape me over your body to beguile everyone you meet."

Cassie thought music, not beauty, was supposed to do the charming, but she didn't bother to correct the plant. "I think honesty is a better approach."

"Snake agrees with me. It's best to lure your enemies into a false sense of security."

"I don't have enemies," Cassie said.

A rustling sound pulled her attention to the something slithering through the leafy ground cover. Snake's head rose from the leaves and swayed with sinuous grace. "Of course you have enemies," it said. A tongue flicked out as if tasting the air. "Friends, also. Trust me, Cassie. The secret to success is pheromones. Smells to entice Jonas so he'll be helpless to your charms."

"Love is more than chemistry. It's trust and mutual respect and caring with all your heart what happens to those you love."

"Silly girl, your first quest was flawless. Science alone provides precise answers. Superstition brings only sorrow and disappointment."

"You're wrong."

"Oh? Have you found your spirit guide? You can't even find your way out of this jungle." Snake burrowed into the underbrush. "Panther and Alligator are weak. You'll get no help from me." It crawled away. The ivy withered and died, releasing a stench of blood and human excrement. It smelled of her own despair. Briars, thickets, and vines formed an impenetrable wall around her. She saw no trace of a path, not even the one that led her here.

Grandfather had always been sure of his way, even in the dark. Cassie closed her eyes. She recalled his voice, worn with age and wisdom. "Head north."

"I have no compass, Grandfather."

"True north is not a point on the compass; it is the direction you move when the heart and spirit align."

The jungle felt alive and she chose not to fear it. She heard animals, insects, and rustling leaves. She smelled flowers, fruit, and rich dark soil. In one direction the scent seemed more fragrant, and the birds sang more sweetly. She opened her eyes and saw an opening, the path Grandfather would have chosen.

At the edge of the jungle the vegetation thinned to reveal a small rise to the east. Cassie recognized it as the place where she had witnessed the take-off of the last chemical rocket. On that spot now perched the *Far Traveler*, its silver hull gleaming in the rays of the setting sun. A final sprint and she would be there.

It was the goal she *really* wanted. The guide was irrelevant. The elders would still complete the operation and let her fly among the stars. She took a step forward. Something felt wrong. Something *smelled* wrong.

She sniffed, and the odors seemed to resolve into a cry for help. It came from the left, in the midst of a dense thicket. With a last glance toward the spaceship, she turned and pushed her way through the barrier.

Crow was trying to catch a caterpillar, who managed to keep a leaf between itself and the hungry bird. "Help!" cried the bug in a tiny, desperate voice.

"Shoo!" shouted Cassie. "Leave it alone." She swatted at Crow.

"Stay out of this," said Crow. "A bird's got to eat."

"No. Not in this place." Cassie grabbed at the occupied leaf, but Crow was faster. It plucked the leaf from the tree and flapped noisily into the air. The captive caterpillar wailed.

"Wait!" Cassie yelled. The bird flew higher. It shifted the leaf and captive worm from beak to claw, the better to laugh at her.

"Wait! I have what you really want!" She yanked Grandfather's totem from her neck and held it to the sky. "A totem of power and beauty." *An object of love I treasure more than anything.*

Crow circled. The circles grew slower and lower until Crow landed on the ground and dropped the bug-bearing leaf. Crow regarded her with suspicion.

She set the totem on the ground.

"You no longer need a guide," said Crow. It snatched up the necklace and flew away. Cassie watched it go and hoped she hadn't made a mistake.

"Thank you," said the caterpillar. "We're nearly done." The voice sounded familiar, or maybe the smell, although Cassie couldn't place it.

"I'll take you with me to the ship. We'll be safe there, at least until I wake up." Cassie looked around and realized she'd lost her sense of direction. No, not exactly lost. Nothing felt better than being exactly where she was. Maybe because she felt tired and sore and the sun was setting. Maybe because she hadn't found her spirit guide and would once again have to admit defeat. She'd deal with that tomorrow. She climbed a tree for safety and fell asleep in a wide fork. The caterpillar remained beside her.

Cassie slept, and she woke to a dream.

"Hello, Granddaughter."

"Grandfather?" Cassie opened her eyes and saw no one. "You sound so real."

"Memories are as real as you make them."

"I couldn't change the past. I'm sorry."

"They're your memories, and the quest has not ended."

"What am I supposed to do?"

"Look at the stars. Think of the space surrounding the star, a hundred billion stars in a galaxy, a hundred billion galaxies in the universe. How does that make you feel?"

"Small," whispered Cassie.

"Small," he agreed. "Wake up, Granddaughter."

She had shrunk to the size of the caterpillar, which labored beside her while spinning a cocoon. It looked safe and warm in a universe grown ever so much larger and more dangerous.

"Join me," Caterpillar said. Now she recognized the smell. Sage.

"*You're* my spirit guide," she said. It felt so right, so obvious. She squeezed into the cocoon and they fell into a sleep akin to death, but without the sense of finality and loss.

In time, the conjoined butterfly awoke and broke free of its confines. The wings unfurled and dried in the sun. It took flight and travelled true north to the ship, high above the domains of Alligator, Snake, and Panther. From atop the *Far Traveler*, the butterfly saw the three totems smile.

We need a name, Sage-Cassie. Yes, we do. Sassie.

***

"Cassie! Sage! Wake up!" Strong arms pulled her from the muddy pit. She coughed water from her lungs and took a breath, not from need but from desire. It felt *good* to breathe, just as it felt good to bask in sunlight. She opened her eyes and saw JP's ecstatic face.

Sassie smiled and looked down at her naked body. Black as coal, just like JP. *Vision. Hearing. This is amazing!* She sniffed. *And smell. He smells like love.*

JP smiled. "I'm catching some of those thoughts... Sassie. Hmm. Appropriate name."

She placed his hand on her abdomen. "The baby?"

"They're fine."

Her eyes widened.

"Twins. Boy and a girl. You're about six weeks along, but with the new genetic structure it's anyone's guess about the due date."

Sassie looked around, making sense of sights, smells, and sounds. Most of the grove celebrated the successful operation, but odors of grief and pain lingered beneath the cheer.

"*Thank you, Elders. We are in your debt,*" said Sassie.

"*Do not think us rude, but we are eager to have this planet all to ourselves again,*" Elder Marjoram puffed.

JP said, "*We couldn't stay here even if we wanted. We're too powerful.*"

Sassie nodded. "*Heralds of change. Immortal beings of great power, whose very touch can heal or kill.*" Grandfather's words? Or some other voice? She had several in her mind now. The voices eased her children's fear as consciousness came far earlier than normal human development. Mastery of biology and genetics created a new species free from the whims of evolution.

The *Far Traveler* gleamed in the sun like a great bird of fire, beckoning to them.

She took JP's hand. "*Somewhere in the galaxy, the designers of this garden world still live, still create. We are the children of these thunderbirds. Let's find them.*"

End

About the author

W. D. County (Dave) has a keen appreciation for technology, drawing on experience as a nuclear reactor operator aboard the ballistic missile submarine USS *Sam Houston* (SSBN 609), a quality assurance manager at the Three Mile Island Nuclear Station, and a developer of custom software for the federal government. His stories have appeared in the e-zine *Spinetingler* and anthologies *Speedloader, Pulp Ink 2,* and the *Aesthetica Creative Writing Annual 2014.*

Dave resides in Lee's Summit, Missouri with his wife and three cats. When not writing, Dave loves to drive his Miata convertible through the back roads at more or less legal speed. Mostly more.

For more information on the author, check out WDCounty.com and www.Facebook.com/WDCounty

CPSIA information can be obtained
at www.ICGtesting.com
Printed in the USA
LVHW081823080519
617104LV00014B/671/P

9 781731 195753